DAUGHTER OF THE NIGHT

ELAINE BERGSTROM

ACE BOOKS, NEW YORK

This Ace Book contains the complete
text of the original edition.

DAUGHTER OF THE NIGHT

An Ace Book / published by arrangement with
the author

PRINTING HISTORY
Jove edition / October 1992
Ace edition / September 1994

ISBN: 0-441-00110-6

ACE®
Ace Books are published by The Berkley Publishing Group,
200 Madison Avenue, New York, New York 10016.
ACE and the "A" design
are trademarks belonging to Charter Communications, Inc.

PRINTED IN THE UNITED STATES OF AMERICA

10 9 8 7 6 5 4 3 2 1

Ace Books by Elaine Bergstrom

BLOOD ALONE
BLOOD RITES
DAUGHTER OF THE NIGHT
SHATTERED GLASS

Dedicated with love to my grandmother
Marie Kiraly,
born 1899.
The first to show me my past.

O what can ail thee, Knight at Arms,
  Alone and palely loitering?
The sedge has withered from the Lake
  And no birds sing!

I met a Lady in the Meads,
  Full beautiful, a faery's child,
Her hair was long, her foot was light
  And her eyes were wild.

                        John Keats

I would like to express my gratitude to the following writers whose valuable research made the writing of *Daughter of the Night* so much easier. Special thanks to Raymond McNally for his highly detailed account of the Countess Bathori's life, *Dracula Was a Woman*. Also to writers Marjorie Rowling and Joseph and Francis Gies for their accounts of day-to-day life in the early Renaissance, to Edward Otetea for his history of Romania, and, above all, to Tekla Domotor whose excellent book *Hungarian Folk Beliefs* first introduced me to the *liderc* and *Kisasszony* legends, the function of the *taltos*, and many of the folk spells and practices that enrich this novel. And, finally, thanks to Mark Paul Stehlik whose extensive library on monsters and myths provided over a dozen books related to the life and times of Elizabeth Bathori.

PART I

CATHERINE

HISTORICAL NOTE

It is a fact that in 1475 Prince Istvan Bathori, at the request of King Matthias Corvinus of Hungary, returned Vlad Tepes, known as the Impaler, to the throne of Wallachia. After fighting numerous battles with the Moslems and the Wallachian landowners who opposed Tepes's rule, Prince Bathori and his troops reached Bucharest, then the major city in Wallachia. Afterward, for reasons never understood, Bathori deserted Tepes, leaving him with only a handful of loyal troops to defend his kingdom against the armies massing to destroy him.

CHAPTER
1

Wallachia, 1475

The chief officer for Prince Istvan Bathori held the chain of the slave fighting in the dusty ring, moving quickly around the outside of the circle, trying to keep the chain from tripping the Impaler's own Turkish champion. In the ring, the two bodies circled—the champion, short and hairy and huge; the slave, tall, oddly long-limbed, fragile it seemed except in the confident way he moved. Both men wore only breeches and their bodies were caked with dust from the ground beneath them.

"Ah, the big one's only got to get his arms around that child and it's over," one of the soldiers said with a trace of sadness though he, like the others, had bet on the Turk.

"But maybe the Turk will want him for something else, hey?" his companion responded. The men around them chuckled at the joke, but uneasily, for with his raven curls and wide-spaced black eyes, the young slave in the ring had a magnetic beauty about him that none in the room could ignore. Since he had been taken near the battle site the day before, he had sat motionless in the back of the crowded common cell. Unlike many of the other prisoners who made frequent moves to escape, he never threatened anyone yet none of the guards had dared approach him.

Word had spread among the soldiers that last night when he had been given a slave's collar, Prince Istvan himself

3

had gone to watch the fitting, that the guards were unable to approach the strange youth, and that, at the end, the prisoner had snapped the hot metal band into place himself. Afterward, it was said, the prince had dismissed his guards, then stood and watched the prisoner for hours. Though no words were exchanged between the pair, the prince had seemed unusually thoughtful afterward, spending the night alone in his quarters. Now tonight, in a move his men thought insane, Prince Bathori had placed the slender youth in the ring against the Impaler's giant and all were prepared to watch the prisoner die.

All save one. In the shadows, in dark corners where torches threw no light, a black-robed figure studied the fight. Once, his dark eyes met those of his kinsman, the slave. —Our father is anxious, Charles. Come home— he said mind to mind in the silent way his people shared their thoughts.

The slave kicked, his foot falling deliberately short of its mark. It would not do for the fight to end too soon. —He is always anxious, little brother, but I never thought he would send you to be my shepherd.—

The youth sprung over the crouched Turk, spinning, wrapping his arms around the huge man's arms and shoulders, laughing as his slow-moving adversary tried to shake him off his back. His head pressed against the Turk's, pushing it sideways and up.

The room grew suddenly hushed and the dark figure watched, waiting to see the inevitable end, the feeding that would come. —Are you so hungry you would betray your own!— he challenged.

Charles's head jerked back, the champion screamed, and a snap was heard by the closest soldiers. The two men fell together, only the young slave moved. —Betray? Never!—

—And when will you come home, Charles?—

The chief officer handed the chain back to his lord and Prince Bathori jerked it, reminding his slave that he took too long. —Home?— Charles responded and Steffen, his brother, detected the silent laughter. —Tell him I'll be home when these creatures no longer amuse me. Tomorrow, most likely.— Charles stood and bowed to the prince, his mockery and respect hidden behind the impassive mask of his face.

"Leave us!" Prince Bathori ordered and the room cleared except for the prince, the slave, the prisoner motionless on the floor, and the dark-robed figure overlooked in the shadows.

"You are hungry?" the prince asked Charles when they were alone.

"Yes, deliberately. I have reason to hate this one."

"If I had known, we could have conducted this match in private."

Charles laughed. "A youth against a seasoned fighter? Didn't I shame him well? Didn't you earn a peasant's fortune on your wagers this night? Besides, he is alive. I broke his arm, not his neck. He'll wake soon. Then you will witness the real struggle. The one you would prefer to see."

"I wish I had your power," the prince said honestly.

"Do you?" This time the mockery almost reached the surface.

The prince detected it. "I am aware that you can leave me anytime you choose. Why did you allow my men to take you? When I offered to free you last night, why did you demand the right to be treated as a slave? And why do you stay?"

"Do you wish the truth, my lord?"

"I do."

Charles kicked the prisoner hard on the arm he had broken. The larger man moaned and began to stir. Charles ignored him, looking intently at the prince as he answered, "I let your men capture me because I understand there is no other role they can play. I let you rule me because my people value the peace your king may bring to this land. I have stayed"—he rested his bare foot on the prisoner's shoulder, holding him pinned to the ground—"because I intend to be well fed."

Prince Bathori chuckled. "I see."

The prisoner stared up into the face of the victor, into eyes that promised to devour him. Charles crouched beside him. "Do you recall a little dark-eyed boy, a child your band ran down last winter in Afold? Do you remember how you all used him before you gutted him to keep him from ever revealing your sin? My son showed me your face. He still screams your name in his nightmares. I promised him this revenge. Now you will be the last to die."

"Not possible! He could not have lived!" the prisoner said, holding his arm, his feet pushing his body away from the thin young slave.

"I came for you. I wear this collar for you. I will record every scream, every plea, every perfect moment of your death. I will share your pain with my son and it will cleanse him of his own."

"How could he still live? How!"

Charles smiled, mouth wide, lips pulled back, revealing long sharp fangs that glistened in the torchlight.

"The Mountain Lords!" the prisoner wailed, then scrambled to his feet and ran. Charles jerked the chain from Prince Bathori's hand and moved so fast he seemed to vanish, reappearing a moment later in front of his target, swinging the heavy metal links, lashing the huge Turk back into the center of the tent. The man routed in a different direction with no better luck. And again. And again. Terror building with every attempt. At last, exhausted, his arm a white-hot bar of pain, he fell where he had fallen for the crowd.

"Beg."

The prisoner shook his head and a bolt of fire blasted into his mind.

—You will— his executioner promised. —Before we're done, you'll beg me the way my son begged you.—

The prince leaned forward, resting his elbows on his knees, his chin in his hands, and watched Charles slowly devour his enemy. The victim's agony built exquisitely in him, a growing silent scream that wove together the prince, the predator, and their shared prey.

Hours passed before Charles dropped the corpse and gripped the chain attached to the collar on his neck. He glanced at the prince who acknowledged the silent question with a quick nod. Charles snapped the chain, then twisted the collar at the joint. When it cracked, Charles pulled the ends apart and dropped the chain and collar on the ground beside the corpse.

"I give you freedom if that is what you wish," Prince Bathori said, almost sincerely. "Now I would like to propose an alliance—your power . . . and mine."

"My kind has no interest in war. We ask only that you leave our lands untouched."

"Such agreements require stability and peace, do they not? Why not stay and rest . . . you and your silent kinsman from the shadows. If I could, I would have a banquet in your honor but the questions . . ." The prince left the thought uncompleted.

"I've had my banquet. As to rest"—Charles glanced at Steffen before responding—"we accept the hospitality you offer." Charles sensed what the prince had been reluctant to request and softly, mind to mind, responded with silent discretion. —It has been a long and bloody day. Perhaps a warm bath would soothe the aches? We could speak of an agreement then.—

"And your kinsman?"

Charles added another suggestion. The prince nodded and called for his guards.

In the center of the camp, a handful of tents displayed the Impaler and Bathori banners, the two dragon symbols challenging the Turks to attack if they had the courage. They didn't; not this night nor for months to come. The three-day battle had swept them from the land in a shameful route they would not soon forget. The largest of the tents in the center of the camp was occupied by Prince Bathori, a second by his concubine and her slaves. Two others were reserved for visiting royalty and the guards escorted Steffen to one of these while Charles followed the prince into his. If the guards thought it unusual for a slave and the obvious close kin of a slave to be treated with such hospitality, they did not speak of it aloud. Prince Bathori was their hero. Tonight he could do no wrong.

The inside of the prince's tent was as sumptuous as a lesser room in his castle in Somolyo. Furs covered and softened the dirt floor, an iron brazier filled with burning coal and incense warmed and perfumed the space, small hooks in the tent walls held draperies of deep gold that waved in the night breeze, and a pair of torches threw an uneasy flickering light. But for all the prince's love of luxury, this was a campaign tent nonetheless and while one corner held a raised bed covered with silks befitting a sultan's chamber, another had a table and chairs, maps and lamps for late-night plotting.

Charles stood just inside the door, his head cocked, amusement dancing in his dark eyes. He waited silently until the servants wheeled in a steaming bath easily large enough for four men, took off their ruler's outer garments, and left without a glance in his direction. "How delightfully Turkish," Charles said.

"I captured my castle from the Turkish Porte. I've learned to appreciate its comforts. Including cleanliness." The prince seemed about to add something, apparently thought better of it, and turned, dipping his hand into the bath, testing its heat. "Are the legends true?" he asked without looking at Charles.

"Yes," Charles said simply. The bond between need and desire was already forming, pulling them together though neither of them was willing to make the first physical move.

"I am far from young and I have never desired a man until now. But then you are not a man, are you?"

—Not mortal, but a man nonetheless.—

"I know appearances deceive. How old are you?"

"I was born in the years that the Szekely tribes began to settle this land. Seven centuries ago, Prince."

Istvan Bathori ran his hand through the water, watching the ripples spread and die, thinking of how one unexpected event could have so many far-reaching consequences. Then he turned and held out a steady hand to Charles. "You gathered far more filth in the ring tonight than I did in this afternoon's battle. Come, lord of the mountains, let me learn more of the legends."

The servants also delivered a smaller bath to the neighboring tent where Steffen had been taken. He looked at each servant with dark suspicious stares. Though he sensed no plots against him or his brother, this place made him wary and he vowed to not sleep until after dawn. Besides, Charles would not object to sharing his pleasure. They often played mental voyeur to each other's passion. He had just lowered himself into the water and lay back, prepared for an evening of vicarious pleasure, when his tent flaps parted and a woman entered.

A veil covered her face, a shapeless brown robe concealed her body, and she walked toward him reluctantly, as if afraid of what she were doing or that she would not please him. He sensed that she was more than a camp whore and unused to this kind of boldness. Perhaps she had decided to come on her own. This would not be the first time his natural magnetism had placed him in this delicate predicament.

He detected a sudden smile beneath the veil and knew she enjoyed his uneasiness. As she threw back her hood, a cascade of auburn hair spilled over her shoulders. Her hands were shaking as she unfastened the hooks on her cape, but she willed them steady and pushed the fabric off her shoulders to lay in a heap around her bare ankles. Beneath it, she wore nothing at all save a single necklace of gold beads and the rings on her tapered fingers.

She stood a moment before lowering the veil. Her lips were full, her brows thick and darker than her hair with a high arch that gave her a child's expression of wonder, her eyes were almond-shaped and slanted, and even in the dim torchlight, he saw they were as black as his own.

"You were sent, yes?" he asked, lightly probing her mind, trying to discover the truth.

"I would have been sent to your kinsman tonight but he is occupied." A flush spread across her cheeks. "You are quieter than he is, I think. Perhaps I will like you better." She tried to sound coy and failed.

"Who are you?"

"I am Ilona Bathori, the prince's daughter."

Daughter! Yet the prince had ordered her to come here. Steffen probed harder, enough that she detected his mental intrusion. Her eyes widened with surprise and fear, a hand automatically rose to cover her mouth.

He knew what the prince wanted, what she had been sent to achieve. It was impossible. He was about to tell the woman as much when she walked past him to the bed.

The faint currents of air in the room drew her scent to him—a mild mix of frankincense and, beneath it, a fainter pungent aroma that seemed natural to her. His head spun, the dizziness pleasant but disquieting. He did not know what had made him so suddenly hard, so ready to take her.

No matter. She would not be the first woman disappointed to discover that some of the legends were untrue. Unless there was a blood sharing between them, he could not give a child to this woman and blood sharings were rightly forbidden.

If he told her the truth, she would not believe him. Besides, it had been a long run from the Vardas Pass through lands reeking of death, crawling with scavengers. His need had not been great, indeed he had fed on one of the Old One's slaves two nights ago and could wait nearly a week before feeling any true hunger. But the woman—her delicious blend of courage and innocence and that damnable scent—oh, yes, he felt hunger now, enough that he rationalized it would be better to leave her with only her pride intact.

Though she lay across his bed, as enticing as any mortal he had seen in his centuries of life, he did not rush the bath. Instead, he leaned his head against the wooden molding and quieted his thoughts, moving his mind out of his body, trying to find the source of his troubling unease. Was it instinct or only the unfamiliar location?

He sent his mind out of the tent and into the prince's where he saw his brother sitting in the bath with Istvan Bathori, their bodies just touching as they talked quietly. Charles, who had been here for days, seemed at peace. The guards standing watch around the camp were the only ones awake and even they appeared weary. Perhaps his unease was a mistake. As he returned his attention to the woman, he sensed her watching him and his concern vanished. Without looking her way, he began to study her thoughts, her reasons for being here. Her sexual likes and dislikes were irrelevant for, as he expected, she was a virgin and her father had sent her here only because he hoped to mate her with a god.

He wondered, with some annoyance, how well he would uphold the family reputation. Seeing no reason to dwell on his uncertainties, he stood and wrapped himself in the cloth left for him and approached her with deliberate languor, savoring her reaction to his approach, her fading fear. Her head turned up, her lips parted, and when he kissed her she responded with unexpected lust, her tongue sliding into his mouth, its tip brushing one and then the other of his long rear fangs.

Steffen drew away from her and growled, "Are you certain now?"

Rather than responding, she rubbed the outside of his thigh with her leg, inviting him to take what he wished. He grabbed her ankle and pushed her leg back as he stared down at her, noting the flush coloring her face as she met his eyes.

"Will someone miss you?" he asked.

"No."

"Then we have the night, yes?" He ran his hand down the inside of her thigh and began to lightly stroke her, his eyes never moving from her face.

Ilona frowned and tried to pull away. "But you must . . ."

"I promise I will give you whatever you desire . . . in its own time."

As she tried to relax, he entered her mind, beginning the soft mental touches he knew so well, feeling her passion starting to grow, that damned elusive scent growing with it. His head spun, and cursing the witch that had mixed this potion, he fell on the woman.

And lost control. Completely—and perhaps tragically—he used her as he would one of his own.

CHAPTER
2

I

Later that morning, Vlad Tepes, recently restored prince of Wallachia, rode into the Bathori camp to visit his son's future bride. Finding her missing from her tent, he went in search of her. The camp's guards, uncertain how much they should restrain the man they had sworn to protect, followed anxiously as he moved to the next tent and, after a quick inquiry regarding its occupant, stepped inside alone. A moment later they heard a single bellow of rage, then nothing.

Prince Bathori, already alerted to Tepes's presence in camp, rushed to the neighboring tent. Charles, his long arms and legs sticking out of the plain brown tunic that covered him, followed. There they saw Tepes, his arms frozen at his sides, his hands shaking as he tried to resist the mental control of his adversary, to pull his sword and slaughter them both. Steffen stood beside the bed, his eyes wide, exerting all his control, yet finding himself barely able to hold a mind as twisted as the Impaler's. Ilona lay between sleep and death, her naked body revealing the deep scratches Steffen's nails had made on her arms and thighs, the marks of his teeth on her neck and breasts. Her hair was tangled, the kohl on her eyes smudged. Her necklace had broken and tiny beads were scattered across the floor, glittering in the sunlight falling though the cracked flap in the tent.

Charles, as furious as Tepes and Prince Bathori, detected

Steffen's bewilderment. —The prince sent her to me . . . —

—Then you ripped her apart! Haven't your years taught you any restraint, little brother?— Charles moved closer to the girl, resting a hand on the side of her wounded neck. As he did, his anger vanished. He looked from the girl to his brother, an odd remote smile on his face.

Steffen heard his silent laughter. It broke his control. Tepes flinched. His hand moved a few inches before it froze again. "*Strigoi*," he whispered, the Wallachian word for vampire.

"Power." Prince Bathori mouthed the word, looking sadly at Charles as, without any trace of anger, he asked, "Is she very hurt?"

"No," Charles answered while his brother stood, his eyes locked on a madman's, fighting to maintain control, fighting to keep his distance. Charles saw how his brother had tensed and knew that Steffen wanted to destroy this creature. From what he had seen of the aftermath of the last battle, Charles hardly blamed Steffen for his reaction.

"Cover my daughter and release Tepes," Prince Bathori ordered.

Charles complied with the first order, pulling a white wool blanket over Ilona's body. Steffen appeared not to have heard the words, continuing to probe Tepes's mind, finally asking, "Should I take this memory from him?"

"You can make him forget what he has seen here?" the prince asked in amazement. This was part of the legend he had not known.

"I can."

"Do it. Then I think it is best that you both leave here."

Steffen nodded and moved toward Tepes, lifting the Impaler's hand from his sword, continuing to hold it, letting the touch strengthen their bond. They stood, their faces only inches apart. Tepes's narrow green eyes flashed red in their depths like rough-cut emeralds. The Mountain Lord's were steady, coal-black and demanding. Though Prince Bathori had reason to fear the Impaler's wrath, he knew the seemingly delicate creature challenging his ally was far more dangerous. Yesterday, when he went to the cells to view his exotic capture, he had felt the power, heard the mocking laughter behind the impassive beautiful mask of Charles's face. Then for the first time, Istvan Bathori believed the stories he had heard from his mother so many years ago and began to set his trap. The timing could not have been more perfect.

As Steffen carefully wiped from Tepes's mind all recollection of the last few minutes of his life, the prince watched, certain he was seeing the old legend meeting the new. The tales King Matthias had spread of the Impaler had already made him a monster throughout the western lands. As Nero and Herod well proved, monsters were always remembered. As to the Mountain Lords, they were as old as this land itself and could never be forgotten.

Then Steffen began moving, pushing Tepes backward toward the tent flap, motioning that Prince Bathori should follow until the two men were outside, Charles and his brother concealed within.

As Tepes's eyes began to focus on their surroundings, the prince purred, "You must have had a long ride, my friend. Come to my tent and I will order you some food and wine."

Tepes looked from his host's face to the tent he had just left and he paused to brush the dust off his austere black jacket before nodding and replying uneasily, "Yes, yes it was. A strange ride too." After they were seated in Prince Bathori's tent, he added, "I had hoped to see Ilona while I was here."

"She is resting. She has not been well."

"Nothing serious, I hope."

"Not at all but it is better that she remain in bed for a day or two."

"You're her father, of course you know best." Tepes paused to take the goblet of wine a servant proffered, then, referring to the wedding, added, "It will be a good match."

It would have been, the prince mentally concurred, as much for temperament as for politics. Then the legends had intervened. If Ilona was pregnant, the power her child would possess must remain in the Bathori family. Besides, weddings of state required time. Tepes might acknowledge his own bastard son as heir, but he would never be willing to extend the same charity to the child of his daughter-in-law. Given his temper, he'd most likely slaughter Ilona as soon as her pregnancy began to show and Istvan would lose his daughter as well as her child.

And yet Prince Bathori had sworn to the king that this marriage would take place. Well, they would not reach Bucharest for at least three weeks. By the time they arrived, he would know for certain if his daughter had conceived and have planned a means out of this predicament. But for now it was better to sip the wine, devour the sweets his slaves had delivered, smile graciously at his barbaric guest, and remember the touch of the Mountain Lord who he was certain he would never see again.

II

Charles and his brother ran across the last battlefield, oblivious to the impaled bodies around them, the wails of women and children. Sometimes a mourner would look up and see dark shadows moving in the distance, lean quick beasts running four-footed, their bodies close to the ground, and they would cross themselves and return to wrapping their dead.

When the pair were well beyond the reach of the prince's soldiers, they took refuge from the midday sun in a thick stand of trees north of the Hungarian encampment. After a quick mental check to determine that the woods were deserted, Charles fell heavily onto the ground beside his brother.

"I feel as if I defeated an army last night. I believe it was worth it. It has been so long since someone looked at me and knew exactly what I am. Exhilarating, yes?" Charles asked with amusement.

"Dangerous," Steffen responded. "Suppose your prince had decided to try and destroy you instead? You weren't exactly in the best position for fight or flight."

"But he didn't. He gave me what I wanted and in exchange ... well, the shame he could almost hide was the perfect spice to his passion. Throughout the night, he kept reminding himself that I am a god. I tried to live up to his fantasies though not nearly with your own ... shall I say, enthusiasm." Charles added a low final chuckle. Since they were old enough to crawl, he'd baited his brother. It had been years since he'd seen Steffen this perfectly confused and he intended to revel in it.

"Being bewitched isn't all that pleasant," Steffen replied with disgust. "Now I have an idea of how our own conquests must feel."

"I doubt it was witchcraft."

"It must have been. I tell you, the moment I smelled her perfume, I lost all control."

"I'll tell you what that 'perfume' reminded me of, little brother, since you've made a point of never smelling it. It's nearly the same scent our women exude when their times to conceive have come. We know they are going to die but we have no choice but to mate with them when their bodies are ready."

"Are you telling me that woman will bear my child?"

"I'm only saying that no spells were involved. Some years ago I was the victim of the same experience. I had been traveling through the Szatmar region near Ecsed . . ." He rested a hand on his brother's arm. "The girl I met . . ."

The memory hit him hard the moment he'd gotten close to Ilona and detected that odd sweet perfume like some ripe exotic fruit. Now he recalled his own enchanter's face. With no real effort, he shared the vision with his brother, their link achieving a focus only the first born could achieve, making the memory as real as the event itself.

. . . The girl's hair shines red-gold in the afternoon sun as she rides past his hiding place to the narrow stream where she stops to rest her horse. She does not see him approaching her from behind and when he grabs her she screams and fights him with surprising strength, fighting even his mental intrusions. With his chest gouged by her nails, he swings her around and takes her facedown in the field, not even trying to arouse her passion, not bothering to wipe her memory when, hours later, his desire finally spent, he leaves her alone and sobbing in the dust . . .

"It wasn't all that many years ago," he added vocally. "And now what's done is done. If she and Ilona conceived, we should be grateful. Our numbers are so few that even half a legend is something to be cherished, yes?"

Steffen looked at his brother with disgust. "You speak of abominations."

Charles laughed. "And I thought I was speaking of babies, little brother. Life is hardly an abomination."

"You haven't changed. You still hold nothing sacred, least of all yourself."

"I'm far too old for absolutes." Charles raised a hand, pointing toward the last battlefield. "And we're not the ones who think life is cheap after all."

For the first time since their meeting, Steffen smiled. "The world is ready for you now, I think."

"Is that an invitation? Did you travel out of the glorious west to try to lure me back to my eternal toil?"

"I would not break our agreement. You'll have your half century of respite. If you want the time, that is. I brought Catherine home."

"Catherine?" Charles sat stunned, fixing the name with the face, the face with the soul, the soul with his memories. He layered the memories quickly, still not certain how to view her return. "Why?" was all he managed to ask.

"Kings are ransomed for far less than it took the family to buy her freedom."

"Buy? Have you resorted to using *money*, Steffen?"

"It was far easier than wiping a hundred minds of her memory," Steffen grumbled.

"And you ran the errand. Little brother, what should I make of that?"

"Necessity. She did not want to return. No one else has a mind strong enough to hold her for so long a journey. Even so, it took all my power to keep the men in our traveling party from slaughtering one another over who would possess her."

"Are you planning to stay awhile?"

"I've done my duty. I leave it to our father to deal with the monster." Though Steffen's words were mocking, Charles detected his regret. Since he had abandoned the keep three centuries before, Steffen had requested nothing from the Old One until now. "Has the Old One treated Matthew well?" Steffen asked.

"Better than I had expected." The thought of returning to the Austra family keep above the Vardas Pass seemed suddenly oppressive, but Charles thought of his son. He could not leave the boy to face Catherine unprotected, especially now when he had the means to end the boy's long nightmare. Thinking of Matthew, he lay back and rolled over on his side, facing his brother. "Where will you go?" he asked.

"North. West. Rachel suggested that I spend some months with James in Stockholm before I begin the family commissions in Austria."

"Church windows?"

"Private houses. Every petty noble must have his castle."

"Take my son with you. This country is no place for the boy."

"Because of Catherine?"

"Because of the war. Because what happened to him three years ago could easily happen again. Because these lands are our heritage, not his. He loathes it here."

"Is his mind any stronger?"

"We're only as strong as our world forces us to be, Steffen. No more. No less."

Steffen rested a hand on his brother's shoulder. "Come with us."

Charles shook his head. "I have years before I agreed to return, little brother, and I do not intend to cut this time short. But now, while we rest, tell me how your work goes and about our sister and the others."

Steffen closed his eyes. With one small part of his mind alert against human intrusion, he began to show his brother the firm's latest works and to convey the messages of affection from the rest of the family. They spoke for hours, neither asleep nor completely awake until the sun began to fall toward the mountain.

The pair traveled to the Vardas in one long run, approaching the narrow twisting mountain paths to the family keep well after dark. Steffen remained in the shelter of a cave below the timberline while Charles climbed the rest of the way alone. The half moon threw the keep's shadow across Charles, and as it touched him, he called to his son, the high-pitched cry of Matthew's name merging with the mental touch.

Matthew rushed outside, smiling, then laughing as Charles greeted him. For a moment it even seemed to Charles that his son was unchanged, the same bright youth who had come here with him five years ago, overflowing with curiosity about the Old One, the ancient family keep, and this barbaric country.

Then, on one of their periodic explorations of the surrounding countryside, they had become separated. Hours later, Charles had found Matthew's bloody, seemingly lifeless body, lying facedown in a trampled field. He knew what had happened even before he carried his son back to the keep, before he shared the nightmares. With a father's lust for blood he sought the men who had violated and tortured his son, destroying them one by one. Now, with his arms wrapped around the boy's thin shoulders, he felt him shiver with the old memory and knew this would be the last time.

"I found them all," Charles whispered, his cheek against the boy's soft hair. "Come." He turned and ran, not at his full speed, but fast enough that Matthew had to fight to keep the pace. They traveled down the mountain, past the timberline into a high treacherous valley of rocky outcroppings, overhangs, and one large cave. At its entrance, he and the boy built a fire, not out of any need of warmth but for the hypnotic effect of the rising smoke and flames.

Father and son sat beside each other, watching the flames grow and die, drawing strength from the stars and the silence. Finally, for the first time since the attack, Charles asked his son to think of more than a face and a name. The boy shook with the remembrance of fear but he obeyed, showing his father every nuance of his helpless rage and his agony.

Eleven. Small even for his kind. How could Matthew have fought off so many? But he'd tried. Charles sensed his shame at his failure along with the rest.

As Matthew finished, Charles held out an arm, wrist upturned. The order was familiar—a call to merge—and Matthew immediately responded. They'd exchanged blood many times on their trip from the west, the sharing able to tighten even a father-son bond. As they lowered their heads and began to drink from each other, Charles joined minds with his son, sharing last night's vengeance. Death provided the strongest emotions, far more potent than the attack that had left the boy screaming, replaying the painful, perfectly detailed memory whenever his control diminished with sleep. Now, the visions of how his attackers had died merged with the boy's memory of the attack itself. Matthew would no longer be able to recall the horror of the first without the satisfaction of the second. Vengeance cleansed, the family was fond of saying. It seemed to Charles that it more aptly coated, reminding them of their nature and that, in the end, their real vengeance came with time.

The memory faded to the tinkle of laughter from the hill below them. Catherine sat cross-legged on a flat rock. Her head was tilted, the waist-length hair that covered her naked body was tangled from days of neglect, her black eyes slitted and maliciously sly.

"You make me long for blood," she hissed the words in the ancient Austra tongue and disappeared into the trees as abruptly as she'd come.

Charles listened to her go, the soft rustle of her body passing across the ground, her feet padding over the fallen needles. Matthew followed her with his mind, traveling with her as far as he was able until she was lost in the mists curling through the forest around them. Charles knew that the boy, like the Old One—like him for that matter—was already maddened by her. Charles recalled the years that he and Catherine had roamed the streets of Florence, taking life where they would. How in awe she had been of his power then, pushing him to excesses he had long ago abandoned until the dark side of his nature forced him into this premature exile. Even now, after so many years apart, he was still as infected with Catherine as some mortal with leprosy. He could hide the sores but they would never heal.

"Why did you bring me here?" Matthew asked, drawing him back from the memories.

"So you could understand what you really are." Killer. Monster. Immortal. Born to powers the old gods would envy. He said none of the last, hardly dared to even think this lest the boy, his mind already strong, would sense them. "It was a mistake and I am sorry for it."

His son lay back, staring up at the stars, breathing in the thin mountain air, so sharp it seemed to cut his lungs. "Did you come here only because of me?" he asked.

"No."

"Then I don't want to go. Not until you're ready."

"And then?"

Matthew didn't answer. In three years he had not left the peaks. Now there was nothing to fear but the country itself, its emptiness and its people. These were more than enough.

Charles found himself losing his resolve for he wanted to keep his son near him. As they walked back to the keep, he began forming desperate plans that would shield the boy from the barbarity that had descended on this haven from the human storms. As they neared the stone walls, Matthew stiffened and began running forward. Charles reacted first to his son, then to the cry of terror that followed.

The high, carved doors of the slaves' quarters were open and the handful of human servants kept there huddled inside, afraid to face the demon who had invaded their sanctuary. The cry came again, louder and sharper, from one of the private sleeping rooms. Matthew reached it first and stopped in the doorway. His father joined him, staring at the horror inside, all their senses drawn by the delicious scent of terror and blood.

Catherine had chosen her victim well. The slave was a year or two older than Matthew and new to the keep. Catherine woke him without the slightest effort to calm him, without any attempt to rouse his passion. Still fearing his masters, he had fought as she expected, giving her the sport she wanted.

Now, with his back pressed against the wall, his head tilted sideways, he could only stand, held by her mind, and let her drink.

His scream came again, a wave of fear rolling out with it. Catherine could have kept her victim silent but instead she drew the family here to witness this sport. "No!" Matthew responded, his hands curled and hard at his side, recalling for a moment the horror of his past.

Catherine whirled, letting her victim go. With only one thought on his mind, the boy tried to bolt from the room, slamming hard into Matthew, pushing him against the stone wall, clawing at Matthew's face as he struggled to find his footing and run. Matthew reacted to the sudden attack as every instinct forced him to respond—his arm lashing out, hitting the boy on the neck with all the force of an iron bar, his sharp nails digging into the boy's soft flesh. The boy fell, his legs and arms twitching.

Catherine's bloodstained lips twisted into a smile that vanished as she, like her kinsmen, felt the powerful presence of the Old One.

His pupils filled his eyes—hard and flat and unreadable. Though Charles was tall by human standards, his father towered nearly a foot above him, the black robe that covered him as motionless as the long, thin body beneath it as if he had materialized from the walls themselves.

"Your child's been spared the ring, at least," Francis said to his son. "Perhaps some talent has come out of my children's haphazard matings after all." Only his eyes moved, fixing on Matthew, crouched beside the wounded slave who struggled to breathe. "Kill him," Francis ordered and stayed only long enough to be certain that Matthew would obey.

The boy fed only as much as was needed to form the bond, then finished the destruction his single blow had begun, killing quickly and kindly as he would an animal. As Charles watched his son trying to focus on the satisfaction of this life and finding only remorse, all doubts about the boy's leaving vanished. He recalled the ritual killings all the Old One's children had been forced to perform. The deadly Austra rite of passage had been intended less to test his strength and instincts than to etch in him forever that he was as superior to humans he resembled as they in turn were to the animals they used for their own food. Unlike Steffen who had viewed the ring as an inevitable necessity, or Claudia, their sister, who had been sickened by it, Charles had immediately thrilled to the slaughter. Even now the memory of it filled him with desire. Now the chance to revel in blood had come again.

The thought returned again a day later as he stood in the high stone tower of the keep and watched his son leave with his brother, taking all need of restraint with him. Carrying no belongings, encumbered only by the plain brown cloaks of pilgrims, they wound their way down the mountain in the waning evening light. Charles followed with his mind until they reached the flatter ground of the pass, then sent Matthew a quick, loving good-bye.

Then with a shrug, Charles turned his face from the mountain and descended the stairs to seek out Catherine—and to fall backward into his past.

In the years that followed, the war that seemed eternal to those who were born and lived and died while it raged on meant only one thing to the creatures who dwelt in the peaks above it.

At night the dragon frost would settle on the grasses of the high mountain meadows and Charles and Catherine would follow the winds that carried its fine grey ash back to the battle where they could feast on the dying and the dark-skinned victors in their pale flowing robes.

Sometimes Catherine would leave him, responding to the powerful summons of the Old One's mind, returning to the pleasures only he could give. Then Charles would hunt alone, surprised by the recurrent old memories of his civilized past and the similar future that would inevitably come.

Soon. All too soon.

CHAPTER
3

Paris, 1536

Jacques Vernet lost his family during an epidemic of the plague in Rouen. His mother took sick after the midsummer's fair and, within days, had died. In spite of the white reeds they had hung on their door and the healing incense the physician had supplied, his sisters followed one after another until only himself and his father were left.

As the plague spread through the city, quarantine was established and convicts were released from prison to act as gravediggers and haulers of the dead. When they came to take his sisters' bodies to be buried in the mass graves on the edge of town, they threatened to drag his father to the plague house. Knowing that his father would never survive in that terrible place, Jacques paid the men to leave, using the last of the family's possessions to buy his father a chance for life.

The bribe didn't help. His father died anyway and when the gravediggers came for one more body, they looked at Jacques—pale, red-eyed from lack of sleep, shaking with hunger—and ordered him to come with them.

Jacques followed, the noon sun hot on his fevered head and the dark shirt he wore. The day reminded him of the next and with a final burst of hope to give him speed, Jacques ran from death through the narrow reeking streets. With the cunning of the doomed, he skirted a makeshift wooden barricade designed to halt traffic through the plague-infested section of town. Though the men stopped pursuing him after only a few minutes, he kept on running until, exhausted, he took shelter in the back of the cathedral.

The cool dry air with its slight hint of incense revived him, and as he went inside to pray for the souls of his family, he saw someone sitting in the center where the light from the windows was brightest. "I'm sorry," Jacques began, not certain who he'd disturbed but knowing from the young man's embroidered cloak and the sheen of the silk of the shirt beneath that he was wealthy. It seemed best not to intrude.

He started to back up, to turn to leave, when the man looked at him with eyes dark and huge and just as weary as his own. A pale, fragile hand framed with a fine lace cuff motioned him to come closer. Jacques obeyed, shuffling uneasily forward until he stood in front of the man. Though he did not mean to stare, he found it impossible not to do so. Though the man's skin was as pale as death himself, Jacques thought he had never seen anyone so beautiful or so serene.

"Is the sun still so bright?" the man asked in an odd lilting accent.

Jacques nodded.

"Since we're both hiding, do you play chess?" The man spoke softly as if he were concerned that someone might overhear.

Jacques, twelve years old, alone and starving, shook his head. "Teach me," he said and swallowed back his tears.

They sat together until the sun was low in the sky. Then the man who introduced himself only as Steffen took Jacques to his nephew's residence on the outskirts of town. To Jacques, the high stone walls seemed to hold a palace, but once inside he could notice nothing save the sorry appearance of the house and courtyard and the strong resemblance between the two men.

"He's lost everything," Steffen said, unconcerned that Jacques was standing beside him, listening hopefully to every word. "He'll be loyal, I assure you, and if you're going to maintain this house you will need at least *one* servant." Steffen's lips curved in a tight smile as he said the last and Jacques glanced at the porticos on three sides of him, their doors into the house boarded and dirty. He looked at the flowerbeds, well arranged but covered with weeds, at the grass growing between the flagstones beneath his feet. One servant! If Jacques had anywhere to run, he would have bolted from the courtyard.

"Need? Whatever for?" Matthew asked.

When Steffen didn't respond, Jacques interjected, trying to sound older than he was and more responsible. "I can clean. And I can cook."

Steffen chuckled and it seemed to Jacques that it must be hard for the man to laugh with his mouth almost closed. "And he can amuse," Steffen added.

Matthew stared at Jacques a moment, then said, "Well, if he's staying, he'll need a bath. A hot one. And wash your clothes as well. I can smell the plague on them."

Jacques had to set a fire in the kitchen before he could heat water and he found only two large jugs of that. He scrubbed himself with the corner of a ragged blanket first, then washed his shirt and pants in the same water. Wrapping the towel around himself, he spread his clothes to dry on the courtyard stones and went searching for food. But though there was water and soap he could find no trace of anything to eat. Reluctant to mention his hunger to the two men sitting and talking in the shaded courtyard, he decided to explore. In a house of over two dozen rooms, with sculptures and paintings, with the tapestries around the beds, and the dark stained glass in the windows, only the main room and his new master's bedroom were not covered with dust.

More uncertain of his future than ever, Jacques returned to the kitchen and crouched in a corner with his knees pressed against his chest. The sun slanted through the narrow windows and traveled up the far wall, but he hardly noticed it. He tried to say the prayers his family recited each evening, but the words made him cry and he had to be an adult now. Finally, exhausted by the day's many tragedies, he slept.

Well after dark, he opened his eyes suddenly as if someone had shook him awake. It took him a moment to recall where he was. Then, curious, he stole into the courtyard in time to see someone coming through the open gate. Jacques crouched and was about to rush inside to warn his new master of the intruder when the man pushed back the hood of his dark cape and looked up at the moon.

Matthew! Jacques was less concerned about his master's violation of curfew than his lack of common sense. At night the gravediggers traveled freely through town robbing those who strayed from their homes, beating and killing those who resisted them.

Though Matthew could have hardly seen him in the dark, he turned directly toward Jacques, threw him a bundle, then walked past him and through the main doors of the house without saying a word.

Jacques took the bundle into the kitchen, lit a candle, and unwrapped it. Inside were a half-dozen rolls, a large round of cheese, and, even more amazing given the time, two clean shirts and pants. He left the shirts wrapped and protected from the dust and wolfed down enough food to fill his stomach, then returned to his place on the floor and slept.

The next morning Jacques rose early, put on his old worn clothes, and went outside. At home, he had been given most of the gardening chores, and deciding to begin his duties with what he knew best, he cleaned out the brackish courtyard pool and cleared the beds around it. He'd been working for hours when he heard the main doors of the house open.

"The house is too much of a job for one person, isn't it?" Matthew pulled up the hood of his dark cape and joined him. He sat on the edge of the pool and slipped on a pair of round dark glasses. Though Jacques had never seen anything like them before, he thought they might be the sort a wealthy blind person would wear to hide the ugliness of cataracts. "I remember the gardens that once grew here," Matthew said. "We had roses there." He pointed to the bed near the south wall. "We planted herbs near the kitchen and this circle around the pool was covered in ivy with tiny star-shaped leaves. There were lilies in the pool and frogs."

"Frogs." Jacques laughed at the thought with just a trace of anxiousness. Matthew seemed so relaxed, so much less an employer than a companion that Jacques felt the need to try to follow suit. "Where did they come from?"

"My father took me to the river to catch them." As Matthew spoke, his mind traveled backward to the old pleasant memories. "At night, I would lie here and look up at the stars and listen to them sing." And as soon as Matthew had turned five the pleasantry had ended and he was forced to endure an hour each afternoon in this courtyard without the protection of hat or shirt. He suffered for months until his body learned to adapt. The memory of the pain was one reason he'd insisted on reopening the house—that and the outlandish hope that when everything was made new again his father would return. Recalling the suffering, he said only, "I like the courtyard best at night. My body detests sunlight. It's a family trait. That's why I wear the hood and the glasses."

"You could plant trees here. They would shade the space and cool the house and you wouldn't need all that protection," Jacques suggested.

"Excellent! Is there a place where we can buy the saplings?"

"There's a gardener living just outside the city walls. He'd know of a place."

"Could you go and discuss this with him?"

"I'd have to leave the city. I don't know what will happen when I try to return." Though Jacques's voice trembled from fear, he told Matthew about the gravediggers and his escape. "If they recognize me, they'll kill me and it would be their right. After all, I might spread the plague."

Matthew didn't appear concerned. "Then we'll have to make certain they don't look twice at you. Come inside and put on the clothes I brought you."

As Jacques dressed, Matthew left the room, coming back a short time later with a bright red sash that he wrapped around Jacques's waist and a white leather doublet with a sewn red insignia over the heart. It seemed familiar to Jacques, but until he stood in front of the mirror and looked at himself, he did not recognize it. Then, seeing it for what it was, the combined alpha and omega letters of the Austra family crest, he turned and stammered to Matthew. "I can't wear this. I'm not a glassmaker's apprentice."

"This is my family's mark as well as their firm's. You are in my employ. Of course you can wear it."

"OW-stra." Jacques pronounced the name carefully and looked at himself again.

"The jacket was mine when I lived here. Now if we just clip your hair no one will suspect . . ." Matthew halted. Something about Jacques caught his eye and he stared at both their reflections in the mirror. Though Jacques's hair was of a lighter black, both had the same loose curls. Both were pale-skinned, though Matthew had far less color to his. Both were slender, and from the length of his limbs, Matthew assumed that Jacques would one day be as tall as himself. "How did you know my family's symbol?" he asked.

"My father was a stonecutter. Sometimes he and the Austra apprentices worked together. He said . . ." Jacques swallowed hard, thinking of all he had lost. "He said he was going to begin teaching me the work on my twelfth birthday. If I showed promise I would have been apprenticed, possibly even to the de Chellets. He had connections there."

"Is that what you wanted?"

Jacques looked at Matthew and frowned. No one had ever given him a choice before. It disgusted him to think that his family's deaths had allowed him one. "I don't know," he admitted.

The resemblance between them gave Matthew an idea, a bold and daring one, and caught by its prospects, he asked, "Jacques, have you had any education?"

"I can read and write. I know a little Latin." He didn't add that when he'd been younger, his family had thought he might have a vocation.

"And figures?" Matthew continued.

Jacques nodded. "Not well," he added honestly.

"Well, Jacques. Steffen was right to bring you here but I don't think you will be a servant. I want to ask his advice on your position before you leave the house. The garden will have to wait a day or two."

Jacques took off the coat. "What should I do next?" he asked.

"Come upstairs with me and choose your room."

"Upstairs! But those are your family's rooms. Shouldn't I have a place in the servants' quarters?"

"I'm alone here, Jacques, and it is a very large house. No matter what we decide your position to be, it will not be that of an ordinary servant."

Jacques had just chosen the airy east bedroom when four men entered the courtyard through the servants' gate. Sent by Matthew's uncle, they set to work with brusque efficiency, moving from one room to the next with their mops and brooms, leaving the windows shining, the floors polished, the tapestry-draped chairs and divans free of dust. They then left as abruptly as they had come and the house smelled of orange pomander and beeswax.

After they were alone, Matthew broke the seal of the note one of the men had delivered. Inside, in Steffen's small precise hand was written, "Noon tomorrow."

"So it begins," Matthew said to himself. He put down the note and looked at his young companion. "Your first duty, Jacques, will be to wake me tomorrow morning at nine."

Jacques woke at dawn. Though he tried, nervousness would not allow him to go back to sleep. Finally, concerned that he would miss the correct time to wake Matthew, he took a makeshift breakfast to the courtyard and watched the shadow move across the sundial.

A bit before nine, Jacques knocked on Matthew's door and heard no reply. A pounding brought no better response, and uncertain of what to do, he went inside. Matthew lay sprawled facedown on top of the covers of his high oversize bed. Though he'd taken off his shirt, he still wore the same brown pants he'd had on when Jacques had gone to bed. One long arm fell over the side, Matthew's fingers brushing the floor.

"M. Austra . . . Matthew." No motion from the thin, pale figure. Convinced he was being tested, Jacques shook him.

Pulled from sleep, Matthew responded, instantly awake and tensed, all instincts alert and ready to face whatever enemy disturbed his morning rest. Jacques sprang back and crossed himself, trying to control the fear of what he'd seen—his brief glimpse of the long rear teeth, the curled hard fingers, the black eyes that had no whites showing. He lost his balance and fell, scrambling backward until he reached the wall behind the door. He began to make the protective circle with his fingers and arm, thought better of it, and settled for squeezing his eyes shut as Matthew approached him.

"Jacques . . ."

"Please. Please let me go. I promise I will never tell anyone what you are. You've been so kind to me, I could never betray you."

"Jacques. I don't want you to go. Look at me."

"Please . . ."

Matthew had never been forced to explain his nature. When he'd been a child, he had been protected from all human contact save with the house servants who had known the family's needs and understood. Later there had been the Old One's slaves, chosen for him for their pliancy. His years in the wilderness with Denys had rarely included human blood. Now, his choices were clear and the most obvious one seemed unthinkable.

"Jacques, damn it, if you value your life open your eyes!"

Jacques obeyed and, with difficulty, focused on Matthew's face. Even its beauty seemed ordinary when compared with a moment before. His fear vanished and he nodded dumbly when Matthew said, "Stay where you are while I dress. Then you will come with me to AustraGlass."

The Austra firm was located a mile outside of town just off the main road to Paris. Though beds of yellow and orange marigolds were planted around the three Austra buildings, no trees grew near any of the structures and the huge woodpile used to heat the furnaces was situated some distance from the buildings. The Eure River ran behind the glass house proper and wind-driven pumps diverted some of its water into two huge cisterns at one end of it. As Matthew led Jacques inside, he noted that the floor slanted slightly uphill toward the water supply. Judging from the smoke in the air from the open fires beneath the ovens and the glowing buckets being carried from the ovens to the pouring tables the precautions were a necessity.

Matthew met his uncle in the smallest building, the one that held the Austra offices and the design studio. While Jacques stood stiffly in Steffen's office under Matthew's mental control, Matthew explained what had happened that morning.

Steffen listened with an unreadable expression, then fixed his cold dark eyes on Matthew. "You are responsible for his discovery. Now you are responsible for his life. Release your hold on him and tell him what he needs to know to make the choice."

"I don't want him to die. I thought that you . . ."

"Could erase his memory? I could, but I won't. I suggest you speak to him most eloquently."

"Steffen, I can't."

"Can't? Then kill him. You're capable of that, aren't you?" Steffen's hands were pressed tightly against the top of his desk as he leaned over it. Matthew could feel his uncle's anger, a pain in his mind as Steffen said, "You think that, after years of doing nothing, you are ready to take a role in this firm? You ask to be placed in charge of a hundred men when you aren't certain you can even control one? You know your responsibilities. Do what must be done. I have work to complete. Call me when you've finished here." Lecture concluded, Steffen left Matthew staring forlornly at what might be his first intentional victim.

"Jacques," Matthew called and woke him.

Jacques trembled but stood his ground. He knew where he was but not how he had come here. He had heard the discussion between Matthew and his uncle but it seemed as if they were speaking of someone else. Nonetheless he pulled in his breath as Matthew approached him, a quick hiss that Matthew feared would mean his death.

"Jacques. You said you would never tell anyone what I am. What do you think I am?"

Some force inside him directed that he answer truthfully. "A demon. A sorcerer. I don't know."

"You're a good Catholic aren't you, Jacques?"

"Yes, but I still would not betray you."

"Why? Is it because of my kindness or is it something more?" Matthew slowly opened the rear office door as he spoke so that Jacques could see beyond him to the main room of the studio where huge wooden tables held a section of the next Austra masterpiece.

Jacques walked toward the door to the studio. Trusting his own instincts, Matthew gave him the freedom to go, waiting in the doorway, his mind observing the boy's to be certain that Jacques did not try to bolt from the building.

Framed sketches ringed the room—Chartres, San Denys, Laon, Notre Dame, and the other great churches whose windows had been created by the Austra craftsmen. Steffen, the same sort of creature as Matthew, worked alone, painting the details on the nearly finished creation, and Jacques stood across the table from him watching his hand shading a section of St. George's armor. The dragon writhed beneath the saint's feet, a horrible demon that needed to be exorcised. He looked up and saw the crucifix on the door of Steffen's office, then walked with a steady step to where Matthew stood in the doorway waiting for him. "What have you decided?" Matthew asked. Though

Matthew looked into his eyes as he said this, Jacques could detect no mental control. This decision would be his own.

"By their works you will know them." Jacques responded with the familiar Bible quote his father had repeated so often on the nights he had come home exhausted by his work. "Whatever you are, you cannot be evil for your windows further the glory of God."

Hearing this, Matthew held out his hand, palm down. Jacques did not understand the significance of the gesture, and after taking Matthew's hand, he pressed his lips against it in the manner of a thankful servant to his master.

Matthew jerked his hand away but, responding to Jacques's pained look, said kindly, "I came here at my uncle's request. I am to be trained to manage the firm. I'll need a great deal of support if I am to succeed. There are servants for hire everywhere. What I desperately need is one knowing friend."

Jacques nodded and said nothing. The truth was, he didn't have the slightest idea what to say.

Matthew glanced out the door and Steffen, hearing the silent call, quit his work and joined them. "So my instincts were correct, yes?" he said to Jacques in the lilting voice of one of the first born.

Jacques stood, silent and confused, enthralled by Steffen's powerful presence in his mind.

"And I know you mean your pledge but these are terrible times and word freely given can be destroyed by force. I want you to take my hands and look at my eyes, Jacques. Be calm, I won't hurt you though you may feel dizzy for a moment."

Matthew moved behind the boy ready to catch him should he fall. But though Jacques swayed, he did not lose consciousness as his mind was selectively altered. When it was over, he would never be able to reveal the Austra secret—not out of foolishness, not even to escape torture or death. Until the moment when he would weaken and try, he would never know what had been done to him. Every Austra servant was under this control. Were they not, the family would have long ago been forced back to the dubious hospitality of the Old One and the cold comfort of the Austra keep.

Their route home that evening took Matthew and Jacques close to the quarantined part of the city. The houses were shuttered and barred as if locks could keep out death and the dusty silence of the streets gave better warning than the barricades that beyond this point no mortal dared pass.

"My house is two streets over," Jacques said and, without thinking, grabbed Matthew's hand and moved closer to him.

Matthew understood and pulled the boy into the shadows of a narrow walkway between two houses. "I can show you the house, Jacques. I can take you there with my mind. Do you really wish to see it?"

Jacques shivered and nodded.

—Close your eyes.—

Jacques moved forward as if he were a bird soaring over the barricades and the houses. He could feel the setting sun brilliant and pressing on the streets and roofs, on the debris that had been dragged onto the narrow dirt road.

The gravediggers had wasted no time before looting. The door to his house hung open, one hinge snapped as if death were a storm that had battered it down. Inside, the older furniture was broken, the beautiful pieces his father had carved so lovingly were gone. As the only son, he had been given a tiny upstairs room and now his spirit flowed up to it, surprised to see that nothing had been taken. Perhaps the looters hadn't known about it, perhaps the narrow ladder leading to it had looked too fragile for their bulky forms. No matter, everything was there—all of it, just as he'd left it, the only part of his life that still remained.

He wanted to cry. They should have taken his treasures with the rest!

He sensed motion in the rooms below, heard someone softly calling his name. From his position in the loft, he could see Little Pere, his closest friend, standing on the bottom rung of the ladder. He had come every day, Jacques somehow knew, looking for him.

"Jacques, are you here? Are you all right?" Pere called as he had so many times before.

—I want him to know— Jacques declared.

A moment's indecision. Assent.

Pere, bolstered by a courage he could hardly understand, began climbing until he sat on the edge of Jacques's bed, mourning his friend. Then, without understanding why, he began sorting through the carvings, taking a half dozen that he hardly thought were the best and wrapping them in the quilt. Slinging it over his shoulder, he descended the ladder, and with a quick look left and right, he crossed the street and stole through the narrow alleyways that bypassed the barricade.

Matthew pulled out of Jacques's mind and Jacques found himself staring at the crumbling bricks of the houses. As Pere approached them, Matthew adjusted Jacques's cape to hide the Austra symbol, then moved into the shadows so the boys could be alone.

"I thought you were dead!" Pere said, his voice lowering to a whisper as he finished the sentence.

"Saved," Jacques answered, lifting the bulky sack from Pere's arms. "I will not come back when the sickness ends and I want you to have the rest of my carvings. Give them . . . give some of them to Jean and Gilles and tell them to think of me."

Jacques hugged the smaller boy and left him standing in the shadows. When Pere came out of the trance into which he'd fallen, Jacques was gone. Recalling the treasure that had been given to him, Pere wiped the tears from his face before stealing across the street and through the alleys leading to what had once been Jacques's home.

When they reached the Austra house, Matthew left Jacques alone, watching from an upstairs window as the boy unwrapped his treasures and lined them up on the edge of the pool. Here were the newborn birds, individually carved to fit together in their nest, given to him on his fifth birthday. It had been the first piece his father had made for him. Here were his own poor copies, made a year later. Here was the castle with the doors that opened and closed given to him when he was six. The griffin and the unicorn, the carved flute and the other presents that marked his years. And here was the quilt from his bed, sewn over months by his mother and sisters.

Dead. All dead.

Matthew fingered the dark amber pendant around his neck, formed from his mother's ashes, and recalled the tragedy that had marked his solitary birth. Was it so odd that he should long for a companion when, unlike his father who had a sister and brother to share his youth, Matthew had never know anyone close to his age until he met the slaves in the keep?

He had thankfully fled from the woman who had drained all life from their ancient home, fled from the land around it, fled from everything that reminded him of his past. And, even now, the uncanny resemblance between Steffen and his father made him want to flee even this. No wonder he felt so terribly unsure of his worth.

Holding the pendant, watching the boy with the blanket pressed against his body crying silently below him, he felt Jacques's sorrow as a rush of emotion echoing his own.

Steffen visited Matthew's house again a week later. During the days since his last visit, three clumps of birch had been planted, shoots of ivy ringed the pool, and the grass between the flagstones had been burned away. The gardener had planted the trees and replaced the stones around them. Jacques had done the rest, and after Steffen praised his work, Matthew thought it an ideal time to raise the subject of Jacques's position in the family. "You've told me that an absence of children makes the family vulnerable to suspicion," Matthew began. "Jacques resembles us. His features and his coloring are nearly perfect. I could raise him as my ward and when the time comes for Denys or . . . my father to take your place in the firm, there will be a past for him."

"So, in just a few years you will be prepared to send the boy away?"

"And to go away myself. Uncle, I doubt I have the talent for the creative work of the firm."

"You haven't tried."

"I don't wish to try. Let James and Rachel teach me about numbers and sales. I can be the firm's representative in the east. My father told me that the land is becoming civilized. There'll be churches and palaces. And you can create their windows, but only if someone arranges for the firm to do the work." He sensed his uncle's anger, dissipated before it surfaced. "Is it so wrong to tell you what I would like to do?"

"Yes, when you haven't tried to learn the work the rest of us know so well."

"Why must I?"

"When you were a baby, your father guarded you from every danger. In the keep the Old One most likely doted on you as much as he is able. Even James let you run wild for far more years than I thought wise. Now I say you have responsibilities and you demand the right to choose." Steffen hesitated, then ran his fingers through the clear water of the pool. "But you are correct in one regard. We do need a family representative in the east. However, as you have seen, the people there are dangerous and unpredictable. If trade is the part of our business that you truly want to pursue, Robert can be sent east. You can take his place in London where our presence is already well established."

Though Matthew said nothing, Steffen sensed his denial and the anger he carefully controlled. "So, it is not the work that interests you but the country itself, yes?" Steffen asked.

Matthew nodded. "I've been thinking about it for years but only recently has the need become clear to me. I must go back. Father may have ended the nightmares but it is up to me to face my past . . . and conquer my fear."

"You should have admitted that from the beginning. Do you think I would not understand?" He scanned the courtyard, thinking of the years past when he and Charles and Claudia had dwelt here together until Miriam came, her time almost upon her, to mate with a first born and wait for death. Claudia fled from the reminder of her fate, joining her cousins in Florence. Steffen had moved into a smaller house near the firm leaving Charles to his sad duty, made all the more tragic by the birth of only a single child. No wonder Matthew had been so protected. Steffen's mind moved quickly over the possibilities, choosing the best one. "Very well, Matthew, I will allow you your nephew. We will call him Jacques Robert Austra."

He had not chosen Charles! "Robert? But Robert isn't . . ."

"Anyone who knew the boy would see through the substitution in an instant. Jacques may resemble the family in some respects but he can never duplicate the accent of a first born. Still, we can provide a past for Robert that will follow him wherever he goes. As to your leaving, the business of the firm will require more discipline than you have displayed so far. Your assumption of those duties will depend on how well you learn the craft you would practice should you stay in France. You understand, yes?"

"I do."

—But you don't approve. Well, one day I think you will. We shall see.—

• • •

Servants came. The steward was a family retainer, entrusted with the Austra secret. The others were hired from the town and knew nothing of their employer's nocturnal habits.

In time, Matthew learned to tolerate the elaborate formal dinners where he hid his inability to consume solid food by playing the role of overdiligent host. He learned to appreciate the necessary splendor of court and, far more, the intimate gatherings his uncle frequently held. Lovers came from unexpected places smiling coyly at him from beneath half-open fans. Chaperoned evening walks led to discreet trysts where he took nothing but blood and the fantasies of passion before he wiped their minds of the few minutes of feeding his needs required. For sex there were serving girls with hair of flax and gold who giggled about him behind closed doors, who gave up their virtue with willing abandon when he stole into their beds callous as an incubus at midnight.

He also learned his craft, discovering talent he never expected to possess and a steadiness that surprised him as well as his uncle. By day he learned the more mundane part of the work with the other apprentices, adding more dangerous aspects of glassmaking at night when he and his uncle were alone. It seemed that he endured a thousand surprise burns Steffen deliberately inflicted until he discovered how to absorb the pain and swallow the high-pitched, alien scream.

As he considered his environment—the stone walls, the carved tables and chairs of oak and pecan—it seemed to him that the family surrounded itself with things so old and solid that none would ever suspect that there was veneer covering the Austra nature. He thought of the lessons he learned at home and at work as a thickening of that veneer until it would become a shell, hard and unbreakable.

Matthew noted the passing of years by watching his young ward mature. And as Jacques learned to wear the cloak of aristocracy as if he had been born to it, Matthew stopped longing for another unknown shelter and thought of this place as home and the boy under his care as his kin.

His peace was abruptly shattered. Deborah Austra sensed her time to conceive was approaching and William, still in exile, agreed to be the father. The pope decided to rebuild St.

Peter's and Steffen, as master craftsman, was required to go to Rome. Steffen visited Matthew at home, breaking the news with brusque directness, concluding only, "Go home. Find your father and tell him that fifty years is too long an exile."

"And if he refuses to return?"

"You will take his place here." Somehow Matthew expected to hear this but not the pride as Steffen added, "You've learned the work well. I would be honored to place you in charge of the firm. But your wishes must likewise be honored. You have earned that right, yes?"

They discussed details. Matthew would leave France first, going to the keep to find his father. William and Deborah would join them by midsummer for Deborah desired to spend her remaining time in the ancestral home. "Should I accompany my father if he returns?" Matthew asked.

"Only as far as Vienna. The firm needs you there. Though it is difficult to predict when Deborah will conceive, it won't be too many years before William and his children will be joining you. Rachel intends to move there as well to help care for the little ones. You won't be alone, Matthew."

"I know. Still, I had hoped to spend some time with my father."

"It is only May. I don't need one of you here until the end of the year. And later, Matthew, I promise that you'll have more time. As for Jacques, he could travel with you as far as Vienna and be waiting for you there when you return. Or if he wishes, he can remain here."

After so many years, Matthew couldn't imagine a future without Jacques. As for Jacques, when Matthew and his uncle presented him with the options he declared he would go all the way to the Vardas or not at all.

"I knew you'd say that," Matthew responded to the ultimatum. His voice softened, friendship overcoming their disagreements as it so often did. "I had hoped you would request this, but I must warn you of the risk. The lands we will pass through are terrible. Peasants are tortured and killed for the slightest insubordination to their betters. Even aristocrats can be disposed of at someone's whim. And when we reach the keep, you will be a slave. My slave but still subject to the whims of the Old One."

"Would that be so harsh?"

"Catherine is with him," Matthew went on. "I watched her kill. I was powerless to stop her. I doubt I possess much more power now."

Jacques turned to Steffen, silently begging him to contradict his nephew.

Steffen complied. "I think my father would honor your bond at least so far as to protect Jacques as he would a servant. Catherine won't be able to touch him."

Not unless he wants to be touched, Matthew thought, recalling Catherine's body, her seductive laughter. Nonetheless, he wanted someone to share his thoughts and understand the need that drove him back to that desolate pile of stones.

And ignoring his misgivings, he agreed.

Some nights later, the family held a blood sharing, not the formal Long Night sharing of winter solstice but one more personal. The brief exchange of a part of each of them strengthened their ties with Matthew, and on the long trip across the continent, he could take comfort in this night.

He and Jacques would take few personal possessions but a number of gifts—bolts of finely woven silk to placate Catherine for their intrusion, a collection of pigments and rolled canvas for Francis, and, from Steffen, a number of books for his father—printed and bound accounts of the discoveries of Columbus, a Bible, an anatomy text, and a book of Greek philosophy. Though isolated by choice from the world around him, the Old One was fanatical about being a creature aware of his time. "If anything will secure fair treatment for Jacques and affection for you, it will be these," Steffen told Matthew as he presented the volumes. "As for you," he said, turning to Jacques, "while Matthew is occupied with his father, you can teach the Old One to read."

Jacques whitened. It had not occurred to him until now that he might have to face Francis Austra alone.

"Just remember, Jacques. You only have to tell him a thing once. Understanding may take longer. Diplomacy will be the difficult part."

"More difficult than dealing with the abbot at Laon?" Jacques asked, reminding them of a particularly meddling, and color-blind, client.

"Only somewhat worse," Steffen said and laughed.

• • •

The pair set out on horseback late the next morning, traveling east through the afternoon, stopping each night so that Jacques could sleep and Matthew could hunt. Though Jacques sometimes sensed men watching him from the forest, they kept their distance. In time, his uneasiness weakened and he learned to sleep. Nothing could harm him, not as long as Matthew was close by.

They left the trade roads at Vienna, traveling east through Hungary. On each anniversary of the day he had met Matthew, Jacques had gone to the great cathedral in Rouen, lit a candle for his family, and dropped as many coins as he could afford into the poor box to help those less fortunate than himself. This year he said the prayers and lit the candle in a tiny stone church in the center of Cluj. Though the church was Orthodox rather than Roman and the date a week too soon, Jacques knew it would be his last chance to give thanks properly.

They sold their last set of horses the following morning, and with their baggage in hand, they disappeared. Rumors spread through the town. The pair had not been taken, they had gone willingly to serve the Mountain Lords. More candles were lit in the small stone church. Someone wanted to dedicate a Mass to them but the country priest dismissed the suggestion with a quick, nervous flutter of his hands. Superstitions. Though he believed them, he would not condone them.

Running at night, unencumbered by possessions or his human companion, Matthew could have made the trip in a week. Instead, it had taken two months and the last few hours of it seemed the worst.

Jacques had a terrible fear of heights, a fear that only revealed itself when they crossed the timberline and the path narrowed to a width that forced them to travel single file. Jacques knew that Matthew longed to run forward, to find his father and greet him alone but he remained behind Jacques, cheering his every half-frozen step. Finally, Jacques's knees gave way altogether and he sat with his back to the steep mountain rocks, looking at Matthew with misery.

—Did it ever occur to you, Matthew, that you could drop your gifts and carry him?—

The words flowed into both of them. Matthew frowned while Jacques found himself instantly mesmerized, staring at some point between this peak and the next, trapped by the beauty of that strange inaudible sound, the bright peals of laughter that followed.

"The Old One?" he asked Matthew.

"Catherine."

"Where is she?"

"Most likely inside the keep. It isn't very far now."

Jacques pulled himself from the waking dream into which she had thrust him. "I won't go the rest of the way on your back," he declared, and pushing himself to his feet, he picked up two of the lighter bundles and began a determined last climb, deliberately keeping his eyes on the path ahead, never looking down.

The ancestral home of his adopted family astounded him. Jacques had expected some fortification such as the castles that seemed to dot every major hill in the surrounding land. Instead, he found himself looking up at a fortress that seemed little more than an extension of the mountain peak—the same hue as the rocks and, with one exception, the same jutting shape. Only the tower seemed to have been formed by other than nature's hands and it stood, a high rocky aerie above the peak.

Jacques looked up and saw a flash of motion on the edge of its wall, then a figure fell from the heights. Thinking someone had been thrown over the edge, Jacques could only watch the fall, stepping back at the last moment so he would not be crushed.

A man landed on hands and feet with all the grace of a young cat. Jacques knew by his resemblance to Matthew's uncle and by Matthew's delighted cry of surprise that this was Charles Austra. Charles hugged his son, then did the same to Jacques, laughing as he picked up a portion of the packages and flung open the high, shaded doors of the keep.

Jacques would remember the strange warm welcome for its contrast to everything that happened later. It was the only joyful moment he would have for weeks.

CHAPTER

4

I

Throughout the afternoon, Matthew showed Jacques the keep. They toured the slaves' quarters, divided into a number of different classes of rooms. The plain barred ones held the Turks and Russians who fought and died in Catherine's arms. The ordinary ones, not unlike his old room in Rouen, provided private space for the servants. The plush, tapestry-lined wing that held the Old One's harem could only be entered through high carved doors in the great hall so Matthew took him through those only with his mind. Three concubines sat together in the main room of their quarters playing a game of cards with a lavishly painted deck.

Three women—one with hair black as Matthew's, another with eyes so blue they rivaled the evening sky, the third so ordinary, so mouse-brown and yet, Jacques knew, she was the Old One's favorite because she gave the most.

Jacques wondered if they were content with the luxury surrounding them. Their baths would always be warm, their food always plentiful and well prepared. They had music and games and the beauty of the peaks should they choose to walk outside. And yet the rooms where they were kept seemed too large for them. There were too many beds, too many private alcoves. Perhaps if there were more of them, they would not seem so lonely and so sad.

—The slaves' quarters are used by the entire family—

Matthew explained. —Once there were many more of us living in this place.—

—You can go there?—

—Whenever I wish.—

Jacques thought of Matthew in the dark one's arms and the vision he had was too lewd to share. Matthew, understanding, let him go, and they rested waiting for Francis to summon them, neither of them feeling calm enough to sleep.

"What did you sense in there?" Jacques asked.

"Nothing," Matthew replied without opening his eyes because they would betray his uneasiness. "Jacques, I want you to promise me one thing."

"Yes?"

"Do not let Catherine touch you."

"Touch? I don't understand."

"She does not possess a mind as strong as my father's or my uncle's. She needs to touch you to form a true bond. Don't let her."

"What did you sense in there?" Jacques repeated, his voice more insistent.

Matthew decided not to spare him the truth. "When I was young there were over a dozen living in those quarters and the rooms were always filled with laughter and music. Now there are only three, and fear darkens the hearts of all of them. I repeat, Jacques. Do not let Catherine touch you."

Jacques paid his respect to Francis and Catherine that evening. He went alone for that was the custom of this place. Unintentionally adding to his nervousness, Matthew had disappeared with his father, perhaps to the plush quarters behind the carved doors. As Jacques walked into the great hall, he kept his eyes straight ahead, concentrating on the people he would meet, not on the walls rising around him or the paintings that covered them. He became acutely aware of his footsteps echoing off the stone floor, ceasing abruptly as his feet sank into the plush Oriental carpet covering the center of the room. Torches ringed the raised dais where Francis sat beside Catherine, unmoving as if he were a part of his surroundings rather than the cause of them. Catherine, for all her beauty, was perpetual nervous motion, her hands fluttering like pale butterflies, revealing her uneasiness over what Matthew's visit might portend. Neither of them attempted to hide what they were. Their eyes were dark and huge, their arms bare revealing their incredible length. Both were sumptuously clad in black vests and loose pants tooled with gold, a king and queen waiting to see what manner of servant had come with their kin.

"He is a beautiful child, is he not?" Catherine said to Francis as Jacques bowed low before them. She spoke French and Jacques knew he was intended to hear the comment. He attempted to think of her words as a compliment, though, at sixteen, he could hardly be called a child anymore. Still, he had the uneasy feeling that she thought of him as less than a man, even less than a child, more like a prize merino sheep best suited to wool and mutton.

"I have lived in Matthew's house for five years." After Jacques said these words, it occurred to him that five years was nothing to the Old One who measured his life in millenniums. He wondered how old Catherine might be.

"And your name, child?" Catherine asked in a lilting voice that made him think of the strange pear liquor he had drank in Cluj—sweet until the burning started.

"Jacques . . . Jacques Robert Austra."

"Steffen is no fool. He does resemble Robert as a child, does he not?" Catherine laughed and leaned toward the Old One. As she did, one flap of her vest fell open, revealing a pale breast. Jacques forced himself to look only at the Old One's face.

Francis studied Jacques carefully. "Do you understand what it means to be one of us?" he asked in his own language.

Though Jacques was not familiar with the Austra family language, the complex inflections coloring the guttural sounds seemed clear in his mind. "I do not *know*. Some of it, I can imagine."

"Then imagine."

Jacques had been warned to respond truthfully. Nonetheless, he weighed his words before replying, "This keep was not made to withstand an army, but to hide from one. To be an Austra is to be lonely, I think."

"Lonely!" Catherine's voice rose in pitch, her words followed by a quick nervous titter.

"You have brought gifts for me?" Francis asked in a French so thickly accented that it took Jacques a moment to realize that his ears alone should be able to understand it.

Jacques nodded and held out the book he'd been carrying. "This one is a Bible, the sacred book . . ."

"I know what a Bible is. You need not instruct me."

Jacques felt the anger like a slap and he flushed.

"Now you will sit beside me and show me what all these beautiful markings mean. Then perhaps I will show you how it feels to be truly alone."

Catherine looked from the Old One to Jacques. Her expression darkened and she lightly brushed her hand down Francis's arm, a gesture all the more seductive for its simplicity. Francis did not look at her, did not seem to notice her in any way even when she left the room, her back stiff, her departure haughty.

Jacques read the Bible, his fingers moving from word to word as he spoke, Francis sitting with his eyes closed, absorbing the letters as they formed in Jacques's mind. When Jacques had finished Genesis, Francis took the book, his fingers moving as Jacques's had moved while he recited word for word. He had only to see a thing once to know it.

Understanding took longer. They discussed the book and the way it had been made until early morning. Then Jacques fell asleep where he sat, waking well after dawn, stretched out beside the Old One on the dais. Later, it seemed that he had not dreamed but a crushing black emptiness remained with him throughout the next day. Was that what Francis had meant when he said he would show Jacques loneliness or was it simply that for the first time since the journey began Jacques felt truly alone?

He didn't know. He didn't want to ask.

He did not see Matthew at all that day. The servant who brought him his meals said that he and Charles were not in the keep. Jacques had expected them to go off alone but to not be told concerned him. Throughout the day he felt abandoned and uneasy, so much so that he welcomed the Old One's summons that evening.

Continuing where they had left off the night before, they read Exodus, but instead of discussing it, Jacques was asked about his home and his family, Rouen and Paris, and what the far-flung Austra family had been doing with their lives. Jacques answered as best he could. Tonight, uncomfortable at sharing a bed, however large, with a man to whom he found himself inexorably drawn, he asked to be excused.

Francis refused and left himself. As Jacques fell asleep, he thought he saw motion on the narrow balcony that ringed the great hall. He though he heard voices but he could not be sure. Comforted, he slept. This time he dreamed of a distant past when tribes hunted for food on the grassy Hungarian plains and built bonfires to keep the *liderc*, the lonely female demon, from claiming their souls as her own.

And as he lay, lost in the vision, he heard a bright peal of laughter, Catherine's whisper, so soft the words could not be known.

The following afternoon, Matthew and his father returned and the Old One disappeared with them. Exhausted by the unfamiliar late hours, Jacques retired early and slept deeply until Catherine began to call to him. He had expected this, an odd beautiful song created just for him to fan his desire. Though he'd been warned to avoid her, the music was too sweet to resist. Without thinking of the consequences, he pulled on his pants and tiptoed barefoot down the long corridor to the great hall.

Torches had been lit throughout the space. The narrow windows along the catwalk had been opened and the chilly night air fell, making the flames dance, the tapestries sway. And along the edge of the huge room, Catherine whirled, her naked body swaying like a reed as she spun, her feet making soft slapping sounds on the stones.

Fairy. Malicious sprite. Demon.

Jacques stood and stared, wanting her, fearing her as she moved, faster, ever faster, swirling in a dervish dance set to the pace of her own private music, her long hair a shiny black cloud around her head. Transfixed, Jacques hardly noticed when she began to move down the long wall toward the place where he stood until she stopped, stock-still in front of him, the expression in her dark slanted eyes one of surprise and delight as she savored how his gaze was drawn to her body. She took one step forward. Two.

Had Catherine raised her arms, she would have touched him and all would have been lost. Instead, she waited for him to give permission.

Like it had once before, Death waited. Jacques, trembling with fear and desire, recalled the memory and fled.

In his room, on his knees, his hands clenched into fists, his fists pressed against his forehead, he prayed.

Hours later, Matthew found Jacques still on his knees, leaning against his bed sleeping. He picked Jacques up, laid him on his bed, and sat beside him stealing the vision of Catherine from his mind.

The room was too small for Matthew to rest there comfortably but he did not dare desert his friend. He stretched out in the corridor where, heedless of the cold hard stones, he slept as well, his body guarding the one entrance to the room, keeping anyone from entering or leaving.

Catherine had sent a warning, he knew. If she had meant to harm Jacques she would have done so. Instead she was telling them both to leave.

He was glad the discussion with his father had gone so easily.

II

Charles Austra had not stayed in the ancient keep this long since he'd been a child. As always, it was home to him, a part of his soul he could never abandon forever. As always, leaving would be at best temporary. Nonetheless, the message his brother had sent was true. If he didn't go soon, he never would and the thought of being trapped here, a prisoner of his nature, seemed even worse than a few decades in civilized France.

They would leave tomorrow, taking nothing, traveling north to the home James had made in Sweden. Better to spend the remaining months with his son in happier surroundings. This place was too uncomfortable for Matthew and too dangerous for his young ward. Even Francis admitted relief when Charles told him that they would be setting out the following afternoon.

But first, whatever else he did, he had to find Catherine and tell her of his decision before she sensed it and misinterpreted its meaning. His mind moved through the keep, seeking her.

He found her in the tower, her body slashed by moonlight and shadow. Though she could not help but hear him as he approached, she refused to turn and look at him. "You know," he said.

She nodded. "I saw the way Matthew looked at me when you returned. I saw the triumph."

"This isn't a battle."

"Someone lost." She hesitated and gripped the wall, squeezing, crumbling the old stones with her fingers. "Francis is with his mouse-brown witch. I wanted to hunt tonight. He refused. He said he needed more." Again she paused, this time for emphasis. She was so transparent, he saw through the words to what she really meant. "He's cold, Charles; so cold that just the touch of his hand drains all the heat from me. Even so, if he hadn't forbidden me his three favorite pets, I would have destroyed them long ago."

Age would devour them. Death would claim them. And Francis, like all of them save Catherine, would find others to replace them. Perhaps that difference is what made Catherine so addicting to them all. She reminded them of what they ought to be. In Paris she had been prohibited the kill for the family's safety. To compensate, she had taken lovers, using them night after night until they had nothing left to give. In the end, she would wipe their minds of even her memory. Charles sometimes encountered them in his work and they would stare at him with dry, lifeless eyes and expressions dull and confused as they tried to remember something wondrous that they had forgotten. "Come with me," he said, regretting the words as soon as he spoke them.

She laughed. "What will I have there? Here, at least, I have my human herd of brutes locked in the slaves' quarters to devour one after another whenever I choose with the rest looking on. You know the fear, Charles, the delicious terror that just my presence inflicts. Think of the potency that only a few drops of their blood can impart, then tell me why I should go back to the churches of France and to hiding what I am."

She untied the shoulders of her long, thin tunic and let it drop onto the stones. He thought she meant to come to him and attempt one final seduction but instead she balanced on the edge of the tower for a moment, just long enough for him to call her name before she jumped. Landing softly in the snow, she ran off, like the lean white wolf she so resembled, to seek her prey.

As he stared down at the shadows where he had once seen her form, he knew that William would not come here, nor Deborah. As long as Catherine was here, this could not be a home to the others.

Only him. He would come back to her. He always did.

In the great hall, Matthew took his turn with the Old One, telling Francis of the family, their wanderings, their triumphs. Francis demanded to know every detail, every bit of the present that Matthew could recall. While they sat together, Charles sorted his things, packing the clothes he had so meticulously embroidered and beaded in his countless hours here, the detailed miniature he had painted of Notre Dame on the day of its dedication. Jacques, who had been ready since that morning, mustered his energy for the trip ahead and slept.

Catherine stole down the corridor leading to Jacques's room, moving on hands and feet, her body close to the ground, her thoughts veiled lest one of the others would sense her and come. Outside Jacques's door, she waited, sending her mind into his, forcing him into a deeper sleep.

Any of the family knew this trick. Weak or strong, they needed to learn it to survive.

Carefully, she unlatched the door and slipped inside, padding to his bed. He dreamed . . .

. . . and he is back in the great hall, watching her dance, watching her body. His shame is gone, taking all fear with it. When she stops in front of him, he reaches for her, pulling her close, kissing her.

Kissing her . . .

Kissing her. His hands were wrapped around her, his chest pressed against her bare breasts when he opened his eyes.

He could not scream. Their bond had formed and she had stolen his voice!

One pale hand pressed against his face, the other flung back his covers and moved slowly up the top of his thighs, leaving a trail of cold, eternal fire in its wake.

Had he a means to remember the words, he would have prayed.

—To lie is a sin. Do you desire me?—

The assent, pulled from him.

—To lie with me is a sin. Will you allow it?—

Again, the assent. Jacques managed a moan. He wanted to scream.

Her hand rubbed his scrotum, his penis—so hard, so shamefully hard.

And he wanted her. Not with a desire forced any longer, but freely, openly, though he be damned for it.

—Matthew stole my lover. Now I shall steal his.— She moved him sideways, across the bed, his head dangling, cradled in her hand, the blood pounding in the veins of his neck. As she stroked him, she lowered her head and began to drink.

Fire consumed him. He had never felt such pain!

As he struggled to scream, she bit deeper and stretched out on top of him, her knees bent. Even in his agony, he could not resist her. His hips rose to meet her, his body rocked with her. As his strength slowly ebbed, the fire grew.

In the great hall, Francis stopped speaking, staring at nothing for a moment. "Jacques," he said.

Matthew, understanding, ran for his friend's room, pausing at the door, fighting her mental barrier, pushing himself through.

—No!— He screamed. He thought. He begged.

Catherine did not raise her head from Jacques's neck, did not stop the quick coupling of her body against his.

Enraged, Matthew reached for her, pulling her off Jacques, placing himself between them. Her face was smeared with Jacques's blood, her thighs were wet, her smile one of predatory triumph.

"He is mine!" she shrieked and, without warning, sprang.

Thrown off guard by what should have been an impossible attack, Matthew reeled back with a long slash on the side of his face, then, ignoring the pain, gripped Catherine's wrists. She struggled, her body slippery with the boy's blood, broke his hold, and attacked him once again, opening four long gashes on his chest.

Too caught up in the battle to comprehend the enormity of her act, Matthew fought her off, wondering how long he could avoid giving her the prize she wanted. Only Jacques's faint stirring kept Matthew from losing hope until he heard the Old One's bellow, "Enough!"

Catherine turned and wiped her face with the back of her hand. "The boy gave permission. That makes him mine."

"He's Matthew's meat, not yours." The Old One hissed the words in the ancient family language. "And Matthew has proven himself far more worthy of the family lineage than you, a first born. Whatever you've done in the past has been nothing compared to this."

"He'll heal," Catherine declared. Indeed, Matthew's wounds had already stopped bleeding.

"You raised your hand to one of your own kind. You know the penalty for such an abomination." The Old One's tone shifted, deepened, the force of his command impossible to ignore. "Catherine, for this crime, you are banished from this keep and from the family. None of your kind will give you shelter, not here and not in the west. I will send word to Steffen and to Denys, to all of them. They will heed this command or I will bring their empire down around them. Now go."

Catherine laughed and walked toward him, her head cocked, her hands palm out at her sides. There was no mistaking her own power, even Matthew could feel the attraction not meant for him. He sensed the Old One weakening for a moment, then his resolve hardened. He built a wall around his body and mind that made it impossible for her to touch him. Forced back, she hissed and turned, running from the room. Only laughter remained, seductive and mocking. Matthew was condemned to remember it perfectly forever.

Matthew had listened carefully to the Old One's curse, trying to follow the ancient language and its curious inflections. One thing shocked him—the Old One's use of the term first born had been given the night inflection. The added meaning implied "pure."

This made no sense. In spite of what she had done, he and Catherine were kin. Perhaps in his rage, the Old One had made a mistake.

Impossible. At a time such as that, he would never be more precise.

A scream echoed in the great hall, a long extended sound of someone dying. Another followed. Another. She was killing the Old One's concubines, yet Francis stood impenetrable as darkness, his stern expression never changing, his thoughts veiled as he watched Matthew tend to his ward. He cared about these last three women as he had not cared about the other slaves he had allowed her to destroy, yet he would not try to save them, would not stand up to her beyond the words he had already spoken.

Matthew understood. This would be Catherine's only vengeance. He would let her have it because he would never rescind his curse.

From a distance, Matthew sensed his father's questioning concern, sensed the Old One's mental reply. His father's wrath grew until it became so strong that only Jacques's soft moans kept Matthew from pressing his arms against his head as if he could somehow shut out the pressure and the pain. Francis, against whom the onslaught was directed, seemed to feel none of it.

—Take care of him— Francis said, the thought mixing concern and pride. He seemed to banish the anger as he had banished Catherine, and Matthew felt it fade.

It faded still as his father moved away from the keep. Defying the Old One's command, he pursued her.

Matthew propped a second pillow beneath Jacques's head, the new angle closing the wound. The bleeding diminished, and heartened, he went for water and clothes. Then, having done all he could do, he sat beside his friend, holding his hand, hoping he would wake, and wondering despondently if he would ever see his father again.

Catherine ran headlong down the mountainside, leaping from one rocky outcropping to another, surefooted as the mountain goats that shared the peaks. Once she tripped on the long silk gown she wore. Furious from the pain of her fall, she ripped the skirt front and back, tying the ends around her ankles in the fashion of harem pants.

Unable to match her rage-driven descent, Charles almost lost her. But on the flatter ground of the pass he used his speed to full advantage, catching up with her as she reached the road heading toward Cluj, swinging her around.

She spit in his face. "You know how he cursed me. Go back to your son and the pretty little catamite he brought with him."

"I am forbidden to give you shelter but I can travel with you and help you for a time."

"I would be happiest traveling alone."

"If you go on looking like that, you will find yourself happily killing men. Let me go back and bring you what you'll need. Even in his rage, Francis will not deny you your clothes and your jewels. You will be a wealthy woman anywhere you go, Catherine."

"If I have need of wealth, there is wealth to be taken wherever I go. I say it again, I'll survive as I always have. Go back to your own, Charles."

He only stood, his head at a slight angle, his expression as determined as her own.

Without warning she sprang, her hands curled and aiming for his eyes. Even surprised as he was, he caught her easily, holding her tightly, feeling her fight on long after she had lost the round.

Her nature should have made it impossible for her to physically harm one of her own yet she had managed to do so three times today. She had to be insane. Charles could conceive of no other explanation for her acts.

She relaxed, pressing her body against him. "Do you really believe we are of one blood?" she asked and, with a sudden lurch, broke free. "It's a lie. You are nothing like me. In your worst nightmare, you could not conceive of being a monster such as me."

Then she raised her hands and touched his temples. Her delicate fingers brushed the sides of his face, and with a tenderness that astonished him, she kissed him. A cloud of passion blinded him, he was lost in her as he had been so many times before. They stood, their bodies barely touching, their minds twined, and for the first time she opened hers completely to him. He felt her loneliness and her rage, the consummate rage that made her want to destroy everything she valued, everything she touched.

—Charles Austra—builder of temples, father of so many children, bearer of so many gifts—you must not stop me.—

She pulled him down against the cold earth, and as his thoughts told her that he cherished her too much to let her go even if going with her would mean his own exile, his head exploded in a ball of pain that dizzied him. With all the speed and strength of one of the mountain born, she struck again and again, leaving him dazed and unmoving at the side of the road.

Through the pain he detected a distant rumble in the earth. Soldiers were coming, at least two dozen on horseback were galloping toward them. With a quick laugh, Catherine ripped the bodice of her dress. Her face contorted into a grimace of pain and she ran toward the men screaming, pressing her body against their leader's boot. He jumped from his horse and she fell into his open arms.

Less concerned about her well-being than in protecting his newfound prize, the soldier questioned her quickly. Between dry-eyed sobs, she blurted out a story of rape and kidnapping, torture and attempted murder. *"Vadember!"* she spat the Hungarian term. Wild-man, something less than human. "Wallachian pig!" she added, appealing to the chauvinism of her Magyar rescuers.

Fanned by her anger, the ancient hate grew in all of them, and even before their leader spoke, they knew what they would do.

"Bury him. Bury him the way the White Knight Hunyadi buried Mircia, son of Dracul. Let him be an example to all the thugs of Wallachia."

An example, Charles thought coldly, *must be known.* These sudden assassins would leave scarcely a trace of him, the only sign of his passing the disturbed earth they were already turning. Charles looked from the leader of this small band to Catherine and sensed her triumph. His mind had been damaged by her blow. Now he would have to find the strength to kill them all if he wished to escape. Slaughter was exactly what she desired.

She would not drive him to it. He wouldn't give her the satisfaction.

Besides, though their leader did not know it, the death they planned for him was the one he had chosen. Charles looked at his executioner as if memorizing his face, and the coldness in his eyes gave the man years of anxious dreams. The man raised his sword ready to strike, then, inexplicably, lowered it. "Tie him tightly. We'll let him feel every last moment."

One of the men emptied a food sack and pulled it over Charles's head, tying it at his waist.

"We're doing you a favor, you know, by using only a sack. You'll die quicker," the leader said.

Charles, fighting his killing rage, said nothing.

The ropes were strong but that didn't concern him. The sack smelled of potatoes and cabbages and onions that it had held days before. They had only their hands for digging but the twelve soon made a deep pit and rolled him into it, covering him with the loose earth, piling stones above it to weight him down.

Dark. Silent and pressing. Charles slowed his breathing to match the air he could pull out of the earth. He waited until he sensed that his head had almost healed, then used his nails to wear through the ropes on his wrists. He tensed and they snapped. He arched his back until his long arms reached his ankles and began chafing at those ropes as well.

When his arms and legs were free, Charles rolled sideways, working his body into every small pocket in the loose earth, digging upward.

It took him two hours to free himself. In that time, the soldiers had moved on, taking Catherine with them. He followed their trail to their camp but by then she had gone, stealing a horse and their gold. Their leader was dead, the men who had been on watch were dead. The others slept, oblivious to her theft. Charles let them live. Like him, they had only been her pawns.

He wondered where she would go, how content she would be in her eternal exile. No matter. His instincts had not altered their conclusion. Someday he would see her again.

III

In the mountains near Deva, a merchant tucked his only child into bed in the two-room cottage he had recently purchased for the family. He blew out the candle, picked up a knife from the dining table, and carried it into the private bedroom he shared with his wife. Irene sat stiffly upright in bed, her long hair plated down her back, a shawl covering her white bedgown, a string of rosary beads wound round the fingers of one hand.

"Did you bar the door?" she asked.

"I did."

"Will Eva sleep?"

"She isn't nervous," the man said. "Only you."

"Is the fire dampened? Did you lock the shutters?" Irene added these questions with a petulant frown.

"Did you say your prayers?" her husband countered and chuckled at her fear.

For the first time that day, Irene smiled. "I've never been so far into the mountains," she said. "It's so quiet."

"Better bears and wolves than Timisoara."

Irene reached for the wooden headboard, gripping it tightly so the dreaded word would pass over her and follow the wood down to the earth. If prayers to Mother Mary were not enough, the old beliefs would give added protection. If sleep would not come, there was wine. She poured a glass and gave it to her husband, then took it from him when he was done and finished it. She giggled nervously as he touched her, then relaxed. He was right, after all, for the first time in weeks they were safe, freed from the threat of invasion and the hungry children who roamed the streets of Timisoara in feral packs, the orphans of the plague that had preceded the war.

Dusk turned to darkness. They had few candles but enough food to last a week or more. Tomorrow, if the hunting was good, her husband would add to that. They had money to buy more, of course, but each trip to town would be risky now. As for tonight, they held each other and slept.

In the darkness, something padded round their cabin, something that walked on hands and feet, something with fingers to test the strength of the shutters, something that could listen at the door and, with more than human cunning, gauge their sleep.

It leapt onto the thatched roof, digging through the reeds, squeezing through the beams beneath it, landing quietly on all fours in the dark room beneath.

Inhales. Exhales. Peaceful sleep. No one knew that death had fallen deliberately into their midst.

The creature stood upright and now no one would think it anything more than a woman fair of face, lean of form.

The woman's eyes, unaffected by darkness, took in the size of the main room as they had the mountains surrounding the cottage, the thick forest that protected it, the steep path that led to it and could be easily concealed.

There would be no surprises here, no intruders on her life.

The creature walked into the bedroom, silent as the moon rising outside, and glutted herself on the man. Only at the end, in death, did her hold vanish and the final spasm of his body wake his wife. The one called Irene shook her husband, shrieking at how limp he had become. Then seeing Catherine's pale body just visible in the moonlight falling through the cracks in the shutters, she shrieked again.

Pulled from her bed by her hair, she was dragged into the main room where her daughter lay, the covers over her head, shivering with fright.

"Please," Irene begged as her attacker threw another handful of sticks on the fire. "Please," she repeated as she was dragged toward her child, unable to break the hold the long, fragile fingers now had on her wrist.

Wrenching the child from the bed, the creature loosened Irene's arm, only to grab her hair once more, pulling her head back. Without letting the child go, she smiled, the growing fire revealing the long rear teeth of her kind. Seeing them, the woman began to tremble, the child screamed and tried to twist out of the creature's grasp.

Begging was useless. Struggling was no better.

Their attacker drank from both of them, and when she had taken her fill, she locked them with the corpse in the bedroom and went to sleep, curled on the child's small bed like a cat.

Late the next day, Irene and her daughter were let out. They ate and washed, all the time Irene kept her eyes on the door, certain they could never reach it. A demon had come to live with them, a beautiful demon with teeth like a lynx. Irene did not ask anything, not even if she could bury her husband, but later in the day when the air grew hot, the woman wrinkled her nose and ordered her to do so.

The monster kept Eva at her side while Irene piled the stones. As long as Irene could not rescue her daughter, she dared not try to escape.

The next morning, the woman unlocked her door earlier, giving her a sack of gold. "Take one of the horses and go to Cluj, to the weavers' street, and find a merchant called Geza Jambor. Tell him you have come for the bolts of cloth ordered for Catherine."

"That is your name?" Irene interrupted. A name would make

this creature seem more a woman somehow.

"Silence!" Irene choked, clutching her throat, unable to breathe while Catherine slowly finished her orders. "Tell him you will deliver the cloth yourself. He will be happy to see you take them. Then you will purchase needles and thread, whatever you need for my garments."

Irene patted her chest, her eyes frantic.

"You are a seamstress, are you not?" the woman said with her broad cat's grin, then released her hold. Irene inhaled deeply and leaned against the table to steady herself as the room spun around. "And while you are gone, this pretty little thing will amuse me." She pointed to the bed where Eva still slept, then to the door. Irene ran.

Irene dared not warn the town, indeed she was not sure what she would warn them of save that a forest demon had come into her house and claimed it as her own. As the demon had said, the merchant was pleased to give her the cloth, asking only for a description of her mistress before he parted with them.

On the way out of town, Irene stopped at St. Michael's Church in Kolozsvar to find a priest to bless her. The younger priests were away, giving last rites to the dying but one old one knelt at the altar, praying as he had been praying for weeks that the plague would abate and leave the town in peace. He was not pleased to have his prayers disturbed, especially now that they seemed to be working, but he did as the woman asked and heard her confession. Cataracts made him nearly blind so he did not note her tears as he gave her absolution.

Afterward, Irene returned to the cabin and set to work. It took a week but when she was finished the bolt of teal and gold silk had been fashioned into a diaphanous shirt and Turkish-style pants, the fine leather into a vest embroidered with gold. Tiny seed pearls covered the bodice of a high-waisted grey satin gown. It seemed barbaric to Irene that the woman would wear clothes so thin that you could see her body through them, but Irene was pleased with her work. She hoped that now that her task had been finished so beautifully, the woman would release them both.

When Catherine tried on the clothes for her final fitting, Eva clapped her tiny hands and tossed her golden curls, declaring, without a trace of guile or fear, that Catherine was the most beautiful woman she had ever seen.

Eva's innocent awe disarmed Catherine. Never had anyone admired her so openly. Catherine made the girl a cap braided from remnants of the teal and gold silk and trimmed it with butterfly wings and pheasant feathers. At night she would sit at the table and tell the girl stories of changling children, left in the forest when their hapless human parents discovered what they were.

Irene listened to the stories and said nothing to the child, complaining obliquely to Catherine, "I see the path your tales take. I know what you're doing."

"And if I ever sense fear in her, I will destroy her. Remember, I will have no need of you if she is gone."

And each night, she locked them in the bedroom and disappeared on a long frantic hunt. Finally, tired of the constant hunger, she went in search of something to slacken it.

In the house beside the same church where Irene had gone for absolution, a priest woke from a light sleep to the sound of distant rapping. Convinced that the sound came from the church, he dressed without waking the others and stole across the courtyard and through the small rear door to the room behind the altar.

No candles were lit in the nave, and in the dark he could hear but not see the intruder, the steady determined rapping puzzling him. He had begun to turn to go for help when the rapping stopped. Curious, he held his breath, listening to the silence until a hand grabbed his wrist. He started to cry out and discovered he could make no sound.

A demon! Only demons moved so softly in the darkness. Yet what would a demon be doing in a church with so long and blessed a history?

Laughter—beautiful and lilting like the running of the stream on the rocks outside of town—surrounded him in the dark, in his mind, and he took comfort in a myth. "Please, there are votive candles in the vestibule. Take me there," he managed to whisper reverently. "Let me see your face."

"My face?" More laughter. "As you wish."

Then he found himself dragged smoothly along, down the blackness of the center aisle to the rear doors and the flickering candlelight. There he found himself looking at a vision so perfect he was convinced that God had chosen him.

Her features were unmarred symmetry, her skin so pale a contrast with the cascade of dark curls falling onto her shoulders. Her gown pressed against her body and as he noticed her form a desire began to grow that was far from holy. This creature had tricked him. She was not the angel that she seemed. "What has brought you here?" he managed to ask, never able to force his voice above a whisper.

"Can you feel the fresh air, priest?"

He did. A steady draft that curled around his bare feet and up his legs. He turned to its source and saw the empty space above the baptismal font. What had she done! These windows were a treasure, made by the Austra family over a century ago.

—And I am a thousand and I will live for thousands more.—

He had not spoken. Neither had she! The priest crossed himself, disheartened when the gesture had no effect on her.

"What did you expect, priest?"

He looked toward the altar but the words of his prayers eluded him. Only her hand gripping his wrist had any substance.

"Did you think I was a vision that would dissolve with a wave of your holy hand? Is your imagination so pure that you have never dreamed of someone like me?" She touched his face, the side of his neck, his chest through his loose cassock, and everywhere her fingers brushed they left a warmth in their wake that astonished him.

"And I am only taking this one small piece of your church. You can replace it, can you not?"

No, he wanted to protest but she was kissing him and he could not say a word, not even when she slipped the cassock from his shoulders, her lips following the cloth to the floor.

The acolytes who came to serve at the dawn mass found the priest lying on his back in front of the altar, his body covered with a hundred small bites, the expression on his face one of such pure rapture that it was said he had either died damned or in a state of perfect grace. Some believed the good tale, others the bad. Still others noted that the theft of St. Lucy's window could have mystical significance. Rumors of witchcraft began to spread.

A year passed. During it twenty-six women were convicted of conspiring with the devil and were burned or hanged depending on their station. The trials ended when the Turks invaded, one great onslaught that brought them to the edges of the Bihor hills. Catherine disappeared each night, returning coated with the blood of her victims, carrying sacks of gold and booty from their camps. The cottage became rich with walls of tapestry and floors of sable. The fingers of all three of the women were gloved with rings and they lived in silk and fur with riches filling the space around them, while above them a huge St. Lucy shed a fantastically hued light over their hoarded treasure.

Irene always went to town to purchase the food she and her daughter needed. Each time she took longer to return, noting, with oddly placed jealousy, that Catherine did not seem to care and her daughter rarely noticed her absence. One day, tired of living in fear and certain that she had lost her daughter's love, she did not return.

In a week, Eva's food ran out. At first, Catherine stole from the army. Then the forces moved on and Catherine fed the child meat and nothing else. Eva grew thinner, and for the first time since Catherine had come to live with them, she cried for her mother and would not be consoled.

Faced with a responsibility she loathed, Catherine drew the child close to her. When Eva's sobs subsided, Catherine kissed her, then gently began to drink. With a tenderness she had never felt before, she slowly devoured the girl, then arranged her pale hair about her face and put the cap on her head before burying her next to her father.

Catherine had not expected to mourn for she had never mourned a human life before. This time, though, she did and the pain she felt made her vow that she would never allow another human to share her life again. The vow was always broken for she wanted that single-minded adoration, needed it more than fear or blood.

She would hear a child crying in the fields and go to it. She would find an orphan of war and carry it to her sumptuous cottage. The children would worship her and amuse her until she grew tired of them, then they would die happily in her arms.

In time, word spread throughout the region—avoid the Bihor hills north of Borsa especially after dark unless you carry a gift with you, something that would be welcomed by the creature who dwells there and who cannot be killed. Travelers brought silk and fine wool, gold and silver cups. One, who sought to tame the beautiful demon, brought furs and a jewel fit to grace a royal hand.

Some died. Others went on their way with odd tales to tell of a creature of impossible beauty who laughed at them from the shadows of the wood, her pale body moving quick as a hummingbird's as she danced on the edge of their sight.

As the tales spread, those who lived in the region gave the demon in their midst a name so feared that to even utter the word became taboo.

Kisasszony. Fair Lady.

And so Catherine, who had once been mistress to a god, acquired her home and her fortune and the protection of legend.

PART II

ELIZIβETH
1563

HISTORICAL NOTE

The Bathori family achieved outstanding successes in the political, religious, and military realms. Among Elizabeth's close relations were a prince, a king, and a cardinal. However, others in the Bathori family suffered from similar mental ailments including blinding headaches, blackouts, and periodic fits of extreme rage in which they attacked and bit the flesh of those who tried to come to their assistance. Though these attacks have not been proved to be hereditary, the Bathori family, like many of the noble houses of Europe, regularly inbred (Elizabeth's parents were cousins). However, the source of their strange aberrations cannot be determined.

CHAPTER
5

I

Elizabeth Bathori was three years old when she bit her wet nurse. Though the event happened by accident while she was nursing, it had a profound effect on her future. Marijo, taken by surprise, reacted as she would have with her own daughter, pushing Elizabeth away and slapping her hard enough that she fell and scraped her arm on the wooden floor of the nursery.

Elizabeth responded with a loud, piercing wail. The sound, so unnatural in the usually stoic baby, echoed through Ecsed manor, drawing the attention of her father. As he entered the nursery, Marijo stammered an apology, then, too frightened to give a verbal explanation for what had happened, the young woman pointed to the bloodstain on the front of her white cotton blouse.

Gyorgi Bathori glanced at his daughter's bleeding arm and, without warning, brought his walking staff down hard on Marijo's breasts and back in a series of blows that left her lying facedown on the floor, sobbing. "You will never, never discipline my daughter again, do you understand!" he bellowed. "If you do, you will find yourself envying this pain."

As he crouched down to comfort his daughter, Elizabeth's face contorted with terror and she pulled out of his grasp, crawling into the corner. There she sat, facing the polished wood wall, screaming, each cry louder than the last as if her own voice fascinated her. Gyorgi stood and, with a contemptuous look at the nurse and his daughter, left Marijo to tend to her wounds and comfort Elizabeth.

Marijo caught her breath and sat up. Knowing she had to silence the child or risk another beating, she ignored her pain and pulled Elizabeth to her, rocking the girl until the cries finally subsided. "See what your naughtiness has done," she said, her gruff tone so at odds with her actions.

Elizabeth did not have a way to explain that she had been startled by a sudden noise in the courtyard. Instead, she pressed herself tightly against the woman's ample chest, nuzzling her breasts, her whimpers growing louder until Marijo untied the string of her blouse so Elizabeth could finish nursing. As she drank, the taste of the blood mixed with the milk, and Elizabeth thrilled to the strange new warmth that filled her.

Later, when her mother woke from her afternoon nap, Elizabeth went to her and, in the universal language of toddlers, announced simply, "Papa hurt Marijo."

Anna Bathori had been informed of what had happened by the servant who woke her. Though she was a gentle mistress to the house staff, she would never dare contradict her husband in any matter. Besides, her daughter's headstrong behavior, already a trial to the placid Anna, had to be tempered. "Your father was right," she said. "We are Marijo's masters. She is here to nurse you, not to treat you as one of her own."

"I hurt her first," Elizabeth responded and began to cry.

Her mother refused to touch her, keeping her hands folded in her lap as she said coldly, "That makes no difference. Your father did his duty. Someday, when you are a grown woman, you will understand." When Elizabeth only stood, watching her mother's face, waiting for some clue as to what her words meant, Anna asked, "Isn't your father taking you and Steven out in the carriage today?"

Elizabeth nodded with no enthusiasm. She hated her older brother and would prefer to stay home.

"Then go and tell Marijo to dress you," Anna said.

Without a word, Elizabeth fled her mother's room. Outside of it, she leaned against the wall and took huge gulps of air. Marijo had gone to her bed, lying on her side and moaning with pain. Her father had done the beating. This was the first act of violence Elizabeth had ever witnessed and she longed for nothing more than someone to come to comfort her. On her way back to the nursery she saw her father in the hall and pressed herself against the wall until he passed, then ran to her rooms as quickly as she was able.

Over the next few days, Elizabeth stayed close to Marijo, but though the woman still took care of her, she would not play with Elizabeth as she had before, nor hold her beyond what was necessary to nurse her, and then with no real affection. Marijo had been painfully reminded of her place and she would never again forget it.

Rejected, Elizabeth soon decided that she hated Marijo. Over the next few months, she made her hatred known in a hundred different ways for she was an intelligent child and very inventive.

All of Marijo's pleas had no effect so Marijo tried to frighten her. She took the child to watch the drowning of the witches and whispered to the girl that they had been disobedient children. "They died," Elizabeth responded, the shaking of her head implying that she knew that witches could not drown.

On the day that Elizabeth poured lye into Marijo's wash water the woman finally threatened her directly. "If you are not good, I will give you to the *Kisasszony*, the Fair Lady who lives in the wood. She loves little children. She loves them until they die."

Elizabeth stuck out her lower lip. "There is no such thing as a *Kisasszony*," she declared. "If there were I would know."

"Would you?" Marijo laughed. "Come upstairs to the kitchen and I will give you a piece of cake and tell you all about her."

If Marijo thought her tales would frighten Elizabeth, she had underestimated the toddler. The more she spoke, the more fascinated Elizabeth became, her questions drawing out one detail after another.

"It is said that in the time after she came to the hills where she lives, ten children were killed in half a year. When their fathers went to take their revenge, they were killed also. No one opposes her now and no one seeks her though she is very beautiful. She is like the perfect mother every little girl wishes she had. When you pine too much for love, she comes and takes you to live with her. And when you cry, she kisses you until you die. She teaches a lesson, you see, that you must not wish for more than you are given."

"Did you ever see her?" Elizabeth asked.

"Once," Marijo lied. "I was hardly more than your age and

I saw her at dusk on the road near our cottage. I ran to my mother and curled up next to her to sleep the night. Mothers can protect their children from the Fair Lady."

She said this because Elizabeth's mother never slept with her, nor with her father unless he demanded it. Sometimes, it seemed that Anna Bathori did not sleep at night at all. Instead, she paced the castle and the grounds caught in a strange nocturnal insomnia no potion could treat. As for protecting Elizabeth, Anna was far too pale and weak.

"But you are strong and you would not dare let anything happen to me." After declaring this, Elizabeth demanded, "You will take me to see her."

"She lives far to the north in the Bihor hills. It would take us two days and a night to get there. Your father would never let us go."

"Then how can you give her to me?"

"I can summon her."

Elizabeth's eyes widened and her lips twisted into a strange, remote smile far too knowing for a child so young. "Witches summon," she said in a whisper implying far more than her words.

Marijo's expression froze. All she had meant to do was frighten the child into obedience, but even a rumor of witchcraft would be enough to earn her questioning and torture, perhaps even death.

Elizabeth pushed her advantage, adding, "If you do not take me, I will tell Papa your stories."

Marijo concentrated on slicing another piece of the poppy-seed cake and placing it in Elizabeth's hand. "If you tell anyone, then they will send me away and I will never be able to take you. But if you are obedient and do what you are told, I promise we will go when you are older, perhaps when the family goes east to the mountains in the summer. We'll be much closer to the *Kisasszony* then."

II

In the next few years, fighting between the Hapsburgs and the Ottoman Empire kept the family away from their summer home in Dejo and Elizabeth eventually stopped mentioning the Fair Lady. During that time, with Elizabeth's firm support, Marijo's position in the Bathori hierarchy of servants rose. It was she who arranged the children's lessons—coordinating the schedules of the special tutors who taught Elizabeth and her brother, Steven, their Latin and Greek, math and music. Though Steven was six years older than Elizabeth, her intelligence went far beyond his and her wit was far sharper than Steven's plodding mind could comprehend. Her intelligence was the one road to earning her father's respect and she reveled in her precociousness. "Be less of a fool," Gyorgi Bathori would tell Steven. "Emulate your sister. You are my son after all."

Steven's anger grew until, on a day that Elizabeth corrected him once too often, punctuating her words with a malicious smirk, he attacked, scattering their books while the old hired tutor ran for help. By the time the servants arrived, Steven had already choked his sister to near unconsciousness and blackened both her eyes. After this, their lessons were conducted separately for Anna Bathori did not want her only son enraged any further by Elizabeth's unseemly skill. Anna hoped that the lack of competition would slow her daughter's progress but Elizabeth surprised her by becoming a scholar entirely for learning's sake.

Sometimes Anna would watch Elizabeth studying one of her texts, her forehead furrowed with concentration, and she would consider that she had not even known how to write when she and Gyorgi were married. He had taught her—saying that a lady should have some education, after all—but only enough that she could read his letters and write her own. It disappointed her that her petite daughter shared her father's intelligence since she would have so few opportunities to put it to good use. Still, it was better that her brother had been given the gifts of size and strength. The boy might become a fighter like so many of the men in the family, and there was always need of warriors in these times. Perhaps he'd make a name for himself someday when his temper had cooled and leveled with age. Now, though Anna Bathori knew that Steven still took every opportunity to privately abuse his little sister—teasing her, pinching her, even beating her in places that would leave no obvious marks—she did not try to stop him. The girl needed to be broken a bit, to know that the way things should be was the way they always had been.

An uneasy truce with the Turks was made more solid with the death of Sultan Suleiman in 1566. Five years later with Transylvania in the hands of Gyorgi Bathori's uncle, the Bathori family, accompanied by their servants and guards, visited their estate in Dejo for the first time since Elizabeth was an infant.

Riding in the carriage with her mother and Marijo, Elizabeth looked out at the mountains, then at Marijo. Though Elizabeth had not mentioned the Fair Lady for years, she never forgot a promise and Marijo was certain she had just been reminded of hers.

One night some weeks later, Elizabeth came to Marijo's room and said, "Papa and Mama are going to Vienna in two days and are taking my brother with them. You will take me to see the *Kisasszony* while they are gone."

Marijo, who had never seen the *Kisasszony*, nonetheless knew that the hills where people reported seeing her were nearby. What harm would there be in indulging the girl's whim, especially since the creature she sought didn't exist at all? An afternoon's ride through the dark forests would be enough to satisfy the girl. To guarantee it, Marijo added, "You know that if the *Kisasszony* does not wish to be seen, she will hide from us. And she can be very dangerous. She may decide to kill us both."

"She will not harm me," Elizabeth said. Her expression was imperious, demanding, every bit the royalty she had become. Nothing would touch her. Nothing would dare! Without another word, Elizabeth spun on her heel and marched off to bed.

The following morning, Elizabeth waved good-bye to her parents, then went to the stable and ordered one of the servants to saddle her horse.

"You are too little to ride alone, small countess," the man replied.

"Marijo is taking me into the hills. Saddle the mare for her."

"With your parents' permission?"

Elizabeth didn't need anyone's permission. She frowned and said nothing.

Even at twelve no one dared question her, certainly not a stablehand. He saddled the horse, holding it steady so

Elizabeth could mount, then doing the same for Marijo. "Where are you going?" he asked Marijo.

"To Borsa." Noticing the man's concern, she added, "I have an errand to run. Elizabeth wishes to go with me."

The man, who had been raised in the area, stood on the drive and crossed himself as he watched them leave. If the Fair Lady put the girl on her platter, one taste of her would be enough. She'd most likely spit the little countess out.

The pair rode for hours before they began the climb. The narrow road grew steeper and the horse slowed her pace. Suddenly, Elizabeth ordered Marijo to stop. She cocked her head, trying to listen as the woman grumbled, "There is nothing here, child. Let's go on."

In response, Elizabeth slid off her horse's back and ran into the forest.

Marijo sat and waited but Elizabeth did not return. Finally, fearful of what would happen to her if she did not find the girl, Marijo dismounted, tied the reins of both mounts to a tree, and followed Elizabeth into the woods.

The forest grew thicker, great stands of oak and fir blocking out the sun. Everything became dark, so suddenly oppressive that fear covered Marijo like a dark cloak. She was afraid to call out for the girl, afraid that someone else would answer.

She headed in the direction she thought would lead to the road but it had vanished. A mist wove through the trees and surrounded her. Finally, panicked, she ran, tripped, and fell silently. As she sat rubbing her ankle, she listened for Elizabeth's voice. When she found the girl she would scold her, then comfort her and make her swear that she would never pull such a dangerous stunt again.

Not a word.

Marijo pushed herself to her feet and limped uphill. The road had to be at the top of the ridge. But when she reached it, nothing greeted her but the waning light of dusk. Nothing moved around her but leaves tossed by the night winds. Nothing made an intelligent sound though the world was filled with danger. The earth had swallowed Marijo's charge, and when Gyorgi Bathori discovered Marijo's part in it, there would be no place she could hide from his wrath. She bowed her head and began to sob.

Elizabeth's cry of fright made Marijo turn. Behind her stood Elizabeth, her back to a tall, pale-skinned woman whose arms circled her neck. The woman wore a tattered lace dress of deep forest-green that swayed in the evening wind. That, her long gaunt body, and her tangled mass of dark hair made her appear less substance than specter though her hold on Elizabeth seemed real enough. As if in response, her grip on Elizabeth tightened, making Elizabeth cry out from the pain. As Marijo looked at her in horror, the woman kissed Elizabeth's cheek, her eyes fixed on Marijo's as she did so. They were huge and dark with tiny points of red at the center as if they had somehow trapped the setting sun in their depths.

"She is the daughter of a count," Marijo managed to blurt.

"What is her position to me?" The woman sang the words. Her delicate hand cupped Elizabeth's chin, lifting it as she kissed the side of her neck.

"The family will not rest until she is at home."

"What is their search to me?"

No one had ever challenged the Bathori family before. Marijo, powerless and terrified, sobbed louder.

"Silence!" Elizabeth shouted at her nurse and twisted loose of the *Kisasszony*'s hold. Instead of running, Elizabeth turned to face her. A long look passed between them, then Elizabeth curtsied as she had when presented to the Emperor Maximilian at his court in Vienna. "I am the Countess Elizabeth Bathori," she said. "And I am honored to meet you."

As always, Catherine had sensed the invasion of her domain since the woman and child had entered it. She might have let them pass through her hills as she often did but her fame had spread. Few traveled through the Bihors and it had been many days since Catherine had feasted on human life. As she approached the pair, she discovered that unlike the usual uneasy travelers through the region, the woman and child were actually looking for her. Curious, she had called to the child from the shadows, and when Elizabeth had run toward her, Catherine had deliberately leapt at her, pouncing like the great cat she so often resembled. But though the child had been startled, she lacked real fear. Catherine attempted to arouse it and found her mental tricks thwarted. Indeed, she could scarcely touch the child's mind at all.

Now this strong-willed girl greeted her as she was meant to be greeted! Fascinated, Catherine snatched her up, and ignoring the frightened wails of the silly desperate woman who had brought this prize to her, she carried the girl deep into the woods, depositing her at last in the corner of her sumptuous cottage.

Elizabeth pushed herself up onto the top of a low oak bureau, smoothed down her hair, and carefully arranged her lace skirts over her crossed legs. She posed pretty as a porcelain doll on display with Catherine's other trinkets, her back stiffly regal, her expression one of intense curiosity. "Tell me what you are," she demanded in a voice already used to giving commands.

Catherine threw back her head and laughed, revealing her long rear teeth, waiting for a cry, a gasp, some surprise, and receiving nothing. "First tell me what you know," she replied.

For the next hour, Elizabeth revealed an amazing—and to Catherine, amusing—collection of legends. Most she had learned from the woman who had brought her here but she had heard other, darker tales as well—of blood drinking and terrible silent torture. Yet Elizabeth displayed fascination rather than fear even when she confessed that, yes, she believed most of them; even when Catherine said, softly for emphasis, "I intend to kill you, you know."

Elizabeth only cocked her head. "Why?" she asked.

"Because I am hungry."

"Marijo is somewhere outside. Take her instead."

"Now why would I want a peasant when I can dine on royal blood?" Amazing! Even now with her fingers around the girl's wrist, the tiny countess sat quietly, her expression steady. Here was someone who would dare anything, who placed herself above everyone.

"Marijo is big. I am small." Elizabeth's voice recited the words like some well-rehearsed child's rhyme and ended with an impish grin. "Besides, if you will allow me, I want to come back and visit you."

"Suppose I do eat Marijo, then keep you here always. Would you like that?"

"Yes. It is quite a pretty house once one is inside and I like all your treasures," Elizabeth answered, lightly touching a golden satyr on a display rack beside a mirror. "But you must not keep me here. Marijo told someone where we were going. My father's servants will come to look for me. Many will come."

She stopped short of saying "too many," of making even the vaguest threat against Catherine. Instead she made the possible invasion sound like a minor inconvenience. This was not diplomacy, Catherine knew, but the child's sincere belief that she and Catherine were on an equal footing.

Not certain exactly what she would do next, Catherine nonetheless threw open the front door and stood under its arch. Her long arms touched the top of the doorframe, her fingers were hooked into the stones above it, her head was bowed as she called, the silent mental summons of predator to victim.

In the woods, Marijo thought she heard Elizabeth crying. She grabbed a stick to use as a walking cane and began to hobble in the direction of the sound, following it until she was almost on top of the clearing and the cottage. Then Catherine sprang forward and, grabbing both Marijo's wrists, dragged her into the house, throwing her to the floor.

When she let go of the sobbing servant, Marijo pressed her body against the fur rugs, too hysterical to even beg. From her perch, Elizabeth looked down at her, saying nothing.

"What are you thinking, young countess?" Catherine asked.

"I am thinking that Marijo only brought me here to frighten me. I am thinking that she is crying only because she knows that if I do not return home my father will find her and rip the flesh from her bones and feed it to her the way Prince Zapolya did to George Doza after his rebellion. I am thinking that she should be made to believe the legends."

"And nothing else?"

Even at twelve, Elizabeth understood. Her aristocratic education combined with youthful candor allowed her to answer, "What value is the life of a servant to me?"

Marijo wailed louder. Catherine ignored her, asking Elizabeth, "If I kill her, will you still be able to come to see me?"

"I do whatever I wish. No one ever stops me from doing anything."

"Suppose I do not come for you when you have entered these hills."

"I will find you."

Catherine fingered a strand of Elizabeth's hair. "That would be difficult."

"But I will order servants to bring me. None will dare disobey me . . . even if my escorts never return to the house with me."

The girl offered victims! Suddenly the self-assured young countess seemed a monster, the human sort that preyed on its own. Yet if she were one of Catherine's kind, she would be the sort of child Catherine would love to conceive—intelligent and perfectly ruthless. She rested a hand on Elizabeth's shoulder, drawing her index finger back, striking. The nail made a deep cut in Elizabeth's neck. Elizabeth responded by tilting her head back and leaning her body forward, allowing Catherine to drink.

As Catherine's lips touched her neck, the girl wrapped her arms around Catherine's shoulders, yielding her mind as she had her body and allowing Catherine to form the mental bond more perfect than any she had ever achieved. Thrilled by her own power, Catherine turned her attention to the terrified servant.

Seeing what the woman had done to Elizabeth, Marijo scuttled crablike across the floor, trying to reach the door, finding her way blocked. She tried again and again until, convinced she was being teased like a mouse in the clutches of a barn cat, she stopped trying to escape.

Catherine sat in a chair, facing a huge gilt-framed mirror leaning against the wall, one of many in the cottage. One hand motioned Marijo to rise, then as the servant obeyed, Catherine handed her a hairbrush.

No words were exchanged. None needed to be. Her hands shaking, Marijo began to brush Catherine's hair, arranging each black curl over her shoulders. As she worked, her eyes, like Elizabeth's, were drawn to the mirror, watching Catherine's face, pale and beautiful and deadly when she finally smiled, her long hands lying so languidly against the arms of her chair until they tensed and curled and revealed their power. Marijo, more frightened with each passing moment, let out a low moan of terror. As soon as she heard it, Catherine whirled, so quickly that Marijo did not notice when she moved from her seat, one fingertip curled beneath Marijo's chin, one long sharp nail pushing Marijo's head back.

Elizabeth, her mind a part of Catherine's, felt Marijo's pulse quicken, saw the beating of the veins in her stretched neck, sensed all the delicacy of her terror. She held her breath as

Catherine drank, trapped in the passion that passed from victim to killer. Catherine pressed Marijo tightly against her, supporting her when she lost consciousness, fastidiously dragging her outside before ending her short mortal life.

When she had finished, Catherine dropped the servant and carefully wiped the blood from her chin, licking it from her fingers, staring through the doorway at Elizabeth.

Though she knew the child's thoughts, she could not comprehend them.

The girl's perfect bow of a mouth was pursed, the edges slightly upturned, making her look both amused and thoughtful. Her dark eyes were steady and dry. Nothing she had experienced had disgusted her, indeed she had reveled in it. "When should I come again?" she asked.

"Whenever you wish. There are animals in the forest. They suffice."

"I will come on Saturday."

"What is today?"

Elizabeth's eyes widened. Torture and death had not startled her. Catherine's ignorance of the day did. "Today is Tuesday," she said. "I will come in four days."

"And you will bring someone?"

Elizabeth nodded. "Tell me who."

Catherine laughed. "Whomever you wish, child. I am hardly particular. You make the choice."

Elizabeth's parents were gone for a month. During their absence, four servants at the summer home disappeared on Elizabeth's outings. Elizabeth explained that Marijo had fallen from her horse while in the mountains and most likely wandered off while Elizabeth napped. The girl had no idea how to find the place she had seen her servant last. A man and a woman had disappeared one after the other. As they were known to be lovers, one of the kitchen maids was bribed to suggest that they had run off together. The fourth, the stablehand who had warned Elizabeth on her first outing, had, Elizabeth declared, been snatched by the *Kisasszony* at the edge of her domain.

Only the last story held any truth and only the last aroused parental disbelief. But though her mother tried to get Elizabeth to recant the tale or to provide details, Elizabeth stubbornly refused. They did not press her. They had only lost a servant and servants were easily replaced, after all.

The night after her parents' return, Elizabeth lay in her bed and giggled. What had begun as a boring summer had become one filled with wonder and dark, potent secrets. As she lay, thinking of the victims and how Catherine had devoured them, their blood seemed to course through her own veins, arousing her as nothing ever had before. Thinking of Catherine, how she had held her victims, the magic of her touch, Elizabeth placed her hand between her thighs and began a steady motion that brought her quickly to climax. She did not make a sound, indeed hardly breathed any quicker because what she did was a sin and she did not want God to hear her.

III

Two days later, the family left for their home at Ecsed Castle.

Surrounded by servants, dining with her parents and her brother, Elizabeth had never felt more alone. She took refuge in education—both from the books given to her by her tutors and in the old tales told by the servants who began to welcome the pale, charming young countess to their nighttime gatherings.

She learned of the Mountain Lords who lived in an aerie castle far to the east in the Vardas, of the satyrs and wild men who dwelt in the forests of the Balkans, of the *liderc*— the succubus—who loved men to death and whose domain was madness of the noonday sun. She heard tales of the *liderc*'s counterpart, the *Kisasszony,* who lived in the night shadows and preyed on children.

The last would make Elizabeth smile. She wondered what they would think if she told them that she had met the *Kisasszony* and that she knew the woman's name.

She remained silent for she had learned well. And the stories made her think of others she had heard from her aunt many years ago. She began sifting memories of her past, trying to sort reality from infant dreams, piecing together the shreds she remembered into one logical whole.

She dropped hints to her mother, mentioning some of the

things she had heard of the *Kisasszony* and the Mountain Lords. Instead of learning more, she was coldly rebuffed as if she had mentioned some past sin her mother refused to acknowledge. But the next time that Elizabeth visited the night gathering in the servants' kitchen, legend abruptly turned to gossip and anxious glances in her direction and, finally, a hesitant suggestion that she return to bed. Afterward, Elizabeth stopped visiting the servants or asking questions altogether.

By day she wore a delicate, agreeable smile perfectly matched to her suddenly placid disposition. At night, she would lie awake, staring at the shadows her candle threw onto the walls, too stubborn to give into her loneliness and cry. Eventually, her longing for Catherine became too great. A heavy gold piece pressed into the proper hand gave her a potion that made her ill. She could keep nothing in her stomach and what stayed down flowed through her. The physician who was summoned could suggest nothing so Anna Bathori, village-raised and seeped in the old traditions, sent for a *taltos,* a healer from the nearby town.

A second coin and a few words whispered in private brought the diagnosis Elizabeth wished to hear. "She needs a change of climate, Countess Anna. Send her to the mountains. The air will do her good."

And Elizabeth, accompanied by her mother, her tutor, and a handful of servants, returned to the summer home and the dark freedom of the Bihor hills.

As the *taltos* had recommended, Elizabeth was given a room on the first floor, one that looked out onto the hills and, when the shutters were open, filled with the scents of grass and autumn flowers. At night Elizabeth would stand in the window and wait for Catherine to come to her and carry her off to the hills to prey on the outlaws who had fled their lords' lands for the dubious shelter of the forests.

As the weather became colder, they hunted the castle, Catherine drinking in silence, the pale tiny countess at her side. A dozen servants died of a strange wasting illness that sent Elizabeth's mother into a frenzy of worry. She ordered the bodies burned rather than buried, a precaution against disease, she told the household. She ordered the shutters closed and barred even on balmy nights lest outlaws from the forest hear of their mishaps and, believing them understaffed, come to pillage the estate. She prayed. Perhaps she even thought her prayers had been answered because, in spite of all the deaths, Elizabeth continued to thrive.

Finally, the snow began to fall and Catherine, unable to hide her all-too-real footprints, came only once more to say good-bye until the following spring.

Elizabeth waited for her in bed, a down feather mattress beneath her, three layers of quilts above. When she saw the shutters swing outward and the familiar dark form against the night sky, she held out her arms. Catherine came to her, her cold body warming against Elizabeth's, her face buried in the girl's soft hair.

For the first time since they met, Elizabeth cried. Catherine held her. "What is it, little countess?" she asked.

"I will be so alone without you. Every night that you do not come seems to last forever."

"And for me. Our bond is a mystery we may never understand."

"Never!" Elizabeth propped herself up on one elbow. "Perhaps I know the answer already. When I was young . . . well, younger," she added in response to Catherine's quick laugh, "Aunt Klara told me a story. She said I was descended from the gods."

"Is that all? That sounds very much like the tales told to kings to convince them that they have the right to rule."

"And you are a goddess," Elizabeth persisted.

Catherine shook her head. "That is foolish, Elizabeth. You know what I am."

"I will see Aunt Klara and ask her to explain again. Now that I am older, I will remember it all."

"Do what you must, child, and know that I will be waiting here for you." Catherine began to pull away and Elizabeth clutched her shoulders.

"Stay with me tonight," the girl begged. "Show me again where you lived, the castle in the mountains. Show it all to me."

Lifting the girl's long dark hair, Catherine pressed her lips against the familiar wound and drank. It occurred to her that the bond could be even tighter, and thinking that a violation of one more family taboo would never be noticed now that she was in exile, she ripped at her own shoulder and pressed the child's lips to the scrape.

They soared together . . . their memories moving south and east to the Vardas and the keep and the family long dispersed throughout the human world.

In the end, when the visions turned to a child's dreams, Catherine left Elizabeth asleep in the last peaceful slumber the girl would enjoy until spring.

When Elizabeth woke the next morning, she found a ring on her pillow, an oval of silver surrounding a gem as hard and black as Catherine's eyes. She placed it in a box on her dressing table, pulling it out often during the day to hold it up to the window and watch its facets trap the sun.

CHAPTER
6

I

As they always did, the Bathori family spent an extended Christmas holiday near Budapest at the estate of a distant cousin. The central location and the festivities in the city attracted many of the family, including her aunt Klara, as well as many of their friends.

Though Elizabeth was far too young to have any interest in marriage, her mother ordered her to go riding each day with one or another of her young suitors. They all seemed so awkward to the girl that she found herself secretly laughing at how tongue-tied they became when they tried to speak to her. She was smarter, braver. If she had her choice, she would follow in the steps of her namesake, Elizabeth Tudor, and refuse to marry anyone.

Finally, weary of a particularly dense companion, she took off in a gallop. A stirrup came unfastened and she fell, bruising the side of her head. Her adolescent suitor placed her on his horse and, leading both animals, walked her home.

That night the servant who had saddled her horse was whipped by the stablemaster. Elizabeth, the cause of his punishment, elected to go to the rear courtyard and watch.

The blows fell until the man's back was a mass of crisscrossed welts and the blood began to flow. The man's screams aroused her, the scent of fresh blood seemed too much a reminder of summer for her to bear.

As Elizabeth turned and silently walked alone back to the house, she noticed her aunt Klara following her. At the top of the stairs, she halted so her aunt could catch up, and though her mother had ordered her to never be alone with Klara whose depravity had made her notorious, Elizabeth invited Klara to her room.

Klara shook her head. "You know what your mother thinks of me," she said.

"But I must speak to you," Elizabeth whispered and added, "privately."

"Must?" Klara started down the hall that led to each of the family's private suites, stopping outside Elizabeth's. She waited until Elizabeth had opened her door to be certain there was no one inside, then said, "If you *must* speak to me, come to my rooms when the house is quiet. I will be waiting." Promise made, the tall, lanky woman swaggered on, her hands deep in the pockets of the breeches she insisted on wearing everywhere, her head thrown back, whistling a jaunty peasant tune. When she reached her room at the far end of the hall, Klara slammed the door behind her hard enough to emphasize that now that she had deposited herself there she intended to stay.

Later, a servant carrying a basin of warm water and towels came to Elizabeth's room. She unhooked Elizabeth's dress, then waited while the girl washed herself. The woman would have stayed and helped Elizabeth get ready for bed but Elizabeth ordered her to go. Slipping on her white cotton nightdress and robe, Elizabeth lay above the covers on her bed hoping the night cold would keep her from sleep.

A clock in the hall rang the hour, and another. Elizabeth heard footsteps outside her door, her brother voicing a slurred lewd comment about some serving girl he had ordered to his room and petulantly noting the sour taste of the Christmas wine. He paused outside her room, and though it had been years since he had dared to lay a hand on her, Elizabeth held her breath and gripped the knife she kept on the table beside her bed until he went on his way.

These were the last voices she heard. Still, Elizabeth waited. If she were discovered alone with her aunt, Klara would be banished from the house before Elizabeth could speak to her. Finally, certain she would not be able to stay awake much longer, Elizabeth arranged her pillows under her blanket to make it appear she was sleeping there and stole down the hall and into Klara's room.

Klara waited on a chaise in front of a low fire, one hand wrapped around the stem of a crystal glass of wine, one long painted nail idly tapping the side. A half-full bottle sat on the table beside her. "I see that you had the good sense not to knock, child. Did anyone see you?"

Elizabeth shook her head.

"Good. Come here." Klara filled the glass and handed it to Elizabeth. The wine was sweet, not at all like what had been served with dinner, and it warmed her throat and chest as she swallowed it. Klara poured her more. This time, Elizabeth sipped it, staring at her aunt all the while.

Klara's lead-powdered face seemed a grotesque imitation of Catherine's porcelain complexion, her henna-dyed curls garish by contrast to Catherine's dark ones. Yet Klara possessed a similar charm, a magnetism that made Elizabeth want to touch her, and an insight that made her hold out her arms to her niece. Elizabeth responded by pressing close to her. Her heart beat fast, the only indication of how nervous she had become, as she waited for her chance to ask about her heritage.

But Klara seemed more interested in Elizabeth's body than family history. She pushed the girl back to arm's length, and with her hands on Elizabeth's shoulders, she looked her up and down. "Soon, Bethy, you will be a woman here . . ." Klara's hands brushed across Elizabeth's chest, pinching the nipples of her half-formed breasts. "And here . . ." Klara's hands moved to Elizabeth's pubis, rubbing the soft skin through the white cotton nightshirt, her eyes narrowing at Elizabeth's quick, indrawn breath. She pulled Elizabeth close to her once more, balancing the girl across her knees, resting a palm on the top of her thighs. "How did you feel while you watched the stablehand being whipped?"

"I . . ." Elizabeth flushed and stopped.

"You can tell me your secrets. I promise that they'll be kept by me."

And one secret might lead to another! "I wanted to be the one holding the whip," Elizabeth answered honestly.

"Do you know why?"

"That is what I came to ask," Elizabeth responded. "This summer, I began to hear odd stories . . ." As she described the stories of the *Kisasszony* and the Mountain Lords, Klara lightly stroked her thighs. Her aunt's hand felt warm against Elizabeth's skin and she wished that Klara would press harder. It was so strange having something moving there that she did not control.

"You are not an ordinary child," Klara said when Elizabeth had finished. "You were born to rule . . . indeed, *bred* to rule. Consider your father and the lands he controls. The blood is even stronger in your cousin. When the landowners made him Prince of Transylvania, their vote was unanimous. And he won't stop there, I assure you. There'll be a crown on his head someday. Do you understand what I am telling you?"

Elizabeth heard little of her aunt's short discourse. "You spoke of blood?" she asked with enough intensity that Klara immediately understood.

"Bethy, how much can you recall of the tales I used to tell you about your family?"

"Only a little. I asked Mother about them but she would not answer."

"That's because my older sister has all the imagination of a milk cow. It seems the fire skipped a generation, and given your brother's apparent potential, you may have inherited it all." Klara laughed. "Bring the bottle and come to bed with me. I'll keep you warm and tell you again about your great-grandmother. Her name was Ilona. She married a man named Gyorgi, like your father. But the child she had was not his . . ."

As Klara told the story, she carefully watched Elizabeth drain her glass, then lifted it from the girl's hand and set in on the floor. When she had finished her tale and answered all of Elizabeth's questions, she threw the extra reading pillows onto the floor, rolled the child over, and drew close to her, Elizabeth's back against her chest, her arms around the girl's waist, her hand against Elizabeth's breasts.

Elizabeth hardly cared what Klara did to her. The wine had made her numb and the words Klara spoke were so exciting. Though Elizabeth was old enough to sense the passion her body aroused, she lay still and let Klara caress her, concentrating less on her touch than her words, storing every small detail.

Kin! She and Catherine were kin!

No, Catherine could never forget her now!

Her eyes closed. She felt herself being moved, Klara's trembling hands fumbling with her nightdress.

Though Elizabeth pretended to be asleep, her aunt knew better. Still, they both maintained the ruse.

If only one of her suitors were as exciting as this . . .

The thought drifted away as Elizabeth switched off her mind and slept.

Elizabeth woke late the following morning in her own bed without recalling how she had gotten there. When she went looking for answers from Klara, she found a servant cleaning Klara's empty rooms. After a loud argument with Elizabeth's mother, Klara had left suddenly for Vienna.

Had they been discovered together? Try as she would, Elizabeth could not remember. Returning to her own rooms, she rang for a servant to dress her, choosing her clothes with special care, demanding that everything be perfect, her make-up applied to hide the circles under her eyes, her hair carefully arranged. She wanted it to look as if she had been up for hours and the maids, knowing her temper, moved frantically around her.

Soon after, her mother summoned her. As Elizabeth sat across from her mother in Anna's drawing room, Anna gave no indication that she knew of last night's indiscretion though her manner was oddly distant. She barely looked at her daughter as the servant poured their tea and placed plates of delicate apricot muffins on the low table between their carved wooden chairs. The woman picked up the cream pitcher to pour but Anna dismissed her with an imperious wave of her hand. As soon as they were alone, she asked Elizabeth, "What do you think of Ferenc Nadasdy?"

Elizabeth frowned. She could not recall the name and her head was pounding. She wanted nothing more than to go back to bed and sleep.

"The young man who rode with you yesterday," her mother added.

Elizabeth carefully broke off a piece of her muffin and ate it while considering a reply. "I think he . . ." She laughed brightly as she thought of just the right turn of phrase and answered in Latin, *"Cogito . . . ego et non ille."*

Her mother apparently did not understand, which was itself understandable. Elizabeth repeated the phrase in Hungarian, "I think . . . and he does not."

"No matter. You are riding with him again today," she said.

"I refuse. I detest him."

"As well as tomorrow," Anna added with icy calm.

"Considering how we got along on our first meeting, I don't believe that would be advisable."

Anna Bathori chose to misinterpret the remark. "Then you will walk with him . . . today, tomorrow, as often as he likes. And in the spring you will be betrothed to him."

"No!" Elizabeth stood so quickly that her teacup overturned, staining the front of her green silk dress. She caught it before it fell and, with a deliberate final glance at its delicate beauty, flung it across the room where it shattered on the stone wall. She would have tossed the pot as well, but her mother was pouring herself a second cup, refusing to let her daughter's outburst ruffle her forced composure. "I refuse," Elizabeth screamed. "He is an idiot! You must have my consent to marry and I will never give it. Never!" After one final cry of rage, she started to bolt from the room.

"Elizabeth," her mother called after her in a voice taut with control. "Do you think that anyone but an idiot would tolerate you?"

So she had known! Elizabeth stood with her face to the door and willed the tears to fall, then, sobbing, ran to her mother, falling to her knees before her, burying her face in Anna's skirt. "You cannot blame me for what happened!" she cried. "You cannot punish me this way!"

"This is not a punishment, child. Your marriage was arranged before Klara lured you to her den. You need to be married to someone and your father, not I, has chosen Ferenc. Do you really wish to oppose him?"

"No," Elizabeth admitted for her father's temper frightened even her. "But do you think I should marry someone like Father—a bully who will do his best to destroy any semblance of independence and intelligence that I possess? Do you approve of my marriage to someone like that? Answer me honestly this one time, Mother. Tell me what you think."

"I hope you will fare better than I did. I've done what I can to assure it," her mother replied with a candor that shocked

Elizabeth. She had never heard Anna Bathori say one word of reproach against her husband before.

"So you approve?" Elizabeth repeated, not certain she understood.

"Yes, for reasons you are probably not old enough to understand."

"But our name . . . our heritage . . ."

"Heritage? Do you believe the rubbish that Klara told you?"

"Yes." Elizabeth dared not confess why she believed so she merely added, "Besides, Ilona's pregnancy lasted so many extra months."

"Did it? Or did she perhaps conceive a child in the weeks after her marriage?"

"That is possible?"

"To miss our cycle and later conceive? Of course, particularly if you believe you are pregnant. And Ilona believed, as her father believed—enough to sacrifice her virginity to a myth."

"What about the one who took her virginity? Was he a myth also?"

Anna paused and decided on the truth. "No. The Mountain Lords exist. I believe I even met one once at court in Vienna. I wisely kept my silence."

Her mother's logic seemed skewed. Why accept one tale and not another? "But what has all this to do with my betrothal?" Elizabeth asked.

"Because your father, like your great-grandfather, believes this tale. And since you do, you may take comfort in knowing that you and young Nadasdy are distant cousins. If the legends are true, you share that blood."

Elizabeth sat back on her heels, thinking about Ferenc with more tolerance. "And you approve of him?" she asked again with less anger than curiosity.

"For a reason that has nothing to do with his blood. Ferenc's prowess with a sword is remarkable. His horsemanship is remarkable. He seems to have some inborn capacity to lead men. One day he will be a great hero."

"And a stupid one," Elizabeth said with obvious disgust.

"Heroes usually are but they are also seldom at home and their self-conceit is large enough that they grant their wives the same freedom your father has always allowed you. Tell me, Bethy, do you wish to be married someday?"

"No," Elizabeth replied immediately though she was unable to pinpoint the reason for her aversion.

"Then, since you must marry, wouldn't you prefer an absent husband who will let you do as you wish to one constantly underfoot, making demands and meddling in your life?" Anna looked down at her teacup and smiled.

Elizabeth stared at her, speechless from the sudden revelation that her mother possessed far greater intelligence than she had ever suspected. She wiped the tears from her face and nodded, then said with a wicked smile, "And perhaps, if I am truly lucky, he'll be sliced in two by a Turkish blade."

Her mother pretended not to hear, saying instead, "Bethy, if you are ever compromised again, be less discreet. Have the good sense to scream as well as fight."

Elizabeth could only watch her mother, seeking some clue as to what she meant.

"Still, those marks you left on Klara's face will stay with her for weeks. Perhaps they'll even scar. Judging from how she damned both of us, she certainly thinks so." Her mother looked at her with the tight-lipped smile reserved for those who know when justice has been delivered. It occurred to Elizabeth that this was the first time her mother ever seemed to wholeheartedly approve of one of her actions. "I am proud of you, daughter," she added, "but I wish you to promise me one thing. Promise me that you will not receive my sister into your home for as long as I live. I have my reasons for requesting that you do this. Please do as I ask."

Elizabeth stammered the correct response and quickly left. Marks? Her aunt had surely been merciful, Elizabeth rapidly concluded. Klara would dare anything, but to protect Elizabeth's reputation, she had marked her own face. Elizabeth would have written her aunt to thank her but the likelihood of a letter being intercepted and read made that courtesy impossible.

As she walked through the hallway to her own rooms her thoughts turned to Ferenc. Women who married soldiers were usually widows at an early age. She had met many in Vienna and Budapest, most of Klara's friends were of that small, independent female aristocracy. Yes, if luck were with her, Ferenc's sword would slip or his horse stumble. Then, if the families believed there had been true devotion between them, Elizabeth could go into mourning forever.

Comforted by that pleasant possibility, Elizabeth rushed to her room, poured a glass of wine, and rang for a servant to help her dress. She would look her best for the day's courting.

During their long afternoon together, Elizabeth laughed at Ferenc's every small jest, pleaded helpless when the time came to mount and dismount her horse, making certain that she pressed against him at the right moments. All of it was designed to give him some sense of the woman she had nearly become.

She was aware of the precise moment when Ferenc decided that he might one day grow to love her. He had been merely tolerating her presence as a necessary duty until she began telling him of the summer, describing how she would sneak away from the house and go riding alone though there were outlaws and runaway Turks in the hills. Her bravery appeared to amuse him at first. Then, as he began to realize that this tiny girl knew exactly the risk she had taken, his voice warmed, his touch became more lingering. His suggestion that they take a carriage and go to Vienna tomorrow had some urgency. He actually wanted to see her alone again.

As for Elizabeth, if she looked only at his body and ignored the mind inside it, her future husband was tolerable enough. If he didn't kill himself before the wedding, he would suffice.

Abruptly, she thought of one of Catherine's victims, a young man far taller and stronger in build than Ferenc. Catherine had taken a fancy to his colorful clothing and, after she had stripped him, to his body. She had seduced him before she fed and he had no choice but to comply with tears running down his face.

Elizabeth had sat in her usual place on the bureau and clapped in time to their coupling. Her presence, Catherine declared afterward, had made her unusually inventive.

When they returned to the stable, Ferenc left Elizabeth in the courtyard while he went with one of the servants to see about a carriage. The covered one he wanted had been taken by Klara. "No wonder she wanted to hide her face," the servant leading their horses commented in a low tone to Ferenc. "She was in a fight, the vicious kind that women have. She had bites on her face and neck. Deep ones."

"Bites?" Elizabeth stood in the doorway, her hand covering her mouth, her voice low, horrified.

"Countess, I'm . . ."

Elizabeth stalked into the stable and swung her riding whip hard across the side of the man's face. "How dare you say that. It's a lie," she screamed.

"But, Countess . . ."

She hit him again and would have continued but Ferenc caught her wrist and pulled the whip out of her hand. "What is it?" he asked, but she only turned, her hand covering her mouth, stifling a scream as she fled.

Within an hour, Gyorgi Bathori heard rumors of what had happened at the stables. He summoned the servant and ordered him to explain. The first few words were enough. "Hang him," he ordered his aides, pointing to the man. "Then let him rot where he hangs. Tell the others that his death serves a lesson. No one will mention my wife's sister again. She is not dead to this house. She never existed. Make them understand."

The next morning, Ferenc passed an open window and noticed his future bride standing in the servants' courtyard, looking at the body swinging outside the barn. Thinking that the sight of it must be painful for Elizabeth, he ran outside and wrapped her in his cloak, holding her small shivering body tightly against his.

"Such a waste," Elizabeth said softly, her eyes still fixed on the swaying corpse.

Assuming that Elizabeth referred to the man's short life, he responded apologetically, "Your father only did what he thought was best. It's over now."

She nodded and pulled away, walking alone back to the house.

II

Ferenc Nadasdy and Elizabeth Bathori were betrothed in the spring of 1572. The engagement was formalized at Sarvar, the Nadasdy family seat in the lowlands of western Hungary.

The Nadasdys, more interested in Elizabeth's heritage than in her fortune, readily agreed to her demand that she keep her family name. Elizabeth's parents also agreed to give the summer home in the Bihors to the young couple as a marriage gift. Strong-willed, set against the match in the beginning, Elizabeth's change of heart delighted them. They would have given her more but this had been her sole request.

In late March, Elizabeth returned to the Bihors accompanied only by an ancient half-blind cousin and a handful of personal servants. It had been a damp spring and the lowlands around the house were covered with shallow ponds and mud. The hills surrounding them looked bare and so dismal that they seemed incapable of spewing forth spring's life. Nonetheless, within hours of their arrival, Elizabeth set off for her usual ride, accompanied by a Czech lad who knew nothing of the local legends.

In spite of his ignorance of the area, the young man seemed ill at ease on the narrow forest path. His eyes scanned the darkness beneath the trees as if he were seeking nightmares.

She did not know his name. She had not chosen him. She preferred to leave the victims to the head maid or the stablemaster—not because of any guilt she might feel—but because the uncertainty lent an extended charm to the game.

She had noticed the lad as she had all the others who accompanied her and her cousin from Ecsed. As she rode in her carriage, talking with her elderly cousin about sewing and household management and the secrets of maintaining a colorful summer garden, Elizabeth had peered out the window watching the riders escorting them through the hills, wondering, *Is the tall dark one in the front the next to die in Catherine's arms? Will it be the silly one who whistles every waking moment and winks at me whenever he catches my eye? Will it be a man at all?*

Now that another had decided on today's victim, her thoughts followed a different path. As she watched him leading his stubborn horse up the mountain path, she wondered if he would die quickly or if Catherine would be attracted to him for more than just blood.

The young Czech began a nervous chatter and Elizabeth immediately ordered him to be silent. This time she didn't just imagine his response. Like Catherine, she felt the warmth of his fear deep inside her.

•   •   •

As soon as Catherine sensed Elizabeth traveling in her hills, she ran through the forest, deliberately avoiding the narrow lane the merchant and his wife had followed so many years before. Grass and scrubby bushes now covered it, obscuring the fact that it had ever existed at all. Catherine's small shelter, like her life, had become isolated.

As she embraced her young friend, Catherine scarcely noticed the youth holding the horses, staring with wide, terrified eyes at his young mistress and the tall pale lady. Finally, immediate danger took precedence over the long-term consequences of abandoning the countess and he bolted down the path. Catherine let him run almost to the limit of her power before she trapped him with her mind and ordered him back. He returned, pale and shaking, so weak with fear that he could hardly stand by the time he reached her. Then, for all of Elizabeth's bloody fantasies, Catherine decided she had wasted time enough and disposed of him quickly. His presence had been, after all, an unwelcome intrusion on their company.

Later in the cabin, Catherine displayed her new plunder, jewelry and silks stolen from a trading company passing through the hills. Catherine dressed the tiny countess like a sultan's daughter in flowing silk pajama bottoms and gold chains strung with coins for her bare chest. She taught the girl an oriental dance, then danced with her, their quick rhythmic movements in time to Catherine's voice and the beating in her mind.

Their feet pounded on the floor, the tiny bells strung to their ankles tinkling as they moved.

In the end, exhausted, Elizabeth sprawled in a heap of pillows on the floor, drinking wine Catherine stole from her wealthy victims while Catherine, hungry for the bond they shared, held the girl's hand, taking tiny intoxicating sips of the girl's blood from the small wound her teeth had made on the soft side of Elizabeth's wrist.

They were an odd pair—more than friends, more intimate than lovers. Inseparable, it seemed, until Elizabeth told of her betrothal, giggling as she described her mother's pragmatic advice.

"If your husband is often absent, won't you have a great deal of work?" Catherine asked, thinking of the Austra firm and estates and all the hours the family spent in managing them.

"That's what servants are for. And when poor Ferenc is off impaling Turks with his men, I can come to you." Elizabeth giggled and lay back, fingering one of the coins, an old Egyptian piece with finely wrought sheaves of wheat on the back.

"Is there a way that you could come here alone?" Catherine asked.

"What?"

"Next time, come alone." The girl's regret only made Catherine more adamant. "I don't want to share you, not even for a little while."

"Is that really the reason?"

"Yes, and the fact that there have been a great many soldiers on the roads lately. I am well fed."

She lied. Elizabeth still could not understand these sudden insights but with Catherine they were strongest of all. Considering the mystery of their odd attraction, she opened the subject Catherine refused to take seriously. "I talked to my aunt," she said and went on to describe everything Klara had told her.

Catherine laughed when Elizabeth began, but later in her story her expression clouded and she found herself unable to hide her amazement. The names of the women were right! Charles had described his savage attack and Steffen's odd seduction to her and, when she discounted Elizabeth's natural exaggeration, even the places matched.

"Do you think the legend is true?" Elizabeth asked when she'd finished.

"You believe it."

Elizabeth jerked her hand out of Catherine's grasp, droplets of her own blood staining her chest. "My mother said that," she declared. "I want to know if they are true."

What did Elizabeth want of her? Reassurance? Catherine refused. On the subject of her family she found it difficult to agree to even a half lie. "I don't know," she said.

"Mother says I may stay at least until June. I think it will be far longer. Now that I am to be taken off her hands, she really doesn't care what I do anymore." Elizabeth stretched and yawned. Had the journey from Ecsed only taken three days? Perhaps it had been the presence of Cousin Eleni that had made it seem so much longer. She would have told Catherine about her cousin but Catherine was rubbing her back, singing an old peasant lullaby, her voice high and soft and clear like the ringing of a fine crystal wineglass. "Have you ever loved a man, Catherine?" she asked when the song was finished.

"Of course I have. You've seen me."

"Not sex. Love. Have you?"

"I don't think I have ever loved anyone until you." Catherine kissed the nape of Elizabeth's neck, her hand still moving across Elizabeth's back in its slow gentle circle. "But there was someone, one of my family. I loved Charles, I think because he was the only one of my kind capable of returning it."

"Was it pleasant?"

"No."

Thinking of what Klara had done to her, Elizabeth rolled over, her hands pushing back Catherine's dark hair. "I'm sorry," she said and kissed Catherine with real passion. Catherine pulled away, more astonished by her surprise than by the girl's action. Her looks had attracted women before, more than enough of them for her to recognize the signs. "Do I have to wait for my marriage before I can be a woman?" Elizabeth asked with no trace of embarrassment.

Catherine answered the only way she knew how. She entered Elizabeth's mind and willed her to sleep.

Later Catherine walked the night, stopping to take one long last look at the face of the boy she had killed. So young. So sweet. So much the sort Catherine used for a night of passion, then sent on their way with only their memories harmed. Did Elizabeth realize what she did or was she already blind to death? The last thought made Catherine shudder for she had much to do with nurturing the blood lust inside that child.

She knew she should order Elizabeth to leave here forever. She possessed the power to do so but she could not. They were bound together. They might even share the same blood. If she sent Elizabeth away now, the consequences to both of them could be enormous.

Was it the loneliness of living without her family or was it something more that made Elizabeth and she incomplete without each other? Could the girl's tales be true? In the months that Elizabeth had been gone, Catherine's emptiness had already raised questions about her own beliefs. And the thrill that coursed through her in the moment she sensed Elizabeth within her domain convinced her that she might be wrong. Now the girl added the correct details to a story Catherine had heard years ago.

Perhaps this summer they would discover the truth.

Four days later, Elizabeth returned home alone. Her white horse was mud-covered and lame. The servant had run off, she said. Had she not been taken in by a local family, she would have died of exposure.

Her maids immediately took charge. One prepared a hot bath. Another placed hot bricks in bed to warm it. A third brought food and all of them looked genuinely relieved at her reappearance. Elizabeth, well rested after three days of lounging in Catherine's palatial lair, first viewed the servants' concern with an amusement that quickly shifted to alarm, then rage. They treated her like a child when she was mistress here! Her mind flew over the possible ways of establishing her position, and recalling how her father dealt with peasants, she picked a ruthless course. She ordered the head maid who sent the Czech lad out with her to be given a hundred lashes for her disastrous choice of escorts.

A chair was brought into the courtyard. There Elizabeth sat, a tiny delicate creature, her face as pale as the starched white ruff of her garment, watching the preparations for the punishment with an impish smile on her lips as if the woman's agony would be nothing more than a game played by a child imitating the adults around her.

The servants were subdued. Had Elizabeth not returned, they might have all been tortured and killed for Gyorgi Bathori had never been known to be merciful. As to the whipping, they believed that their young mistress would most likely call it off as soon as she heard the servant scream. The bailiff even said as much to the head maid as he tied her wrists to one of the high stone posts that later in the summer would be covered with vines.

Elizabeth's smile froze on her face as the first screams—high-pitched, raw, and primal—tore into her like a sword heated in a fire. She would have ordered the beating to stop but the words stuck in her throat. All she could do was watch, feeling the waves of agony course through her until the woman lost consciousness and the incredible sounds ended. As Elizabeth stood, she swayed. Then, forcing her body to remain upright, she gave one final imperious order. The woman would be left hanging until morning.

Late that night, Elizabeth woke and, with a dark robe hiding her body, its cowl pulled tightly over her head, she stole outside to her still-unconscious victim. Someone had covered the maid's back with a damp towel and turned her around so her wounds would be protected from the gnats that invaded the area every spring. Standing on tiptoe, Elizabeth tilted the woman's head back, ripped off what was left of the woman's blouse, and bit her breast, sucking as she had so many years before. Moving to the neck, she bit again, drinking the blood as she had seen Catherine drink.

The woman moaned. The vibration against Elizabeth's lips telling her that the servant was close to consciousness. The clouds covering the half moon blew past and the courtyard was bathed in a milky white light. Forgetting for a moment that she ruled this small kingdom and held the power of life and death over her hapless subjects, Elizabeth turned and, like the child she still was, rushed back to the house shaking with the fear of discovery and punishment.

Alone in her room, she poured herself a glass of wine and tried to wash the taste of blood from her mouth. Her head began to pound, and with fingers moving convulsively over the stem of her goblet, she lay in bed and prayed for sleep.

In the morning, she rushed to her window and saw that the servant had been cut down.

How dare they treat her like a child! Elizabeth screamed for her chambermaid who, with eyes downcast from fright, answered simply, "She died in the night, Countess."

"Oh." Elizabeth hesitated, dismissed the thought of demanding to see the body, and settled for asking instead, "The beating killed her?"

"We're . . . not certain, my lady. We think perhaps some animal."

"Well . . ." The obvious question was on Elizabeth's lips but she did not ask it. Instead she motioned toward her closet. "I want to wear the green dress today . . . and my black boots. I am going riding."

The maid rushed to get it. "Do you wish me to request someone to accompany you?"

"No. Not today."

"But, Countess, is that wise after your accident?"

Elizabeth raised her chin. "Come here," she ordered.

The woman folded the dress across her arm and walked to her mistress. Elizabeth raised her hand and slapped the servant with all the force she possessed. A petite thirteen, Elizabeth didn't possess enough strength to hurt more than the servant's dignity, but the maid wiped her tears and continued assembling Elizabeth's wardrobe without saying a word of reproach.

Elizabeth had hit her servants before but never had she seen a reaction such as this one. Like all the servants, her maid had seen the whipping and knew that Elizabeth was capable of ordering another. What she had done last night made her the undisputed mistress here.

That was as it should be. Elizabeth wanted no one to question her again.

In an hour she was gone, riding alone as fast as her mare would carry her high into the hills, to Catherine.

III

Weeks passed with Elizabeth gone two nights out of three. Even a half-blind old woman could hear rumors. With a common sense born of years of compromise, Eleni Bathori avoided direct confrontation with her cousin. Instead she sent a letter to Elizabeth's mother, informing her of the strange events at the house, making certain that her own conclusions were hinted at but never set to paper. Anna Bathori responded immediately, ordering her daughter to leave for her future in-laws' home in Sarvar by the end of the month.

Elizabeth read her mother's letter as her maid was fixing her hair. It took her a moment to realize what had occurred before she exploded, brushing her hand against the hot curling iron as she flung the message across the room. The light parchment fluttered to the floor, and as the maid went to retrieve it, Elizabeth kicked her out of the way. The maid fell on the iron, and hearing her scream, Elizabeth kicked her again before grabbing the paper and flinging it into the fire.

She pulled off her blue silk dress with such force that she

ripped the tight-fitting bodice and threw it to the sobbing woman. "See that it's repaired before I return," she said, then, without waiting for help, pulled on her loose grey riding breeches and jacket. Soon, her unbound hair flying around her head, she took off into the hills.

From her spot in an upper-floor window, a servant of Eleni Bathori's noted Elizabeth's departure and conveyed it to her mistress. Eleni went to the window, saw the blur of horse and rider, and sighed. The direction Elizabeth traveled was always the same and now she always went alone. She must have found a lover, the old woman had long since concluded. Girls lost their innocence so early these days. Well, she had done her duty to the family though she pitied the child her good-byes. Turning from the window, the woman picked up her sewing—a cream satin nightdress, the collar quilted and embroidered with tiny pink rosebuds—and, holding it close to her fading eyes, continued with her handmade gift for Elizabeth's trousseau.

Today Elizabeth did not wait for Catherine to come for her. She tethered the horse at the end of the narrow path and ran headlong through the forest. They met midway, Elizabeth with tears streaming down her face, hands clenched into tight angry fists. She shrugged off Catherine's attempts to hold her and stormed past her to the cottage. "They can't make me leave. I won't go!" she cried.

"Leave?" Catherine asked softly. The winter's loneliness had been harsh enough. Catherine had thought that they would at least have the summer.

"I am ordered to go to Sarvar, to Ursula," Elizabeth spat her future mother-in-law's name. "Suppose I refuse to go? What could my mother do then?"

Catherine smiled and tried to sound light as she asked, "What?"

"Enough." Tears had mixed with the dust from Elizabeth's hands leaving long dark streaks on her face. She looked tinier than she was, less miserable than frightened.

"Elizabeth, what's really wrong?" Catherine asked.

"In Sarvar I will be Ursula's prisoner. She will watch my every move and allow me no freedom. Catherine, I do not want to be a virgin when I marry."

This child who had faced death without a shudder was afraid of her wedding night! The idea seemed so absurd that Catherine laughed. "Why not? Surely it cannot be because you desire some man?"

Elizabeth's bow-shaped mouth turned up at the edges. In another less-assured adolescent the gesture would have indicated uneasiness. Not in Elizabeth. There was no mistaking her determination. "No. But I have heard that my husband-to-be has bedded more than his share of lovers. I don't wish to be less than his equal."

"Elizabeth, it is not seemly for a woman to demonstrate too much knowledge on her wedding night."

It was Elizabeth's turn to laugh though she responded seriously. "I would rather have Ferenc furious than thinking that I have given my maidenhead to my *arranged* husband."

Her point made perfect sense. "And what kind of a man would you like?" Catherine asked.

Elizabeth opened a locket that Ferenc had given her and showed Catherine a stylized miniature of him. "Since this was painted he has grown a mustache. He is tall and athletic. Find me someone who looks like him. That way later, there will be no surprises."

"Find *me*!" Catherine laughed again, a sound so warm and so beautiful that Elizabeth wanted to abandon her past and her future and remain here forever. "Countess, there are always surprises. But if you truly want to make love to a man, I think you should be the one to find and bed him. You don't need my help for that."

"I don't?"

Catherine pointed to the girl's reflection in a gold-framed mirror. "Look at your face and your body. You've become quite a beauty. No, Elizabeth. See to your own trysts."

CHAPTER
7

I

Imre Josika, eldest son of a lesser landowner whose holding bordered the Bathori estates, took advantage of the warm spring weather to organize an early fishing party on the Somes River.

The group caught far more than they expected and Imre decided to split the catch. Sending all but a single servant home with the evening dinner, he took the remainder of the large brown trout to the Bathori house.

Though he had hoped to see his old friend, Steven Bathori, the young man had not yet arrived for the summer. Instead, Eleni Bathori came down the curving stone stairs to meet him. She gripped the decorative iron rail as well as the arm of a maid who carried her cane. The servant whispered Imre's name to Eleni as she held out her hand. As Imre bent to kiss it, she moved her face close to his for one long clear look at him. They had exchanged only a few words when she asked him to stay for dinner. Given the effort it had taken her to meet her social obligation and his father's chastisement if he did not take every opportunity to ingratiate himself to the Bathori family, Imre could hardly refuse.

A fire was lit in the large blue and gold drawing room, plain save for a huge tapestry on one wall woven with the Bathori dragon's teeth coat of arms. The simplicity of the room as well as the high stone wall surrounding the house served as a reminder that this estate, like his own, was on the frontier, subject to attack the moment the political winds shifted. But today their world was at peace and, God willing, would remain so.

A maid brought wine and pastry from the kitchen and Imre sat on a long black velvet settee with the aged countess, trying to pay attention to her words and not the bronze hunting clock clicking loudly above the carved satyrs and trees of the polished wood mantel.

The windows had been opened to let in the afternoon warmth and Imre found himself distracted from Eleni's monolog by the sound of a single horse's hooves on the stones outside. A moment later Elizabeth entered the room.

Though he and Elizabeth had played together when they were young, Imre had last spoken to her three years earlier in Ecsed. Since then, he had only seen the young countess in a distance, usually riding alone, dressed as she was today in loose men's clothing, her hair pinned up under a plain brown riding cap. He would have found the recklessness fetching in a servant girl. In a member of the ruling aristocracy, it seemed indecent as well as dangerous.

He noted that she had not grown much in those three years though other changes in her were nonetheless apparent. A maid rushed to hold the door for her and take her riding cape. A second brought a glass for her wine and a cup and saucer for her tea. The pair moved with frantic efficiency, never quite meeting their young mistress's eyes.

They fear her, Imre thought. He had heard rumors concerning Elizabeth's odd disappearances, the death of a servant earlier in the year, and how the household staff seemed so anxious to risk their lives by running away from the Bathori estate.

"Did you have a good ride, Countess?" he asked.

Elizabeth simply nodded as she sipped her wine and stared at him so rudely that he was convinced he had spoken his thoughts aloud.

Eleni took advantage of the silence. "I've asked Imre to stay for dinner."

"Have you?" Elizabeth's eyes never left his face as, without a pause, she added, "It's a long ride after dark. Perhaps he should stay the night as well." Without waiting for his assent, she rang for a servant and requested that the house ready a guest bedroom for his use. "I'll send one of my servants to your home with a note for your father. He'll bring you back a change of clothes."

She picked up her wineglass and left the room. Imre heard her soft voice giving the order to a servant, her light footsteps on the stone stairs.

They ate dinner in the west-facing solarium, its tall windows closed now, the black quarry tiles of the floor and dark wainscoting warming in the late-afternoon sun. Eleni, dressed in plain black, sat at the end of the table, Elizabeth across from Imre. Elizabeth's long dark hair hung loose over her shoulders and wisps of it had been curled French style around her face. The effect softened the girl's features and emphasized her deep-set eyes while the plain black dress she wore drew attention to her pale, translucent skin. The change also made her look younger than her years—a beautiful child made up to be a woman.

They discussed Elizabeth's wedding at dinner and afterward Eleni excused herself early, leaving the pair sitting in the light of the setting sun. As soon as it was polite to do so, Imre stood and began to ask a servant to show him to his room.

"I'll take you upstairs," Elizabeth said.

Carrying the candle, she went ahead of him. Then, as she paused outside his door, she confessed candidly that she desired him.

Even if he cared for her, she had manipulated him once too often today. "If you were a few years older, Elizabeth, I would be more than willing," he responded in a voice that barely remained civil. "But I do not desire children however lovely they may be."

Elizabeth's expression froze, only a flush spreading across her cheeks revealed any sign of anger or embarrassment. Nonetheless, she had the presence of mind to respond with a face-saving reply. "I'm sorry, Imre. I am not usually so direct but I was recently betrothed and I do not approve of my father's choice. Our combined estates will be far-flung and difficult to manage. Besides, I love this country and I do not want to leave it."

Though he could hardly compete with Ferenc Nadasdy in social standing, Elizabeth was right. The Bathori and Josika estates bordered each other. Imre suggested that they take a morning ride over both their properties before he left.

Imre expected Elizabeth to slap his face. He deserved it. His remark had been rude, and if her proposition hadn't taken him by surprise, he would have thought of a better response. But either the girl was too stupid to know when she had been insulted or, more likely, she had outwitted him again when she accepted.

Either way, the result was the same and by morning Imre had cursed his stupidity more than once. Elizabeth Bathori was already betrothed, and no matter what her opinion of her future husband, she would not be able to back out of the match. But second marriages were often less socially correct. What harm could there be in cultivating a closer friendship with the girl?

So they went for their ride though the day was gloomy and mists covered the lowlands. He and Elizabeth led with his servant in the rear. They headed east first, then northwest into the hills. Though he had heard the warnings about the mountain roads, his household had never experienced any problem, and with two men mounted and ready for trouble, he allowed himself to relax. As to the legend of these hills, it had always struck him as ridiculous.

Then he saw Catherine standing by the side of the road, clothed in diaphanous red silks like some eastern princess. Imre reined in his horse, ready to call to Elizabeth to turn and flee, but Elizabeth had already dismounted and was running to the apparition, embracing her as a friend. Imre smiled and relaxed, thinking he had finally solved the mystery of the countess's odd disappearances and wondering how he could make the most of this strange encounter.

"Welcome to my woods," Catherine said to him softly. "Let me show you the comforts of my house."

"Would you like to ride?" Imre asked. "My servant could walk behind."

A long look passed between Elizabeth and the woman. Then the woman responded, "I will share his mount and show you the way." With no help, she jumped up behind the rider. Her long arms circled the servant's waist, and as they rode, she pressed her body against him. With her thighs over his knees, she pushed herself up so she could reach his neck and drink. As he lost consciousness, her fingers lifted the reins from his.

Imre was afraid to look at Catherine, afraid that her beauty would cause him to make a fool of himself in front of Elizabeth. So, riding in the rear of their little caravan, he kept his eyes fixed on Elizabeth's back.

They soon reached a cottage that Imre riding alone would have missed seeing altogether. The windows were shuttered, they and the walls were covered over with vines that extended across the roof as well. There was no sign of servants or stable, no sign of even a garden for food. More curious than wary, Imre helped Elizabeth dismount, then went to help Catherine. Instead of taking his hand, she dropped the servant at his feet. The man landed on his back, his lifeless open eyes staring at the sky, the side of his neck a bloody hole as if it had been gnawed at by some beast.

Imre looked up at Catherine, at her beautiful lips rouged with his servant's blood. Imre's mouth hung open but he could not say a single word. Shock and Catherine had stolen his voice. To Elizabeth, he looked most like a frightened carp on a hook.

Catherine took his hand and slipped off the horse, then without letting go of him, she led him inside, ordered him to sit and relax and forget for the moment what he had just seen.

Catherine's face was so flawless and her body so magnificent that Imre longed to be at peace here and forget the horror that had gripped him outside. Desire made control simple and in a moment he was sitting cross-legged on the fur-covered floor with Elizabeth lounging beside him.

Catherine's attention shifted to the countess. "You could have done with this without me," she said sternly. "Why is he here?"

"I only have the rest of the week," Elizabeth explained, her cold voice hiding all the pain of the rejection. "He is my choice but he refused. He insulted me and I want you to . . ."

"Look at her!" Imre exploded. "She is only thirteen, hardly old enough to . . ."

—Silence!— Catherine ordered and Imre swallowed the rest of his words, looking so shocked that Elizabeth was certain he was about to choke on them.

Elizabeth giggled, then demanded, "Make him take off his clothes." Concerned that she may have gone too far, her voice rose to a child's plea, "Please, he is my choice. Make him love me."

Imre shuddered. Something was about to happen, something he could scarcely understand but he was certain that his will no longer had any bearing on the event. He was helpless against this woman, and if she wished it, he would do whatever she asked.

. He reached out, trying to take the woman's hand and beg her to let him go. But she only pulled away and walked behind him, running her long fingers down his cheeks and neck, lifting his chin, kissing him on his closed lips.

"He does look pretty, doesn't he?" Catherine purred. "I could devour him as I did his servant and cut his fine purple shirt into ribbons for my hair. Or perhaps, if he performs as well as he thinks he is able, he might live to see the sunset."

"Live?" Imre's hands closed into tight fists. He wanted to fight or run but the woman's touch seemed to freeze his body. He could not move.

—Undress— Catherine ordered.

"What?"

"You heard her," Elizabeth said, rubbing the back of his hand with her thin white fingers. "So did I, now do as she demands."

Imre refused. A wave of pain washed through him, so strong it left him shaking. Catherine kissed the side of his neck, and as he flinched from the touch, she tilted his head back once again and smiled. At the moment he saw her long rear teeth and tried to pull away, she moved far faster than he could ever conceive of moving. Her teeth rent the flesh of his neck and she drank.

—Undress— Catherine repeated.

The bond formed. He saw himself through her eyes, saw how much she cherished his life, and dizzy from fear and desire, he had no choice but to obey this command, knowing it was only the first of many that would follow.

When he stood naked in the center of the room, Elizabeth sat and studied him. Unlike Catherine or Klara or even Marijo who had felt so soft when Elizabeth hugged her, this man aroused nothing in her except disgust. Anxious to get her ordeal finished, Elizabeth stripped and lay across Catherine's bed, heaping pillows behind her head so that she could watch what he did.

—Go to her.—

This time, Imre recognized the source of the words. He looked at Catherine but her expression remained impassive.

—You will regret it if you do not perform as well as you are able.—

—She's a child— Imre thought the words, wondering if Catherine could hear them. —I have no desire.—

—You will. When the time is right, I promise you that.—

Imre walked to the bed and touched Elizabeth's leg. As he did, a charge ran through him, its intensity making him shudder. Suddenly, he wanted this girl, desired her more than anyone he had ever known. Forgetting Catherine, he kissed the top of Elizabeth's foot, her ankle, then his hands began moving up the inside of her legs.

Elizabeth sensed the moment when Catherine entered Imre's mind for it was the same moment when Catherine entered hers. She and this haughty young man cared nothing for each other so Catherine aroused the attraction each of them felt for her, playing both parts for the time it took them to complete the act. And it all seemed so perfect until, as Imre pounded his body against the girl's, Elizabeth began to claw at Imre's back, pulling him down to kiss her, sinking her teeth into his lower lip, biting it through. Imre responded with a grunt of pain but wisely did not try to pull away.

—Elizabeth, let him go!— Catherine ordered but the girl was swooning from the blood and the passion and if she heard, she did not obey.

Catherine rushed to the bed and, placing her hands on either side of the girl's face, repeated her order. This time the results were better and Imre was able to raise his head and stare dully, with his blood dripping down his chin, into Catherine's eyes.

Beneath him, Elizabeth was struggling, scratching at Imre's shoulders and neck, trying to pull him down and drink from him again. Catherine's mind was hardly a match for the girl's now so she gripped Elizabeth's wrists and held them over her head, kissing her, murmuring reassuring words as she built their passion once more.

When it was over and Imre and Elizabeth, exhausted by their coupling, slept, Catherine looked down at the girl. Her face was smeared with Imre's blood. Her fingernails were caked with it as well. With horror, Catherine began to wonder what kind of a wedding night the young countess would have.

Well, Catherine would have time to dwell on that problem later. Now, she had to consider what to do with Imre Josika. For all her boasting to Elizabeth on the day they first met, Catherine knew her limits. She might have killed the girl and her female servant—at the time, there were outlaws in the hills who would have been blamed for the crimes. She often killed wealthy travelers along with area peasants who disappeared with frightening regularity without her help. However, devouring the eldest son of a local landowner was another matter.

And though Elizabeth had not given the problem any thought, she would certainly be questioned if young Josika disappeared.

However, the Josika family lived within two hours' ride of her mountains, giving Catherine an idea about how to save her and Elizabeth a great deal of difficulty. She went to the bed and kissed the young man, drinking from his wound. His eyes opened for a moment and he tried to struggle.

—Quiet, Imre. I have no need of your life. Not yet. Perhaps never.—

Calmed, Imre sighed and, as she willed, returned to a deep, silent sleep. Looking down at him, Catherine thought of the slaves, the *cows*, kept in the Austra keep. He would fit in there well with that young body, so full of beauty and passion. Yes, he was perfect. He would be her first lover-in-exile, strong enough to see her through months of use before he died. Perhaps he would even be enough to give her the courage to do what must be done today.

She and Elizabeth were alone when the girl woke that afternoon. There were tears in Elizabeth's eyes as she washed and dressed and Catherine knew that the girl wanted some reassurance that her future would be happier than this morning. Catherine could not give it. Instead, she touched the girl and showed her everything she had done to Imre, leaving Elizabeth sobbing and shaking in her arms.

"What happened need never happen again, child. I want you to leave me now and forever. I care for you as I would for my own daughter, and for that reason, I do not want you to ever return here again."

"But that won't help!" Elizabeth managed to blurt before the sobs started again. When she was able, Elizabeth told her about Klara and the servant and what little she could recall about Marijo, speaking with an odd soft focus as if she had witnessed rather than caused the wounds. "It isn't *you* that created this need in me, don't you see? I was like you long before we ever met and now I am so frightened of what will happen."

On her wedding night, Catherine thought again.

And when the morning after came and her bridegroom could not go out to face the well-wishers at the wedding breakfast, what would he do with his new bride?

He could lock her away in the castle, send her to a convent to live out her years, or he could have her declared a witch or a blood-drinking *mora* and the authorities would burn her. Every answer was tragic, and Catherine decided she would do anything to help this child even if it meant facing the world once again.

"Catherine," Elizabeth said, her voice soft but strained as if she were afraid that someone would hear her next words. "I know what you did last night. I want you to know that it would not make any difference if it were Imre or Ferenc or some other man in my arms. I don't desire any of them. I only desire you."

"Elizabeth, you cannot help that. You . . ."

"And if I had not met you, I would have loved some other woman. I am cursed like Klara. I always knew it, I think. But Klara was given to a man over twice her age, already an invalid when they married. I am being given to Ferenc and every time he touches me, I will have to struggle to keep from screaming."

"Elizabeth, can you be certain of what you are?"

"Don't tell me I am too young to know what I want or need." She held out her arms.

Catherine moved toward her, lowering her head to plant the first of many kisses on Elizabeth's bloodstained lips.

II

Imre Josika was found by a sharp-eyed servant who had spotted his horse in the fields near his home. He was half-dazed, the wound on his lip still raw and bloody. His clothes were torn and mud-stained and the side of his head had a huge, dark bruise.

He could remember nothing save leaving Elizabeth when he and his servant reached the main road.

"You were attacked?" his father asked after Imre had been washed and placed in bed.

Imre could only close his eyes. His head hurt when he tried to remember what had happened. It hurt even more when he tried to recall if Elizabeth had been alone when she had ridden away.

The physician blamed the head wound for the boy's confusion and brewed a tea of gentian and henbane to quiet his nerves and help him sleep. Not convinced that his son's problem stemmed entirely from attack and fever, Imre's father rode to the Bathori house to question Elizabeth and found her and her servants in the midst of a flurry of activity as the household made the final preparations for their long trip across Hungary to Sarvar. The girl was charming, every inch the lady of the house as she took time from overseeing the packing to order refreshments and answer his questions. She could be of no help. The attack had occurred after she had left Imre on the road. Charmed by her, the elder Josika thought of additional questions only after he had left the estate, but when he returned a day later, Elizabeth and her servants had gone.

Though Imre's wounds healed, his mind did not recover. At night, with his hands frozen at his side, he would see those dark, lonely eyes and pale, beautiful face hovering over him, he would feel her kisses on his lips and neck. His passion would grow until he was allowed to hold her and the creature that at first seemed no more substantial than moonlight felt warm and solid in his arms.

They never spoke to each other and Imre had no illusions about how much he meant to her. When he died she would find another and another, substituting countless lives for the one she could not have. He knew this, knew that he should even be able to remember this creature's name but none came to him, in the end not even those of his old lovers.

Month by month, he grew paler and weaker. Finally, a servant came to him while he was sleeping, trimmed a lock of his hair, and gave it to a *taltos*. The healer mixed it with ashes from the kitchen hearth and buried it in the garden. She then boiled coal with water and, when it had cooled, took it upstairs and poured it into a vase of wild roses in Imre's room.

The releasing spells did not work. Imre slept later each day, his mind ever more confused. Still the beautiful creature came, devouring him slowly with her love.

The winter storms became fierce in mid-November and though the family worried over Imre's frail health, he inexplicably rallied. By Christmas he had even become almost the same lighthearted young man that family and servants alike remembered and loved.

He remained in good health until the spring thaw. The physician thought the night air brought his malady and ordered his shutters closed and barred. But in the morning the servants would often find them open, Imre lying dazed and naked across his bed.

Finally, a letter came for Imre. It had been sealed with the Bathori crest, but that evening when Imre opened it in the privacy of his room, a second sealed envelope was inside addressed simply to *Catherine*. He placed it on his bureau, then sat in a chair and let all the willed-forgotten memories that name aroused surface in him. He shook. He swore. He cried but he knew what he must do.

And while the house slept, he sat and waited. When Catherine came, he handed her the letter and ordered her to go. She didn't say a word but the pain in her eyes as she took the envelope haunted him long after she had gone.

The return of his memory hadn't released him. He was still under her spell and finally he rode off alone to beg the *Kisasszony* to give him back his soul.

With effort, he found the cottage but the doors were open, the inside, emptied of its sumptuous treasures, cold. A loneliness so pressing that he no longer desired to live accompanied him home. He caught a chill on the way. The sniffles became a cough and the cough settled in his chest. He could have fought it off. He didn't want to.

He died a month before Elizabeth Bathori was married in Varanno. The Josika family, in deep mourning, never suspected that through two bodies—one human, the other immortal—a part of Imre lived on.

CHAPTER
8

I

Anna Bathori stood in front of her dressing-room mirror while her servants made the final adjustments to her cream-colored satin gown. It had been a long and painful year, but in an hour Elizabeth would be married and Anna's responsibilities to her daughter would be over. Oddly, her self-satisfaction had become bittersweet. The crisis they had faced together during the last year had brought her and Elizabeth closer than they had ever been.

It began with a letter Elizabeth sent her in mid-June. Its angry, frightened tone alarmed Anna and she had done as Elizabeth demanded and rushed to Sarvar. Intending to comfort the girl, she instead found herself facing a pregnant child. Her daughter's morning sickness had already begun causing gossip among the Sarvar servants though, Elizabeth was quick to explain, she made certain there was always blood on her underclothes at the appropriate time each month.

"Who was it!" Anna Bathori had not screamed the words, indeed she scarcely spoke above a whisper lest a Nadasdy servant overhear their conversation.

"Imre Josika," Elizabeth replied.

Anna lifted a crucifix from its place on the wall and held it out to the girl. "Do you swear on your immortal soul that what you say is true."

Elizabeth rested her hand on the cross and said evenly, "I do."

Anna had put the cross back in its place and gone to the window, staring out at the countryside. "Well, you cannot remain here." When she turned, she noted her daughter's relieved expression. In her letter Elizabeth had confessed that she loathed Sarvar, Ursula Nadasdy—her future mother-in-law—the servants, even the land itself, complaining bitterly of the plague of summer heat and gnats and the stench from the lowland swamps that added to her misery day and night.

"The Bihor house would be the best for your confinement. It will be cooler through the summer and it is the most remote of our holdings. But considering that the father lives so close . . . ?" She left the rest of the question unspoken, watching her daughter's face for the answer.

"He doesn't have to know," Elizabeth countered.

Elizabeth did not show the slightest emotion when she discussed the man. Anger or contempt, Anna could understand, but not this. "Imre meant nothing to you, did he?"

"Experience."

Without thinking, Anna slapped her daughter with a force hard enough that Elizabeth lost her balance. She broke her fall by grabbing the carved stone mantel of the room's small fireplace. Her body went rigid, her arms began to shake. As abruptly as the rage had surfaced, it vanished. When she turned to her mother, her face had become a rigid mask hiding what seemed inexplicably like fear.

"I have no choice as to whom I will marry," Elizabeth said coldly. "I made what choice I could. No one knew what we did, I can swear to that as well. Take me there or wherever you wish so long as we leave this house."

"And what of the child?"

"The child is of no concern to me. There will be other children, that I am capable of having them seems clear enough."

Anna had composed herself well enough to face Ferenc's mother and declare that the summer heat in Sarvar had caused the return of an old fever. Before any other plans could be made to move Elizabeth, Anna had spirited her daughter off to her cousin's country estate near Somolyo. And in those months, Anna had been the strong one, hiding Elizabeth away when the family came to call, sympathetically allaying her daughter's fear as her time for delivery approached.

A child was born on St. Lucy's day and, within hours of the difficult delivery, was sent away in the care of a maid who would receive ten gold talars a year to raise the child as her own. The amount was twice what Anna needed to spend but she wanted the child raised with some luxury. Duty to your own blood demanded that much. Elizabeth never asked what had been done with the child. If Anna had ordered it destroyed, she sensed her daughter would not have cared. Afterward, Elizabeth returned to Sarvar for the holidays. She had apparently performed well there for Ursula Nadasdy's letters to Anna were full of praise.

Now, with the greatest hurdle to her daughter's marriage overcome, Anna watched while her maid put the final pins in her hair and added the tight cap accented with intricate gold embroidery. After one last appraisal of her attire, Anna went to join her daughter on her wedding day.

Anna heard someone crying as soon as she stepped into Elizabeth's private drawing room. She went slowly to the unlatched dressing-room door and pushed it open, ready to order out the servants and comfort her daughter.

But the sight in Elizabeth's chamber was far from what Anna expected. A servant was on her knees in front of Elizabeth, sobbing as she tried to dab away a spot of blood on Elizabeth's hooped underskirt. As Elizabeth wiped the blood off the black ring on her finger, she looked down at the woman kneeling in front of her, her eyes fixed intently on the woman's shaking hands as if nothing happening today was as important as the pain she had inflicted. The servant worked quickly but the cold water was only spreading the stain, making it more noticeable and the woman more frantic. While she worked, the blood seeped slowly from a jagged wound on her cheek, flowing down her face. In a moment it would drip on the outer skirts and the damage might be impossible to undo. How could her daughter be so stupid as to let this continue.

"Loosen the skirt and slide the stain to the back where it will be hidden by the overskirt," Anna ordered. "Not you," she added in alarm as the servant with the bloody cheek began to lift Elizabeth's gown to find the hooks. Another lifted the fabric from the wounded woman's arms and did as Anna asked.

When they had finished, Anna dismissed them and took a moment to study her daughter. Elizabeth's hands shook, her eyes staring into the mirror, disapproving of everything she saw. "I wanted it to be so perfect, everything in place, and that stupid cow nearly scorched the collar with her iron. I had to make it clear . . ."

"A servant's mistake is not important," Anna interrupted, then added a reassurance. "What's important is how beautiful you look. Turn around and let me see the back."

Elizabeth's wedding dress was teal with a pale mauve linen collar accented with matching lace and seed pearls. The pearls spilled off the décolleté neckline, falling like dewdrops down a line of dark green leaves, then scattered over the full ruffles of the four-tiered skirt open in the front to reveal embroidered darker mauve rosebuds on the hooped underskirt. Anna had never seen her daughter dressed more joyously, her face so pale, her expression—now that the servants had gone and she could drop her facade—so resigned.

Though Elizabeth's answer would make no difference, Anna asked, "Are you and Ferenc compatible?"

"I don't know," the girl replied woodenly. "He has been patrolling on the southern frontier. He came here three days ago and leaves again at the end of the next week. I promised I would go with him." She began to walk through her sitting room to the outside door, paused, and turned back to her mother. "He seems to understand why I must be with him. Perhaps we will get along well enough after all."

"Where will you go?" Anna asked.

"He intends to fortify the castle in Sarvar."

"And Ursula?" Anna asked, knowing that Sarvar was Ursula's home and hoping that Elizabeth and the woman had reached some understanding.

"She will be in Vienna for the summer. By the time she returns to Sarvar, it will be my house with my servants. I have already begun to assure that." Anna knew she meant the words and woe to any house peasant who dared oppose her.

Anna kissed her daughter's cheek, then they went together down the hall to the wide curved stairway to the chapel. On either side of the stone steps long banners with the family crests gave color to the plain walls. The Bathori crest with its knights and dragon's teeth seemed oddly juxtapositioned beside the Nadasdy one of ducks and water as if the masculine and feminine had somehow become confused. As Anna wondered, not for the first time, if Ferenc was strong enough to control her headstrong daughter, she saw him waiting at the entrance to the chapel.

Ferenc Nadasdy had matured since the betrothal. Now, as Elizabeth went and joined him, Anna saw that he towered over his bride, his thin bearded form making him seem so much older than the seven years separating them. He wore black hose and jacket, full satin breeches of dark green. The breeches and the matching sleeves of the jacket were slashed in the Swiss style, revealing a gold underfabric. His beard and hair had been trimmed making him appear less a soldier than a poet, and when he looked at Elizabeth, Anna saw an affection in his eyes that heartened her.

Had the families been Catholic, the couple could have married in the town church with the entire community at the service. Instead they used the third-level chapel in Varanno Castle. While beautifully designed with high narrow windows and carved Gothic-inspired arches, the chapel was small and could hold no more than fifty guests. As a result, only the immediate families and a representative of the monarchy would be present for the short service while the majority of the guests had been invited to the banquet and evening receptions starting immediately after the service in the great hall below.

And instead of the fine stained windows of the older churches, the glass here was of a pale opaque green that gave the guests a sickly pallor and altered the subtle mauve collar and trim of Elizabeth's gown to a dingy grey.

"To think that Melanchanton once preached here," Elizabeth commented bitterly to Ferenc as they waited in the rear of the chapel while the court representatives went to their seats.

Ferenc looked at the room as if noticing its ugliness for the first time. Raised Lutheran when the country was still seeped in religious intolerance, he impetuously decided on a fitting gift for his bride. "I vow, Elizabeth, that with God's help I will one day build you a chapel of our faith with windows that will rival the masterpieces of France. You need only name the place."

Elizabeth hesitated before acknowledging his offer, staring at the church thoughtfully before lifting her chin and looking directly at him. For the first time today, a radiant, triumphant smile softened her features, making her look innocent and hopeful. A moment later the musicians began to play their lutes and recorders, the clear high notes of the wedding song signaling the beginning of the service. Anna kissed her daughter on the cheek and rushed to take her place in the front row. Then, with their cousin, Count Thurzo, sent as the royal witness for the match, Elizabeth and Ferenc marched to the alter. Fourteen and twenty-one. So young, Anna thought, and so hopeful.

II

Near the heart of the Hapsburg Empire, Varanno Castle had been gradually remodeled to resemble less a military outpost than a lavish country home. Recently decorated in the Renaissance style, the great room featured carved marble pillars and an oak and walnut parquet floor whose intricate geometric design had taken nearly a year to complete. The frescoes on the walls dated from an earlier time and depicted elaborate hunting scenes. The deer being chased had genuine antlers. These hung from the walls and held the sconces that lit the hall making it seem as if the deer were carrying light into the room. The raised platform that had held the wedding couple's table at the earlier banquet had long since been cleared and the seating on the floor replaced with two huge tables on one side of the hall. One was covered with pastries and pitchers of wine. The other displayed the wedding gifts. At the far end of the room, a second raised platform held the musicians and singers. When all was ready, the chamberlain opened the doors, the trumpets gave a joyous fanfare, and the guests filed inside.

The wedding party entered last and, Anna noted, her daughter stood in the arched doorway, her eyes scanning the room, veiled disappointment registering in them. She had been looking for someone who had not yet arrived. Given the hour, it was unlikely anyone else would.

The madrigals stopped, the orchestra began to play, and Ferenc led Elizabeth to the floor. Midway through the dance, a woman joined the musicians on their platform. Dressed in a deep blue evening gown with cream lace on the sleeves and underskirt and strings of black amethysts around her neck, she looked less like a performer than one of the guests and Elizabeth's quick cry of delight confirmed this. One of the men made a remark that the lady had probably had too much wine, then glanced at her face and found himself trapped by its beauty. Others had the same reaction and a hush spread through the room.

Then, a capella, the lady began to sing an old song of crossed lovers' tragic meetings. Her voice rang through the room as clear as the winter sky she described, with overtones so sensual that woman found themselves reaching for their partners, Ferenc stealing a kiss from his enraptured bride. The musicians joined with her, picking up the melody as her voice moved in its own slow and sensual harmony, a song that quickened, moving faster and faster until the players broke into a raucous *czardas,* the national dance of Hungary. The singer jumped down from the platform and pulled an old man from his chair to join the dancing, her voice as perfect as it had been when she began, rising and falling as she wove with the others through the room.

From her place in the archway leading to the gardens, Anna Bathori watched the stranger. Her expression was carefully poised to hide her uneasiness as the woman sang and danced, then warmly greeted her daughter, embracing her as if they were close friends.

All Anna's worst suspicions were true.

Fair Lady—not of the shadows but of the mountains, one of the ancient race whose blood was rumored to be mixed with her own. She thought of the servants who had disappeared while riding with Elizabeth, of the others who had died, of her daughter's strange fascination with the family legend. Anna tried to get the woman's attention but they always seemed to be on opposite sides of the room. At last, Anna drew aside the chamberlain to ask the woman's name.

"I believe that is the Baroness Catherine."

"Baroness?"

"I am sorry, Countess. That is the only name I was given. She is on your daughter's special guest list so I assumed you knew her."

"It's been a long time," Anna responded. "When did she arrive?"

"At the beginning of the service, Countess. We showed her to her room to rest."

"Then she will be staying the night?"

"Yes. Your daughter requested she be given the green room in the tower."

The room was two stories above the bridal suite. No human could scale those stone walls but the mountain people had no such limits. Anna's mind focused abruptly on how cold her daughter had looked at the injured woman serving her, as if she longed to continue the beating. Could Elizabeth and that woman have planned Ferenc's death?

Elizabeth danced with her husband, a slow *landar* perfectly suited for a bride and groom. Her head was raised so she could look at Ferenc and her expression was one of perfectly acted adoration to a man she scarcely knew. With horror, Anna realized that her daughter was capable of any atrocity.

The revelation stunned her. She handed her glass to one of the servants and moved toward the door. When Anna reached the table holding the gifts, she stopped and scanned them, seeing immediately the one the ancient "baroness" must have brought.

Hardly larger than her hand, the tiny satyr was fashioned of gold, the face and body and fur of his loins so lifelike it seemed less formed than gilded. The eyes were lapis, the flute it played was hollow crystal. Anna lifted the statue and felt its solid weight.

Elizabeth and the woman were more than friends. The woman's presence in itself had made that much clear, the gift only confirmed this. As someone proposed one more toast to the bride, Anna made her escape, and stood in the deserted stone foyer trying to decide what course she should take.

III

Catherine had whispered her reassuring words to Elizabeth and danced enough for one evening. Now she disappeared as abruptly as she arrived, using an inside exit that led to a smaller paneled room with broad wood beams and carved corbels. An octagonal table surrounded by straight-backed chairs were its only furnishings. One entire wall, from the floor to the height of Catherine's head, was devoted to shelves and books. Catherine stared at them, studying their dyed and tooled leather bindings, their gold-leafed titles. Some might have been Latin—

at least the words looked like those in the book Jacques had presented to the Old One and on the sheets of crisp parchment on which the monks had written when they taught Charles and the others to read. The family had been so eager to learn, so obsessed with the desire to change as the world changed, as if each new invention rendered the past obsolete.

She had thought the heavy boxed manuscript a human oddity, like the endless parade of fabrics and laces that defined fashion from one year to the next. Now it seemed that knowledge had taken on more importance than she had ever expected, and not for the first time, she found herself longing for the innocent barbarity of her past.

The library walls seemed to press down on her and she opened another narrow door that led outside. A moment later she crossed the broad wooden causeway spanning the brackish lake around Varanno and found solitude in the spacious gardens beyond the castle walls. The sweetbriers and mock orange were in full bloom, the lilacs long past their prime giving a heady undertone to the more delicate scents. The May weather was warm and the starched collar of Catherine's formal gown chafed her skin. Had her dressmaker been present she would kill him again and this time be far more painful in her method. If she had no obligations tonight, she would strip completely and run free with the deer in the woods and let their deaths renew her. She had need of that renewal for she hated this place and the presence of so many people that forced her to use all her power to remain constantly on guard.

Well, tomorrow would bring relief. Tomorrow she could abandon this ruse and begin the journey back to her little retreat and the treasures she had hidden in its dried-out well.

And soon, as always, Elizabeth promised to return to the hills. Next time the house would be hers, and with no husband or family to tell her otherwise, she could stay as long as she wished.

Catherine heard someone crossing the gate. Without turning, she sensed the sex and the age. Neither was any surprise, and she was pleased to note that the man was a performer who would not be missed by the wedding party. Rather than confront him in view of the house, she disappeared into the hedge maze, her mind soaring, showing her the shortest distance to the center. There she waited for him, a spider in a web of greenery. As he sought her, she began toying with his desire, feeling it grow with every empty turn. At the end, he ran the final long tunnel to where she sat on the iron bench beneath the wisteria vines, waiting for his kiss.

Sometime later, she stepped out of the maze and began crossing the causeway. As the shadow of Varanno touched her, she gripped the woven iron railing and looked up at the stone wall rising in front of her, remembering for a moment the Austra keep—so austere compared to this luxury, so old that the century this castle had stood seemed no more than weeks.

Did she miss her past? Sometimes, even after so many years, she could hear Francis calling to her, promising her forgiveness if only she would come home and ask for it.

Yes, he must be lonely too. She took consolation in this thought as she climbed the worn servants' stairs to her tower room, pushed open the door, and saw Anna Bathori standing inside, her hands clenched, her lips pressed together in determination.

Catherine knew the woman instantly. Though they had never met, she had seen her face in Elizabeth's mind and noted her portrait in the great hall of the Bathori summer home on the nights that she and Elizabeth had hunted the house.

"Why are you here, Countess?" she asked, her dark eyes wary as they met the woman's.

"To ask you . . . no, to beg you, to leave my daughter in peace."

"As she begged me to come?" Catherine replied, her voice lilting, mocking. "The price of my attendance has just reached six lives and you tell me to go after only a few hours of revelry."

"I have seen the results of your presence in Borsa. And I ask again, if you care for Elizabeth at all, leave her now."

Catherine's arms were rigid and she stepped back, putting some distance between her rage and this woman. "She sought me out and I would never harm her."

"Never? Then why did she ask that you be given this particular room?"

"I cannot tell you that."

And Anna would not say the truth. She didn't need to. Even a mortal woman could have seen what she believed written clearly on her face.

"Answer me one thing. Why do you care so much for my daughter?" Anna asked.

"You know the answer to that. As for me, I will not speak of it."

"And so you came here."

"To sing at Elizabeth's wedding. To dance. To leave gifts. To wish her well for the rest of her life."

To kill her husband, Anna thought and saw the slow nod of Catherine's head.

"No one will ever suspect your daughter," Catherine said. "I will assure it."

"The most precious gift you could give her would be forgetfulness."

Catherine shook her head. "We've known each other far too long for that."

"But now she can start a new life with her husband and with the children she will undoubtedly bear. She need never return to the Bihors, to anywhere that will remind her of you. If you care for her, can you deny her all that you cannot have?"

Catherine frowned and countered, "She need not forget me to be happy."

"No? There are rooms in this castle where couples are holding each other trying to be satisfied with mortal flesh now that they have seen and touched you. You possess more beauty than any of them will ever know until they reach the godhead. How can anyone ignore your allure?"

"How do you know that? How did you know what I am?"

Instead of replying, Anna fell into a chair and began to cry. "Fair Lady, please! Give my daughter the only chance she will ever have to be truly happy."

Catherine stared into the blackness beyond her narrow chamber window as she asked the question uppermost in her mind. "Countess, you do not love your daughter and you scarcely know the bridegroom. Why do you care enough to risk your life by coming to me?"

But Anna would not answer. Hysteria was building in her to an intensity that Catherine could not comprehend.

—Look at me!— Catherine demanded, the mental command as powerful as she could make it.

Anna only shook her head. Like her daughter, she seemed

immune to much of the Austra powers.

"Tell me how you knew!"

When the woman only continued to sob, Catherine knelt in front of her, one hand gripping Anna's shoulder, the other forcing Anna's chin up, her mind compelling Anna to meet her eyes. When they did, Catherine probed and felt nothing. She raised the woman's wrist to her lips, bit hard and drank and probed again.

And discovered only a familiar wall. The woman was prohibited from speaking any name by a power far greater than Catherine's own. One of the family had touched her, used her, and only half managed to wipe the memory.

Catherine let the woman go and Anna's head fell forward into her lap. "Go to your room, Countess. Go to sleep."

As Anna woodenly obeyed, Catherine impulsively reached for her. The blood tie was still strong, strong enough that Catherine's merciful message managed to reach her as the one so many years before had not.

—Forget me. Forget the other as well. Go. Sleep. Forget.—

As soon as Anna left, Catherine barred her chamber door and stripped off her finery, replacing it with black knit leggings and hooded shirt. She stood at the window for a moment, looking out at the gardens and the forest beyond them. Elizabeth had been the best of her loves, but with her mortal limitations, she could hardly be the last.

Yes, Catherine loved her as she had never loved anyone. Perhaps it was best if she did not wait to say good-bye.

Resigned, Catherine stuffed the most precious of her treasures in a small leather sack that she attached to the rope coiled around her waist. Then she hooked her fingers around the latrine pipe that ran down the side of the tower and began her descent.

IV

The drapes around the marriage bed were thick and dark, and in spite of the night candle on the bureau, Ferenc could not see beyond them. But as he caressed his petite bride, memories of the strange woman's song became more vivid, the music still floating in the darkness beyond the bed. A shadow crossed the window briefly blocking the stars before it moved to the shaded top of the bed.

Elizabeth sighed and, for the first time tonight, relaxed and raised her arms straight above her head, reaching through the bed drapes.

And it seemed to Ferenc that his vision blurred for there were white fingers curling around his wife's wrists and the song that had been only in his memory became suddenly real.

And what had begun as a mechanical, ritual coupling turned into more than that. Ferenc shook with desire, his wife below him panting as well, her hips rising to meet his downward thrusts.

Bewitched by her, that's what he was. He had always dreamed of such a lucky match and now it had happened. He shut his eyes, for when they were opened, they saw hands holding his wife's chin, the bed drapes moving inward over Elizabeth's face.

Then, with his eyes still shut, he felt Elizabeth kissing him, her teeth biting his lip ever so slightly. His own blood crazed him, he had never felt more aroused. He heard Elizabeth crying with passion and his voice joined hers in unexpected ecstasy.

They went on and on, one climax flowing into another and another until the candle flickered and died. The music moved back into his mind. The shadow left as it came and Elizabeth lay wrapped in her husband's arms.

Hours later when Elizabeth woke and looked up at her husband's face, she had a moment in which, dazed, she felt an undefined sadness as she mourned something she could not remember.

As quickly as it came, it departed. She clapped her hands to wake him and jumped out of bed, laughing as she threw a hooded cape to Ferenc and slipped on her own, belting it to hide her body. "It will be hours until dawn. Let's go downstairs into the maze and make love beneath the stars," she said and followed that with a mischievous giggle.

"Let's take the wine," Ferenc added and a moment later they stole down the servants' stairs and through the hall to the main door.

A night guard stopped them. "You should not go out there," he said.

"What harm can there be in a walk with my bride?" Ferenc demanded.

"There are wolves hunting the estate."

"Wolves?" Elizabeth asked.

"One of the musicians was attacked and killed in the maze."

"Killed?" Elizabeth gripped her husband's arm. The room had begun to spin.

Ferenc looked at Elizabeth with concern. Her voice had become so flat and strange.

"We won't be able to pick up their tracks until the morning so you see it isn't wise . . ." The servant halted in midsentence. Ferenc caught Elizabeth before her body could hit the ground.

Ferenc held Elizabeth upright on a bench just outside the main doors and moistened her lips with the wine until she recovered from her faint. Without a word, she wrapped her arms around him and kissed him with a ferocity he did not comprehend.

She felt so light in his arms, so perfectly fragile as he lifted her and carried her up the stairs to their room.

From her hiding place on the far side of the garden, Catherine had seen the servants with their torches carry the body from the maze. She had felt the moment when Elizabeth and Ferenc, left with only her mental suggestion, discovered that they would be forever bound by the passion she had planted in them. And she had laughed silently as, in her own private chamber, Anna Bathori looked in puzzlement at the little satyr she had stolen from the wedding table and, without any logical reason, wrapped it carefully and packed it in the bottom of her trunk. It was a treasure, of course, but one Elizabeth could afford to lose. After all, her best gift had been given in the bridal chamber. She thought of the words she had used, *You will care for each other and desire each other, only each other for as long as you both shall live.*

What more perfect wedding gift for an arranged marriage than a spell such as that?

And they would be gentle and kind to each other, Catherine had seen to that as well. This wasn't the consuming passion the young countess wanted but it was the best one if she was to survive and prosper in her world.

Now, with miles between her and her remote lair in the Bihors, Catherine tried to find some satisfaction from her sacrifice but all she could feel was an empty despair.

There would be others. There would have to be others. The loneliness would allow her no choice any longer.

V

That evening the servants broke down the locked door to Catherine's abandoned room. Outside of some clothes and a glass on the table, nothing indicated that the room had been used the night before. The chamberlain questioned Elizabeth, but the bride only shook her head, declaring that she had not known the woman.

Since no harm had been done, the chamberlain refused to press her. Instead, he examined the room and the window ledge, then showed Ferenc what he had found. "The room was above yours. The dirt on the ledge is smudged and there are marks on the pipe. She might have been a paid assassin who failed in her mission."

Ferenc examined the evidence, then asked the chamberlain to accompany him to their own room. The same smudges were on the ledge there as well. "Throw out all the linens in this room and from the one above. They may carry the plague," Ferenc told the chamberlain. "Have everything burned. Dump any wine or food left downstairs. Let no one eat what is not prepared fresh today." The commands were given easily and Ferenc hoped that no one noticed his alarm. Last night, someone had been in their room, he remembered that much, he even recalled a whisper, pieces of a song.

As he walked downstairs to his child bride, he noted her pale face, her dark expressive eyes. He was on his way to becoming a powerful man. Powerful men had enemies and families were always a weakness.

"Order your maids to begin packing," he whispered to her. "We leave for Sarvar tonight. And if any of them cross you in any way, you tell me and I will see that they never disobey you again."

"I can handle that myself," Elizabeth responded coldly, then broke into a warm smile and kissed him.

No, he refused to believe that he had been in any danger last night—passion alone had altered his senses.

The thought stayed with him during the trip from Varanno to Sarvar. They stopped at inns along the way, often until late in the morning for Ferenc had a hunger for his new bride. Her every wish was granted and immediately for the couple soon demonstrated what would happen to an unfortunate servant who did not rush to obey their commands. The maid who failed to warm their bed was flogged when Elizabeth complained of being chilled. The cook who oversalted their evening meal was burned on the cheek with the lid of his stewpot. Ferenc ordered the discipline with cold detachment. As a soldier, he was used to inflicting it. Not so Elizabeth, and when Ferenc saw how violence excited her, he grew more demanding. Everything had to be perfect for his bride, as perfect as the nights when they lay together.

Their reputation preceded them, and by the time they reached Sarvar, the house was ready for them. The meals were exquisite, the service superb, and for the time that Ferenc remained with Elizabeth, all remained serene.

Everything changed when, with the castle fortified, he left to see to the outlying lands. Elizabeth's cycle had been a week late when he left but the next day she began to bleed. Ferenc would be so disappointed. As she lay on her bed, sobbing with misery, the voices began, strange lilting whispers so soft that Elizabeth could scarcely hear them at all, tied somehow to the scent of her own blood.

The voices stayed with her in the weeks that followed— a sibilant connection of syllables not quite speech but more than gibberish. Elizabeth concentrated on the sound, her mind focused inward, seeking the barrier to understanding. Around her, the world continued on. Maids dressed her and brought her meals. They turned back her bed in the evening and opened her drapes in the morning. She scarcely noticed them or the passing of time. Nothing broke the monotony of life in Sarvar, not even one bright soul for conversation.

Two weeks after Ferenc left for the frontier, Elizabeth sat at one end of the marble-topped table in the dining room opening a belated wedding gift and letter from her aunt Klara. The gift—

a licentiously illustrated French copy of the *Decameron*—was, Klara wrote, intended to inspire her and Ferenc on their nights together. The rest of the letter was oddly apologetic, as if it were Klara's doing that she had not been invited to the wedding. In a way, Elizabeth supposed, it had been.

The past mingled with the present as Elizabeth paged through the book and recalled what little she could of her night with Klara with a pleasure that seemed sinful as if the event over which she had no control had made her unfaithful to her husband. At that moment, a tall, dour-faced Slovak maid knocked and entered and began cleaning the ashes from the fireplace. Elizabeth stared at her, at her huge chapped hands shoveling the coals into the bucket, at her breasts pressed against her thin summer blouse. Thoughts came back to her—of Klara and Marijo—and the woman, sensing she was being watched, turned and glanced at Elizabeth and the book she held.

Elizabeth shook. Her face, always pale, turned even whiter, and with an angry shriek, Elizabeth kicked the ash pail, scattering hot cinders against the crouched woman's face and chest. The woman screamed, brushing the coals onto the carpet. Elizabeth, frenzied by the cries, grabbed the shovel and began tossing glowing coals at the servant from the hearth, ordering her to beat out the smoldering carpet with her bare feet. The woman, too frightened to bolt from the room, tried to obey, screaming all the while. Finally, Elizabeth swung the shovel against the side of the woman's head and, not bothering to glance at the damage she had done, dropped the weapon beside the inert woman, picked up the book from the table, and left the room.

Her passion dissipated, Elizabeth went to her bedroom. There she lay across her bed weeping—not for Ferenc who she missed terribly but for herself. A great calm followed this outburst and she slept, deeply, for the first time in days.

When she woke, it was dark and servants were whispering outside her door. She rang the bell, intending to ask that the evening meal be brought here, and the voices fell silent. "Who is there?" she called out, thinking of the plots Ferenc feared so much.

No one responded. "Who is it?" she called again with some alarm.

The door swung open. A servant shuffled reluctantly in. The side of her face was bruised and cut, her chest was bandaged.

Behind her stood Katia Szezany, the headmistress, pushing her forward. "I want to . . . to tell you that I am sorry for my . . . my mistake, Countess," the woman blurted.

Elizabeth frowned. What could this woman mean? Lapses in her memory were common enough that she easily hid her confusion. "Just be more careful in the future," she said.

Though the woman was ugly, her chapped hands shook as she spoke, and they seemed to Elizabeth to be the most beautiful hands she had ever seen. "Now bring me my dinner," she said.

"Yes, Countess," Katia responded.

Elizabeth scowled. "Not you, Katia. Let this woman bring it. I want her to serve me for as long as it takes her to heal. It will be easier than her usual work, I think. And make sure her feet are tightly wrapped. I don't want blood on the carpet."

Food came—tiny plum dumplings with apricot sauce and a thick spicy partridge stew. The woman, who had never served before, spilled the wine, then looked at Elizabeth so fearfully that Elizabeth had to press her lips together to keep from laughing.

"Bring me my writing desk," she ordered. When the woman only looked confused, Elizabeth giggled at her ignorance and pointed at the shallow wooden box on the table beside her bed. Though she intended to keep her promise to her mother and refuse to admit Klara to her home, the correspondence with her wicked aunt would cheer her and shorten the days until Ferenc returned. Humming to herself, she composed a reply to Klara's letter, describing her married life with as many lewd details as she dared set on paper. One letter led to others. Elizabeth wrote her mother, her cousins, then penned brief messages to those who had come to her wedding. She invited her favorites to Sarvar and, after sending the letters, ordered the guest rooms swept and washed and readied for the guests she had invited.

The activity kept the voices at bay, but when the work was over and there was nothing left to do, the loneliness closed in and they started their strange soft whispering once again. And once again, Elizabeth became withdrawn and silent, hardly speaking a word. The servants, who were becoming well acquainted with her moods, shuddered and wondered who would be the next to endure her torment.

As the years passed, the voices grew louder but no more distinct and her moods became more extreme. She fawned on her husband when he was at home, deferring to his wishes as if she were a slave at Sarvar, enduring his caresses with a displaced passion that seemed to come from outside her body. Rage built in her for the weeks he remained at Sarvar, and once he left for the frontier, she would explode. Her victims were always her own sex for she despised it and the stupid games women played with men not nearly their equal.

Eventually, the servants began to draw lots for who would serve the countess when the inevitable explosions neared. Still, they were hardly worse off than peasants on other estates, better perhaps for their lord and lady were wealthy and kept them well clothed and fed.

Long reprieves also cheered them. Elizabeth, and Ferenc when he was home, often traveled to Vienna or to their other estates leaving the servants to their own devices. A decade later, during a rare few years of peace, Elizabeth bore three daughters and a son. In the years that followed, Elizabeth became so engrossed in her family that the whispers became so faint she rarely noticed them at all.

CHAPTER

9

I

1599

Ayn Darvulia had been informally betrothed to Martin Uhrban for six months before they dared approach Count Nadasdy and ask for permission to wed. His approval had been his last gesture to the servants before he left with his men and Elizabeth had stood at his side, beaming as he announced that the wedding would take place on the anniversary of his own. Everything had seemed so perfect, so peaceful in Sarvar until the count and countess returned from Anna Bathori's funeral in Ecsed.

The countess brought crates with her, carefully packed china and other treasures from her mother's estate. As Ayn helped Katia Szezany unpack, the countess examined each piece, making certain it had not been damaged in the trip, then gave it back to Katia to wash. The countess paused at each piece, letting them remind her of the past, Ayn thought, but longest at the strange golden satyr. Then, with a reverence that seemed strange, the countess herself dipped it into the vinegar and water, wiping the golden limbs with the dry cotton cloth, polishing its tiny crystal flute.

"Leave me," she said to them, and as they obeyed Ayn looked over her shoulder to where the countess sat, holding the satyr up to the fire, watching its golden fleece glow in the flames, her expression troubled.

When the pair were called back sometime later, the satyr

was not with the other pieces on the display rack in the countess's sitting room. Ayn later learned that it sat on the table beside Elizabeth's bed, a candle always burning beside it. It was rumored among the servants that the countess hardly slept at all and they waited for the next painful outburst.

Countess Klara Bathori arrived a few weeks later. Though well past fifty, she was still an athletic woman and the half-moon scar on her cheek that she could never quite cover with makeup gave her a rakish air. She came accompanied by two young women and a half-dozen armed escorts. The unruliness of the group troubled the house servants. The women were not ladies-in-waiting but nobility who, like Klara, enjoyed the pleasures of their own sex and their public licentiousness troubled everyone. The men were worse. They did nothing but eat and drink, beating any servant who dared to cross them, taking advantage of any woman who caught their eye. Ayn had been wary but one of the men surprised her in the barn when she went for the morning milking.

Ayn thought it would be best if she didn't fight the attack but he slapped her face anyway, then began roughly pinching her breasts. He'd be sure to leave marks on her. Martin would see them and he'd risk his life to kill the man, then afterward turn on her because she had not fought. Decision made, she kicked hard into the man's groin. The suddenness of her attack threw the rapist off guard and she ran toward the barn door. There she grabbed a pitchfork and, still hoping to keep her honor without her fiancé learning what had happened, turned and pointed the tines at her attacker. Unable to stop in time, he impaled himself on the sharp tips.

Had he died silently, the servants could have hid his body and their future might have been utterly different. Instead, he fell slowly to his knees, holding the fork handle as he bellowed for his companions until he could scream no longer. By the time the household collected at the barn, he was dead and Ayn was kneeling on the ground beside the body, staring at the blood—black in the dim light—coating the dirt and straw; and at the dying man's expression, still holding shreds of his earlier lust and rage. Someone had thrown a blanket over her and helped her to her feet when Countess Klara Bathori came through the barn door.

Her face without its makeup was reddened by dissipation,

her short henna hair tangled from sleep, and the cloak she had thrown over her body barely covered her. Her irritation turned to amusement when she saw the corpse. "Who did this?" she demanded with a twisted smile as she pointed more at the puddle of blood than the man.

"I did," Ayn admitted, clutching what remained of her dress against her chest. He had deserved to die, after all.

Klara rolled the man onto his back and pulled the fork from his stomach, holding the bloody points close to Ayn's face. "Defending your honor, were you?"

Ayn shut her eyes. "Yes," she said softly.

"Stand straight, girl," Klara ordered. "Now put your arms at your side. That's it, let the dress and blanket fall. We all have the greatest interest in seeing what you had to defend at the price of a man's life."

Ayn glanced past her to where the Countess Elizabeth stood in the doorway. "Please, Countess," she called. "I did not mean to kill him. He . . ."

"Strip," the countess said coldly. "I too would like to see what she defended."

"No!" Martin pulled himself away from the men who were holding him back and worked his way to Ayn, pushing Klara away from her.

Katia Szezany moved to Elizabeth's side and whispered, "There are three horses lame because last night these men rode through the fields when they were drunk. Later they built up the kitchen hearth fire so high I thought the castle would burn. If Ayn had not fought, she would not have been the first woman raped. I intended to speak to you about these matters sometime today."

If Katia hoped to soothe her mistress, Martin Uhrban's actions had already made that impossible. "Stand away from her," Elizabeth called to him. "Now, Ayn, do as you were told or I will order the men to do it for you."

When Ayn had finished and stood naked before everyone, a flush spread from her face to her chest. No matter what the verdict, she would never forgive her mistress for this indignity. Klara rephrased her question. "Was your body worth a man's life?"

Ayn looked at the men around her, some of them lowering their heads, a few of the bolder ones leering at her. She looked at Martin, straining to control the fury that could doom them both. Then her eyes moved from her mistress to the Countess Klara and she gave the only answer she knew would save her life. "Yes," she replied proudly, her eyes never moving from Klara's face as she spoke.

"A life for a life," Elizabeth responded. Though she spoke softly all had been hushed, waiting for her reply as they now waited for her to name the means of Ayn's execution.

Klara cocked her head and looked thoughtfully at Ayn. "Elizabeth," she called. "More justice would be done if you gave her to me. A servant for a servant."

"Give?" the countess asked.

"Someday I'll return her. I think you'll be pleased with her education."

Ayn expected Martin to explode. Instead, the young man looked at his feet. Now that he had considered the situation, he had wisely decided that cowardice suited him better than a futile brave stand. Resigned, Ayn wrapped herself as best she could in her grey linen dress and followed her new mistress inside where the papers were signed legally passing her ownership to the Countess Klara Bathori.

Her education began that night in Klara's chambers, the pleasure she received far more distressing than any pain would have been. When it was over, she stole the countess's cloak and went searching for Martin, intending to beg him to run away with her. Though the penalty would certainly be death if they were caught, any risk was better than submitting to those horrible embraces again.

She didn't find him. From the kitchen servants she learned that Elizabeth had offered him freedom and a gold talar if he left the estate immediately. When Ayn heard the news, she began to cry and covered her face with her hands to hide her grief. She expected someone to come and comfort her but no one did. Finally, with her shoulders squared, her back straight, she walked to the door that led to the great hall, whirling at the end and seeing only relief and satisfaction and, saddest of all, a pair of odd twisted smiles on the faces of the women who had once been her friends.

I will remember this moment, she thought. *I will remember it clearly until the day I die.*

Ayn waited for word from him for a month and every day that passed made her more bitter. Isolated from her old companions in the kitchen, she sat alone in the room that had been prepared for her, finally pouring out her thoughts to the only person who ever stayed with her long enough for a conversation. When she had finished, Klara Bathori responded in a voice flat with conviction, "You have a lesson to learn, my dear. Men are not worth considering."

"Do you hate them?" Ayn asked.

"Hate?" Klara laughed as she sat at the table by the tall north window, smoking a carved ivory pipe. "Hate is too strong an emotion to waste on a man. Despise is a better word, don't you think?"

"Yes," Ayn answered truthfully. Martin had said he loved her, had lain with her, had promised to protect her always. Then, when she needed him most, he had chosen the coin over her. Once betrayed, she vowed she would never let it happen again.

"I thought so. I saw that defiance in your eyes in the courtyard and I sensed something more as well. You are already a powerful woman, Ayn Darvulia, and I will add to your power. When I am through, you will teach my niece everything you have learned about pleasure and pain." She held out the pipe and Ayn gladly reached for it, already addicted to the euphoria its contents brought, the languor that allowed her to endure Klara's kisses and all that followed, to endure even the presence of Countess Elizabeth sitting in a chair in the corner of the room watching everything that was done to her, her face pale as parchment, her hands and lips trembling with disgust and desire.

When Klara's visit was over, Ayn went with her to Vienna and every day that passed under Klara's instruction made her harder and more merciless, more willing to bury her past beneath the layers of pain Klara Bathori taught her to inflict on their well-paid victims.

She quickly learned something else about her new mistress. Klara Bathori never let time interfere with revenge. Wounded and banished she saw, through Ayn, a way to take her vengeance on what remained of her sister's family. Now Ayn sensed that she waited, like the plague, for the moment of weakness when she would strike. "What is my family to you?" she said with cold fury the one time that Ayn hesitantly spoke in defense of her previous mistress. "My charming niece would have killed you had I not intervened. And had I suggested that she flay you alive, she would have done so with relish. Spare me your pity, Ayn. It doesn't become a woman, not a true one that is."

"But vengeance, Klara. How can you possible achieve it?"

"Don't you know? Can't you even guess? You dear, silly child, I intend to make her just like me."

II

During the four years that followed, Ferenc Nadasdy drove the Turks from the lands south and west of Sarvar, his ruthlessness earning him a nickname used by friends and foes alike—"the Black Knight." Tales of his deeds preceded him home from each battle. Elizabeth, with her daughters grown and married, her son in the hands of a tutor she despised, responded with a ruthlessness of her own. His every victory was paid for with his servants' lives as Elizabeth strove to mimic his heroic deeds on a domestic scale. Each time he returned home, the Sarvar estate was above reproach—everything from the family chambers to the barns and fields perfectly manicured.

As for the bodies of those servants who had misread Elizabeth's orders, Ferenc no longer heard of them for the survivors had learned it was better to avoid mentioning them than to risk the count's rage when they criticized his beloved wife.

To all of them, he seemed as strong as ever. He kept the weakness to himself, knowing long before it became apparent to the family that his days were numbered.

And by the end of 1603, after nearly thirty years of marriage, Ferenc Nadasdy was dying—not the warrior's death Elizabeth had always imagined would claim him but something slow and lingering, something that left him in pain, crying out for mercy for days on end. His breath became foul so the sickroom smelled of it and his skin had a jaundiced cast. The doctor who examined him told Elizabeth he could linger for months in this terrible half death. Country-raised, Elizabeth

sent for a *taltos* from the village but the healer said fearfully that
she could do nothing. Though she expected a beating for her
honesty, Elizabeth was too horrified with the news to order one.
Instead, she wrote Klara a quick letter describing the attacks.
Klara once told her that she practiced the black arts. If need
be, Elizabeth would sell her soul to save her husband.

Klara responded by sending Ayn home. The woman who
had once been so bright and merry, so quick to laugh, came
dressed in a black wool dress and cape, her light brown hair
pulled up in a severe bun. She arrived in one of Klara's
carriages bringing a valise of clothes and another containing
paper-wrapped packets of potent herbs and tiny glass bottles
of elixirs. She came prepared to use her power on a woman
desperate enough to need it.

A disheveled near-hysterical Elizabeth met Ayn on the steps
outside, not even letting her slip off her traveling cape before
leading her to the sickroom where Ferenc lay. He was covered with a pile of blankets, his bed close to the fire on the
hearth but he still shivered, his once-powerful body wasted
so his joints seemed only grotesque knobs over skin-covered
bones.

He pulled himself to consciousness and managed a wan smile
when Elizabeth entered the room. Another woman would have
felt some pity, not Ayn. She ordered Elizabeth to leave, then
set to work, opening the windows to the winter cold, bathing
the man in a blend of alcohol and herbs, giving him something
to drink that made him alert for the first time in days. When
Elizabeth was allowed to see him later that afternoon, she
found him sitting up in bed, smiling at her. And the room
smelled wonderful, like almonds and oranges. "My ears ring
and my words seem to come from far away but the pain is
gone," Ferenc told her.

For days, Elizabeth had been afraid to touch him, using only
the sound of her voice to let him know she was near. Now she
held him while she told him what she had been doing, every frantic detail she could remember until she noticed his eyes closing
and left him to his rest.

In her room across the hall from the sickroom, Ayn Darvulia
sat by the window, smoking a pipe and looking out over the
snow-covered countryside. She had her instructions, and by the

time Elizabeth came to thank her for Ferenc's sudden health, Ayn was ready for her with the brutality of truth. "I only gave him potions to make him stronger and to mask his pain. But the pain is still there, Countess, and when the drugs wear off it will come again."

"Then give him more."

"They will only work for so long and in the end they will poison him." Ayn saw how stiff the countess had become. She understood the outburst that was coming for she had seen the same expression on Klara's face often enough. Nonetheless, Ayn said bluntly, "You have the blood of gods in your veins. You should face death squarely. Do you understand me, Countess?"

Elizabeth moved beyond her to a chair by the fire and sat there with her back to Ayn and watched the flames. Her shoulders slumped forward, her head slowly bowed. "His son will see him tonight," she said and added the final words after a long pause. "Then you may do what must be done."

Ayn pressed her power. "You, Countess. You should be the one for he loves you so much."

"Yes, in the morning," Elizabeth said in a tiny child's voice, automatically holding out her hand for the glass of wine Ayn had poured for her. As the warmth spread through her, exhaustion claimed her and she fell asleep where she sat.

The house was quiet when Elizabeth woke and stole into the room where her husband lay so still it seemed he was already dead. She looked at him in alarm until she saw his chest rise and fall with a labored breath. No, he was not dead, not yet, but he was fading and she could feel their love fading with him.

Elizabeth tried to pray for him but the words would not come. Instead, she saw all the blank hours of her past so suddenly vivid that it seemed it had never been gone at all. "The bodies were mine, Ferenc," she whispered. "The deaths. The blood. All of it, mine. I pray that God does not damn you for any of it."

And as the dead showed their faces to her, Catherine's passionate kisses on her victims began the familiar coursing ecstasy of

blood that finally climaxed with the memory of that last night
in the Bihors in Catherine's embrace. "Ferenc!" she screamed
in terror. "Ferenc, you must not leave me to face this past
alone!" Her hands began to shake, her thin lips contort with
rage. How dare he go! How could she have loved someone who
would leave her this way? How could she have even tolerated
his touch? She turned to leave him and she must have done so
because she woke in her room, slumped in front of her chair.

When she went to look in on Ferenc, he was dead as she had
expected. A strip of bloody cloth was wrapped around his neck,
and though her hands shook, Elizabeth unwrapped it and looked
down at the deep rip on his throat, then at her own bloody hands.
She retied the bandage, adjusted the covers around him, turned,
and saw Ayn standing in the doorway.

"I covered the wound," Ayn said, her voice hardly more than
a whisper as if she had guessed the truth and would keep the
secret. "If we dress him in his uniform with the high collar,
no one need ever know."

Elizabeth looked from her to Ferenc, then, giving in to
exhaustion and remorse, she fell to her knees beside the body,
buried her face in her hands, and began to cry.

The ground would be frozen for months making burial
impossible so the servants placed Ferenc in the marble sar-
cophagus in the burial shed. Before closing it, Elizabeth laid
his sword on his chest. It would not be buried with him for it
would be given to his son, Paul, but Elizabeth hoped it would
be a comfort to Ferenc through the long winter before the
burial. Then the family closed the doors to the funeral shed,
leaving Ferenc to wait for spring and interment. There he lay in
his sumptuous casket surrounded by servants wrapped naked in
unbleached cloth, the ones who had died of the lumbar plague
at Christmas, the three that Elizabeth had killed in her frequent
rages during his final days.

In the weeks that followed, Elizabeth went to the shed often,
examining her victims, then opening the casket and looking
down at her husband's frost-covered face. He looked so empty,
so sad, as if he had never obtained what he really wanted in
life. And that was true, she thought bitterly, he had possessed
her instead.

"We were bewitched, Ferenc," she finally whispered, for now the familiar voice had become louder, and today the words whispered on her wedding night though still soft were completely clear—a parting gift that seemed no better than a curse. She had never really loved him, could never truly love any man at all.

She walked from the burial shed, across the courtyard toward her house, a tiny black island in the swirling snow.

In her room upstairs, she held the golden satyr reverently in both hands, folded slowly to the floor, crossing her legs, arranging her skirt over her knees as she had arranged it so many times before.

"Catherine," she said softly. The name released something deep inside her and she began to cry. As she wiped her tears away with the back of her hand, she looked down at the dark stone ring on her hand. Why had she never questioned its origins until now?

Catherine had betrayed her, had taken even the memory of her past. She wondered if Catherine still dwelt in the Bihor hills and if she would allow herself to be found. No matter. Elizabeth would find her if it took a fortune to do so.

But even if they never met again, one thing would still be certain, they were kin. They lived on blood. Nothing could change that. As she returned the statue to its place beside her bed, a tear fell on her arm.

It would be the last one she ever shed.

Later, Ayn found her facedown on her bed, shaking with this new, more terrible grief. When she touched the countess's shoulder, Elizabeth rolled over and held up her arms. "Help me, Ayn," she moaned. "Help me become the creature I know I am."

"Klara sent me to be with you always," Ayn responded, holding Elizabeth as she spoke with a warmth in her voice she could no longer truly feel. "Klara told me exactly what to do."

Ayn had been told enough about Elizabeth to understand that her next move was a dangerous one. Nonetheless, she was also far younger than Elizabeth with a natural beauty that years of dissipation had not yet erased. Knowing the power that Elizabeth's passion would give her, she slowly raised Elizabeth's chin and looked at each part of her face.

"Forgive me this intimacy, Countess," she whispered. "You are so beautiful!"

Then she kissed the countess lightly, not moving forward nor retreating either. Instead, emulating her own experience with Klara so many years ago, she waited for Elizabeth to respond.

As the thin arms wrapped around her neck, Ayn felt a shallow stab of pity as she recalled Klara's parting words, "You won't have to force her as I did you. No, she will take all your instruction gladly. I know what she is and I have seen her worst."

The pity departed as the months took their terrible toll. As Ayn well knew, the murder of a single servant meant nothing to the high nobility. The deaths of a dozen over time would scarcely be noted. But in the half year after Ayn came to Sarvar, over twenty women died in the tower room above Elizabeth's private chambers.

Ayn had been skilled in the art of pain but hers was a subtle art, the occasional death a mistake rather than intentional. Now the sheer audacity of Elizabeth's violence astonished her. Perhaps the countess did not believe that anyone would be powerful enough to stop her murders. More likely, Ayn thought, Elizabeth did not give the matter any consideration at all.

No, the countess had become lost in her own internal rhythm of lucid calm and deadly explosions. And when the latter struck and Elizabeth ordered the beatings to begin, every scream made her grimace with delight, every sobbed plea for mercy made her order the torment increased. And the blood she drank from the open wounds gave her an orgasmic satisfaction.

But when each life was over and each body lay cooling on the stones at her feet, all Ayn could detect in the countess was a self-directed regret.

"It isn't the same." Elizabeth would say each time.

"What isn't?" Ayn would ask.

"There is no warmth from their deaths. I don't feel their life flowing in me."

Then one of her more trusted servants would drag the body away. Another would sweep the stones clean of blood. Another would pour their blood-soaked mistress a bath. As she washed, Ayn would kiss her and tell her she was beautiful. Ayn would suggest a new color of gown, the countess's hair fixed a new way. But no matter what she did to distract her mistress, the rage would always come again.

And as Ayn dreaded, someone did notice. Imre Megyery, tutor and legal guardian to Elizabeth's son, Paul, began inquiring among Elizabeth's servants. When he had finished, he wrote a long account to send to the authorities, then delivered a second copy of his letter to Elizabeth. With it, he included a written ultimatum. She would leave this house before she compromised her family further. She would take up residence at the unused family estate of her choice and trouble her son's conscience no longer. If she did not, Megyery would go to the authorities, declare her insane, and have her locked away forever.

Ayn did not see the letter but Megyery told her exactly what it contained and cautioned her to be certain her mistress heeded his threat. Ayn waited the hours she knew would be necessary to calm Elizabeth's rage before going to her. But instead of fury, she found her mistress sitting in front of the gilded pretzel-shaped mirror made of salt dough baked the required seven times for healing. She did not notice Ayn and instead continued staring at her face, scrutinizing every tiny wrinkle, every blemish, every ruddy patch of age on her cheeks.

Ayn quietly sat in a chair on the edge of Elizabeth's vision, waiting for her to break her reverie and speak. When she did, the words were a surprise. "It is this place that is destroying me," Elizabeth said. "This was Ursula's house and now it is my son's. I am going to go away to the Bihor house that is mine. And then I will find the one I need to show me what must be done."

"Then, if you will have no need of me . . ." Ayn began.

"But I do. You were given to me to be my companion."

"Please, Countess, I miss Klara. And she is so old. She needs me."

"If you go, I will tell the authorities that you bewitched me and that your power forced me to kill. Don't make me take that course with you, Annika my love. Don't ever try to leave me."

She'd been doubly trapped, Ayn knew. First by Klara, now by Elizabeth. For the authorities would never listen to a commoner, never place her truth above a countess's lies. And when they had ripped her limbs from her body and thrown her into the fire, Elizabeth could kill again and the blame would still belong to the witch, Ayn Darvulia.

Trapped, with a mistress so clearly insane.

"I love you, Annika. I love you so much," Elizabeth whispered.

Resigned, Ayn stood and went to where the countess sat waiting with her arms outstretched, her pale face tilted upward, a gentle child's smile playing mischievously over her thin red lips.

III

To reach the Bihors, Elizabeth and her retinue traveled a crescent north and west through the Hapsburg-held territories. Throughout the journey, Elizabeth stopped at a number of royal estates where the entire company was fed and housed. But between these infrequent sojourns, Elizabeth set a frantic pace and they reached the house, nearly three hundred miles from Sarvar, in six weeks.

No one had been alerted that the countess was coming. In the years since Elizabeth had been given the estate, the main house had been closed while the overseer and a handful of servants needed to look after the lands lived in separate smaller homes. When they realized that their mistress had come home, they set up her lavish traveling tent, acquiring food and drink from the nearby town along with laborers to clean the interior.

Elizabeth did not remain to oversee the work. Instead, as soon as the horses were fed and rested, she ordered a pair saddled, and covering her bright green gown with a plain black cape, she rode into the hills with a reluctant Ayn behind her.

After so many years, the distinctive oak tree that marked the turnoff from the main road had been damaged and died. The faint trail itself had been overgrown with weeds and scrubby trees. Nonetheless, the path was fixed in Elizabeth's memory and she found the house as easily as she had when she was twelve years old.

The thatch roof had rotted and caved into the interior. The inside rooms had been stripped of their treasures and ruined by the winter storms. Mice had taken shelter in the rubble and an owl, frightened from its perch on a splintered crossbeam, flew out of the open space where St. Lucy had once been mounted, staring pensively down at their pagan revels.

As Elizabeth viewed this devastation that remained of her dream, the sorrow in her expression made Ayn wary so that her complaints were less sharp than they'd been on the road. Nonetheless, she asked, "Countess, why have we come to this place?"

Instead of answering, Elizabeth circled the house, coming at last on a pile of bones in the little hollow behind it. Only the scattering of skulls among them made it clear that they were human instead of animal. She stared at them a moment, then spun quickly, peering into the shadows looking for the creature that reason told her must be long gone.

Ayn moved beside her, reaching for Elizabeth's hand, squeezing it lightly as she repeated her question.

This time, Elizabeth answered. "Isn't it strange, Ayn. To learn what I am, I must first view the ruins of my past."

After a long pause, she whispered a single name, "Catherine," then stopped and listened to the forest as if expecting some response.

The wind through the ancient trees gave the only answer.

Elizabeth clenched her fists like an angry child, then bellowed the name, "Catherine!"

As Ayn expected, nothing answered. Without waiting for Ayn's prompting, Elizabeth walked back to the trail where they had left their horses and rode quickly to the main road.

On the way back to the estate, Elizabeth spoke with anxious speed, "We will not remain here. We will go to a place such as she would choose, a place like her old home, wild and isolated, a place where I can be just like her, where I can kill just like her. You will show me, Ayn, you will show me everything I must do to be just like her."

"Like Catherine?"

"You must never say her name again, do you understand? You must never say it to me even when we are alone! There is a penalty for saying that name again, do you understand?"

Ayn nodded, then bowed her head. She had thought the countess's stories were a delusion until now. But the bones and the hut told her otherwise. What kind of a creature had been the real mother to this woman? What had she learned in this place?

"Will you continue to look for her?" Ayn asked.

"Forever."

"And where will we go, Countess?"

"North. East. Into the White Carpathians. The family owns a castle there that is just like the Old One's home. It will be so perfect, Ayn, with just you and me." Stopping at the edge of the forest, she unbound her long dark hair, then with a clear, lilting laugh rode quickly like an excited child back to the house where the servants were laboring to finish the rooms she would never occupy.

PART III

MARGUERI
1609

CHAPTER
10

I

Though nightmares plagued him for years afterward, Jacques Robert Vernet-Austra recovered from his wounds. He served his adopted family well in Prague and Vienna, then returned to Paris with Matthew when Matthew decided that he was finally ready to manage the family firm.

Through all their years together, Jacques's religious fervor never waned, his love for the family that had saved him from death never diminished, but finally in Paris he found another love, Monique Lupin. And she was perfect! As the daughter of one of the Austra firm's most skilled craftsmen, she had been raised as one of the privileged few who knew the Austra secret and accepted it.

She had deep brown eyes and a dusky complexion inherited from an Indian grandmother who had traveled with her English lover across the seas to this oddly civilized land. Like her ancestor, Monique had a passion for travel, a need to see the world. This passion drew her to Jacques the moment they met.

Though she was scarcely eighteen and Jacques nearly sixty, she was fascinated by his tales of faraway cities and his adventures with Matthew during Matthew's necessary years of exile. Everything she longed to do, Jacques had done.

"She doesn't love me, she loves where I've been," Jacques complained to Matthew.

"Well, I can only give you fair warning. Marry her and you'll never spend more than a year in a single place."

Matthew's prediction proved true. Jacques Robert Vernet-Austra and Monique Lupin were married in the cathedral at Rouen where Jacques had first met Steffen Austra. It was, Steffen had remarked with cryptic humor, the first time that an Austra had been the center of a ceremony in any of their public creations. The couple then moved into a section of the house Jacques had helped restore but they did not stay there long.

Their only child was conceived in London, born in Paris, raised in Brussels and The Hague. By the time Margueri was seventeen, she spoke five languages and had lived in six countries. She possessed all the charm and independence of the continent itself. And now, for the first time since her birth, she was coming to the town her father considered home.

Their carriage lurched and Margueri's mother swore with an eloquence becoming a Calais fisherman. Jacques stifled a moan and chuckled. "You should be used to the rigors of travel, Monique."

Monique's only reply was to brush back a strand of her auburn hair, careful to hide the shaking of her hand. Jacques noticed it, as did Margueri. Neither said a word. They were bound by a silent conspiracy Monique refused to accept—that this would be Jacques's last journey save the one to the grave. The coachmen had mounted a pallet across the facing seats so Jacques could stretch out his legs and sleep when necessary. Monique faced him, Margueri sat beside him, pressing his hand, feeling its warmth. The fever that had plagued him in Italy had returned during travel.

They should have taken a boat, Margueri thought, but her father would not allow it. Now, though the weather was rainy and the uncommon May damp probably dangerous to his health, Jacques sat with the window slid open, looking at the familiar countryside with love and desire.

He had his will and instructions for burial written and sealed, given to Margueri for safekeeping. When he died, Margueri would give them not to her mother but to Matthew Austra, and Matthew, Jacques had assured her, would see to the details. It was better that way, he said, better than entrusting such responsibility to Monique who possessed little business sense, better than leaving the matter to Margueri who might not have the authority to do what must be done.

Margueri wished that she had not been entrusted with this, that she were the flighty one, the passionate one; that she not have to spend a lifetime in her mother's brilliant shadow. Having already lived more adventures than a dozen women, Margueri nonetheless approached each new situation with such innate common sense that all romance was drained from the event. Sadly, she was intelligent enough to know it and mourn the loss.

Her mother would have hardly understood, but in a rare moment of candor, she had confessed her need for independence to her father. As a result, the letter in the bag resting at her feet split her father's inheritance making her, in effect, a free woman unencumbered by any dictates but her own. She could go to the university at Bologna and study painting with Lavinia Fontana as she had always longed to do or she could travel to her grandmother's native land or even to the new settlements in the Americas.

And if she did, would life be any different for her than here somewhere in France on this ill-maintained road with the carriage roof leaking onto her shoulder?

She smiled to herself, that tiny private smile of inward contemplation that her mother petulantly said reminded her of that strange painting by Leonardo. No, the moment her father told her of his intentions she realized that the only real change came from within.

Had he known this insight would be the result of his action? Thinking he did, Margueri squeezed his hand with affection. She would miss him when he was gone, all the more because, with the difference in their ages and the constant buffering presence of her mother and the servants, she had hardly known him at all.

They rode through the night, reaching Rouen the following morning. Rachel Austra was there to greet them while the servants took the baggage to their rooms. Though a meal would be ready soon and Jacques was more than willing to hide his illness and his fatigue and join them, Rachel apparently discovered his condition from a kiss on the cheek and sent servants to heat a bath and prepare a tray to be served in his room.

On the way up the curving marble stairs, Jacques faltered, and after a quick glance around to make certain they were alone, Rachel scooped him up and carried him the rest of the way, placing him on a divan by the window. The weather had cleared and the sunlight covered him, its soothing warmth making him drowsy. "This was my room from the time I came here," he said to Margueri, then closed his eyes and dozed off until breakfast.

In the meantime, Rachel took Margueri on a quick tour of the house and grounds, leading her through the garden by her hand as if she were still a small girl. "It was a difficult trip, was it not?" Rachel asked.

"I was frightened for my father," Margueri responded and, with a perception she scarcely understood, noticed an odd concern in Rachel's dark eyes. Later in the kitchen, Rachel prepared Jacques an herb tea, its bitterness only slightly masked by the honey she mixed with it. The brew served its purpose well, and by the time Matthew arrived from AustraGlass some hours later, Jacques was alert and ready to see him.

As they sat together around a table in her father's room, Margueri tried not to stare at their host. Though she knew the Austras did not age, she was not emotionally prepared to meet a friend of her father's who seemed as young as herself. Once, Matthew caught her looking at him and he winked a reply. A flush colored her face and she hid it by looking down at her plate.

The old friends talked of their past and their work while Margueri listened, so silent they often forgot she was in the room at all. Matthew stayed home the next few days, taking the women riding through the hills or on trips into Rouen while Jacques napped. He had last seen Margueri when she was an infant. A lady now, her narrow face with its wide-spaced dark eyes reminded him of Jacques when he was young, her expressions brought back memories, and her lips, full and red like her mother's, made him think of how pleasant it would be to kiss her. The depth of her silence intrigued him. But it was the infrequent laughter that attracted him most, for it was bright and quick as moonlight on running water. Some days later, as he and Jacques sat alone in the courtyard where the trees now blocked the sun, he confessed that he wished he could hear it more often.

"Is this the first time that you've fallen in love?" Jacques asked him.

"Love? Say rather that I find myself distracted at the most awkward moments."

"I never thought you would be like Steffen and the others. I expected that you would admit how you feel."

"Jacques, it is never love with us, at least not exactly, and there can be no lasting future for us—no marriage, no children. I know you wouldn't want anything less for her."

"I have learned many lessons in all my years, Matthew, but I think the most valuable is the reason why Monique so desired me. I have seen how other women live and I have the conceit to hope that Margueri will someday make as fortunate a match as her mother."

"Jacques, do I understand you correctly?"

"Am I giving you my blessing? No. But I have given Margueri her independence. She is free to do as she wishes since she will do as she wishes in any event. I ask only one favor, do not seduce her. Let her decision be her own. Has she given any indication that she cares for you?"

"Nothing more than that of a friend."

"Then give her time. You have enough of that to spare."

Margueri's window looked down on the courtyard, and concealed by the draperies, she watched the pair talking and guessed that she was the subject. She had seen how Matthew watched her, how he always seemed to display an uneasiness in her presence so similar to her own. Yet, their reasons were different. He desired her but she could never return his affection. In spite of the nature that her mother said would make him a consummate lover, he would still be a sensible choice. So gentle. So kind. And so much a disaster from the moment she dared open her mind to him.

Yet her father loved him so much. How could she refuse him when he finally spoke of his desire?

It would be soon. She sensed that and dreaded their ride tomorrow.

Death intervened. Her father's fever attacked again in the night. With no strength left to fight it, he died peacefully before morning. At the end, Matthew sat beside him holding his hand, sharing his final thoughts with Margueri while across the room Monique stood with her back to death, sobbing in Steffen's arms.

As soon as the silence descended on the room, Margueri retrieved her father's letter and will and, without a word, handed them to Matthew. Knowing there was no need to explain any of it, she went to her rooms to mourn alone.

II

On the road leading from the coast to Rouen, Charles Austra reined in his mount beneath the welcome shelter of a copse of trees and surveyed the countryside. The fields stretched around him, parched and cracked, their few grains of wheat baking on the stalks in the infernal July sun. He estimated that the harvest would be less than a quarter of usual and farmers were already becoming wary of the night thieves. Charles had passed the bodies of a man and a child hanging beside the road, their mutilated corpses left as a warning to others who might be desperate enough to try to steal to eat.

It was, Charles reflected, a terrible year.

His own problems began when he lost the coin toss with his brother and spent five months in London on behalf of the Austra glass house only to be told, long after the matter had been settled, that all efforts to rebuild St. Paul's were being delayed. Furthermore, when they were renewed, a Catholic firm would not be considered to design the windows. Charles might have forced him to agree—his powers were certainly equal to the mind of one intolerant cleric—but the man would most likely be in his grave before any definite plans were made. Instead, Charles settled on a diplomatic exit remark concerning the Austra firm's respect of different creeds, mentally adding a vivid image of what he thought the cleric should do to his mother, reinforcing the incestuous fantasy so that it would vividly plague the unfortunate man's mind for months.

Charles hoped the cleric believed in the virtues of flagellation.

On the other hand, the cold reception in London pointed out a serious shortcoming in the family firm, one he intended to share with the family as soon as a meeting could be arranged. Catholicism was a dying religion. What would replace it, now that the religious wars were coming to an end, would be a building to rival the Gothic glory of France. And if the family was seen as too closely allied to the pope, the firm would never become a part of it. No, they would slowly fade, turning out pretty palaces and stemware, vases and ornaments.

He'd have no part of that.

A group of beggars approached Charles's patch of shade making a request for water rather than alms. Charles carried two bottles of the thin dilution of the Tarda water bottled for the family in their homeland. One was sufficient for his needs. He drank from the second and passed it to the men, each of them thankful, each noting its odd, salty taste. "It will protect you from the dangers of the sun," Charles explained, and pulling his cape low to shade his face, he left them the rest and rode on.

He reached Matthew's estate after nightfall. The horse, sensing that food and water were nearby, quickened his pace. Inside the courtyard, Charles left him at the fountain with the lone servant who met him when he rode up. "Don't let him drink too much," Charles warned. "Is my . . . is Matthew Austra at home?" He had almost said *my son* though their apparent ages now made that relationship impossible to publically maintain.

"He is occupied, sir. Shall I announce who is . . ."

"I'll see myself in, if you please." Charles pushed past him, through the doors, so beautifully restored that only a rounding of their carved edges revealed their age, and into the darkness of the foyer. He sensed the family before he heard their music flowing softly from behind the closed doors to the principal room. Their singing was quick and soft accompanied by the double-necked stringed *naizet* on which Steffen excelled. Outside of the stablehand, the house was empty of servants.

A private night. What better reception could he find on his return.

Cloaking his presence long enough to slip inside, he joined them in the final phrases of their song. Then Steffen stopped playing, he, Rachel and James sending their warm mental welcomes as Matthew rushed to embrace him.

With an arm across Matthew's shoulders, Charles scanned the gathering.

A fire on the huge stone hearth provided the room's only

light. Steffen sat cross-legged on one of the low divans, an auburn-haired woman beside him with one hand resting on his bare ankle, a veiled expression of satisfaction on her face as if her passion gave her more than the bond of simple use. Well, his brother hadn't waited long to satisfy the attraction that had been there from the time Monique had been in her teens. He had apparently decided that like a fine vintage she had aged enough. Charles studied her a moment longer, then said to her, "Madame Vernet, I have been away so many months. Please allow me to offer my belated condolences."

Monique Vernet's magnificent dark eyes stared into his with a disarming trace of mischief. "Thank you," she said. "Jacques led a long and happy life. I am sure he wishes me the same for the rest of mine."

Monique meant it. So in all the years he had been afraid to probe for the truth she had loved her husband. Surprised to find himself without any reply, he said a quick greeting to his cousins, Rachel and James, then turned his attention to the young woman looking up at him from her place on the carpet at Monique's feet.

"Margueri?" he asked.

"I assumed that you always knew," she said, her expression one of guileless inquiry.

"Not unless I wish to know. Tonight, I prefer the delight of surprise. You've grown to resemble your father."

"And my mother," she said, reaching back to squeeze Monique Vernet's hand in support.

"How did business go in London?" James asked, his thoughts—as always—concerned with the success of the firm.

Charles poured himself a glass of water from the pitcher on the sideboard, drinking it all before replying. "Damp, dreary, and futile. In that last respect, far too much like Rome," that last a reminder of his brother's failure at St. Peter's when Michelangelo and Bernini had formed an unbreakable alliance and created a religious crypt of stone and paint and mosaic, one less suited to lofty thoughts than those of the grave.

"Business is best discussed in the daylight," Steffen commented.

"Particularly when it isn't going well?" Charles asked.

"Not as poorly as you believe. Now, will you sing with me?"

Charles laughed, then suggested, "'The Sun and the Moon'?"
Steffen nodded and split the *naizet* into two halves, handing
one to Charles. Soon their slow notes blended, followed by
the old haunting song of the love the sun had for the moon, a
hopeless love that left them never touching, only longing for
each other across the space of an empty sky.

Their voices wove and broke, rose and fell in a complex
harmony. They sang in their own language, mentally translating
for their human companions. When they had finished Margueri
wiped the tears from her eyes and pushed herself to her feet.
"I wish . . ." she began, looking from Steffen to Charles.

"Yes?" Charles asked.

But Margueri only nodded a quick good night and fled
upstairs to the room still kept for her.

Had he been alone, Charles would have followed her at least
with his mind. He had a desire to study her, to understand the
misery that had nothing to do with her father's death, to share
his own. Now was not the time, perhaps never for he saw in his
son's expression the first signs of the deadly desire the flame
has for the moth that circles it.

They heard distant voices on the road, soft singing, someone
pounding a makeshift drum. "A group of traveling musicians
performed tonight. We sent the servants to town to watch
them," Matthew said.

"I prefer to travel the road home alone," James said and bid
them all a hasty good night, leaving the doors open behind
him.

The singing grew louder as the group approached and more
of the travelers joined in. The rear gates of the Austra house
swung open. A woman laughed, a high drunken titter, and a
man answered in a low whisper.

"I want to join them for a while," Charles said.

"I'll go with you," Rachel added, moving beside him.

He glanced at her with some surprise. Rachel was a forest
hunter. Outside of an occasional lasting lover, she rarely touched
man. "I think it is the music, cousin, or perhaps the way they
sound, so lighthearted even if only for a little while. It makes me
want to share their pleasure." Rachel lifted Charles's hand and
kissed it, then pulled him through the door and into the night.

They mingled with the crowd on the dark road where the
torches made masks of everyone's faces. They joined in the

laughter, the jokes and songs from the evening's performance, then slowly split a young couple from the group, drawing them into the darkness of a stand of trees beside the Seine where they stood like two pairs of lovers, locked in each other's arms.

They left the couple holding each other, half-dazed, recalling only a swift pleasant memory, gone as quickly as it came. By the time their wits returned completely, Charles and Rachel were long gone, laughing silently as they padded across the dry fields to the untapped forest in the hills.

In the house they had left, Matthew sat with his uncle and Jacques's widow, staring into the fire. Monique touched Steffen's arm, received a quick response to her private question, and moved beside Matthew, taking his hand. "You want to ask me something, do you not?"

"I wish to ask your advice. We are pouring a number of different tones of glass on Wednesday. Margueri has asked to come and watch the process. I was wondering what you might suggest that we do afterward."

Monique laughed. "I know that compared to Steffen and the others, you're hardly more than a youth but, Matthew, must you sound this young? All right, all right, I'll tell you what little a girl her age shares with her mother. Take her riding afterward. Then to the little inn north of Elbeuf. Suggest that she order the orange chocolate that Spanish owner smuggles in from Seville."

"Monique, I hardly need an aphrodisiac!"

"Don't believe every story you hear concerning what you cannot consume. We both became quite fond of orange chocolate when we lived in Spain and it excited no carnal desires."

"And after we've stopped?"

"It's up to her . . . and to you." Monique stood and smoothed her skirts before reaching for Steffen.

"I'll be up in a moment, Monique. I wish to speak privately with Matthew for a bit." With a puzzled frown, Monique kissed Matthew on the cheek and left them, going upstairs to the guest room that had been prepared for her.

Steffen still sat cross-legged on the divan while Matthew stood and stared into the darkness beyond the open window. "You don't approve of my attraction to Margueri, do you?"

"Years ago, I desired Monique Lupin. If I had been ready for exile, she and I might have seen the world together, but since I had just returned to the firm, I could not have left no matter what my desire. Because I did not wish to deny her what she truly wanted, I held back her attraction for me. She believes she made a good match."

"What does this have to do with Margueri?"

"I am attracted to her in a way I never was to Monique. So are Rachel and James. The moment that Charles brushed her mind, I sensed his desire as well. Even Claudia wrote me from Florence late last year to describe how magnificent the girl had become. I assure you that I have never heard my sister sing the praises of another woman."

"So I should avoid her because we all desire her. Explain . . . if you can."

"She appeals to something at the core of us, something that dark beast within us wishes to consume."

"Margueri?" Matthew laughed uneasily. "Steffen, you must be wrong. I have never met a more even-tempered or sensible woman in my life."

"There are times you must trust a stronger mind. I cannot tell you that she did this or she did that and so you must avoid her. But the calm on her surface hides some deep inner turmoil. I cannot explain precisely what I sense but I will not risk my self-control by touching her."

"Why should you? You have the mother, after all." Matthew did not try to hide the disapproval in his tone.

"And she almost keeps my mind off the daughter."

"That's why you seduced her?"

"Seduced? Her arms were open. I just fell into them, yes?"

"Are you forbidding me to court Margueri?" Matthew used the chivalrous term because it best suited the purity of his feelings.

"Forbid? You are an adult. You earned the right to make your own choices many years ago. Consider this a warning instead."

"And if I don't heed it?"

"You'll know when to retreat. I am certain of this as well." Steffen stretched and stood. "Now, I think I shall go to that delightful distraction waiting for me."

Alone, Matthew stared into the fire, thinking it would be unwise to go upstairs just yet and cope with the passion that would be flowing from his uncle's room with Margueri sleeping peacefully nearby, so unaware of how much he longed for her. Not for the first time, he found himself thankful that Margueri and her mother had moved their permanent residence into a wing of the larger Austra chateau north of Rouen that Rachel shared with Steffen.

One of the servants smelled the smoke from the fire and, thinking everyone had long since gone to bed, came inside to dampen the coals. Seeing Matthew, the woman began an embarrassed retreat. "Stay," Matthew said, then abruptly changed his mind, waving her out of the room.

After spreading the coals and adjusting the screen to keep the sparks off the rug, Matthew stripped off his shirt and exited by the rear window. A short drop to the ground and he was off, his mind already showing him the way to where Rachel and his father ran swiftly through the woods, heedless of anyone noting their revels on this moonless night.

III

In deference to the scorching summer weather, Matthew arrived to escort Margueri early in the morning, wishing to take her through the building before the heat of the day became too intense. She met him in the foyer of the single-story perpendicular Gothic home. The stones held the night air, cooling the room. The walls, more glass than windows, had been designed with the family needs in mind, their subdued light providing beauty and sustenance as well as protection from the sun.

"I want to see how these are made," Margueri said, waving at the colored windows around them. As she did, she brushed against him and Matthew pulled back, his hands shaking. He did not feel nervous, only constrained. His uncle's warning troubled him and he did not trust his desire.

As they rode toward the firm, Matthew explained to Margueri that in the last year the Austra glass house had run with half the staff it was capable of supporting. Denys, now in Tirol, and William in Amsterdam kept the creative aspects of the family business afloat with private orders while the firm shifted much of its work to the production of transparent window glass and occasional pale shades to highlight leaded estate windows. This order for a private chapel in the country estate of the Duke of Medina called for the first pourings of deeply colored glass that year.

Though hardly unexpected, the death of her father had thrust Margueri into a profound depression and today was the first time she had ventured into the firm. Now she stood in the doorway, shaded by the broad porch above her, watching Charles overseeing the pourings in the main building. "The bricks on the ovens are not mortared in the front," Matthew explained. "When the melt is ready for pouring, the bricks are taken down and the clay pot pulled from the fire. They're doing that now, watch them. Now see, they skim the impurities off the top."

"Like soup," she commented.

"Exactly. And then they fill the buckets and carry them to the table."

"Why does it take two men to carry such a small bucket and why do they hold it between them on a stick?"

"Were they splashed by the melt it would burn through their clothes and their flesh down to the bone. This way the splashes are all on the floor. See them?"

Glowing red droplets fell from the bucket, changing to the color of the pour as soon as they hit the cool stones. Margueri watched twelve sheets poured, set, and moved. She watched Charles order a second oven cracked with rapt attention.

He led her across the main room and down the long open walkway to the designing rooms where Steffen and Rachel supervised the work of cutting and finishing the complex patterns for local churches and private houses. Others packed and crated individual panes for shipment to England and Scandinavia and across the ocean to the viceroyalties of New Spain and Peru where churches were already beginning to dot the once-heathen landscapes.

"So far away," Margueri said wistfully. "And because of them you can travel where you wish?"

"We always could. But because of them we have public places of refuge from the sun and the exhaustion it brings. We can conserve our strength. Because of it, our needs become less demanding."

"For blood?"

Matthew glanced around the room. No one was near enough to have heard her. —Yes, for blood.—

She nodded, leaning closer to him as if to catch the silent words more easily, then backed away so suddenly he could not fail to notice. "Perhaps we should ride back now," she said.

"Later. There is one more place I would like to show you."

He took her to a separate building divided into five large rooms. The largest of these was sumptuously decorated with two low tables surrounded by chairs and divans. The walls were hung with Charles's paintings of the churches the firm had helped create. The southern wall had a semicircular window designed by Steffen, a half rose patterned in predominant tones of blue and ruby surrounded by a mosaic of shades representing, Matthew explained, the color range of the firm.

As she had with the other sights of the tour, Margueri said nothing. The space was self-explanatory. Only one question came to her and before she could ask it, Matthew answered. "When your father was first told what we are and agreed to honor our secret, it was in this room."

"Show me. Show me my father when he was young. I want to see everything."

The urgency in her tone troubled Matthew. "Margueri, is something wrong?"

"Only that . . ."

"That we all seem so young and Jacques died of old age."

"Yes. And more. The night your father came home and I watched him sing with Steffen. He is so young, so vital, and I could not help but compare you and him with my father and me. I wish I had known my father when he was a young man. By the time I was old enough to remember him, he seemed only grey and far too religious, like some ancient friar giving orders for my life. You're so fortunate. Your family never changes."

"Never?" Her mind seemed so fixed on externals but then, Matthew reminded himself, for all her poise she was very young. "No, Margueri. Age may not change our features but it certainly changes us inside. We store the past, layering one year on the next like pages in a book, but we never forget any of it even when we wish we could. Our minds are incapable of losing details."

"And so the older you become, the more your lives are governed by your will."

"Our wills?" Matthew had never considered this but Margueri was correct. There were many things he had buried and he had no desire to expose them to the surface again. "Yes," he said after a time.

"And you can share the past, can you not?"

"We share the best at winter solstice."

"I don't wish to wait so long. Please, show me my father when he was young. Show me the day you first met."

Such a simple request, yet to do it would have to touch her, to merge with her. Could he control his desire then? Not certain but determined to try, he took her hands, leading her to a bench beneath the window, seeing himself colored by the soothing light reflected in her eyes as he began.

An hour later, Matthew brought her back to the present. There were tears on her cheeks and a bittersweet smile frozen on her lips. "Thank you," she said. "Thank you for being his friend for all these years."

"At the end, I thanked him. Real friendship is always precious to us."

She looked down to where their hands were still joined and carefully pulled hers away. "I think I should like to go now."

"Would you like to ride? We could stop . . ."

"Home, Matthew, if you please."

Though he tried to draw her out on the ride back to his uncle's house, he did not succeed. As usual, she said only a few words to him on the ride and he left her in the foyer, the deep blue windows making her look even paler than usual, younger and more alone.

CHAPTER
11

I

In the weeks that followed, Margueri began appearing at the
glass house often, standing in the doorway as she had on the
day of her tour, watching the Austras work. Matthew was always
aware of her presence, but knowing she did not wish to disturb
him, he did his best to ignore her. Usually, by the time they
had finished for the day, she would be gone. If Matthew did
have a chance to escort her home, she would ride in silence,
her expression as well as her thoughts guarded.

The work grew steadily heavier, fueled by a sweeping desire
for private chapels. "At least if you have a church in your
house, you can worship the same god from week to week,"
Charles commented to Margueri on a day when she noted
that the workers seemed unusually rushed. "In this case, a
cart overturned on the way to the docks. Hopefully, we can
replace what was broken before the ship sails."

Margueri stood in her usual spot just outside the door as eight
different tones were poured, furnaces ripped down and rebuilt
only moments later as the workers struggled to finish a week's
production in two days. Yet everything proceeded efficiently
until as the workers pulled one of the larger pots from an oven,
the rush of cool air cracked the clay. The side of the pot gave
way and the molten glass flowed onto the stone floor.

A worker reacted too slowly and stepped in it. Even through
his boots, the burning reached him. In shock, he began to fall,

caught at the last moment by Charles who scooped him up before he hit the puddle and tossed him to safety, then turned and fled into an empty office.

Like the others Matthew had been watching the worker but he had felt the full measure of his father's pain. Now he thought only of shielding one of his own from any prying eyes and placed himself between the open door to the room where his father had gone and the men pouring water on the fiery tide and tending to the workers. Margueri, who had seen everything, disappeared into the room where Charles had taken refuge and closed the door behind her.

She found him leaning against a dusty desk, white-lipped to keep from screaming as he stripped off the protective glove that had hardened when the glass had solidified, bits of his flesh ripping off with the charred leather, exposing a bloody hand with varying depths of burn from blistered to blackened. The corners of his mouth leaked his own blood. He had sank his rear fangs into the flesh inside of his cheeks, sucking and swallowing, devouring a small part of himself to ease the pain. He looked up at Margueri, his black eyes flinty from the agony. "Go," he mouthed.

"Let me help you."

He swallowed one final time and responded through clenched jaws. "Stay back! Do you understand me? It is dangerous to be here. Stay back."

"Let me see the miracle."

"Like you've been watching the miracles outside? Go, Margueri." He started walking toward the cupboards, then stopped, leaning against the desk, his face ashen. It had been years since he had received this deep a burn. Nerves were always the first to heal and the brief moment of numbness had already passed. Now fire seemed to burn still, invisible flames devouring the wound as the real ones had his flesh.

"You need help, do you not?" Margueri asked.

He nodded toward the cupboard. "On the bottom shelf there are corked bottles of water. Open one and bring it here."

She did as he asked, pulling the cork with her teeth, keeping her distance as he poured some of the water over the wound and drank the rest of the bottle. By the time he had finished it, he had stopped shaking and his hand was beginning to heal. He looked at her, his expression mocking. "You can go now," he said.

"Should I?" she asked.

There was no mistaking the tone, not after he had heard similar ones over centuries of life. "Having seen all the ancient wonders of the world, now you wish to bed one, yes?" he asked.

As he expected, her eyes glazed with anger and he caught her arm before she could strike. She looked at his long fingers curling around it, then, without warning, leaned against him, putting all the passion she believed she possessed into one frantic kiss.

He pushed her to arm's length, then gripping her wrist he raised it to his lips and bit, devouring her anger along with the lust she had never admitted until now, the lust that had kept her coming here week after week to watch not the work, not the family, but him.

The bond that had formed could be broken just as easily and he let her go, watching her stare at his hand as the skin moved across the wound, the flesh beneath following more slowly. "So quickly," she said. "I hadn't expected that."

He pulled a strip of fabric from the cupboard and tossed it to her, then began rolling up the charred edges on the sleeve of his brown cotton shirt. "You've given me what I needed. Now bind your wound and go."

Instead, she walked to the door of the office and bolted it, then stood and unclasped her cape, letting it fall onto the sooty dirt floor.

A small smile played around his lips as she began to unhook the bodice of her dress. Hiding his wounded hand beneath his black leather doublet, he walked toward her, then past her, cracking the door open only far enough to leave, standing outside until, furious, she shook the dust off her cape and left.

Though Charles had refused her advance, he had insulted her without any thought to his son's affection for her. However, after the shipment had been completed, crated, and shipped, he sought out Matthew to explain what had happened and discovered that he had left hours before.

Matthew did not come home that evening, and well after midnight, Charles changed into running clothes and padded barefoot through the forest to his brother's house. Though he had expected to find Matthew here, he had been mistaken. As he turned to leave, a flash of white at a second-floor window caught his attention; Margueri stood at the open window staring down at the lawn. The distance and the darkness meant nothing to his eyes and he focused on her and saw her tears, felt her sorrow. Until today she had never been anything but quietly acquiescent, perfectly polite. He had taken her first act of true independence and thrown it back in her face. Earlier she had been furious. Now all he sensed was shame.

—Margueri.—

Her eyes widened. She brushed at her eyes and scanned the darkness, looking for him.

—Margueri, I am sorry.—

By the time he told her this she had already vanished into the house. By the time he guessed what she intended, she was running across the misty lawn in her long white nightdress. A moment later she kissed him in a way that made him wonder if he had ever been kissed before.

"Margueri, you should not be here. I only called to you because I want to tell you . . ."

"Shhh. I am going to finish this and I prefer the silence." She untied the cord of her gathered gown and let it fall in a lacy white ring at her feet, then raised her chin and tilted her head sideways and back.

Body. Blood. Spirit.

Whatever foolish illusions he had brought here vanished in an instant. Months of loneliness in London had made him weak. In a moment he was holding her, his hands, his lips, his mind caressing her. Only when he knew he could not control her voice much longer and that soon her cries would flow back to the house and compromise them both did he fumble with his clothes. Leaning against the slanting trunk of an oak, he lifted her and lowered her onto him, feeling the slight resistance before he pushed through.

So young. Had he cared to look he would have known.

Margueri. Virgin.

As they rocked together, he lowered his head, his lips brushing the side of her neck, finding through her pulse the perfect spot to drink.

When he'd taken all he dared consume, he found himself only wanting more. With effort, he moved away from her, pulling on his own clothes while she dressed. "You should have waited," he told her.

"For something more civilized than this. No, this was how I imagined my first time would be." As she spoke, she looked

down at his hand, so smooth in the moonlight that it seemed
it had never been burned at all.

"You've made a pathetic choice," he said and added a
warning, "I am not a kind creature and I am far too old to
change. Besides, I'll be leaving here in a few months and I
intend to leave alone."

"Then we should make the most of what time we have," she
responded with a bright laugh that even to her rang false.

Just before dawn, Charles entered the house he shared with
his son and found Matthew sitting in the dim grey light waiting
for him. Charles stopped just inside the open terrace doors, his
mind touching his son's, recoiling from the anger.

Charles walked past him and up the stairs to his room.
Margueri's scent was all over him and there was no apology
he could make unless he was also willing to give her up.

But the next day, he was surprised to find Matthew waiting for
him so they could ride together to AustraGlass as they often did.
Though they were both thinking of Margueri, neither spoke of
her until they approached the firm. Then Matthew said simply,
"She has made her choice. Whatever feelings I had for her are
no longer relevant, are they, Father?"

This time Charles did not correct his son's use of their tie.
Their past was of the utmost importance now, the one bond
that truly mattered.

"What did you feel when you used her?" Matthew asked
in the family language, using the specific night word *arige,*
implying "drink/use/satisfaction."

"Na arige," his father replied and added honestly, "joy."

Matthew did not respond. A mental wall guarded his thoughts
but in the next few weeks their relationship became, if anything,
warmer, Matthew's anger inexplicably directed toward Steffen
rather than his father.

II

Margueri Austra had been given her independence and she made
good use of it. In the months that followed, she purchased an
elegant home on the edge of Rouen, one well suited to the

necessary small parties that would lead to her acceptance in the town's society. The Austras often came to her gatherings—their charm and family name along with Margueri's sudden wealth and unattached status rendering her fetes irresistible.

Often Margueri would look at Charles standing across the room, his long arms hidden by the loose sleeves of his jackets with their dark velvet fabrics slashed to reveal bright contrasts in gold and red satins, the lace collar of his shirt perfectly knotted at the neck. Such a dandy he seemed and it amused her to think that she was among the few who knew better. Discreetly, she would catch his eye. His frequent mental inquiries would be quickly answered. Then through the night, she would feel his mind in hers arousing her as easily as he could with his body and she would catch her breath, her look beginning to smolder behind her half-open fan. Later, alone, he would undress her, each unfastened hook of her gown, each unstrung stay another brush of his mind until, naked and trembling, she would lay over his knees with her head stretched back so perfectly ready for his feast.

But always, at the end, when his teeth had just pierced her skin, she would pull sideways. The wound would rip and she would give a short cry of pain. He should have been warned by that habit but he was simply too distracted by her to care.

"Why did you choose me?" he asked her one evening as they lay side by side in her bed.

She rolled up on one elbow and brushed the dark curls from his forehead. "On the night you came home, you entered the room and everything changed. You were so honest, I thought I could be open with you."

"And have I disappointed you?"

"You lied to me. You said you weren't kind," she responded with a faint hint of reproach.

They were lovers through late spring and autumn while letters from William discussed orders being received in the east. Most were for glass only, the nearly clear panes destined for estates and country homes near Vienna and in Tirol. But there were commissions for design as well, these for a Lutheran church in Bratislava, two others for private chapels in Graz, and the now recently tolerant Bucharest.

"It's all so ordinary," Charles commented to his brother one afternoon after the two had finished discussing the details.

"Ordinary?" Steffen asked. "The church won't be ordinary. The chapels even less so."

"I had expected that by now Catherine would be demanding temples in her honor."

Steffen didn't reply, not even with a change of expression to show the displeasure the sudden mention of her name invoked. "Do you miss her?" he asked instead.

"Don't you?" Charles stared down at the orders and the pages of sketches William had sent for the church as he asked, "Little brother, what will we do if Catherine ever contacts us?"

"She won't."

"Do you think the Old One's edict will keep us from feeling her pain if it comes to that. Steffen, if I can, I intend to find her and learn how she has fared." When Steffen only nodded, Charles pushed the point. "What will we do if she ever needs help?"

"It will be a family vote, not my decision alone. I doubt it would go in her favor." Noticing Charles about to protest, he quickly added, "So you are going east, yes?"

"I told Margueri that I would not be in France much longer."

"That doesn't mean you can't change your mind and stay."

"I have to leave eventually. Later will only make going more difficult."

But there was time, nonetheless. No decisions would be made until after the winter solstice. Even then the family member assigned to the work would not leave until spring or early summer when the main routes would be hard and dry, suitable for carting the crated glass.

Charles never discussed his decision with Margueri. Nothing should cloud these moments.

But as the weeks moved by, the flaws in his lover became more distinct. Margueri hoarded experience with the same avidity her mother devoted to landscape, and unfamiliar terrain held the most interest.

He became fully aware of this on the night that they stood on the spot in the market square at Rouen where Jeanne d'Arc had been burned at the stake. With her eyes closed, her body pressed against him, her face covered by his flowing grey cape, he showed Margueri the crowd, shared the pain of the fire and the final thoughts of the young martyr. "The last of her voices was mine," he told her.

"Why did you come to her execution? Why did you want to feel her agony?"

Charles only shrugged. He had always been drawn to the potent emotions of pain and fear. In his youth, he had often inflicted both but he didn't bother any longer. The world inflicted enough without his help. "You are the first truly pure thing to happen to me in centuries," he confessed.

A lesser woman would have smiled, a foolish one would have preened. Margueri only looked at the darkened stones at her feet and said nothing.

After that evening, Margueri's simple questions turned to requests and these became demands. She would see a beggar on the road and want to know his history; a crying child would invite a dozen inquiries. She had a skill for tapping the darker side of his nature, a side that Charles fought to keep buried from the world.

On the evening they went to visit her father's grave, he finally asked, "Why do you want me to touch these things?"

She hesitated before replying, then gave a response he suspected had been carefully planned. "All my life I have been wealthy. I have never experienced any real adversity. I have never known hunger or pain. I suppose I should be happy that I can experience it through your mind instead of firsthand. Still, I envy my father his early life."

She looked past him to the stone her mother had purchased for the family plot. *Vernet* it said. In death Jacques had claimed his true name. "Once when we were still in Italy, the fever made him delirious and he called out to someone named Catherine. I asked him about her later but he would not tell me who she was. Did you know her?"

Charles probed and caught a shred of her memory—Jacques bathed in sweat, his hands tight fists as he fought her still. "That I will not share," he said.

"Then tell me, what did she do to him?"

"No more than I did to others in my youth," he said. "Do you want to know that as well? To feel what I did?"

She shook her head but she didn't mean it. Well, it would be better this way. If they were to feed on the darkness in each other, she should know exactly the sort of creature she could drive him to become. He gripped her wrist and pulled her away from the grave to the carriage waiting on the road to take her home.

There were tears in her eyes as he lit the fire in her room while she undressed herself, asking for help only with the snaps in the back. Even then he kept his distance, touching her flesh only when necessary, avoiding looking at her when she sat naked in a straight-backed chair, her skin golden in the firelight.

Apprehensive, even frightened, she had never felt more aroused than now as she watched him undress.

He had told her this was dangerous. He had refused to even hint why.

Then he turned to her, his face leaner than usual, the hollows of his cheeks more pronounced, the pupils of his eyes growing larger until no white remained. His fingers tensed and curled, and as he crouched in front of her, he rested them on her thighs with the nails pressing into her flesh. When he looked up at her, his lips were flattened and pulled back, showing the long, sharp second canines his usual expression never revealed.

She knew in a general way what he was, of course, but until now he had only hinted of the beast inside him. Indeed, in an age when demons seemed all too real, some confidants might know of the Austra need for blood, lovers might obtain hints of their immortality but only a few mortals had ever witnessed an Austra with the human facade fully dropped and most of those were enemies who died soon after.

He expected her to recoil, perhaps to even scream. Instead she placed her hands above his and pressed his nails into her flesh. "Why did you hide this beauty from me when it was what I desired all along?" she asked.

"Desired?" he managed to ask.

She lifted his hands and turned them over. After staring at his bloodstained fingers a moment, she licked them, tasting herself, then fell forward on her knees, straddling him.

She kissed his hands, the hollows of his cheeks. Her fingers brushed his eyelids, the hard bands of muscles on his arms and shoulders. "Show me everything. Use me as you would use a slave in your father's house."

"In my father's house I inflict pain, Margueri. I kill for the pleasure that death gives me. Do you wish to risk touching that?"

"I trust you to know when to stop."

With a low growl of frustration and desire, he rolled her onto her back, his body pressing her against the carpet, his hands around her wrists, his knees forcing her legs far apart, then sliding under her raising her hips.

"Please, I'm not ready." She looked up into his dark eyes and for the first time began to shake, a delicious trembling that made his grip on her tighten. "Please . . ." Her voice trailed off. She had forgotten his name, everything about him save that he was her master, her not-human master, and this was the night of her death.

. . . The carpet grows thicker, the fire broader and more dim, the walls high above her in the slave's chamber. She is stretched in front of him, her voice frozen by his mind, her body unable to move as he begins to kiss her, each kiss ending with a bloody wound, each drop consumed.

There is no beauty here. No passion save that of perfect fear. No reality save that found behind those lightless eyes.

And death.

Her knees relax. Her hands move to press him closer. Perhaps she will live, perhaps not. No matter. This is what she desires, why she chose him. This . . .

Hours later, she woke untouched except for the scratches on her thighs, the familiar wounds on her neck, new ones on her breasts, and dark bruises on her wrists.

He slept beside her, his slumber that of the deathlike dawn lethargy that always claimed his kind. She kissed his cheek, nuzzled the side of his neck. "Yes," she whispered softly, then, not knowing if he'd heard, she returned to sleep.

When she woke, he had gone. Though her hands were shaking she wrote a letter to him explaining that she did not forgive him for the night for there was nothing to forgive, that the marks were nothing and the passion welcomed. She thought a moment, then added an honest *I love you,* sealed the letter, and entrusted it to a servant to take to AustraGlass.

Charles did not reply. Instead, he vowed to stay away from Margueri. He did not come to her the next night nor for a week after. Instead, he hunted in the forests, letting his predatory nature loose, satisfying it as best he could with things that ran four-footed for he did not trust himself to touch her or anyone until the darkness she had forced him to remember had passed from his mind.

Even in this his nature betrayed him. He found himself wandering aimlessly at night through the squalid parts of town, carefully sidestepping the rubbish littering the narrow streets while his clothes and the jewels on his long fingers invited attack. When it finally happened and he looked down at the ravaged bodies of the pair of thieves who had thought to surprise him in the shadows, he understood that the beast she touched in him must be appeased.

So when the terrible hunger struck once more, as he knew it would, he went back to her to play the vicious game again, this time increasing the amount of blood he drank, the amount of pain he inflicted, because they both desired it.

CHAPTER
12

I

Erszi Majorova sat cross-legged on the ledge in front of her one-room cottage in the dense pine forest of the Carpathian foothills. She had sat here in the warm August sunlight as she had every afternoon for the past thirty days, dressed in her best linen gown waiting for the countess.

She had no doubt that the countess would come one day when the sun just reached the top of the great oak on the rise behind her cottage. She knew this because she had seen herself sitting here, the countess kneeling before her and the sun at just that angle. A dream, yes, but her dreams always came true in their own good time. She also knew that the countess had been thinking of her for weeks since her servant, the pig of a half witch on her estate, had moved close to death. Desperate, lonely, knowing—as Erszi did—that her game had no effect on her beauty, the countess would have no choice but to come to her for there was no greater power in this land not even in the churches with their new scowling god.

The church burned the half witches. It drowned the unfortunate dabbler in the ancient pagan rites. More than once Erszi had stood in front of St. Martin's Church in Vishine and watched them die, her eyes but one set of eyes in the crowd, her stare so intent that the executioners would seek her out in the crowd and unconsciously make the sign to ward off the binding spell. The crowd would laugh and Erszi would

173

pull her hood closer over her face and golden hair, serene in her power.

No one touched a true witch. A true witch could do as she pleased.

Erszi had been watching the countess since she had come to Cachtice with her beloved servant, that pig Darvulia, who masqueraded as a *taltos,* yet knew nothing of healing, let alone the darker arts.

If she had, she could have healed her own illness. Instead her potions had only made her more ill. Her death was imminent, the rumors said, and Erszi rejoiced hoping the countess would soon follow.

In the years since the countess had settled in the estate, ruling the land with all the mercy of a spider, the village women had begun to disappear. There was illness at Cachtice, so the officials who inquired at the castle were told, but Erszi knew the illness was of the spirit not the body and the source of it was the countess herself.

Women came to Erszi, leaving offerings outside her half-open door. Old ones begged loudly for the lives of their daughters now held in Cachtice. Young ones pleaded for a potion that would render them immune to the countess's powers. Even fathers came, that hated sex asking so humbly for her aid that she almost found herself pitying them for their love. They left bread and cloth, mean gifts yet this was a poor country and it was all the peasants had to give. And Erszi was thankful for no one could accuse her of using her powers for personal gain.

Yes, Erszi would give her aid and soon.

The sun fell beneath the top of the oak. No, the countess would not come today. Sighing, Erszi stood and stretched and went inside.

Three more days passed before Erszi heard the sound of riders on the trail that ran past her forest cottage. The sun seemed too high, yet the riders held back. Perhaps they could not find her home. Perhaps they were not the countess's men.

But as the sun moved lower, Erszi saw a lone woman walking toward her through the pines. The countess seemed so tiny close up, her skin paler than Erszi had expected, her dark eyes sad with a gentleness that seemed so at odds with her bloody reputation. Though they were nearly the same age, the countess seemed younger and less assured. Her thin hands held a bronze urn that she set at Erszi's feet before kneeling before her. At that moment, the shadow of the tall pine moved over them, exactly as Erszi's dream had foreseen.

"What has brought you to my forest?" Erszi asked softly.

"Pain," the countess said. "I beg you to use your power and end it."

Any common woman would have been asked to sit and rest but Erszi took pleasure in seeing the countess on her knees. Not certain how far she could go, she extended her hand. Instead of using it as an invitation to stand, Elizabeth kissed the back of it, holding it, stating merely, "Please."

"You speak of pain?" Erszi asked, her voice devoid of any warmth or mercy. She would save those emotions for those who deserved it.

"My servant, Darvulia, is dying. I need some potion to cast off her sickness."

"And what of your own pain, Countess Bathori?" Noting the countess's confused expression, she added, "Your future? The enemies that group to destroy you?"

"I came only for my servant but if you will help me with this, I will pay you more." She lifted the top of the urn and Erszi saw that it was filled with gold. "There will be more, Erszi Majorova. You need only name your price."

"First you must trust me and tell me every difficulty. It may take some time." She held out her hand again and this time the countess used it to steady herself as she stood. "Sit beside me. Tell everything to me and to the forest around us that is also blessed with its own power."

With her guards well out of earshot, Elizabeth told her about her search for Catherine, her struggle to obtain eternal youth.

Erszi nodded through the account. At the beginning she'd had to carefully hide her desire to laugh; at the end to conceal her rage at the butchery. "I need to come to the castle to see your servant if I am to treat her," Erszi said, buying time to develop a plan to deal with the countess.

"Come now."

"But it is so late. I must stay in these woods each night. The source of my power lies in the darkness around me. I must draw on it before I come if I am to be of any help."

"Then come tomorrow. Stay as long as you must. I will have a room ready for you."

Erszi hardly slept that night, sitting instead beneath the stars, looking at their distant flames as she considered what must be done. She could poison Ayn Darvulia and the countess. If she chose a potion slow to work, one of the herbs that seems to give life and energy as it destroys, she might even escape suspicion for a time.

But there would be joyful whispers in the village of Cachtice. The authorities would hear them and they would come for her. No, as her mentor had so often reminded her, a true witch must also respect the limits of her power. Cunning would have to accomplish what direct action could not.

By the time she sat beside the countess in the great hall of Cachtice with its parquet floor of a dozen exotic woods, the tapestries on the walls, each of a battle won by the men of her family, the great Bathori crest with its helmet and dragon's teeth mounted above the stone hearth, she had her plan. Erszi forced her eyes to remain firmly fixed on her adversary's. Milky green, the pupils drugged to a pinpoint of darkness at their centers, she knew how compelling they could be and she used them to her best advantage as she spoke. "Your beauty is beyond that of any common woman, Countess. But this beauty cannot be maintained by the drinking of common blood. Noble blood, Countess. You must drink the blood of your own people."

Elizabeth's pale skin became even whiter as she grasped the full implication of Erszi's words. They made perfect sense and yet the danger of such an action frightened her. Killing servants was a simple matter. Nobles had always tortured and killed those who served them. It was even said that the most faithful of Bathori warriors had been sacrificed so that their blood could be spilled into the center of the Cachtice walls to make them impenetrable. But the blood ties of Hungarian nobility meant that each of them, no matter how humble, had powerful relations who would not stop until she was destroyed.

Seeing the countess vacillate, Erszi pressed her position. "You are powerful beyond any of them, even the king himself. You can do what you wish and none of them will be able to touch you."

"None . . ." The countess's voice trailed off. Her thin hands gripped the carved arms of her chair. Insane and desperate, she wanted to believe these words.

"Darvulia will recover. She will help you. You said to me yourself—she always knows what must be done. As for your enemies, I will give you an incantation to recite to keep them at bay."

"And Catherine?"

"I have seen her on the edge of my visions, hiding in my trees and watching you. When she knows that you are truly one of her kind, she will come and share her life with you once more. But you must be strong, Countess. Resolute, even in the most terrible adversity. Then, yes, Catherine will come." Erszi spoke with some emotion now. Though she lied, like the countess, she would do whatever was necessary to see one of the old gods in the flesh.

"You will never speak that name to another human soul," Elizabeth said.

"That is understood, Countess. No, I will never utter it to a mortal." But Erszi would begin the call and perhaps, if she was fortunate, the goddess of the wind and forest would carry the message to Catherine.

During the days while Erszi tended to her beloved Ayn, Elizabeth considered the advice she had been given and carefully weighed the consequences. She made a list of potential victims, managing to think of seven young women who had the necessary lineage and the lack of any real protectors. But even with these she would have to be discreet and space the deaths far apart. Nobles also traveled with their own servants and to murder these as well as their mistresses would certainly invite suspicion. To counter this she would have to be certain that the screams of their mistresses were never heard. After the women had been killed, the bodies, of course, would present their own problems. They could not be dumped as the peasant corpses were for the families would demand that their children be shipped home for burial. The plague, of course, would give her some leeway. A few could die of that and be immediately buried in the churchyard connected to Cachtice. Accidents could account for some of the wounds.

More excuses were hardly a problem since there were so few

candidates. But when Ayn was well enough, she would think of others. In the meantime, Elizabeth would do what she could.

She sent a pair of letters first, both to aging countesses from lesser estates bordering the Bathori lands in Ecsed. Describing her loneliness since the death of Ferenc, she invited their daughters to come to Cachtice and be her companions through the winter. In exchange, she promised to present them at court. Then, as she waited for a response to invitations no socially conscious mother would refuse, she began a personal exploration of the lowest levels of the castle, seeking out the deepest chambers from which the screams could never be overheard.

Masons were hired from the neighboring town of Trencin, and following Elizabeth's instructions, they added to the labyrinth of rooms and tunnels beneath and through the Cachtice towers. When everything was done to Elizabeth's satisfaction, the men were paid and set out on foot from the castle, escorted through the town of Cachtice by the countess's guards who left them at the main road leading to Trencin.

The masons never arrived home. It was rumored that bandits had heard of the gold the men carried and had robbed and murdered the small group. Some said the countess had stolen back her coins until she personally delivered the agreed-to payment to the widows and families, her grief so real that the rumors were ignored.

II

A week before Christmas, soon after Ayn Darvulia was finally able to accompany the countess on her morning rides, the petite young countess Demeter Zichy arrived from Ecsed. Her carriage had been accompanied by a half-dozen escorts and she had brought with her the eldest daughter of their estate's chamberlain, a tall and beautiful girl named Marta. The two of them were given adjoining rooms and were often seen riding with Elizabeth on warmer winter days.

The Countess Demeter's letters home were cheerful, detailing the socials she had attended, the people she had met, the gowns that Elizabeth had ordered for her. *We even traveled to Vienna,* she wrote her mother, *and the countess was kind enough to give*

me and Marta our own carriage so we could be more comfort-
able. We traveled through the night some distance apart and
were stopped once when one of the estate's servants attempted
to run away. We heard the shouts and saw the men running with
torches through the trees. I never saw clearly what happened
later but apparently the girl was found and brought back and
we continued on our way.

We reached Vienna two days later. I was so frightened that
my legs hardly held me when I curtsied before the king but he
was kind to me, even dancing with me when the music started
and laughing the one time I stepped on his foot. "What damage
could a woman so light do to me," he said and I responded
with a smile that seemed correct though I was not certain
what he said was intended as a compliment. I wish I could
be as poised as the Countess Elizabeth. Nobles flock to her
side. I think it is her detachment even more than her beauty.
She looks as if she simply does not care whether she is noticed
or not though she demanded that her servants make her hair
and makeup and gown perfect. We stayed in Vienna four days,
and as we were preparing to go, a German baron said he will
write you and ask for permission to call on me at Cachtice.
Please ask Father's permission for this man is very handsome
and probably a better match for me than Simeon would be.

The only real problem I have experienced at Cachtice may
be a dream. I woke one night certain that someone was in my
room. I called out for Marta and the shadow, if indeed there had
been a shadow, vanished. I mentioned it to the countess the next
afternoon and she said that valuable things have been recently
missing from the castle and that I should take to barring my door
at night. I have done as she asked though it is a nuisance to have
to get up in the morning to let in the servant carrying our wash-
basins. I would call for Marta but she has the small room in the
back separated from me by a hall and would scarcely hear me.

You will be pleased to know that my Latin studies are
continuing. The countess is far less rigid than any of my
tutors. Last night we spent all of dinnertime speaking solely
in proverbs. Needless to say, we ate little but laughed a great
deal. Ride si sapis, *Demeter.*

Demeter sealed the letter and gave it to Marta to deliver to
her guards, then sat in her tower room, looking down at the
courtyard where they were preparing to leave, and wondering

if she had made the correct choice when she decided to remain at Cachtice.

For when the carriage had stopped on the road to Vienna, a guard had ridden back and requested that they remain inside. With her curiosity now completely whetted, Demeter had slipped on her black traveling cape and, keeping to the shadowed side of the road, had made her way forward in time to see a poor bloody girl far tinier than herself dragged from the trees. Released, she flung herself at the countess's feet and begged for mercy. Thinking that it would surely be given for the girl must have suffered enough for her attempted escape, Demeter was surprised to hear the countess order her stripped, and as the girl stood naked and shivering, the guards poured cold water over her and when she fell unconscious, they kept on pouring until the girl was no more than a bright patch of ice beside the moon-lit road.

"She had the right to kill the girl," Marta told her mistress as Demeter lay trembling in her arms. "You would have the right to do the same to me if I disobeyed you."

"I could never . . ." Demeter began, her thought broken by another sob.

"You do what you must," Marta said, rubbing Demeter's back with her strong hands. "And you close your eyes and ears to what does not concern you. My father told me that was a lesson for nobles as well as their servants."

"She was so vicious."

"You don't *know* what the servant did," Marta said. There were places for each of them and the line would not be crossed by her. "You said it many times. Countess Elizabeth has been more than kind to you."

And she remained kind in Vienna, enough that Demeter began to understand Marta's surprising support for their hostess, enough that when the king's judicial administrator, Count George Thurzo, asked pointedly if everything was to her liking at Cachtice, she replied with loyal enthusiasm. Demeter had thought of the serving girl, however, and not been able to look him directly in the eye.

On the return journey, she and the countess had ridden together, sharing news from court and the countess's concern that her petition for payment of the royal debt owed to her late husband would never be granted. "Seventeen thousand guildens is more than the Turks paid to ransom their sultan when Ferenc had him imprisoned. I would settle for half of it if they would only take my case seriously. If Ferenc were alive, he'd have his army surround Vienna but no one listens to a woman," Elizabeth said.

Demeter impulsively reached across the seat and held Elizabeth's hand. "I will ask Papa to write in your behalf. He will find others who fought with your husband and they will do the same. Count Nadasdy was a hero, everyone knows the tales of the Black Knight and reveres his name. The king will have to listen."

Elizabeth hugged her, then laid her hands on Demeter's shoulders, looking into her eyes. "You are so kind to me," she said with an affectionate smile and brushed the girl's cheek with her lips.

That night, Marta barred the door as always and retired. Demeter found it difficult to sleep for she had spent the afternoon resting from the trip. She had just gotten up to dampen the fire when she heard a floorboard creak. As she turned toward the sound, a heavy blanket was thrown over her face making it impossible to scream, a rope held her arms at her side and she was dragged by her feet down a winding flight of stairs into the dampness of the cellars.

Marta woke hours later from the smell of smoke and the pounding at the door. She ran down the hall into her mistress's room and saw Demeter on the floor, her nightclothes in flames, the bed drapes about to follow. Coughing, her eyes watering, Marta ripped the blanket off the bed and smothered the fire before unbarring the door.

"Countess Elizabeth thought something was burning," a maid called as she opened the door, then cried out as she saw Marta on her knees frantically searching for some sign of life in her mistress. "Such a tragedy!" the woman wailed. "Such a terrible thing!"

"If only she'd called out for me," Marta said.

The maid lit the lamp on the table and held it close to Demeter's face. A long purple bruise angled across Demeter's forehead. "She must have fallen near the fire and hit her head on the hearth before she was burned. No wonder she never screamed."

"This is my fault. I should have slept in here with her."

"Then you might have died with her," Ayn Darvulia said from the doorway. Marta did not know how long the woman had been standing there but her words were spoken with no trace of sympathy. "Now you will do what you must do. Take your mistress home and tell the family what happened."

Marta looked at what remained of Demeter—the burned flesh, the welt on her forehead, the strange dark circles on her wrists. Perhaps they had been caused by the wide embroidered cuffs of her robe burning longer than the rest of her garment. Marta wanted to believe that but she had to be certain. "Send for someone to wrap the body, please," she begged. Then the moment Darvulia was gone, she examined the corpse. Burns had not made the slash on her neck, nor the deep cuts on her breasts. And burns had not left the bloody scuffs on the wood floor. She looked from the body directly into the eyes of the servant crouched beside her holding the light. The woman's eyes met hers for a moment, then shifted sideways, staring at some point across the room. Marta made one final examination, this time of the servant's dress. There were sooty smudges on one sleeve and, at the hem of her skirt, a reddish stain that might have been blood.

Darvulia stayed away longer than she needed and when she returned she found Marta kneeling on the floor, washing the soot off what remained of Demeter's beautiful auburn hair.

"Perhaps you should leave at dawn," Darvulia suggested. "The countess is awake and writing a letter of sympathy to Count Zichy."

Marta nodded without speaking. Her rage would show if she spoke and so she continued to cry, sobbing as the body was wrapped and crated and carried down the tower stairs to the coach and horses waiting in the ward near the gatehouse. As Marta started down from the second level, Darvulia stopped her. "The countess wants to give you the letter," she said and led Marta down the hallway to Elizabeth's private chambers.

She found the countess sitting with her back to the door, her eyes fixed on her own reflection in a gilded pretzel-shaped mirror. "Here is the letter," she said, holding out a sealed envelope, her face never turning from its self-contemplation. Marta moved slowly forward, taking the letter without touching the countess's hand and looked at the countess's reflection, preparing for the moment that their eyes would meet. But Elizabeth Bathori took no further notice of her than those few quick words, continuing to stare into her own half-open eyes.

"See that you take better care of it than you did your mistress," the countess said with cold, clipped words as Marta reached the door and Marta realized with a sudden chill exactly what accusations this letter must contain.

Nonetheless, she tucked it safely in her traveling bag, waiting until they had crossed the outer bridge before speaking to the body crated and strapped to the seat across from her. "I promise that I will tell everyone what happened here, Demeter, and I will never rest until someone listens."

Count Mihaly Zichy read Elizabeth's letter before he questioned Marta. As Marta expected, the letter was filled with accusations but the sheer number of them made it unconvincing. Marta had been a companion to Demeter since the countess was six and Marta eleven, and while the girl was less a servant than a friend to his daughter, Zichy could never believe that Marta had been willful and defiant or that, on the night of the accident, had been found in a drunken stupor in her bed.

With the seeds of doubt already planted, he listened carefully to Marta's account of the evening, then examined his daughter's remains in order to decide for himself what must have occurred.

The winter made everything certain, for during the days it took the coach and escorts to travel from Cachtice to Ecsed, Demeter's body had frozen. Every mark was there for the count to view. Unlike Marta who only guessed that the wounds were not caused by burns, Count Zichy recognized what he saw. His daughter had been tortured, from the depth of the rope burns on her wrists, it had taken her hours to die.

Enraged, he ordered six of his most trusted soldiers to meet him in the courtyard and sent them west with a pair of letters. One was addressed to the king himself, a second to Count George Thurzo, the king's palatine in Hungary. Thurzo might be Elizabeth Bathori's cousin but he owed his allegiance to the crown. Nonetheless, Zichy ordered the riders to split when they reached Bystrica, one group going north to the Thurzo family

seat in Bytca while the others rode west to King Matthias's
court in Bratislava.

It would take months to receive an answer. In the meantime,
he sent letters to every noble of any rank in Erdelyi province
to come to his home and view the body of his favorite child.

III

The nobles of Erdelyi reacted with outrage. Letters were sent
to Count Thurzo who responded with vague promises simply because he did not know what to do. His own home in
Bytca was close enough to Cachtice that he had heard the
rumors concerning his cousin's atrocities, but now she had
gone too far and he left unexpectedly for Cachtice as soon
as the spring roads were passable. Elizabeth had expected
some inquiry into the girl's death. She took him into the
tower and showed him the girl's room, the gowns she had
purchased for the young countess, then reminded him of the
letters she had written to friends at court on behalf of the girl.
Sensing his growing belief in her innocence, she sidestepped
his questions about the death with smooth and persuasive
replies.

Perhaps too smooth. His words were harsh as he responded,
"Count Zichy has demanded an investigation by the crown. No
matter what the outcome, it will be awkward, Elizabeth. I think
King Matthias will ignore the charges . . ."

"What difference does it make? I've done nothing wrong,"
she countered sharply, hardly realizing that she had interrupted him.

"I think he will ignore them if you cease to be an embarrassment to him, Elizabeth. Whatever you have done here in the
past must remain in the past. Cease the acts that have caused
the shadow of guilt to fall on you. Stay away from Vienna,
forget the money Matthias owes you . . ."

"I am not guilty, George." The pitch of her voice had risen
nearly an octave. Though she spoke softly, she sounded as if
she had screamed the words.

"Do you think guilt or innocence will make any real difference to Matthias, Elizabeth?"

"You are telling me there is no justice, aren't you, George?"

"There are other ways out of your situation, cousin. Surely a woman with a name so noble and a face that is still so incredibly beautiful can think of one."

"So the only justice given to a woman is the sort she receives on her back? They would not ignore my husband if he were still alive and they will not ignore me. I am able to . . ." She caught herself before she revealed anything that might be construed as sorcery and asked if he would like to stay the night, relieved when he declined.

Elizabeth repeated the conversation to Ayn Darvulia as they shared dinner in the privacy of Elizabeth's dressing room. Occasionally, she would pause to look at her reflection in the pretzel mirror, frowning at the tiny lines that were still visible around her eyes, the dryness of her lips.

Fifty-one. She had to remind herself that she looked at least ten years younger, that she was still considered the beauty of court on the rare occasions when she put in an appearance. Not that she would ever go there again. "Thurzo advised me to live more frugally, to see to my lands as I did when Ferenc was alive, and to be more discreet. The fool has even suggested that I should find a wealthy man to marry." She laughed as she told Ayn the last, pleased to see how saddened Ayn appeared at the suggestion.

"I don't need a man." Elizabeth lifted Ayn's hand, kissing the palm. "I certainly don't want one."

"What do you want, Countess?"

"To be like her. Nothing works completely, not even little Demeter's blood though I think it did make me look better."

Ayn responded as she was expected to. "You look magnificent. You don't need anything else. Why don't we go away, you and I. We could go to one of your smaller estates, taking just a few servants to see to our needs. We could be comfortable and happy for the time we have left."

"Sweet Annika. I know you are trying to spare me pain but I finally see clearly what must be done. The witch said I must consume my own kind but the blood that flows in me is more than noble. No, to be complete I must find Catherine or someone like her. That is the blood I must drink to become what I was meant to be."

"But how will you find them?"

"I have been thinking on that ever since Demeter died. I recall a few things that might give hints of where to find them. There was a church window in Catherine's cottage. She said the light was soothing, so soothing that she took the huge window with her other treasures."

"There are so many churches, Countess. And if the light is soothing, she has her own," Ayn cautioned.

"No matter. I sense them waiting somewhere for me."

"Shall I let the women go?" Darvulia had four servants recruited from Piestany locked in the dungeons. There had been six but two had died from the cold.

"Let them stay where they are. Take particular care with the tall blond one. She's one of Thurzo's daughters, though I doubt he even knows she exists." She ran one tapered nail over the wood grain in the tabletop as she asked, "Ayn, do you suppose that noble blood is noble blood even when it is not acknowledged?"

"Of course it is, Countess," Ayn responded, seeing a way out of a costly and far too dangerous pursuit.

"When we go, we'll need a traveling companion, someone strong enough to last. We'll take the blond one then."

Elizabeth finished her wine and set the glass on the tray with the rest of the dishes, then sent for a pair of her most trusted servants to come to her. When they arrived, she ordered them to stand silently beside the door while she rang for a maid, lit a candle, and began her nightly chant.

"Hear me, O dark wind, blow through the minds of my enemies leaving them speechless with no way to harm me. Send a plague of ravens to haunt their dreams, cats to steal the breath from their children. Send a plague of rats to devour their grain and feast on their dead. Hear me, for I have given homage . . ."

A servant knocked on the door.

" . . . to you. I sacrifice for you. Do homage to you . . ."

Elizabeth waved toward the door and Ayn opened it. The woman entered, almost certain of what she would find, crying out nonetheless as the two serving women grabbed her left arm, dragging her toward the fire while Ayn gripped her right, using her dagger to cut the skin on the woman's wrist. As the blood began to flow, her other hand was forced over the flames.

The cry of fear became a sharper cry of pain cutting through Elizabeth's final words, " . . . I drink and I am powerful."

Elizabeth moved her face closer to the servant's arm, her thin fingers curling with each scream as she lapped the drops delicately with quick upward strokes of her tongue.

IV

In the woods that night, as she had for so many nights before, Erszi Majorova continued her call. At first she had not believed the Countess Elizabeth's story, but as her self-induced trances grew deeper, she sensed a presence at the end of her thoughts—the beautiful, deadly female that the countess had described. And now, after so many attempts, she had managed to attract Catherine's attention. She set a time for her calls—beginning two hours after sunset when the stars first became clear in the sky—continuing until exhaustion claimed her.

Now, after so many attempts, she could soar through the shell of the world to the crystalline sanctuary that circled it, and surrounded by its purity, they could almost touch.

Cachtice, she would call. *Come to the woods north of Cachtice and I will worship you.* The response was always laughter—exquisite, bitter. Yet she continued to try until the day she thought of Elizabeth and found herself flung back into her body with such force that she thought this human shell would break.

Anger had not inspired such rage. Only love could provide it.

Heartened, Erszi deepened her trance, calling again, forcing her mind into Catherine's thoughts, holding her place there with all the strength she possessed as she relayed what Elizabeth had told her.

CHAPTER
13

The Austra family meeting and the Long Night celebration were held at one of the remote family estates in the hills near Cailly. The land had been deeded to the family by the church, a payment in kind for their work on the cathedrals of the province. The roads that had once led to the monastery had been deliberately neglected and the only way to reach the half-ruined monastic settlement on the estate was on foot or by horseback. Wood for the fireplaces and food for the human guests had been carried in by servants for some days before the meeting. Afterward, with the rooms in the intact building swept and the bed linens changed, the servants left and the Austras began returning home.

The first arrivals were those in exile who came from the most distant points. Often disguised as beggars or pilgrims, they arrived alone or in pairs, their ragged clothing immediately discarded and saved for the return journey. They had no need of fire to warm them or for the food stored in the snow-lined pits outside the great hall. For them, the game alone sufficed and the hunting was always good. By the time the others arrived, venison had been added to the supplies in the pit, enough to feed the gathering for the days they would remain.

Margueri went to her first solstice sharing with some uneasiness. The nights with Charles were their secret, a passionate one, and she did not wish to reveal the details to anyone. Meanwhile the ride, like every effort of the past few weeks, exhausted her and the modest wool dress she wore to hide the bites and bruises did not keep out the winter chill. She pulled her fur-lined cape tightly against her body and gripped the mare with her knees as she quickened her pace. Margueri came as part of a small group including Charles, Steffen, Matthew, and her mother. All of them politely left her to her own musings, and so far as she was able, she could discern none trying to touch her thoughts.

But as their horses left the main roads and followed the narrow twisting path that led to their destination, a sense of wonder filled her. She thought she heard music, singing so faint it might have only touched her mind. At the edge of the forest, she looked over the snow-covered fields surrounding the two ancient structures and saw pale shadows moving across the ground from the rise behind the buildings.

Matthew quickened his mount's pace first, then halted and looked back at his uncle who was already on the ground handing the reins to Monique. The other Austras did the same and soon Margueri and her mother were left alone.

Margueri looked at the reins in her hand. "Do you think we have to hold these?" she asked.

Monique only shook her head and headed off alone.

Margueri followed. The singing grew louder, the riderless horses followed, apparently drawn by the sound.

That evening, while the human friends of the family amused themselves as they wished in the main hall of the intact building, the Austra family met in the other. This had once been a temple, one more ancient than any the family had helped to build—one that, if rumors were true, had its foundations laid before the Romans conquered Gaul. Now only the ancient stone walls were standing, the roof and beams long since gone.

Occasionally, a human guest would climb the stairs to the second floor and stand in a window looking down on the temple ruins. It was always a disappointment for the family met in silence, their bodies still as their minds merged, collectively discussing their work and the year to come. They touched on political and religious events, trying to decide the best courses as the world changed around them. Even combined, their intellects weren't equal to more than a fraction of that task, but nonetheless they did what they were able. Afterward, they began dealing with the complex juggling of birth dates and positions that kept their immortality a secret from the world.

Changes were made. Denys, in exile for the last forty years, could come home—reborn, renamed, and decades younger than when he had left. William could do the same with James replacing him in Vienna. Rachel, who had a flair for acting, had aged herself to well past fifty. She could go no further and so decided to return to Florence for a short visit with Claudia. There her death would be noted and recorded in city records, the ruse accomplished with such ease that the family regularly joked about the easy passings of Florence. Steffen, informal head of the family and current director of the firm, had five years before he would have to prepare for exile. He could extend his time with the family if he wished; two or three years of personal latitude were always granted. Now, they all expected Charles to make the same request.

He didn't. Instead he surprised them by stating that he wanted to leave immediately.

No reasons were given. None were needed. There were no real secrets among them on this night.

When the group broke for a time, Matthew took Charles aside to complain privately. "Your leaving is too abrupt," he said. He cared for Margueri but he loved his father more.

"William can accompany me to Vienna and in a few months return to France. His children are here. He deserves his time with them as I had my time with you."

"Father . . ."

"You are too old to think of me that way," Charles admonished gently.

"I'm sorry. But if you must leave, go to Florence and stay with Claudia. You were away from us for so many months last time, don't go so far away again."

"Our work is in the east, Matthew."

"Then let me go with you instead of James."

"Not yet. Stay and comfort Margueri. She will have need of you once I am gone."

"I don't understand."

"Eventually, you will." He looked back at the fire, where the family was already forming the final circle, each of them getting ready for the sorrow of the next few hours when they would recall and honor their dead.

Twenty-three of the Austra family came to the meeting. Throughout the rest of the night, every member of the family, including the five who could not make the journey here, was discussed. Catherine's name was never mentioned.

But on the next night, when the sharing was at its height and the minds of the family, their lovers, and their friends perfectly merged, when the sparks from the bonfire danced with the stars in the sky, Charles dared to think of *her*.

A collective cry of denial pushed him away from the net their thoughts had made, leaving him briefly alone. So, Catherine's exile was more than the prohibition of a bitter, ancient creature who seemed less a part of this family than the human lovers in their midst. Understanding, sadly in need of their comfort on this last day among them, he purged her memory from his mind and joined the rest.

They shared their past, their hopes, their joys until dawn.

Afterward, Charles slept until midday. When Margueri woke and reached across the bed for him, he had left without a good-bye, without a note that said anything at all.

She would not cry. Margueri promised herself that as the evening revels began. They would be repeated for one more day when all but the family would go back to Rouen and Paris for the Christmas celebrations. Midway through the night, Margueri realized she could not wait that long.

Matthew said he would see her home but if he thought she wanted his comfort, he was wrong. They traveled in silence until after the long day's ride to her house, she ordered him to leave.

He stood until her door had shut behind her, then went back to the gathering where he belonged.

How much time would it take for her to love him? He only knew he would wait.

Weeks passed and he did not try to see her, hoping instead that she would send for him. Finally, he was rewarded not with a summons but with a short note. *Do you know how sad your absence has made me? I have lost a lover. Must I also lose a friend?*

That night he went to her and found her expecting him. His father's leavings, he thought as he looked at her, but he did not care. They said very little as they sat by the fire. She had lost a lover, he a father. Hers, Matthew reflected, was the worse loss for she did not possess his luxury of time. And when she began to cry, as he expected she would, he held her gently, trying to think of himself solely as her comforter, afraid that if he weakened the night would end in one more use of her.

"You are the only one I can turn to now," she said softly.

He responded to the invitation and instinctively merged with her.

Then saw what she wanted, everything she and his father had done.

Like all his kind he was a killer, a thief of life. In time the others had taught him restraint, taught him to give the passion the victims wanted and drink their response through their blood. The game had always seemed so simple until now. For a moment, the darker side of his nature responded, overwhelming all control. He pressed Margueri against him, heedless of how hard he held her, the pain he had already begun to inflict.

He ripped at the neckline of her dress, and as the tiny hooks scattered, he saw the pale scars of his father's marks on her neck, saw them together reveling in her pain.

And for one terrible moment, the worst of his past focused in his memory with bloody clarity. He saw himself motionless on the cold stones of the great room in the Austra keep, saw his father bring in the first victim trembling with fear and paralyzed by the power of a first born's mind, saw the cut made, the wound lowered against his flaccid lips. It had taken three lives to pull him out of the grip of death. He would never forget their pain or his own.

Remorse filled him, then self-disgust. He could never love Margueri the way his father had. He would never dare! Only one of the first born possessed enough control to safely give her what she desired. "Now I know why you chose him," he growled. He pushed himself to his feet and left her sobbing on the floor in front of the fire.

His body taut with need, Matthew went to the only place he thought he would find comfort. Steffen answered the late-night pounding on his door, letting Matthew in, taking him upstairs to where Monique had hurriedly dressed to receive him.

Matthew's body still shook as he blurted out one name, "Margueri," then fell silent. Unable to find the words to explain what had happened tonight, he used his mind instead. The blood left Monique's face as Matthew shared everything he had seen.

"I left her. There was nothing else I could do," he concluded, the words clipped through his clenched jaws.

Furious, Monique looked at Steffen who nodded slightly. After a deep breath, Monique turned to Matthew. "I'll go to her," she said.

With Matthew as her reluctant escort, Monique rode through the empty streets to the house where Margueri still lay where she had fallen. Monique rushed to her, rolling her over. Her expression darkened as she saw the old bruises. "Get out!" she screamed to Matthew as if he had been responsible, then held her daughter against her chest as the girl began to cry. "We'll leave here," she crooned. "We'll go to Florence and bask in the sunshine. We'll go to Livorno and walk by the sea. Rachel will go with us. And Claudia is there. Between the three of us, we'll make you forget what he did to you, I promise you."

Matthew wanted to speak, to say the words that would exonerate his father, but he knew Monique would not listen. At the door, he looked back at the mother far too belatedly holding her child and heard Margueri's broken cry. "He only gave me what I desired."

Matthew did not stay to hear Monique Vernet's response. Some people held darkness within them, others light. Matthew suspected they were born that way.

PART IV

CHARLES

CHAPTER
14

I

Bratislava, 1610

The noontime dedication of St. Martins's Lutheran Church in Bratislava was the most joyous event Charles had witnessed in his centuries of creative work. But then, he reminded himself, his family had begun designing their windows when Catholicism was already an old and accepted religion. What the nobility and commoners filing into church felt today must be akin to the satisfaction the sons and daughters of martyrs felt when their first public church was erected on the blood-soaked soil of Rome.

Charles had sensed the fervor as soon as he'd arrived. He had fed on it through the months of building, and now, he reflected that he had never created more beautiful designs. He found particular beauty in the history of this event, how in centuries to come, worshipers would walk into this—the first major Lutheran church in Bratislava—and marvel at what he had done.

As for his own family, he had seen to their needs as well. The special glass created to sustain his family had to be poured and shipped from France. Since it comprised only a small percentage of the glass needed for the designs, he had concentrated it in the southwest-facing window, its sustaining rays of light directed to three small spaces inside. Now, as he stood in one of these and studied the figures depicted there, it seemed to him that the Martha serving bread to Jesus looked very much like Margueri. The resemblance had not been intentional but perhaps his deliberate suppression of her memory had caused his hands to recall what his mind refused to consider.

Had it really been over a year since he'd left her? He could still taste the glory of her pain. And the hunger she had awakened in him still could not be fully controlled. As the angels announcing the birth of the savior were mounted on their wooden frames, as the Lord carried his cross to Golgotha, men died their slow silent deaths to feed Charles's dark needs. From what little he bothered to discern about his victims, they were human predators who deserved to die and he took what comfort he could from that.

As he left the church with the others, he glimpsed a petite woman in an elegantly embroidered cape staring at him from across the square. The intensity of her gaze intrigued him and he was about to work his way to her through the crowd when one of the main sponsors for the church moved beside him, wishing to compliment him on the work. Later Charles looked for the woman but she had gone along with many of the others who had filled the square.

When he worked alone overseeing the local guilds that assisted him, he usually chose to reside with the religious order that had commissioned the Austra firm. Most were proud to open their doors to him. Unlike the architects and stonecutters who labored on the exterior of the buildings, his windows seemed less craft than art—art linked directly with the godhead. This time there was no order involved so he had leased a row house located between the Danube and the church and hired an elderly German tutor to act as his butler and secretary.

The day was already warm, but as he walked through the streets toward what had been his home for the last half year, a thin mist began to roll off the cool waters of the river. For a moment Charles felt oddly in need of shelter and quickened his pace.

His servant met him at the door. "There's a woman here to see you, Herr Austra," Anton Shiller whispered to Charles. The broad feminine term implied that to the class-conscious German this visitor was neither noble nor wealthy. Curious, Charles went inside.

The middle-aged visitor standing in the chilly room he used

as an office was dressed severely in black wool. In what passed for the latest style in women's garb, her neck was entirely covered by a Spanish-style pleated ruff that extended to the edge of her shoulders, making it seem that her head rested on a platter. She had a narrow face, pale grey eyes that might have once been striking, and thin tight lips that were frozen in a disapproving expression. Nonetheless, she was flustered, her manicured hands moving nervously as she spoke. Now and again, she noted their lack of control and buried them deep in the fur muff that seemed her only real luxury. Charles asked her to take a seat and leaned against the windowsill, his face shadowed as they talked.

"I am Ayn Darvulia. I have come in place of Countess Elizabeth Bathori. She wishes to hire you."

"To hire AustraGlass?" Charles corrected, already probing her mind, trying to determine if she told the truth.

"You. When she saw your work at the dedication, she decided that she would not hire anyone else."

"Tell her that I thank her," Charles responded, feigning pride while trying to determine exactly what the woman wanted.

"On her wedding day, her husband promised that he would build her a chapel with windows to rival the Catholic churches of France. He died before he could keep that promise. Now the countess wishes to build one in memory of him." Ayn said the words exactly as she had been hurriedly instructed to do an hour earlier, then fell silent.

"I am familiar with the name Bathori but who precisely is your mistress?" Charles asked.

"She is the widow of Ferenc Nadasdy. She is cousin to Steven Bathori, the king of Poland, cousin to Prince Gabor Bathori, ruler of Transylvania, sister of . . ."

"I understand. And her faith?" Charles interrupted.

The woman looked amazed that he did not know. "Lutheran," she responded after a moment.

Charles considered what suddenly seemed a promising offer. "Do you have drawings?"

"Drawings?"

Charles did his best to hide his exasperation. "The builder's drawings. They would show the sizes and placement of the windows. These are the things I must know if I am to price the work and begin the designs."

The woman shook her head. "It isn't a church but a chapel. The space already exists in Cachtice Castle."

Hearing the castle name, Charles finally realized who this woman's mistress must be. "Is she the same Countess Bathori they speak of at court in Vienna, the one making claims against the throne?" He mentioned only the facts, discounting the rumors he had heard about the countess's barbaric practices.

"Those are not *claims,* sir," the woman answered with indignation. "She only demands the money rightfully owed the estate by the crown."

"I understand that her husband financed Matthias's last onslaught into Turkish lands. Nonetheless, true debt or no, I doubt the crown will part with the funds. So assuming I can reach some arrangement with the countess, I will also need assurances that my firm will be paid for my work."

The woman did not even falter at the insult. "You will be paid. When can you come to Cachtice?"

"I am needed elsewhere. I should be done with that commission by the end of August. In the meantime, a representative of the firm will contact the countess to discuss details."

He expected the woman to push him to come immediately, at least to see the structure, but the woman seemed relieved. "My mistress will be waiting for you," she said.

As soon as the woman had gone, Charles called Shiller into the room. "I wish to keep you on a bit longer, Anton. After I have left for Vienna, I want you to make inquiries about the Countess Elizabeth Bathori on behalf of my family. I believe that she has an estate in Bekov and the woman mentioned Cachtice. Send me a letter detailing everything you discover concerning her. Leave nothing out, no matter how trivial. After I have read it, I may decide to send you to Cachtice to make the arrangements. I'll leave a letter authorizing your visit."

"Did something about that woman trouble you?"

"She is quite devoted to her mistress yet she seemed terrified that I would refuse the countess's request."

"Forgive my criticism, Herr Austra," the German began with trained reluctance. "The Hungarian nobility is always harsh on their servants. Like an occupying army, they prefer to instill fear rather than loyalty. I have received offers to teach children of Hungarian families in Gyor and Kozeg. I refused them. Perhaps it would be wisest for you to do the same in this case."

Charles shook his head. He had a number of reasons for wishing to cultivate the countess as a client—her name and social standing would bring other powerful Lutheran families to the firm, and there was the matter of her strange family heritage. Yet he sensed that her servant had been deliberately left ignorant of the true reason he was being summoned to Cachtice. The last trap he had knowingly entered had been set by a Bathori. Now, unlike a century ago, he had no compelling reason to spring one. "Send the information you collect to me by July, Anton. I'll make my decision then."

When Charles finished his brief letter, he scanned the nearly empty room. Its Spartan interior had been deliberately left unchanged to remind him that this was not a time to focus on personal luxury. Nonetheless, he had enjoyed the city and the hours he spent with those who had sacrificed so much of their fortunes to build their church. His eyes rested on the two small bags of clothing packed and waiting by the door.

"Are you certain you would not prefer to wait until tomorrow?" Shiller asked.

"I'll stop somewhere for the night," Charles lied. Shiller assumed Charles to be in his mid-twenties and, in spite of his command of the various dialects of the region, ignorant of the dangers of its countryside. As a result, Shiller was always concerned for Charles's safety and Charles repaid the affection by never worrying the German needlessly, always retiring for the night and bolting his door before stealing out the window to hunt the streets of the town. At the front door, Charles turned to Shiller and, for the first time since they had begun working together, embraced his servant with real affection. "The house is yours, Anton, for the next three months."

"Three months?" Shiller had expected to clean and close the house the following day.

"You will need a place to stay while you collect your information and find a new position. I've written letters of recommendation for you. They're in my desk. Send them where you will. And there is an account for you with my bankers. Draw your salary as well as whatever expenses are necessary to obtain the information I require."

"Thank you. And, Herr Austra, be careful."

"I have less need of care than you, Anton. I've noted your taste in literature." With this he pointed to a pair of books on his writing desk, hastily written novels of swordplay and revolution. "Promise me that you won't take any needless risks." After waiting for Shiller's response, Charles hooked the handles of his bags together, slung them over one shoulder, and started down the narrow street to the stables.

Anton watched him go with regret. He had never known a master who had shown him such respect. Perhaps he should go west, he thought. Perhaps there were other such men in France. But first he would conclude this final task and do the best job he was able.

II

Charles had sorely underestimated Anton Shiller's need for romance. As Shiller sat and planned his strategy throughout the afternoon, he reflected that for the first time in his dull life he was entirely his own master with only the single edict that he be as thorough as possible. And thorough, he promised himself, he would be. Since Bratislava was the nearest major city to both Bekov and Cachtice, the countess must undoubtedly make many purchases here. He therefore began his quest for information by visiting the weavers and dressmakers district the following morning.

The shopkeepers there had little to report. The countess still made purchases, even coming into the shops herself on occasion. They still gave her credit though her payments came somewhat later than before. One of the clerks did note an odd change in her buying habits. In the past she had purchased silks and fine velvets but the most recent order had been for a dozen bolts of sackcloth. "Perhaps they are replanting the vineyards around Cachtice and need bags to carry the grapes," the owner suggested. "When I was a younger man, Cachtice produced a number of fine wines."

Shiller nodded. If the countess was short of funds an enterprise such as that would make sense. As would the chapel, he reasoned. Farmers thought it wise to discuss the weather with the Creator.

Convinced he had discovered something significant, Shiller called on barrel makers and glassworkers but though they knew her name, the countess had never made purchases from them save for one odd item—a representative of the countess had indentured the daughter of one of the barrel makers to serve her mistress.

"A representative?" Shiller asked the man.

"Her name was Szilay. She sent seven girls to Cachtice along with my Emma."

"Where does the woman live?" Shiller asked, hiding his excitement.

The barrel maker shook his head. "She is gone. Maybe to Cachtice. Maybe to some other city. My Emma is gone as well. She died of the plague at Cachtice."

Shiller might have asked something else but he noticed how bright the man's eyes had become and decided not to press him.

The next day he made his first draw on the accounts Charles Austra had left open for him and made arrangements to visit the town of Bekov, in the shadow of one of the countess's estates. He planned well, taking just enough coins for his purse to satisfy any robber he might meet on the road and hiding the rest in the lining of his jerkin after first wrapping them so they would not jingle when he moved. Since he did not speak the Slovak dialect of the countryside, he also hired a young Slovak to act as translator and guide.

The four-day ride took him and his younger companion, Mark Kalti, through lands that would have been magnificent in another time and circumstance. After a two-day ride, they reached Bekov and discovered it in a sorry state. An early spring deluge had flooded the Vah River, destroying fields and houses alike. The villagers would by custom look to the landowner for assistance but Elizabeth Bathori had pawned her castle and lands and they were not even certain who now laid claim to the fields they farmed. "Someone will come in the fall. They'll demand their fees. I'll give them their share of nothing, and gladly," an older peasant said with a fatalistic laugh.

They arranged for a room at an inn near the center of town, not even bartering on the price. City-raised, Shiller had never seen such poverty, its misery made all the more tragic by how neat the remaining houses seemed, how at odds with the sad expressions of their inhabitants. One of the innkeepers' sons caught a number of trout in the river and they were served in a watery

stew seasoned with onions and pepper. As Shiller carefully
separated the fish from the few thin bones remaining attached
to the flesh, the innkeeper took a spot on the bench across the
table from him and asked where they were traveling.

Shiller took the opening, explaining through Kalti that they
were seeking information on the countess. Not used to subter-
fuge, he added that the firm he represented wanted to be certain
that the countess was financially able to pay for the building.

As Kalti spoke, Shiller watched the man's expression move
from relief to something hard and resigned. "When you said her
name I thought you were bringing us word from the authorities,"
the innkeeper said sadly.

"Word about what?" Kalti asked.

The man seemed reluctant to elaborate. Thinking he understood, Shiller took two coins from his purse and slid them across
the table. Their effect was immediate. The man pushed them
back and, so furious he could not speak, motioned Shiller and
Kalti to accompany him.

They filed through the growing dark to a field on the edge
of town. The innkeeper pointed across it to a small wooden
hut, its whitewashed boards caked with mud, its thatch room
caved in along one edge. The field was still puddled from the
flood and they walked along the higher ground on the edge of
it. As they neared their destination, Shiller detected a scent,
something musky and evil, and he covered his nose trying not
to retch as the innkeeper swung open the door.

The hut's thatch roof had caved in along one side, throwing
enough light inside that Shiller could see the bodies lying close
together on the ground. Shiller pulled back, took a deep breath,
and looked again, counting twelve corpses. From their size he
guessed these to be ten women and two half-grown children.

"The flood covered all the land from here to fields beneath
the castle. As the waters receded, these bodies washed down
the river." The innkeeper pointed to a sharp rise of land north
of where they stood, the stark stone walls of the castle on its
crest etched against the grey evening sky. "These women were
said to have died from the plague." As Kalti translated this, he
stepped back, crossing himself and adding the words of a quick
charm for protection. The innkeeper looked at him with disgust.
"If they had, I would not have brought you here." He rushed
past Shiller, pulling the cloth off the nearest victim. "Look at

these wounds and tell me the plague killed this woman. And here . . ." He exposed a second body. "Her legs were burned. Her hands. Look at her face and what remains of her breasts. Something ate her."

"Wolves?" Shiller suggested.

"No!" The man, whether for grief or rage, began pulling the covers off the other corpses. "All of them have these wounds. Would an animal be so particular? No, the only animal here is a woman, that witch of a countess, may her body burn in hell!" He moved through the narrow space at the feet of the bodies to where one of the smaller corpses lay still covered and began to weep.

"Your child?" Kalti asked.

The man nodded and turned to look at them, his face half in shadow, half in the evening light, his tears the only bright spot in the makeshift crypt. He looked away and began to cover the bodies, speaking woodenly as he did, "Her wrists were cut. Her neck was gouged away. She was burned" —he paused, laying his hand on his crotch—"here."

Shiller felt the bile rising in his throat and he turned and walked back the way he had come letting Kalti and the inn-keeper follow while he tried to decide if he dared continue this quest.

Hadn't he learned enough to warn off his young master?

He wasn't certain and he became even less certain as he and Kalti later sat and shared the innkeeper's grief and fury. "Our priest sent a report to the authorities as soon as we found the bodies," the innkeeper explained. "Nothing happened. Nothing ever does."

"We're going back to Bratislava now, aren't we?" Kalti asked when the man had gone to the kitchen for another bottle.

Shiller didn't answer immediately. He had been sifting the information he had learned, trying to make sense of it. When the innkeeper returned and lowered himself onto the bench, Shiller asked his decisive question, "When the bodies were pulled from the flood, were they in caskets?"

"Caskets? We saw no sign of caskets. No, they had been sewn into sacks before being buried, if they were ever buried at all."

How many sacks could be made from one bolt of cloth? And the countess had ordered a dozen. This matter had abruptly

become more important than an Austra commission. Would
the authorities believe him? Shiller doubted it. But unlike these
poor people, someone had given him the funds to look into the
matter directly.

Driven by what he had seen today, Shiller decided to go to
Cachtice.

But not tonight. Tonight Shiller had to reconcile the horror
of that makeshift crypt with his need for sleep. Resigned, he
held out an empty glass and watched the amber liquid rise to
the rim once more.

After breakfast the following morning, Shiller sent Kalti to
the stables for their horses while he began his letter to Charles
Austra. After describing what he had seen in Bekov, he decided
to keep a running account of their adventure, mailing what information he had collected before he and Kalti reached Cachtice,
the town so dangerously close to the countess's lair.

Later that week, he continued the letter. *We have been riding
through drier and more pleasant country. After negotiating an
exorbitant fee to continue on with me, Mark Kalti has proven
to be a lively companion with a good knowledge of the area.
He claims to be the bastard son of a count he refuses to name,
cut off from any support when his mother died. Though his
German is atrocious and his rational processes abominable, I
believe his story. Listening to him speak, one can easily picture
how his father charmed his way into the arms of a commoner.
Though Kalti is hardly older than yourself, he claims to have
been a trader and apprenticed to a mason and to have fought
against the Turks. Given the softness of his build, I suspect
that he hardly knows how to hold a sword let alone a trowel,
and for all his claims of bravery, he is not at all pleased about
continuing this undertaking. He reminds me very much of some
of the young students I taught who lied to make themselves feel
heroic and who talked incessantly when they were nervous. If
so, I should be thankful the man claims to have led such an
interesting life for he will undoubtedly fabricate outrageous
details before this journey is finished.*

*In Piestany, I had my chance to thwart the countess in
one small way. We discovered a stonemason who had been
approached by a representative of the countess and managed
to dissuade him from sending his daughter to serve at Cachtice.*

Kalti told him there was a plague in the Bathori castle, refusing to explain to the man that it is the human kind. I would warn everyone if I could but Kalti would refuse to translate or even to go on with me if I did so.

"If one whisper of what we are doing reaches the countess's ears, her people will be waiting for us in Cachtice," he tells me and adds that if she is so enterprising with the torture of her women, he shudders to think what she would do to a man. He then went on to describe some particularly grotesque form of mutilation practiced by the Turks, which most likely more fiction than fact, I will not bother to describe to you. I understand the correctness of his position, however, though it galls me to accept it.

I know that I have gone well beyond what you asked of me but I have always thought of my own needs first. Now, presented with the plight of these poor people trapped in their remote towns with no knowledge of the danger and no recourse when they are wronged, I cannot turn my back on them. Please, Charles Austra. Your firm has high connections. Share this warning to you with someone who can see that justice is done.

I do not wish to sound despondent about my future. I do intend to take your advice and place myself in no danger. I am also forced to listen to the demands of my body and stop for a few days in Trencin to let my back and knees rest before riding the last few miles to Cachtice. I intend to send this letter through the trading guild offices there. Do not wait to hear from me again before you act.

Trencin seemed immune to the depression that had gripped Hungary during the endless wars with the Turks. Situated on the main trade route between Vienna and Kassa, the center of the city had a vast open-air market with independent stalls selling bakery and wine, food and flowers, jewelry and cloth. By afternoon, the pair had stabled their horses, arranged lodging, and were sitting on a sunny bench on the edge of the market eating kolach and washing down the dry pastry with a bitter local ale.

"Do you suppose the countess shops here?" Kalti asked.

"I was wondering where to begin," Shiller responded.

"With the swordsmith," Kalti retorted with a hearty laugh.

"Or a jeweler."

"Vain nobility, eh? Well, let's go. The sooner it's done, the sooner we can relax." Kalti attached the handle of his cup to his belt and, ignoring the thin drip of ale running down the front of his pants, began moving through the crowd. They stopped at a number of stalls where the jewelers displayed their handiwork but none of them offered anything fine enough to interest a countess. Finally, tired of the search, Shiller took Kalti's suggestion and the pair went to the covered stalls where the swords and daggers were displayed.

"I want a blade fit for a prince," Kalti declared as he eyed a case of bronze hairpins decorated with tiny golden rosebuds.

"And priced for a vagrant," the round-faced woman attending the stall retorted with a disparaging look at Kalti's travel-worn clothes. She adjusted her flowered scarf, tucking in the thin wisps of grey hair that had worked their way loose in the breeze, and turned her attention to a better-dressed customer.

"Tell her that my employer's daughter is being married. He has asked me to purchase gifts for his future son-in-law as well as a small dagger suitable for a countess to carry for protection," Shiller whispered.

The moment Kalti told her this, the woman attentively began showing Shiller a collection of short blades, their hilts elaborately decorated with tricolor golden flowers. "He wants something unique," Shiller explained through Kalti. "Perhaps something incorporating the family crest."

"My son can do that. He has before . . . even one for the Countess Isabel Zapolya."

"May this man speak with him?" Kalti asked.

The woman's expression became less hopeful. "He isn't here."

"Then we can speak to one of the other smiths."

"Look around you. There are only three good smiths in town and all of them are gone."

"Where did they go?"

"To trade," the woman responded evasively.

"When will they return."

The woman only shrugged. "When they are finished."

Though Kalti pressed her for more information, she wouldn't add anything more.

Shiller tried a bold move. "Has he ever designed anything for the Countess Bathori who lives in Cachtice?" he asked, carefully watching her expression as Kalti translated his question.

"No, he has not," the woman responded and pointedly turned her back on him to help another customer already testing the balance of an inexpensive steel blade.

Other booths offered even less information, and convinced that any further attempts would only arouse suspicion, Shiller finally abandoned the effort, walking back to their lodging for a few hours' rest while Kalti filled his cup again and found a spot to recline in the sun.

He was dozing off when someone sat behind him. "You are going to Cachtice?" a young voice asked nervously.

"What business is it of yours where we go?" Kalti responded, turning his head sideways so he could look at his visitor, a girl of around ten dressed in a drab-grey work gown with a bright blue ribbon holding back her dirty hair.

"If you were going to Cachtice, would you look for my friend Lazos? He went to work there with my father. Would you tell him that Sonya wishes he were still at home?" Kalti started to sit up. "No!" the girl exclaimed. "Don't let them see that you're awake."

"And where might I find Lazos?"

"At the castle with my father."

"Why can't you talk openly to me?"

"Because I'm not supposed to know where they've gone. Even my mother does not know."

"And what does your father do?"

"He is a smith."

"Well, if I go to Cachtice and if I see him, I promise I will give him your message."

"Thank you. I—I will light a candle for you on Sunday."

Candles, Kalti thought as he waited for the girl to disappear into the crowd. *Perhaps that's not such a bad idea given what we're doing.* He debated not passing this news onto Shiller but decided against it. Like Shiller, he was caught up in this quest and willing to risk a bit more danger before deciding on a retreat. Waiting a while after the girl disappeared into the crowd, he sat up and stretched, then went in search of his partner.

Shiller digested the news slowly, his mind trying to make sense out of what Kalti had been told. "Are you certain someone didn't send her to trick you?" he asked.

Kalti admitted that he hadn't considered this.

"Let's rest here one more day, then set out to the west and circle around to have a look at the castle."

"Call it off, Anton. You have enough information. Collect any more and you may not live to send your letter."

"I'll send what I have before we leave. If you don't wish to go any further, I will understand and go alone." After presenting what amounted to a challenge, Shiller pulled the letter from his pocket, quill and ink bottle from his bag, and began to add the most recent news. Hours later, he finished, pocketed the letter, and slept.

Early the following morning, he went to the austere house of the Hanseatic League, leaving the letter and the delivery fee with one of their traders who would be traveling toward Vienna by the end of the month. When he returned to the lodge, he found Kalti sitting on a bench beside the door eating a bowl of ripe apricots. "I'm going with you," he said.

"What made you decide?"

"Your age, Anton."

The German bristled. "I'm quite capable of riding another half day . . ."

"I take pity on a man who waits until he has grey hair to go on his first real adventure."

Shiller sat beside Kalti and pulled an apricot from the bowl. "Is that what you think this is?"

"What else?"

"Justice."

"Maybe I should reconsider. Justice is far more dangerous, after all."

CHAPTER
15

I

They set out the next morning, leaving most of their belongings in their room and telling the innkeeper that they wished to see some of the countryside. After riding north out of town, they veered west, following the Vah River until they had their first glimpse of the castle.

Kalti looked up at the stone walls jutting from a high hill on the edge of the western Carpathians, his mouth hanging open in fear and awe. Shiller's eyes narrowed as he felt his first real foreboding. Even though they were nearly a mile away, the walls seemed ready to encircle him, trapping him forever. The place had a wild, evil air that made even the warm day seem chilly and foreboding. Had Charles been with them, he might have remarked that Cachtice Castle reminded him a great deal of home.

Because of the castle's inaccessible location, the town of Cachtice had been built some distance from it, the two connected by a winding road in need of repair. The wariness that Shiller had noted in Bekov seemed clearer now, the men staring suspiciously at him and Kalti as they rode through the town, the women subdued and fearful as the pair stopped for a drink at the town's well. Cachtice had no inn and when the pair asked where they must go to purchase something to eat, they were directed to the castle. Kalti managed to purchase feed for their horses only by pointing out that they would not be able to leave if their mounts were hungry.

"If we don't start back soon, Anton, we will be spending the night in a tree," Kalti complained as the pair sat by the abandoned town market sharing bread they had carried from Trencin.

Shiller had also been weighing what must be done, reaching a decision only when he spoke the words. "We'll leave by midafternoon but not yet."

"Not yet! There's no sign of our metalworkers. No one will speak to us. We should go now before someone important takes note of our presence."

Shiller quietly pointed in the direction of a small church, its bricks whitened with lime. The statue of St. Methodius, converter of the Hungarian tribes, was placed in an arched stone enclosure beside the front door, indicating that the church was Catholic, tolerated by the countess though not financially supported by her. "The hills are so dangerous. I think we should go to confession before starting back." Though Shiller considered religion superstitious nonsense, he crossed himself reverently and walked with head bowed toward the door, cracked open to invite the faithful, while Kalti, confused and far less penitent, followed.

The pastor, a young priest with intense brown eyes, had been recently sent to the church from a small German parish in Styria. Pleased that he would finally be able to question someone about the countess directly, Shiller requested that the priest absolve his sins. As soon as he was kneeling in the dark confessional, he began with the usual opening, then, separated from the priest by a gathered length of cloth, explained why he had come to the town.

"Have you asked for the seal of confession to protect yourself?" the priest interrupted, anger evident in his trained low voice.

"To protect all of us. My companion and I are being watched. If someone comes into the church, they will assume you are giving me the sacrament."

"That may be wise to do before you leave but I am in no danger. I have already sent my complaint. No one listened. Later, it is said that she killed a young noblewoman. The authorities came quickly enough then, but they only went up to the castle, questioned the countess, and went away." The priest's voice began to tremble as he continued. "Sometimes, the wind used to blow from just the right direction and I could hear the screams. I went to the castle with a formal protest and the screams stopped. Lately I think she has moved her bloody deeds into the earth."

"Earth?"

"There are caves beneath the castle and rooms hewn out of the rock. Once they were used for fermentation of the wine but now a different kind of liquid flows there. Some say that she drinks the blood. Others believe she bathes in it. All I know is that her victims die slowly and that, God help me, I have heard their screams. May she be damned for what she has done, damned to lasting torment of hell." Following a long pause, the priest began to recite the words of general absolution, then left the confessional. Shiller followed.

"It is better to speak of these things in the light. Come and share what I have," the priest said.

The three went through a low doorway to the back of the church where the priest had a pair of rooms. In contrast to the well-swept church, these were dark and dirty. The plaster on the stone walls had begun to chip, the reeds on the dirt floor had not been freshened for months, and the chamber pot in its narrow alcove gave off a horrible stench. The priest lit a single candle on the table and served them bread and dried meat. As they ate, Shiller told him everything he had discovered since leaving Bratislava and, in turn, learned from the priest that bodies had also been disposed of here. "There is a rocky crevasse behind the castle. One of the villagers came across a pile of corpses we think were thrown from the tower. As soon as I heard of this, I sent my complaint."

"Have you heard any rumors of a chapel being built in Cachtice?" Shiller asked.

"Chapel? Temple, perhaps, to one of the old bloodthirsty gods." The priest beat his fist against the wall, breaking his skin. "There is nothing we can do but warn who we can. I rescued some of the girls going up there and now Darvulia tells her newly indentured servants that I am an insane zealot, not to be trusted. When I speak to the women they look at me politely and then go anyway. I think their blood is on my hands because I do not preach that the town should rise up and destroy the countess and all who aid her."

"Then you would have the villagers' blood on your conscience as well. The authorities would make an example of all of you."

The priest covered his face with his hands and began to cry. Kalti, who saw wine as an antidote for all strong emotions, poured the man a glass and placed it in front of him. The priest managed to compose himself on his own leaving the glass untouched. "For a while the countess went away," he said. "I have been told that she went to King Matthias's court in Vienna, then to Bratislava with her daughter. We had hoped she would never come back but now she is here again building some new device."

"What is it?" Kalti questioned.

"Something so terrible that the men who are doing the work are not allowed to come to town lest they speak of it."

Perhaps they had also been killed, Shiller thought. "Metalworkers?" he asked.

The priest nodded. "They are working beneath the castle in the places where the blood flows. I have thought of going to see what they are doing but it will make no difference save to add to my nightmares."

"There is a way inside?" Shiller asked. As he spoke the words, Kalti groaned softly and slowly shook his head.

"The vineyards were on the lands east of the castle. They were connected to the fermentation cisterns by a deep cave. It has been abandoned for decades but I don't think it has been sealed."

"Can you take us to the entrance?"

"Take *you*," Kalti interjected. Apparently, he had gone as close to the countess as he dared.

"Mark, I can't go alone."

"Why go at all? You have enough to convict the woman twice. If the authorities don't heed this information, more won't help."

"Information? Authorities?" The faint bit of hope allowed the priest to shake off his despair. He looked stronger now, ready to act. "My people have had all their courage drained from them. They need a sign, some reason to believe that their prayers will be answered. Can you give it to them?"

Shiller was too honest to promise more than he could deliver so he explained his employer's request and how he had done so much more than had been asked. "But his family is powerful and has close ties to the Catholic Church. If any commoners could get the attention of the authorities, it would be them."

"And if you die, they'll never learn the half of it," Kalti grumbled.

"Which is why you will stay behind to send the last letter to Charles Austra if we don't return by morning," Shiller said.

"It isn't far," the priest said. "With your horses it should take less than an hour to reach the entrance."

They decided to leave immediately after Shiller finished his letter. When it was done and given to Kalti along with his wages and money to deliver the message, Shiller set out on what could be a fool's mission with a man who might be only half-sane.

Deranged or not, the priest took the venture seriously. Though it took them in the wrong direction, the priest chose the western route out of town, then circled it before riding on narrow paths through the hills to the edge of Cachtice.

The shadows of scrubby mountain pines hid their approach until they were a quarter mile from the base of the castle. At that point the woods opened onto a sunny meadow dotted with golden yarrow and purple thistles. After tying the horses in the trees, the pair made their way on foot through the grass and wild vines on their decaying fences. For the better part of an hour, their presence could not have been hidden from anyone looking down from the castle wall and Shiller watched hopefully as the shadow of the castle grew longer as they approached it. He thought he would relax when they reached its cover, but as it fell over him, he shuddered and wondered what foolishness had led him here.

"The town could have tended the vines," the priest complained as they walked. "They could graze sheep or milk cows here. Instead they let all these promises rot like the fools they are. I tell the peasants, 'Go and work it yourselves. The Bathoris will have no reason to complain if you give them their share,' but they say they are afraid of the ghosts that dwell here and the sounds they make in the night." He pointed to a black hole, darker than the grey cliffs beneath the castle. "That is how I know what she does there."

Shiller took one last look at the countryside, bright and

colorful in the afternoon sun, then not at all certain he would ever see it again, he followed the priest inside. It occurred to him, with additional uneasiness, that when he had written his letter he had referred to his ally as "the priest in Cachtice." Yet the priest held Shiller's life in his hands. "What is your name?" Shiller asked as they lit the torches they had brought with them.

"Father Ignatius. And like my namesake, I am a scholar and most likely a fool." With that he began moving slowly through the black tunnel that slanted steadily upward into the base of the castle. They walked as softly as they were able through the spiderwebs near the edge of the door, past a swarm of sleeping bats hanging from the beams farther inside. They communicated in whispers or, when possible, solely with the motion of their hands lest their voices carry to anyone on guard inside.

Shiller thought of the prisoners the castle must have held over its centuries. Had they been carried through these tunnels? Were they buried somewhere outside or had they, like the castle's more recent victims, been left for the pickings of scavengers?

Morbid thoughts but perhaps less morbid than what they would soon face. Shiller quickened his pace.

As they continued through the tunnel, they passed a number of rooms set on the lower levels. The smell of old wine still clung to the stones, scores of dusty bottles still lined one storage-room wall waiting to be filled, and from another where the smell was strongest, Shiller heard a clanging from somewhere above them—the sound of metal being formed. He held his torch high and saw a narrow pipe and spigot descending from the ceiling. The sound was strongest when he stood just beneath it. If this had been the bottling room, the pipe must connect to the fermentation vats and the work was being done near them. He pointed upward and the priest nodded his understanding.

After the next turn the tunnel widened and appeared better kept, indicating that it still saw some use. The incline also steepened and stairs were carved into the stone to make the ascent easier, their worn edges a sign of how many feet had walked over them. The priest moved more quickly, Shiller following some distance behind, his older, heavier body protesting the steepness of the stairs. Then, in a space where the tunnel widened, the priest halted and gave a low cry while the hand holding the torch began to tremble, the flames flickering in the darkness.

Shiller pressed himself against the damp stone wall, certain they had been discovered. But no shouts came from the room above, only the priest's quick breathing and the slow shuffling of his leather shoes on the stone floor. Shiller wedged the handle of his torch into a crack in the wall and moved cautiously forward, keeping in the shadows until he saw what had made the priest cry out not in fear but in awe.

In the center of the room rested the gilded statue of a woman facing the corridor from which they had come. To Shiller, the sculpture seemed far too beautiful to have been modeled on any living creature. Her long curls were wrought in fine gold, her eyes black onyx, her lips a darker alloy. Everything was so perfectly formed that even the lacquered folds of her dress seemed ready to move in the smallest breeze. Kneeling, she was more than the height of a man, her arms slightly bent at her side, the nails on her long-fingered hands colored bloodred. She had a crown on her head of thin spun gold. A huge cut stone decorated the front of it surrounded by a star of deep blue gems.

As Shiller walked up the tunnel toward the statue, the priest touched its hands and face, his hands shaking as he reached up to grasp the golden crown.

"Father, no!" Shiller called out, realizing far too late what it was he saw.

But the priest had already lifted the crown setting off the deadly trap for anyone who had managed to escape this far. The statue's arms shot up hugging the priest around the waist as the inside of the statue sprang open revealing the needle-sharp daggers lining the inside of the body. And from the bowels of this statue came the nauseating stench of countless deaths.

As Shiller rushed through the cave to help his ally, he heard a creaking above him and jumped back just in time to avoid being impaled by a pair of iron gates, spiked on the bottom. Had he been farther up the tunnel they would have closed his escape route. Now they made it impossible for him to go any farther or to save the priest dying slowly just beyond his reach.

Set with one arm raised higher than the other, the springs of the iron maiden slowly closed drawing Father Ignatius into the hollow body. As the daggers entered his flesh, the priest stopped all motion and speaking through clenched jaws he managed to give a final warning. "Run, Anton. I can't fight the pain much longer. Run, before they hear me scream."

Shiller gave one final impotent tug on the gates, whirled and scrambled down the passage. The priest fought as long as he could, then stopped straining at the levers, gripping the spikes instead, using what strength remained to pull his body onto them. Only one scream escaped his lips before he died.

Shiller stopped running only when he reached the safety of the woods. As he caught his breath, he wondered why Father Ignatius had touched the crown. Had it been out of greed? Out of desire to improve the lot of his people? For revenge? Perhaps the answer was simpler yet. The wreath had glittered with such magnificent irresistibility he may have reached for it merely because it was beautiful.

Shiller rested while he planned his next move. Though he trembled at even the thought, he would use the letter Charles Austra had given him to go into the castle, and learn what he could of the countess's bloodthirst.

But before he did this, he must be certain that Kalti had sent his letter. Shiller had to take that caution because he realized that, deep inside, he was no hero but someone who could be broken. As soon as the torture started, he would reveal everything he knew.

And so he decided to remain in hiding until tomorrow. Then, if his ruse was discovered he could tell the truth with no regrets and pray, like poor Father Ignatius, for his unlikely miracle.

II

In town, Kalti had barred the church doors and sat in the dingy living quarters finishing the bottle of wine the priest had opened. Afterward, he stretched out on the straw mattress that served the priest as a bed and slept.

He woke from his nap to the sound of voices outside, then

a loud beating on the church door. Though still somewhat dizzy from the wine, Kalti pulled the letter out of his bag and stuffed it through a ripped seam in the bed, burying it deep in the straw.

"Unbar the door or we'll have to break it down," a deep voice shouted.

Kalti picked up the bottle, splashed a bit on his clothes, ruffled his hair, and went to obey. "Who is it?" he called.

"Lazos Zilahy, bailiff for Countess Bathori."

"Do bailiffs have a right to break down church doors?" Kalti asked when he'd opened it.

Kalti expected a beating. Instead, the three men pushed past him without a word. Two of them were lightly built with the nasty expressions of small men with absolute power. The third resembled a bear, tall and stocky with unruly black hair and a jagged burn across one cheek. "Where's the priest?" Zilahy the bear asked.

Kalti shrugged. "Gone."

"Where?"

"Somewhere with my master. They had only two horses so they left me behind in this fetid hole that papist calls a dwelling, may they both rot . . ."

Zilahy waved his men forward and the pair grabbed Kalti's arms, holding him while Zilahy pulled out his knife. "Where?" he asked again, pressing its tip against Kalti's stomach. "I will ask again but then you'll talk to end the pain. Talk now and save your life."

"Sarvar," Kalti responded, thinking that the falling out between Elizabeth and her son would make the Nadasdy estate a likely destination.

The lie was accepted. The knife slowly retreated. As hope began its first flutters in Kalti's mind, the beating began. He felt a dozen blows, then nothing.

His own coughing woke him some time later and he looked in horror at the flames spreading across the rushes on the floor and up the reed wattle in the walls. He crawled to the doors but they were barred from the outside. The single narrow window was separated from him by a wall of flames. He began screaming for help, fighting the coughing, breathing deeply with each cry. If no one rescued him, he prayed that he would lose consciousness before the fire touched him. And as his eyes mercifully closed, he saw the priest's bed devoured by the rising hungry light.

III

As Shiller rode up to the gates of Cachtice Castle at noon the following day, it occurred to him that it might be best to return to the town and let Kalti know that he was still alive. He had even reined in his horse and begun to turn when he decided that was only cowardice making a bid for safety. With a resigned sigh, he continued on.

Getting inside was simple—as a representative of the Austras, he was expected, after all. And as the guard led him across the ward yard, he saw that the woman sitting on the covered porch outside the great hall was Ayn Darvulia. She greeted him with unexpected warmth, asking him to sit beside her and, if he was hungry, to share her meal. Famished, Shiller soon found himself devouring a hearty smoked beef stew, heavily flavored with leeks and peppers, sopping the gravy with slices of bread.

When they had finished, the remains of the supper were carried across the ward yard to a bench where a number of men reclined in the shade. "Are they castle guards?" Shiller asked.

"Masons and smiths," Ayn responded. "The countess has been here five years. During that time, we have discovered much that needs repair. I will show you the chapel now."

She led him through the great hall to the inside steps of the east tower. From the second level to the conical top twenty feet above the floor was a series of narrow arched windows, covered with thick yellowing glass. There was no altar nor any seats for the congregation. Behind the balcony where the family would sit with their noble guests, one window was missing altogether and a number of birds had built nests in the ceiling beams. "My mistress now worships in the privacy of her room," Darvulia explained.

Shiller could well understand why. "Do you have measurements for these spaces?" he asked.

"I can provide them before you go."

"And does Trencin have the nearest glass house?"

"I don't know. The countess is away just now. She would probably have the answer."

Shiller made a pretense of examining the space trying to think of something else to ask. Nothing came to him. The woman apparently did not know enough to guess his ignorance, suggesting instead, "You've had a long ride. Why not rest while I have the spaces measured. Will that be all you require?"

"For now, madam." He hesitated, then added, "This could be a magnificent room."

"I suppose," she said as if she truly didn't care.

Shiller sat in the kitchen garden at the corner of the inner ward, lulled by the scents of herbs. When the smiths returned to their work, he began to walk across the ward hoping to get a glimpse of their project. Too many eyes followed his movements and he returned to his seat.

A maid brought him an apricot tart and a pitcher of lemon balm tea. Still trying to discover what he could, he commented on the burn on the back of her left hand and the deep cut on her right wrist. "A foolish mistake," she said, seemed about to add something, then apparently changed her mind. "Will there be more workers coming?" she asked.

"Soon."

"Good."

"Good?" He laughed. "I'm surprised you say that since their presence will mean so much more work for you."

"We are . . . are so isolated here. It is a pleasure to meet people from elsewhere."

"It is that," Ayn Darvulia said from the kitchen doorway. The maid reddened, turned, and rushed inside. Without further comment, Darvulia brought him a rough drawing of the layout of the chapel with the size and placement of each window noted. "Is this what you requested?" she asked. He nodded and she went on, "Then take this information back to him. Tell him that he will be expected on . . ."

"September first," Shiller supplied a date but if his report was heeded, Charles Austra would never come here at all. He left the castle as soon as possible. On the way down the hill to the main road, he passed three men also on horseback. Waving amiably to them, he continued on until, sheltered by the trees shading the road to the town, he dismounted and vomited everything he had eaten at the castle.

Light-headed and shaking, he rode into Cachtice and viewed the smoking ruins of the church. "Was anyone killed?" he asked the villagers sifting through the rubble.

"The priest," one responded without even looking at him.

"You found his body?"

"We found a body. Burned. Most likely his." The man finished sifting through the ashes in his shovel, stooping to pick up a penny. "Did you know the . . ."

But Shiller had already begun riding away, as quickly as he was able to travel.

The following morning, surrounded by Kalti's belongings, Shiller sat in his room in Trencin and rewrote his entire account, describing Kalti's death with a fatalism he hoped would hide how much his conscience troubled him.

I didn't ask to see poor Kalti's body for, had I done so, I would have revealed my grief and aroused suspicion. I also didn't want to take the time. I suspect that once the countess's thugs speak to Darvulia they will be looking for me. I will therefore be setting out from here tomorrow, posting the letter before I leave.

As to the priest, I wish I had never let curiosity lead us both into such danger so needlessly.

The secrets of the Cachtice cellars are still unknown. However, I do know this, Herr Austra, even though the countess has the empty spaces in need of your artistry and the coin to pay you when you are done, she is evil and dangerous. I saw the bodies. I saw the marks on her servant's wrist and I sensed fear in the unfortunate servants who share her castle. Do not underestimate her power for she has surrounded herself with others who satisfy her every murderous whim. I implore you, do not go there. Instead, share this letter and use your power to destroy the countess and all who do her bidding. You may write me in Bratislava if there is anything further you wish me to do.

But the very points that horrified Shiller provided Charles with the most compelling reasons for going to Cachtice. The marks on the women, the fear, even the location of the estates themselves, all gave evidence of Catherine's presence. Though Charles did not mention his suspicion to James, by the time

Charles had finished the letters James delivered to him, he wanted to go to Cachtice far more than he wanted to work on that damned summer house near Sopron no matter how beautiful the site.

"I thought we had already decided to stay well away from the countess when the first letter arrived," James countered. His concern made the advice sound like an order and he hastily modified his tone. "The crown is considering an investigation into her activities. If you go now, you may find yourself in the middle of it with royal fingers pointing in your direction. It's too dangerous to the family."

Charles knew that if Catherine were at Cachtice, she would leave at the first sign of trouble. Nonetheless, James was correct. By spring the investigation would be resolved and the family would know whether or not they had a countess able to pay for their work.

Though Charles wished it could be otherwise, he agreed to write Countess Bathori and tell her he could not come to Cachtice until next year. In the meantime, he could console himself with the anticipation of only four more months of work, then a long barbaric winter in the Old One's keep. Perhaps on his way there, he would stop close to Cachtice and call for Catherine.

"What shall we do with Shiller's letters?" James asked.

"Nothing," Charles replied. "I will not destroy them but I will not become involved with the authorities either, at least not yet." Charles sensed that Catherine had touched both of them and he would not be the one to destroy a fellow victim of her love. Let others have the satisfaction; he would feel only guilt.

CHAPTER
16

I

The evening tide rolled in, the waves nearly touching Margueri's boots before she retreated to the top of the dunes. In the distance she saw Elba rising through the grey spring mists, its hills low shadows against the pale western sky, and to her right the ship anchored in the harbor that would leave for France tomorrow night.

Her mother was sitting on the porch of the summer house they had borrowed from a friend of Claudia's and undoubtedly Margueri was being watched. Even so, this was the first time since they came to Italy that Margueri felt truly alone.

She could almost understand her mother's logic—who could better heal her of a disastrous affair with an Austra male than an Austra female—but she had never been consulted about where they would go. Claudia, Steffen, and Charles were also triplets and the woman looked so much like Charles that every time they were together, Margueri could not help but think of him. Worse yet, Claudia confessed to an erotic passion for her brother that, with the Austra acceptance of incest, had been well sated in the past. Margueri was no fool; she knew exactly why Claudia had confessed this to her.

Anything Charles had done to her, Claudia could also do.

And yet the aloof Austra woman had seemed so sympathetic that Margueri began to unburden herself and confess how much she longed for him. After, when she began to cry, it seemed so natural that Claudia would move beside her, hold her, and comfort her. But the moment their bodies touched, she felt a charge far too similar to the first time she had touched Charles Austra that night under the stars. For a moment she actually considered yielding to the woman but had been saved from the temptation by the abrupt arrival of Rachel. And as the oldest of the Austra women entered the room a cold look passed between her and Claudia, one that Margueri immediately recognized as jealousy.

Perhaps because these were women vying for her, Margueri finally noted what Steffen had observed from the beginning—they all desired her. She fled the room, the house, catching herself only outside the door. To remain where she was seemed pointless, to return to the house dangerous, so she walked through the courtyard gates and down the street to a church where afternoon confessions were about to begin.

This was the answer! Hadn't her father told her so often that she must put her faith in God when all other hope failed? But as she sat on the hard narrow bench in the center of the nave, her eyes were constantly drawn to the windows around her, a reminder of him. And the vivid scenes of martyrdoms brought their own shameful, glorious memories. As she watched the first of the penitents enter the confessional, she began to collect her sins but there would be no way she could confess them all and the omission would make any absolution useless.

And yet, for the first time in days, she sat in a place where she could think clearly and she used the isolation to arrive at a plan. When she thought it through, she returned to Claudia's home, where she found Claudia, Rachel, and her mother sitting in the courtyard waiting for her, her mother's natural magnificence muted by the two Austra women. Margueri took a deep breath and, with a voice louder and stronger than she expected, said simply, "I have to leave this place. I have to go home."

"If you wait a few more months, I can travel to Rouen with you," Rachel suggested.

"I have to go now."

"What about your students, Margueri?" Claudia asked.

The Italian states were rapidly becoming the trade center of the world. As a result, a number of Florentine traders had been sending their sons to Margueri for language instruction. She had organized her students into separate classes for

English, German, and French and had collected the money in advance. "I hadn't thought of them," Margueri admitted, some of the strength draining from her voice. She suddenly felt very foolish.

Rachel came to her rescue. "If you plan to sail, there will not be a ship departing Livorno until the middle of April. That leaves only a week of classes. I'll finish the lessons for you."

"It's too dangerous to travel alone. I'll go with you, Margueri," her mother said.

"I want to go alone." Unwilling to face further argument, Margueri spun and went upstairs.

That confrontation had taken place weeks ago and now that she had only one more night with her mother, she wondered if she had the resolve to say good-bye.

She started back to the summer house where her mother sat shaded by the vines on the trellis above the porch. As Margueri neared the house, her mother poured her a glass of wine and sliced off pieces of fruit and bread and cheese for her lunch, arranging them artistically on her plate as she had done when Margueri was a child. "It isn't too late for me to leave with you," Monique said, her voice slurred from too much wine.

Her mother always drank too much whenever she felt the need to say something honest and unpleasant that might later require some excuse. Well, this time Margueri would not passively listen. "I already told you what I intend to do, Mother. I doubt that I'm the reason you want to return."

Monique shook her head. "No, I would not go back because of Steffen. Those few weeks satisfied my curiosity, and the truth is, I prefer my men far more vulnerable and he wishes his lovers far more passive." Monique looked down at her hands, a gesture both contrite and anxious. "I want to go with you because we are kin, the only kin that each of us has and we should support each other."

"I am old enough to travel alone, Mother. This is only a voyage, after all. Port to port, a dozen armed men could not keep a ship from sinking or pirates from attacking if God so wills."

"I should not have brought you here."

Margueri nodded and belatedly sat. She might have eaten something but her appetite had vanished. She sipped her wine instead.

"My father's parents died before I could really know them," her mother continued. "My father had no siblings and my mother no family on this half of the world. The Austras became my family, you see. I called Steffen and Matthew 'uncle' long after I knew the truth about their natures. When we traveled we would stay on Austra estates, sharing them with the family. Where else could I turn but to the people I love when my daughter was in such pain?"

"I wish you had told me sooner." Margueri reached for her mother's hand, and when she held it, she pulled herself forward, kneeling at Monique's feet, laying her head on Monique's knees, remembering how, as a child, she had sat this way in the carriages when they traveled.

Monique slowly stroked her hair. "Promise me one thing, Margueri. You will write from wherever you go and tell me that you are well."

"You're the traveler so you will be the one doing the writing, Mother."

Monique said nothing but as her hand brushed Margueri's forehead, Margueri felt it shake.

Early in May, as Margueri stood on the deck, gripping the rail, her eyes fixed on the choppy water of the North Sea, she wondered if her mother had known Margueri would not disembark in France even before Margueri realized it herself. She scarcely thought of Charles now, though her entire quest would now be to find him. No, the adventure itself took precedence and the farther the ship took her from her mother and the sad memories at her home in Rouen, the freer she felt. This was the first journey of many, the first of so many. Laughing as a spray hit her face, she took the coin she had carried onto the deck and tossed it as far away from the boat as she could and watched it sink into the sea.

In spite of her youth, years of travel had made her the most seasoned of the passengers. From the beginning when she had royally tipped the captain's mate to reserve the private berth nearest the hatchway for her use, the other passengers looked up to her. On board, her food was always the best, for she had brought her own private stores and shared them equally with the cook. At the ports where they sometimes disembarked for a few days, she acted as translator and intermediary, arranging the best currency trades for their Venetian coins, gracefully accepting their offers of a percent of the savings. And during the long days at sea, she charmed them all with her tales of Florence and Vienna, London and Madrid, reveling completely in the admiration of the company now that there was no father to watch over, no mother to shade her light.

She left the ship in Stralsund and continued her travel with a group of Lutheran pilgrims to their destination in Wittenberg. There she was forced to wait a few weeks until another group formed to travel the dangerous roads to Vienna. As a result, she did not arrive in Vienna until early August, appearing unannounced at the Austra trade offices in midmorning.

James had a mind that worked best when following a single path. Since he had replaced William a few months earlier, it had been entirely devoted to learning the detailed and mundane aspects of Viennese trade and he looked on Margueri's sudden appearance as an unwelcome distraction. He also disapproved of his cousin's passionate affair as he did of any relationship with a mortal that even hinted of equality and he anticipated with perverse pleasure the moment when an unsuspecting Charles would return to Vienna and find himself facing his old love. In the meantime, the wisest course he could take was to keep her well away from his cousin. "Charles is working with a local guild in a small town south of here. It would not be seemly for you to visit him now. You can stay here, of course, you and your . . ."

"I came alone," Margueri responded, not bothering to hide her self-satisfaction.

"You rode all night?" he asked, amazed at her foolishness.

"My traveling party arrived too late to enter the city last night. We stayed at an inn outside the gates. I made no arrangements for today though I had considered the Hotel Porcia."

If she stayed at a hotel when the Austra family had a home in town, rumors would start, and in an era when the Austras had to be above reproach, rumors were serious problems. "You are welcome to move into the family house, of course. You may even have your old room, if you wish."

Her eyes were bright as she thanked him and James wondered if the rush of emotion was disappointment or nostalgia. It occurred to him that after so long in the close-knit company of travelers she might be lonely here without any friends and he had neither time nor inclination to fill the role. "Claudio Monteverdi is at court now. There will be a performance of *L'Orfeo* on the feast of the Ascension. Would you care to accompany me? It would be a worthy introduction to Viennese society."

"I brought nothing suitable to wear."

"There should be sufficient time to alleviate that problem. I'll have the housekeeper arrange for a seamstress to come tomorrow morning. In the meantime, perhaps you would like to rest awhile. You look as if you've had a hard journey."

"Hard?" She thought of the storm on the North Sea that had threatened to sink their ship, of the bandits that had ambushed them a few miles from Berlin and how the men in their party had captured a pair, beat them nearly to death, then healed them and let them go as an act of Christian piety. She was not the woman that Charles Austra had left behind. Perhaps, she was ready for him now. "No," she said, unaware of how closely James followed her thoughts. "Every moment was magnificent."

Margueri wished to choose her own fabrics, and in the company of a woman who seemed more artist than seamstress, she visited the street where the tailors and cloth dealers had their shops. The selection disappointed her yet there seemed to be more than enough high-paying customers to support finer quality goods. She wondered how much money a well-run caravan might raise. She mentioned the idea to one of the more prosperous merchants, asking him about the quality of cloth available in the north while hinting of a joint venture. He responded by showing her a bolt of pale green brocade that she immediately purchased for half again what she would have paid in Florence and considered herself lucky.

Then she became an observer in the process as the seamstress purchased yards of gold braid, cream lace, and emerald ribbon. Margueri's only requirements were that the farthingale hoop be narrow rather than the currently fashionable wide oval and that the gown not include a ruff around the neckline. Though she clucked over Margueri's dated style, the woman set to work and the result was stunning.

The design was Italian, the skirt open in the front to reveal the cream lace petticoat, the collar forming a low V-shaped neckline, rising on the sides and back in a graceful arch that framed Margueri's head without covering it. Her hair was gathered under an emerald velvet cap with tight ringlets falling down the sides and across her high forehead.

When she joined James beside their carriage, turning slowly to show him the entire effect, he praised her choice. "There is no reason to follow the latest fashion particularly when something more classic is so perfectly becoming."

"As it is for you," she responded. Instead of the current men's style with its hose, short doublets, and tight-fitting sleeves, he hid his long-limbed body under knee-length Dutch breeches in red satin barred with silver and belted with a wide black sash. A matching full jerkin, black hose and shoes, and a broad-brimmed cavalier's hat completed the outfit. "If anyone asks, Cousin Margueri, tell them that this is the latest fashion in Paris," James told her. "For all I know, it is."

As the carriage started moving, he handed her a velvet box. "It isn't mine to give," he said. "But when you showed me the fabric for your dress, I thought of this. It belonged to Miriam. Wear it tonight."

Margueri opened the box and saw a choker of tiny green gems woven on a golden vine and matching circular earrings. As she held an earring up to the light, she asked a question that would have seemed impolite to any other escort. "Are they real?"

"Some are real, others are our glass. I think only a skilled jeweler could see the difference."

"And do you use it to help convince your clients of the worth of the Austra skill?" she asked as she lowered her head so he could slip the choker around her neck. As he did, his fingers brushed her skin and she felt the familiar charge.

He pulled back, watching her put on the earrings. "William and Charles often did. I haven't had the opportunity yet. This is my first public appearance since my arrival."

"And you loathe the idea of going?"

"Does it show so much?" he asked.

"It does." Margueri sat stiffly, not wishing to disturb the carefully arranged collar of her gown. "James, if you could do anything you wished, what would it be?"

"Nothing," he answered.

"You love your work that much?" she asked. She had guessed that he hated it.

"I lived nearly a millennium in the mountain keep. Nothing, Margueri, suits me best. Nothing being impossible, I would settle for a life that did not require me to be clad in hose and boots and damnable starched collars. I leave that to the dandies in the family like my dear cousin Charles who seems to thrive on discomfort."

Margueri laughed. "Have you heard from Charles yet?"

"Given the distance, ten days is hardly long enough for a reply, Margueri."

"Where will he go next?"

"Here." He looked out the window at the gardens surrounding the Hofburg palace. Without dark glasses, the sunlight must hurt his eyes but it was better, Margueri knew, than meeting her gaze while trying to lie. Having exchanged more words in the last quarter hour than they had since her arrival, they rode in silence, down the cobblestone road and through the lacy iron gates that led to the ballroom entrance.

▌▌

When Margueri walked into the king's hall with its polished marble floor and gilt-framed frescoed walls, she was well aware of how many eyes were fixed on her and James, both of them new arrivals at these gatherings. As soon as their names were announced, they were directed to the balcony at the rear of the ballroom where Monteverdi was speaking to admirers. Dressed ascetically in plain brown velvet, he looked more a cleric than a musician. "I had hoped you would come," he said to James. "Your family's windows are the inspiration for so many of my songs."

"And your music for so many of our designs."

"We enrich each other. That is as art should be." Monteverdi moved closer to James, whispering the next words, "There are some people here you should meet. Can you stay for a few hours after the other guests leave?"

"Margueri, would you forgive me?" James asked.

"I understand. I'll send the carriage back for you," she replied.

"I requested that your seats be near the front of the balcony.

I would have preferred to use the church for this performance but because of the pagan nature of *L'Orfeo* and the size of the orchestra, the bishop would not allow it. But at least the acoustics here will make the hours bearable."

"Thank you," Margueri said and moved a bit away from the two men, studying the magnificent hall that she had not seen since she had been twelve years old. Men moved on the floor beneath her in tight-fitting clothes and starched ruffs that seemed designed to separate the mind from the carnal pleasures of the body. The women were more severely dressed, which drew attention to their faces with the pale makeup and bright blushed cheeks.

It occurred to her that there might be guests here who had known her years before and she scanned the crowd, looking for familiar faces.

She did not see any but noted a woman dressed in grey lace with a pale blue overgown staring intently at James's back. Could the woman have known him in France? It wasn't all that unlikely. She would have asked James if he knew her but he was still speaking with the musician so, well versed in James's alias, Margueri walked down the stairs and wove her way through the crowd to the woman's side to deflect any questions before they were asked. After a quick, almost rude self-introduction that was not reciprocated, she commented, "My cousin James looks very much like his father, doesn't he?"

The woman's dark eyes widened with surprise and Margueri wondered if she knew that she'd been staring. "Is that what it is?" she asked. "Yes, I believe he does. And you are?"

So the woman had been that entranced with James. Margueri should have known. "Margueri Austra," she repeated.

The name seemed to focus the woman's attention entirely on her. "Forgive me," she said sweetly, "I am the Countess Elizabeth Bathori. You say that James Austra is your cousin?"

"Yes."

"And you are newly arrived in Vienna?"

"Yes, but my family lived here when I was young."

"Young?"

"Well, younger." Margueri smiled.

The countess nodded as if Margueri had said something important.

"Lately, I have lived in Florence," Margueri added because

she could not think of anything else to say.

"That explains your gown. That neckline is quite daring by Viennese standards."

"Is it?" Margueri blushed.

"And extremely becoming." The countess waved a finger at the frescoed walls. "Consider how we are surrounded by paintings of portly naked females while, for fashion's sake, we are required to cover every strip of skin beneath layers of wire and bone and fabric. What does that tell you about our men?"

"Perhaps that they lack imagination," Margueri answered happily. She was beginning to warm to the countess.

"Since you speak Italian, perhaps you would sit by me tonight and translate from time to time. I am unused to being ignorant. Had I ever suspected that I would have a need to know Italian at this court, I would have learned it."

Margueri glanced up at James. He and the composer had been joined by a number of guests, and if the richness of their clothing was any indication of their station, this would be a profitable night for the firm. When she caught his eye, she passed the mental question to him and received a quick nod for a reply. "I would be pleased, Countess. Let's sit to the side where my whispering won't disturb the others."

Servants began carrying in the benches, and when the hall was half-full, guests were motioned to the seats. The countess chose a pair near the exit door. Margueri wondered how many of the words would be audible but she need not have worried. From the moment the muted trombones sounded the first discordant notes of the Tocatta, the countess was entranced. Margueri let her take the lead, answering questions when asked, explaining between movements how Orpheus marries the beautiful Eurydice, how she dies, how he follows her to Hades and gains her freedom only to lose her to the strength of his own desire. Near the end, as Orpheus was led into the lonely pleasure of heaven, the countess dabbed at her eyes with a black lace handkerchief. "To remain in Hades with his beloved would have been a happier conclusion," she said when it was over.

Margueri, who recognized the parallels to her own quest, agreed and followed the countess into the hallway where wine and cakes were being served. Since James was still absent, she sat with the countess, surprised that a woman with a title so long and noble should be so shunned by the gathering. And when

the time came to leave, the countess offered to share her own
carriage. Since the countess lived only a short distance from
the Hofburg while the Austra firm and house were across the
city near St. Ruprecht's Church, Margueri tried to decline. The
countess insisted, however, adding that Margueri should come
to her house for lunch the following day. James had scarcely
spoken to her for the past few weeks and Margueri eagerly
accepted.

By the next afternoon, Margueri had been informed of the
rumors concerning the countess and she made a point of walking
to the Bathori house in the company of a servant to whom she
gave explicit instructions. He was not to leave without her
personal permission no matter what anyone else told him. He
was also not to go inside.

But whatever misgivings she had about the countess vanished
that afternoon. Though the woman was vain, she also had a sharp
wit and sharper intelligence and they spent that afternoon and
the following together while Margueri entertained her hostess
with tales of Italy and her journey. On the third day, the
countess's coach stopped at the Austra house and the two
women rode through Vienna, finally picnicking on the edge
of the great woods to the west of town. Margueri, not certain
she had been wise to come to such a remote location with only
the Bathori escorts for protection, frequently glanced toward
the trees and the men relaxing at a polite distance. When the
countess sensed the girl's continuing unease, she immediately
took steps to alleviate it. She began by repeating every terrible
rumor that Margueri could have heard in a cold even voice.
"Yes, I know of these whispers," she went on. "They are always
soft enough to be polite, loud enough that I can just make out
the words. Why do you think I would have sat alone through
L'Orfeo save for your kindness?"

"They say such terrible things," Margueri responded, hoping
she sounded sympathetic, hoping desperately that the countess
would deny them.

"You understand what is happening, you must!" Elizabeth
exclaimed with a burst of anger that seemed so at odds with
her serene facade. "My estates are on the frontier. It is wild
country. Few of these soft nobles would dare to visit there. King
Matthias can make up whatever lies he wishes concerning me

and when enough of the emperor's court believe them, he can drag me to my arranged trial, find me guilty, and strip me of my lands and my fortune and happily forget the debt he owes to my family. The only way to combat such calumny is with my wits. So I come here and bow before Rudolph and try to force Matthias to repeat the lies to my face. So far, he hasn't dared."

"But isn't it dangerous for you to come to Vienna, Countess?"

"I am descended from warriors who have never turned away from danger," the countess responded. "I may be a woman and considered too weak to ride into battle but I am no less brave."

"That is admirable," Margueri commented.

"And I need the money for something even more admirable. I am finishing the chapel in Cachtice. Your family will be creating the window designs. We recently agreed on the contract."

"And the one who will be in charge of the work?" Margueri asked, already certain she knew the name.

"Charles Austra."

Margueri whitened. "What is it, child?" Elizabeth asked.

"When did you make that agreement?"

"Over a month ago. James Austra sent me the news."

Margueri jumped to her feet, pacing, thinking the words her mother might use at a time like this though Margueri was far too polite to utter them. "When is he expected at Cachtice?" she asked.

The countess looked evenly at her, concern clear in her wide dark eyes. "I don't really know," she said, then asked, "Why?"

"You speak of bravery. I speak of deceit. I implore you to help me," Margueri finally managed to say. Though any revelation of family matters was frowned on, she continued, telling the countess what she could of her love for Charles, how he had left her, and how she had traveled all the way from Florence to see him. "And now James has been lying to me, refusing to tell me where Charles will be going."

"Perhaps he does not want you to make such a long journey on your own. If you like, I will take your lover a message from you. He is expected in just a few weeks. When he comes, I will intercede and tell him exactly how you feel."

"It isn't enough. Take me!" Margueri exclaimed, all rumors about the Countess Bathori completely forgotten.

"Forgive me my directness, child, but were you intimate?"

"Yes," Margueri admitted.

"Then this becomes a matter of honor. Of course I will take you."

"They . . . my family must not know that I have gone with you."

"I understand. We could leave letters to be delivered after we are safely at Cachtice."

"No." Margueri stood with her back to the countess, hiding her tears as she said, "If Charles knew I was there, he might not come at all."

"I refuse to believe that, not after you traveled so far."

"Nonetheless, I don't want him to know I'm waiting for him."

"Of course. Worry has been known to make a man see what he truly desires. I had been intending to leave for Cachtice next week but we can leave earlier if you wish. Even tomorrow."

Margueri knew she had to go soon. If James sensed anything odd in her behavior, he would quiz her or, worse, steal her plans from her mind and prevent her from leaving. "Tomorrow?" she asked, hoping the countess had been serious.

"Very well. Go home. Pack very little and no one need know we have gone until we have at least a day's start."

Her excitement must show, Margueri knew. She walked too quickly through the Austra house and spoke far more than usual. A servant even looked at her oddly. Nonetheless, no one questioned Margueri when she said that this had been an exhausting day and she wished to retire early.

James did not come home until early morning at a time when he would have scarcely expected her to be on hand to greet him. He had been doing this with such frequency that Margueri had begun to suspect that he wished she would vanish altogether. As she stole out of the house the following morning, clutching a single bag, she wondered what he would think now that she had finally obliged him.

CHAPTER
17

I

As she had every morning for the last year, Ayn Darvulia woke with a moan. Her joints ached, her head pounded, and her feet seemed barely able to take her weight.

Knowing that only one course of action would allow her to face the day, she reached for the pipe that Klara had given her so long ago, then rang for her tea. A maid brought it quickly, well aware of the penalty should she delay this request. As always, it was tepid enough that Ayn could drink it in a few quick gulps, then continue swallowing to keep it down. Sometimes she suspected that the witch Majorova had deliberately added the herb that made it taste so disgusting not for Ayn's welfare but out of a sort of petulant desire to nauseate the countess's favorite every day for the rest of her life.

The drugs immediately began their work on her pain and fatigue and in only a few minutes she was ready to begin what she could of the day's work. As soon as her servant had dressed and groomed her, she ordered the master smith to her sitting room to give an accounting of yesterday's progress.

"The cistern is finished. Today we will begin to cut and weld the bars. In a day or two, everything should be complete. Will you be coming to inspect the work?"

Ayn shook her head. "The countess sent word that she will be arriving here this afternoon. She will inspect the area personally tomorrow morning."

As soon as the man had gone, Ayn sat at the table beneath the narrow window of her chamber and opened the account books. Since Elizabeth had placed her in charge of the castle funds, she had watched them being slowly depleted with no income to take their place. The woman who had been so adept at managing the estates had turned into a single-minded instrument of death, intent on destroying every bit of fortune she possessed.

Ayn wished that her mistress would show some restraint and stop when the screams stopped. Indentured servants were expensive, educated commoners even more so, but purchasing strangers who could pass as nobility was far less dangerous than luring the genuine items to Cachtice. When the need for blood struck, the countess could not tell the difference. Besides, nobles and commoners were the same in the end.

Consumed. Dead. Useless.

The countess would die just as her aunt Klara had died and her parents had died. Nothing could alter her death—not wealth, not even blood. With a sigh, Ayn pushed herself to her feet and went downstairs to find Dorca and Katarina and tell them to prepare the countess's rooms for her arrival and the tower guest room for their latest victim.

The countess and her escorts rode into the inner ward in midafternoon. The countess was on horseback rather than in her coach and the animals had been ridden hard. Ayn expected her mistress to be tired and cross but Elizabeth was at her most charming, personally showing her companion to the guest room, ordering supper sent to them there. Displeased with being kept ignorant, Ayn waited impatiently in her own rooms for the countess to summon her.

When Elizabeth finally called Ayn to her dressing room, she deliberately did not mention the young woman, discussing instead the work in the caverns and the rumors about the investigation the king had ordered. The countess spoke of the latter with a misplaced enthusiasm that Ayn found disturbing. "If they come, what shall we do?" Ayn asked.

"They will not come. Not anymore. I have what I need to keep them away, I think."

"The woman?"

"Perhaps. Perhaps not. I don't really know but it makes no difference."

No difference? What kind of words could these be? "Who is that woman, Countess?" Ayn asked.

"Annika, I can tell you everything now. Charles Austra was once *her* lover, do you understand?"

"The one from your childhood? The *Kisasszony*?"

"Yes," Elizabeth said happily. "And the woman who came here with me is Margueri Austra and she was *his* lover."

"And one of the same people as . . ." Ayn always found herself speaking in partial sentences for she was still forbidden to speak Catherine's name.

"I don't know. I don't think so. The . . . other always knew what I was thinking. This one doesn't or she would have never come here with me. And on the way, we stopped for the night and she ate with me. The other one lived only on blood. Margueri doesn't look like the woman, either. The man does. When I saw him in Bratislava, I knew instantly what he must be."

"They all may not have the same powers," Ayn suggested.

"Powers or no, this one has lived a long time, I think. We spoke of her travels. No one could have gone to so many places in her apparent twenty years. They are a close group, or so she implied. He will come for her and when he does I will possess a power that can stand up to any king, a power that can even call Catherine back to me. And if I am truly fortunate, Erszi Majorova's words will indeed prove true. She said I must drink the blood of my own kind. Who else is more . . . ?" She left the hopeful thought unfinished and began unpinning her hair.

Ayn rushed to help her, uncurling the bun, picking up a brush, and running it through Elizabeth's long dark hair. "It is so pleasant to play the lady's maid for you, Countess. Your hair is so thick, so lovely. And when I am through you will be so beautiful."

Elizabeth swung around and kissed the back of Ayn's hand. "No one knows how to soothe me the way you do, Annika."

"And it is an honor."

II

As they traveled the distance from Vienna to Cachtice, Margueri
had felt as if she were moving back in time. The ordered cobblestone roads and neat villages gave way to rutted tracks hardly
wide enough for a single cart. The tidy villages of Austria
with their tile-roofed houses and straight brick streets became
disorderly groups of wattle and thatch huts with garbage piles
behind them and rats waiting in the shadows for the fall of
night. Riding through them, Margueri saw only glimpses of the
old and the infants, peering suspiciously at her party through
half-open doors as if the helpless had hidden away the young
and strong.

But in Cachtice, with all its barbaric splendor, Margueri
thought she had found an oasis where she could safely rest
and wait for Charles to come. Her single tower room was
magnificently appointed, the great four-poster that dominated it
swathed on three sides in an elegant cream brocade. Its dressing
table was equipped with pots of scented lanolin and rouge, its
closet filled with the clothes she had not been able to bring.
Maids moved efficiently through the room, one unpacking the
few belongings she had brought, another carrying up steaming
water from the kitchen to warm the bath that had already been
prepared, a third following with wine, a loaf of bread, and
delicately spiced chicken stew that she set on a long table
underneath the room's sole window. Margueri requested to
be left alone, and as soon as she had finished with her bath,
she sat at the table, eating and examining a stack of books that
had apparently been left for her.

She had already read the more popular French novels but
had never even heard of the German history of the early years
of Sappho. Idly, she carried it to the bed, slipped off her outer
clothes, lay above the covers, and read.

The story began innocently enough, but as soon as Sappho
arrived at the girls' school, the narrative quickly descended
into a lewd account of pleasure and pain that Margueri found
as compelling as she did distasteful. She had seen books like
these but they had always dealt with masculine fantasies. This
had been written for women and the coarse language only made
the scenes more arousing. No decent woman would admit to
owning a volume such as this, let alone leave it in a guest

room for a casual visitor, not unless there was a motive.

She thought of the way the countess had looked at her during their ride, as if Margueri were less a companion than a treasure, something to be protected and jealously held. She noted the resemblance between her attitude and that of Rachel and Claudia but now the Austra women's motives seemed so much more pure.

She finished the book in one sitting, trying to imagine what she would do if someone used her the way poor Sappho was used in this fictional account. Would she be inclined to fall in love, to write such beautiful verse? Circling the room, Margueri stopped at the table, ate a few bites of the food and poured some wine, then went to the window and looked down at the courtyard much too far below her. Unlike the naive Countess Demeter, Margueri understood that this journey had placed her in great danger, but as it had on her nights with Charles, her nature thrilled to it.

From somewhere deep within the castle, she heard a single extended scream. The guards in the ward yard below did not seem concerned. Perhaps the rumors about the countess were correct and this was a sound frequently heard at Cachtice. Convinced that someone was watching her, Margueri latched the window and went to bed.

In the morning, the book she had read had been replaced by two others with similar sexual themes and a gown of deep green lay neatly across two chairs. Ringing for a servant, she laid back and closed her eyes, listening all the while for the footsteps and, as she expected, the click of the outside bolt on her door.

Instead of the maid, a severely dressed woman of around thirty entered. "My name is Ayn Darvulia. I am the Countess Elizabeth's companion. She requested that I look in on you and ask if you had slept well."

"So well that a servant prepared me for the day without my ever becoming aware," Margueri responded, not bothering to hide her irritation.

The woman chose to ignore her tone. "Perhaps you learned to sleep more soundly during your travels. Inns can be such noisy places. Will you be coming downstairs for breakfast?"

"I think not. I would rather rest and read." Margueri's hand rested on one of the books, a point she was certain that Ayn Darvulia did not overlook.

"For supper. Then we three can talk. You've just come from

Vienna, I hear. Such a beautiful city." She sounded so wistful
that Margueri wondered if she was also a prisoner here.

With no direct way of inquiring, Margueri could only look
for clues. "Are you from Vienna?" she asked.

"I lived there for many years. The countess and I have visited
since but this is my home now."

Not a prisoner but a companion. Margueri was beginning to
understand.

She did join them for supper, wearing the dress that had
been loaned to her. The three women ate and talked, Margueri
giving no notice that she sensed anything amiss. She asked
about Charles, of course—it was what a girl hopelessly in love
ought to do—but now she acted her part. The stupidity of her
actions had cooled her passion considerably.

But not her wits. When she retired for the night, she had a
knife in her pocket. As she undressed, she slipped it under her
pillow and later, her hand resting on its handle, she managed
to sleep.

A noise awakened her; not a scream this time but a soft
constant whimper that, like a night fog or a dream, seemed
to surround her. The curtains on the inside of her bed swayed
from some hidden draft. The flame of her night candle danced.
Gripping her knife, she brushed the heavy fabric and found a
place where two edges overlapped. She ran to the bed, bringing
back the candle, turning its reflective metal mirror to shine the
light against the curtains, then slowly pushed them back. A rush
of cold damp air extinguished the flame but in that brief moment
she saw a narrow hallway, a second room beyond hers.

As her eyes slowly adjusted to the darkness, she detected a
faint light coming from the hallway. She was meant to seek out
its source, but if she did not, they could come for her anyway.
Decision made, she put on her dressing gown, tied it tightly at
the waist, and padded barefoot toward the light.

It came from a steep staircase that circled the lower floors
of the tower. On every third stair, a candle flickered in a glass
holder and shadows of Margueri danced around her as she
slowly began her descent. With every step the sobbing seemed
closer but more faint, and by the time she reached the base of
the stairs and the beginning of a second passageway, the sound
had stopped altogether.

She smelled woodsmoke, saw the golden light of flames on the far wall. Walking carefully, trying to make as little sound as possible, Margueri moved forward until the room just came into view.

Stone walls. High ceilings. A fire pit that could easily heat the entire castle. She took it all in with a single sweep of her eyes, then stared in horror at the sight in the center of the room.

For a moment she did not recognize the countess for the plain, brown-clad woman with the uncombed hair bore little resemblance to the elegantly dressed and coiffed woman who inhabited the upper floors. Her manner was different too, the controlled movements of the salon replaced with a frenzied motion of her hands, an impatient twitching of her lips. A naked woman lay motionless at her feet. Another, her mouth bound with strips of cloth so she could not make a sound, had been tied to an X-shaped cross in the center of the room. Her wrists were bloody from the strength of her struggles and her head was bent forward, a thin trickle of blood sliding down her chest.

Stifling any display of terror, Margueri took a step backward. But before she could bolt down the hall for the dubious safety of the upper floors, the countess turned to her, holding out a silver goblet. "Welcome, kinswoman," she said, her regal tone so at odds with her dress and surroundings. "Come. You have needs as I do. The first victim was mine. I saved the stronger one for you."

For the first time, Margueri noticed Ayn Darvulia standing in the shadows behind the countess and two older women dressed in blood-soaked rags standing by, waiting perhaps for additional orders.

Margueri's mind raced as she tried to make sense out of the words the countess had spoken. Only one possibility came to her, only one course of action was open. Drawing on every ounce of courage that remained in her, Margueri walked forward and lifted the cup from the countess's hands.

Blood. She had expected that and her hands were steady as she lifted the goblet and drained it. But as she did, the woman at her feet groaned and rolled over so that she could see the face of one of the serving girls who had waited on her yesterday evening.

The goblet fell from Margueri's fingers, the firelight folded inward, and she fainted at the countess's feet.

III

When he arrived in Vienna, James Austra had hired two couples to act as servants. One had been recently married, the other pair were lovers. At night, he would stand outside his chosen victims' door, happily goading on their lovemaking until at the height of ecstasy he would join them, drinking from each, then with the ease of a first born wiping their memories of his presence. By day, he treated them all with the respect a true patrician owes his inferiors. In turn, the small staff worshiped their reserved employer and, like James, regarded Margueri's presence as an unwelcome intrusion on the order of their lives.

Aware of this, Margueri had kept to her own rooms, rarely seeking anyone's company or advice. So when one of the servants finally noticed Margueri's absence and reported it to James, he was hardly alarmed. He had decided to treat her much like he would one of the women in his own family. She wanted her independence. She had it. His only hope was that she had found a new lover to take Charles's place and would leave them all in peace. The clothes missing from Margueri's room only assured him this must be true. With that happy idea firmly fixed in his mind, he rode off to meet with a merchant in Baden and present his drawings for the family's estate.

As a result, the countess's letter was placed unopened in an envelope along with other correspondence addressed to Charles, and Margueri's absence was completely ignored. Days later, the packet of correspondence was shipped to Charles at the nearly finished summer house on the lake north of Sopron.

Late at night, Charles sat at the table in his room in the nearly finished house sifting through the correspondence. By the unnecessary light of a glass-cased candle, Charles read the long letters from Steffen and Rachel, then opened the Bathori note. He scanned it first and, seeing it was not at all what he'd expected, went back to the beginning and absorbed every word.

I received the communication in which you expressed your regret that you could not come to Cachtice until next year, the countess wrote in flawless French. *I had hoped that you would be able to rearrange your schedule, but after so many weeks I assume you cannot. Now, however, I am certain that you will wish to make a short visit to view the chapel immediately and, at that time, perhaps reconcile with your cousin, Margueri Austra.*

Mademoiselle Austra was most adamant about coming to Cachtice with me and escaping all memories of her unhappy affair. I, of course, am pleased to be her hostess as she is a charming young woman. I knew that you would be concerned about her, particularly if you have heard the vicious rumors that are being circulated concerning my habits. I felt that I must write and put your mind at rest. These stories are without any foundation. However, Margueri seemed so sorrowful in the days before we departed that I do fear for her health and, to be blunt, her sanity and I am afraid that she may do herself some harm. I therefore entreat you to reconsider your refusal and come alone to reconcile with her. I will be eagerly awaiting your arrival at Cachtice and assure you that in the time it will take you to reach the castle, Margueri will be watched over and kept safe and well.

The countess had been clever. Her words seemed less threat than sisterly concern and the key sentence, *come alone to reconcile with her,* read like the most innocent solicitude. Yet Charles knew otherwise. The thought of Cachtice sent a cold river of fear through him. This was a place his instincts warned him to avoid, but Margueri was there and he had to go to her. His hands shook with rage and he must have made some sound because Count Nemeth groaned and rolled over, scattering the covers Charles had piled on him. He reeked of wine, nonetheless as soon as he'd sat up in bed, he immediately straightened his coat and smoothed back his wispy blond hair. "How much did I lose," he groaned.

"I haven't tallied my winnings yet, Count."

"What! You call me count instead of Jules? You mean I didn't gamble away my title to you? Well, that's something I suppose." The count swung his feet over the side of the bed and, gripping the footboard, pulled himself upright. "The room is spinning. Did I drink too much?"

"No, Jules. I did."

"You?" Nemeth frowned a moment, then began to laugh.

"That's a joke, isn't it? You only had a glass as I recall." He opened the box on the table that held his coins and slammed it shut. "You've made a pact with the devil, that's what it is," he grumbled good-naturedly.

"I warned you when we started, play on chance alone. I always know when someone is bluffing."

"Is that it?" Nemeth fell into the chair he'd used for so many hours the night before. "My father used to tell me that a noble who can gamble will always have his honor and always be wealthy. So far I'm something of a disappointment to his memory. I know! I'll give you five hundred guildens if you make me into a demon at cards."

"I don't think I'll have the time." Charles rested a hand on the letter he'd been reading.

Count Nemeth seemed to sober immediately. "Troubling news?" he asked.

"Yes."

"Then perhaps I should leave you to compose a reply?"

Charles shook his head. "I have need of your advice," he said. Charles went to the cupboard, pulling out Shiller's letters and laying them out on the table in front of the count.

"I care for the woman and I need to know how to best handle this matter," Charles said when the count had finished reading.

Count Nemeth paused before answering, his expression remote as he considered the implications of these notes. "Rumors move like fire through these lands. They spread. They grow. They spread faster," he finally replied. "I heard stories of killings at Sarvar. I didn't believe them. And the reason was a simple one—the Bathori family is noted for its honor and they did nothing to stop her. Now I think I understand." He handed the letters back to Charles before continuing. "Count Thurzo is the king's representative in the north but he is also a cousin to the Countess Elizabeth. If he had been informed of the full measure of the local complaints and the plans for an investigation of Elizabeth, he would have taken steps to stop her himself. I assume, therefore, that he was deliberately left uninformed."

"Deliberately?"

"If the countess is found guilty of murder, then all estates in her name become the property of the crown. The debt to the family will also be forgiven. A great deal of money is involved. Do you see?"

"Yes. And my best course?"

"You refer to the quickest one, I presume. Very well, leave these letters with me but take copies of all of them to Count Thurzo in Bytca. I will write him and tell him that I possess the originals. I will likewise swear to never reveal their contents should he act immediately. If he chooses to ignore his cousin's atrocities, you must tell him that the letters will be sent to King Matthias. We may be forcing him to take action against his cousin; however, given how many months it has been since he last visited Bratislava, I tend to doubt that. I think he will owe us both a debt of gratitude when this is over. He should. I intend to remind him of this as well."

Someday, Charles suspected, someone would order Count Nemeth killed and the victim would take satisfaction in the fact that the assassins would be forced to strike from behind. "I'll have to take the letters to him personally," Charles said.

"It would be wisest." Count Nemeth's voice remained smooth, nearly hiding his regret.

"The local craftsmen can finish the windows."

"Are they capable?"

"The main designs are nearly complete. The guild can handle the mounting."

"When will you leave?"

"Tomorrow afternoon. It will take that long to finish what only I can do. I think it best that I work through the rest of the night."

"Then I'll go." The count had his hand on the doorknob when Charles signaled him to be silent. A moment later, footsteps passed in the hall outside.

Count Nemeth chuckled. "You need not be so discreet for me. The servants know where I spend my nights and if any is so unwise as to tell my mother that I've gambled away a small fortune since you came here, he will find himself flung from the highest tower window. Besides, Mother would not say a word of reproach. She worships me, you know." He tilted his head, his thin smile cocky but utterly sincere.

Charles followed the count to the door. There he rested a hand on the side of the count's face, locking eyes with him for a moment, willing him again to forget the oddities of their nights, remembering only the affection that bound them.

CHAPTER
18

I

Margueri woke suddenly. The taste of blood clung to her mouth. She could smell it when she inhaled, feel it lying like sour wine in her stomach. Inwardly she moaned as she thought of last night's deadly atrocities and swallowed the bile that rose in her throat. Then, as she had for days, she rolled over and brushed her hand over the countess's hair, whispering a good morning in the most loving voice she possessed.

Elizabeth responded with her own soft greeting, then propped the pillows behind her head to watch Margueri dress, looking at her as if she expected something more than the caresses and the kisses of the night before.

Margueri displayed no modesty, revealed no loathing for what they did during their long bloody nights. Someone spying on them at this moment would have no indication that they were anything less than profane lovers, caught in a passion that defied all convention. The truth was something far more terrible. There were ten bodies in the tunnels below Cachtice. Ficzko and Dorca, the servants who assisted them in their bloody acts, had bagged each corpse and coated it with lime. Nonetheless, the smell seeped through the tunnels and into the ward yard where a casual visitor could not help but notice it.

Last night, at Ayn's whispered urging, Margueri had finally found the courage to complain. She did so in the imperious voice that Elizabeth expected from her and, cowed, the servants promised to bury them outside the walls this afternoon.

When Margueri had dressed, she pulled the covers closer around the countess, kissing her before going downstairs. There Ayn Darvulia would be waiting for her at the breakfast table, sitting stiffly in her black linen gown with its severe starched collar and cuffs, frowning silently like some sullen mother superior forced to share bread with an errant novice.

Today, Ayn did not even look at anything more than Margueri's hands as she poured the cider into her cup, laid one of the cheese kolaches on her plate, passing over the single knife so that Margueri could spread it with a coating of butter. They shared the same food every morning, though the portions were hardly equal. It seemed to Margueri that she was the only one in the castle with any appetite at all. As she looked down at the coarsely ground wheat of the kolach, Margueri thought longingly of the flaky sweet croissants and honey-soaked strawberries that she might be eating in Paris.

"Did the countess sleep well?" Ayn asked her as she did each morning.

Margueri nodded.

"I don't want her hurt," Ayn added with sudden candor.

The wit and courage the countess had displayed in Vienna had vanished, replaced by a compulsive and deadly insanity so degrading that Margueri could not help but pity her. "I don't want the countess hurt either," Margueri said honestly.

"She was given up to my care years ago. In spite of what she is, I have come to love her and I do not want her betrayed even by falsehoods."

"Speak directly, if you can."

"If your blood will give her immortality, share it. Let her be what you are. When you do, this barbarity will end."

Margueri shivered as if someone had trickled cold water down her spine. "The blood must be shared willingly," Margueri said carefully, repeating the old legend. "That I would gladly do but first the countess must be tested and found worthy by . . . by one of the first born."

"First born?"

"When my lover arrives, he will judge her. Nothing is possible until then."

"Meanwhile, too many women die."

To Margueri, Ayn sounded like a miserly steward grumbling

over the inventory. "There are always more," she responded coldly. "And if there aren't enough, you can procure more. That is your purpose here, isn't it?"

The words were intended to wound, and in spite of Ayn's impassive expression, Margueri sensed that they had hit their mark. And was her own heartlessness entirely false? Margueri wondered. She found herself thinking of the torture she had ordered last night, how the little dark girl had died so quickly. She had been more careful with the second for she had not wanted to be responsible for two lives when one should have sufficed. She didn't look at their faces anymore, only let their screams course through her. And if she stayed here for months, for years, would she grow to love the sport as Ayn almost seemed to do?

She ate in silence until midway through the meal when the countess joined them. Elizabeth wore only a morning dress and her hair was still rumpled from sleep. She had lost a great deal of weight in the last half month and there were dark circles under her eyes. She sat across from Margueri, winding one strand of her black hair around an index finger, pulling it tight, and letting it fall as if trying to create the distinctive Austra curls. Ayn took the countess's hand, kissing it before asking, "Will you eat something this morning?"

"I dined last night," Elizabeth replied as she always did. For days she had lived on nothing but blood.

"You are like me, Countess," she said carefully. "We are not the first born. We need more than blood to survive." She filled a cup with apricot cider and held it out to the countess, relieved when Elizabeth lifted it and drank.

"Margueri has been telling me that only a first born can judge you worthy for immortality," Ayn said.

"Like Catherine?" Elizabeth asked Margueri. When Margueri nodded, the countess gave her an accusing look. "It has been twelve days since the firm received my letter," she said. "When will Charles come?"

Margueri looked down and said nothing. Perhaps the letter had never reached him. Perhaps he read it and decided that in spite of their bond, he would not come for her.

"How many more days?" The countess's voice had become shrill, demanding.

"I don't know," she said.

"Strangers rode through the town yesterday. My servants believe they came from the king and that Matthias's investigation is about to begin. I need to know when Charles will come."

"I said that I don't know. If you will both excuse me, I would like to sleep a bit longer." She stood and began moving toward the door when the countess spoke again, in a voice so soft that Margueri could barely discern the words. This was the voice Margueri feared, the one that seemed to come from the other Elizabeth beneath the civilized facade.

"You have shared blood with him?" Elizabeth asked.

Margueri still faced the door as she replied, "I have told you so. We were lovers after all."

"Then the bond between you is very tight."

Margueri felt the color leave her face.

"Tight enough that your agony would draw him."

Margueri spun, pointing one finger at the countess, then at Ayn, sitting with such satisfaction beside Elizabeth. "If you dare to touch me, he will destroy you both. You saw how Catherine's victims died and her power is nothing beside his, nothing at all."

With her arms rigid at her side, Margueri walked from the room, closing the doors behind her. In the hall, she hesitated, looking from the narrow stairs that led to her chamber to the open front door and the sunny ward yard. A pair of horses were tethered to a post on the far side of it. If she could somehow reach them without being noticed, she might escape. The chance was slim but she only had enough courage left for flight. Trying to look as nonchalant as possible, she walked outside and down the length of the covered porch.

Servants working in the yard glanced at her but only Dorca, Elizabeth's maid, acted as if something was amiss, calling out to her, asking where she was going. Margueri waved at Dorca and then sat at one of the shaded tables until the woman went inside.

As soon as Dorca had gone, Margueri stretched and stood and moved toward the center of the court, then bolted for the pair of mounts.

If they had been tied in the usual manner she might have escaped but the knots were nothing a normal rider would have used. She was frantically trying to unhook the reins when the huge wooden gates of Cachtice began to close. Margueri ran but servants were waiting for her, enough that even had she possessed the strength of an Austra she might have been brought down.

When the struggle was over, Margueri had no will for anything but surrender. As she was lifted and carried through the yard and down the narrow stone steps to the dungeons below, she heard the countess's hysterical laughter following her and knew how easily she had been tricked.

In the space below, with her arms held securely by the castle guards, Elizabeth inspected the damage the struggle had caused. Margueri panted, glaring at the countess as she ran her fingers over the bruises on Margueri's face, dipped her finger in the blood flowing from the deep cut on her forehead, then tasted it thoughtfully.

"You should not have run," she said. "It reveals how mortal you are." Then softly, as if she were kissing a lover, she pressed her lips to the wound, sucking, swallowing, intoxicated with the taste and the fear and the pain.

Margueri's knees buckled. She would have fallen had she not been held. Instead they let her sink slowly before the countess. She raised her head, the blood dripping down one side of her face, her lips slightly parted as she waited for the countess's kiss.

As their lips touched, she thought of Charles. What he had awakened in her would be exorcised here. If she was lucky, her sanity might survive.

II

To walk into danger, no matter how compelling the reason, was counter to all Austra instinct. Therefore, when Charles found it difficult but not impossible to enter Cachtice, he knew a trap had been set for him, that it most likely would be sprung and that he would survive. Surprise would be the novelty in this game. The challenge amused him and the endings, as always, would be bloody and satisfying.

Though it was late afternoon, no guards greeted him at the gates. The ward yard was empty of any servants save one deformed man who gave a quick cry of warning and disappeared inside. A moment later a woman opened the main doors and came outside. She was dressed in simple black, her pale long-fingered hands a stark contrast against its fabric. Though she could hardly be called a beauty, something about the wide spacing of her dark eyes and the high arched brows reminded him of Claudia. If his sister ever had a human child she might look like this. His mind moved quickly through hers seeking nothing more than recognition, discovering a great deal more than he had expected. —Greetings, Countess— he said mind to mind.

Not at all surprised, she responded in kind. —Greetings, Charles Austra. Kinsman. Once lover to Catherine.—

Catherine. She was not here, had probably never been here, yet Charles could sense her presence in the fear flowing from the walls around him. —Do you know where she can be found?— he asked.

The countess slowly shook her head. "Perhaps we can find her together. That is one of the reasons I summoned you here though hardly the only one," she responded.

He hadn't expected her voice to be so naturally soft or so compelling. Then slowly, as if he could do her no real harm, she turned and let him follow her inside and up the stairs to a room where Margueri's scent lay heavy on the bedclothes. "There is clean water for your use in the pitcher on the table," the countess said. "I could send for wine if you like, or food." The last was said with a trace of humor and he knew she was toying with him.

"You know I cannot eat."

"Then you are like my lover. I am honored to have you here, Charles Austra, first born."

"Where is Margueri? May I speak with her?"

"In time. Rest now. Then you can go to her."

She turned, her hand on the latch when Charles used all his power to repeat his question. —Where is Margueri?—

She looked at him over her shoulder, her eyes not quite focused, her smile not quite sane. Whatever delusions controlled her life seemed to also shield her mind from his power. "Later," she whispered.

As the door closed behind her, he heard the click of its bolts and his instincts screamed their belated warning.

He could break the door down. It was only wood after all. He was less than fifty feet above the ground, an easy jump

for one of his kind. But flight made no sense. He had come
here for Margueri and he would not leave without her. He
sat cross-legged on the floor, his eyes shut, his mind moving
through the castle looking for her. He reached her, touched
her briefly. Her cry of relief and delight forced him back to
his body, his head turning immediately toward the bed and
the hallway hidden behind it. He pulled back the covers and
started down the same stairs Margueri had taken so many days
before.

Unlike Margueri's descent, there was no light to guide his
way, no screams to draw him to the cellars below. Margueri
was there, and as Elizabeth had suspected, Margueri was all
the lure he needed.

He descended the stairs carefully, his mind moving before
him, seeking anyone waiting to attack, but all he sensed were
the caged and the dead. He walked past the center room where
the floor was soaked in blood, the air reeked of death-given,
and the walls still seemed to echo with the screams. He walked
down the halls where hands reached through the bars and
whispers entreated him to free them. He closed his senses to
their voices, barricaded himself against the warning twinges of
his instincts, concentrating instead on Margueri trapped in the
caverns somewhere beneath him.

The twisting passage finally opened onto a second large room,
empty save for the cage holding Margueri. It hung from a chain
near the ceiling, well beyond Charles's reach. Circular, about
ten feet in diameter, it had long inward-aimed spikes welded
to the bars that made up the sides and outer edges of the floor.
Margueri sat motionless in the center with her legs spread apart
to maintain her balance. Her eyes were frantic with fear and he
sensed in her less hope than resignation.

As he looked at her, as he softly called her name, the cage
began to swing. She gripped the nearest spikes, trying to hold
herself still as the swaying intensified. A spike pierced her arm.
Her cry of pain ripped through him, followed a moment later
by the familiar scent of her blood. Her instant of panic made
the cage swing faster. In a moment she would be impaled.

"Brace yourself," he called and jumped the distance, grabbing
on to the floor bars as close to the center as possible, feeling the
welcome press of Margueri's hands on his. His weight stopped
the swaying, but as he hung from the bottom of the cage, the

two entrances to the room began to shut. His instincts shrieked a warning and he obeyed, letting go, intending to run for the door. He might have escaped but the floor gave way beneath him and he fell an extra thirty feet into a wide metal-lined cistern whose woven metal grate snapped shut above him.

He heard someone laughing, looked up and saw the countess smiling down at him. "This is how you trap an animal, even an immortal one. Charles Austra, am I worthy of immortality?"

Charles responded by summoning all his speed and strength into a single upward leap that fell short of the grate by the length of his body. He ran his hands over the walls of the cistern, tried to dig his nails into its surface.

Iron. In a week, perhaps, he could gouge out the first two handholds. In two months, he might reach the bars, but if they were as strong as the walls, he would not be able to break them.

Though the countess had moved back from the edge of the cistern, he heard her mocking laughter. There were other ways out after all, and with all the power he had, he thrust himself painfully into her mind. —Free me!—

He could take comfort only in her startled cry. "It will be harder than that, Charles Austra. We are kin, after all."

Kin? More likely deranged. But no matter the reason, he still could not touch her. Carefully, with his voice at its most compelling, he asked, "Why did you ask me here, then trap me this way?"

"Because it is the only way I can assure that you will help me."

"Help you, Countess?"

"I want you to call to Catherine so that she comes for me."

Charles squatted on his heels, his back against the metal wall, looking at the dim circle of light so far above him. "I thought she might be nearby," he answered. "I called to her but she did not answer."

"Then you'll stay where you are. She'll feel your hunger and she'll come."

"She'll destroy you if you harm me," Charles countered. Was it only his rage that made him want to scream or were his instincts warning him that he had pressed his luck too far? He had no way of knowing but he was amazed that his voice could sound so cold.

"She destroyed me already. And this pretty thing . . ." Elizabeth pulled on the chain that rocked Margueri's cage. Margueri cried out from surprise and pain, then stifled the sound. "If the king's men come to arrest me, I will have time enough to be sure that she dies. If you manage to escape, I will scream your secret to the world. If I am harmed in any way by my servants, remember, I have the only key to this prison and it is well hidden. See that I am kept safe and well."

"And our future?" Charles asked.

"Is up to Catherine to decide."

She would not come. Even if she knew how he had been trapped, she would not come. Desperate, Charles tried a different ploy. His voice at its most persuasive, his mind brushing hers, willing her to accept his words, he said, "You called me kinsman. Indeed, if you share that bond with me, you can be."

He felt Elizabeth hesitate. Even without his subtle push, she would still want to believe. "How?" she asked.

"By sharing my blood."

"Liar!" She jerked the chain to Margueri's cage with all the strength she had. Margueri screamed as her hand slipped and a spike cut into her arm. Charles covered his ears too late. Her agony was in his mind, the dark beauty of it already seducing him. So near yet beyond his reach and he understood—Elizabeth Bathori intended to drive him mad.

"But did Catherine wish to make you immortal?" he asked, the words as even as he could make them.

"I don't know."

"Did she sing the ritual? Did you drink simultaneously from each other?"

"No," Elizabeth admitted.

"But you can be immortal if I will it."

"Why would you?"

"To save a life. To add a powerful soul to the numbers of my family. These are reasons enough if you are worthy of the change."

"I will consider this," she replied, her tone as guarded as her thoughts. The circle of light grew fainter, then disappeared altogether as Ayn and the countess left the lower chambers. Somewhere in the distance, a heavy door slammed shut and a collective sigh rose from the souls trapped in the cells above him. The countess had come and gone and they were all still alive.

"Charles?" Margueri called.

"Shhh . . ." —Think your words. Someone may be listening.—

—I'm sorry. I had hoped that we'd meet in better circumstances.— Inwardly she giggled with a sort of hysterical bravery he could well understand.

—Can you lie down to rest, Margueri?—

He heard the creaking of the cage above him, sensed Margueri's fear as she moved in the darkness, doing her best to avoid the points. She managed to lie in a tight ball, then stretched her legs and arms as far as she could through the spikes to relieve some of the pressure on her back. Her wounded arm was flat against the bottom of the cage and the blood flowing from it dripped through the bars. By some miracle, the drops fell through the tiny holes at the top of the cistern. He watched them descend through the darkness, so slow they seemed as they fell into his waiting palm. He licked them and sent her a warm mental caress before willing her to sleep.

His hands pressed against the iron floor, his mind moved slowly along the wall of the cistern, searching for the faintest cracks, finding nothing. The air felt thick and heavy as if the smooth perfection of these iron walls had compacted it. Was it only his dislike of closed spaces that threatened him with panic? Was it something more?

One thing was certain. If the countess was as strong as he suspected, he would have to fight for every meal.

Later Margueri woke to an unfamiliar sound. Lying in the darkness, she listened, finally understanding that what she heard was Charles's nails scraping on the cistern, digging out the first step of the long climb.

CHAPTER
19

Following a long afternoon's nap, the Countess Elizabeth sat in front of her mirror, her head resting on a pillow braced on the back of her chair, her eyes shut. Dorca carefully wiped away her daytime makeup with a soft damp cloth while Ayn searched the closet, collecting the pieces of the ensembles Elizabeth wished to consider. "I have never felt more sure of myself," Elizabeth said, seeming to speak more to herself than to the women in the room. "The king will not be able to touch me now. Catherine will come. And if the one trapped below speaks the truth, I will be like her. Would you like to be like Catherine, Ayn? Would you like your body young and healthy again, perfect forever?"

"Immortal? No, Countess. I would not like it."

"Even to avoid damnation?"

"God will be merciful, Countess."

"Merciful? Why? Will you tell Him I was to blame for the blood spilled in Cachtice and Sarvar?"

Though Elizabeth's voice had not risen, Ayn detected the fury. "No, Countess. I will explain that you are different. You have needs."

"Good. You tell Him that."

In the quiet moment of relief, Ayn sensed the presence in her mind. Elizabeth had told her that the man caught in the cistern could read her thoughts even over a distance so she had expected to feel him. What surprised her was that he did not try to control her or ask to be freed. Instead he simply sat somewhere at the center of her being, using her eyes to observe what went on in this room. What did he make of Elizabeth's atrocities? she wondered. Did he know what the countess planned for tonight?

—There are thirteen women imprisoned around me. Two will die tonight after as long and painful an agony as the countess is able to inflict. That is how she intends to prove that she is worthy to be immortal.—

Words unspoken, yet so clear, so loud, so filled with contempt! Startled, Ayn dropped the gown she carried from the closet and leaned against a chair.

"Ayn, are you well?" the countess inquired with no real concern.

"Just clumsy." Ayn picked up the dress, brushing the dust off the bodice, laying it with the others on the bed.

"Then come and do my hair. Make it perfect, Annika, as only you are able. I won't even look until you are done."

Ayn's hands shook as she picked up the brush and began her work. The mind sharing her body slowly released her and withdrew, leaving her to wonder if he understood the countess's endearment and if he would use it against her.

As she worked, a vision formed in her mind. She guessed who it must be for the countess had described Catherine to her often enough. As carefully as she was able, Ayn duplicated the hairstyle, pulling back the sides and braiding them at the top of the head with a bright green ribbon, using the iron to form Elizabeth's damp hair into tight curls at the forehead and down the back. When she had finished, the countess opened her eyes and stared at her reflection.

And laughed. And danced through the room, pausing only long enough to kiss Ayn. "How did you know? How could you have possibly known? It is so perfect, you've made me look so much like her." She ran her hands over each of the gowns, pausing at the forest-green one, then running her hands lightly over the low-cut bodice. "I will wear this one tonight, Ayn. It was *her* color—the color of the shadows, she used to call it. And if I am to be like her, I must look like her, is that not so?"

The countess was nearly fifty. Hardly the dark princess anymore. "Of course," Ayn responded, then helped her snap up the back and arrange the curls across her forehead with planned abandon.

While Dorca and Ayn had assisted the countess, Ficzko and Helena Jo were in the cellars, making the final arrangements for the night's revels. The St. Andrew's cross on which Elizabeth bound her victims had been moved to the edge of the cistern, the fire laid on the huge stone hearth in the adjoining chamber. The room smelled of smoke and hot iron along with the more subtle reek of sweat and fear.

Margueri was awake and wisely silent. The victims were moving in their cells. Some whimpered in the corners. Some faced the future stoically. Those who had the comfort of a partner in their cell held each other. Charles heard a distant chant, then silence as the countess walked down the row of cells, Ayn holding the torch high so that the countess could study each of them.

No one knew how to act. No one knew what would suit her fancy from one night to the next, or even when she would come. Some of them had been here for months, others only a few days.

When the countess arrived, Charles tried to ignore the cries as they dragged the woman from her cell and across the rough stones to the cross. He concentrated instead on the next few hours, still not certain what he must do.

Should he force the countess to feel the pain she inflicted on her victims? It was an easy trick, one even an Austra child could do. But then she would vent her rage on Margueri. He dare not try to torment any of the others either for they were all too close to the countess. He focused on them—Dorca, the old woman who took such pleasure in destroying the young and the beautiful; Ficzko, dim-witted and deformed; Helena Jo, as twisted as the countess herself. Last, he returned to Ayn—the one weak link, the one most difficult to deal with because, of all of them, she alone loved her mistress.

"Look at me, Charles Austra," the countess called down. She held a torch as she stood on the edge of the cistern's grate. "Am I not beautiful? Now, I shall show you that I am worthy as well."

He heard a scream, felt the victim struggling in her bonds. He tried to retreat, to shield his mind, but it was too late. All his senses were acutely aware of the agony, and the approaching death he would not be allowed to share.

And suddenly, with perfect clarity, he knew what must be done.

—Give me this woman, Countess— he called privately to her. —Give her to me and I will use her to summon Catherine.—

He had expected questions, an argument, not this sudden surge of excitement. "And you will share the pain with me? You will let me feel this woman's life course through your body?"

Charles had never experienced such a rush of pity or revulsion. In her loneliness, Catherine had created a monster. "Yes," he answered.

"Ficzko, Dorca, bring that creature here," the countess ordered, her voice taut with anticipation. She disappeared for a moment and the bars moved back just far enough for the woman to be dropped through, then snapped shut once more. Charles caught the victim and barely held her for her skin was coated with blood. He let her go and concentrated on the countess sitting cross-legged at the edge of his prison, holding a torch above her head, trying to watch him so far below her.

—I provide my own light.—

The words cut through the darkness. Elizabeth saw Charles clearly, the woman on her knees before him trying to brush the bloodstains from his dark breeches, hoping to prove the only way left to her that she was worthy of release, would be a good servant if he would only let her live. When he finally looked at her, when she finally had the courage to speak, she found the words to beg him trapped in her throat.

His eyes were dark, implacable as he shook his head. Anything he would say to calm her would only diminish her terror. His hands burned where they touched her, her heart pounded.

Elizabeth sucked in her breath in a long audible hiss. "Delicious fear," she whispered.

Though the others could not see what she saw, all eyes followed the direction of her gaze while above them, Margueri did what had to be done, rubbing her wrist across one sharp point until it bled, holding the wound over the place where Charles knelt. He raised his head, caught the blood on his tongue and, with an ease born of so many intimate nights, drew her into his mental net. Then, with one soul trapped, he concentrated on what he knew best.

—Look at me, my chosen. Look at my face.—

Obedient, still so hopeful, the woman obeyed. Drawn by his beauty, she stood, her hands on his cheeks, the tips of her fingers daring to brush his dark hair. She did not wonder how she could see him so clearly in the darkness. For a moment even her fear was gone.

She moved closer, wondering if he would let her kiss him when his lips pulled back, his tongue moving from one rear fang to the next, wetting them, drawing her attention to them, then to the growing darkness of his eyes.

Mute, trapped, her body trembled as he pressed it against him.

"That's it," the countess whispered, her eyes glittering with excitement. "Do what she would have done."

—No, Catherine only destroys. I can share something far more exquisite.—

He began playing with his victim's emotions, blending desire and pain, fear and regret, going far beyond any of the destructive games he had played with Margueri, far beyond anything that Catherine's limited powers could accomplish. At the end, with all his victim's emotions so perfectly balanced, with the woman so placid and ready in his arms, he showed them death in all her burning glory.

And as his victim began her final, desperate struggle, he began to devour her—blood, spirit, soul.

Life filled him, carrying with it a tide of emotion so strong it could not be contained. He channeled it, channeled the extra support Margueri's silent presence brought, and together the three screamed her name . . .

——Catherine!!!——

It was not a focused cry, for he had no idea where she might be, but it was a powerful one. James might hear it. Even the Old One might come. As for Catherine, he sensed her for a moment. The countess had gotten her wish.

Elizabeth sat trapped in her rapture. He felt her joy as he drank, as they both cherished the warmth given by the life ebbing in his arms.

And because he wanted her to know what she ended with such reckless abandon, he stayed with his victim to the end, coming so close to death that only his instinctive recoil kept him from being trapped in Her embrace forever.

As his sight returned, he heard the countess's shallow breathing, Margueri's desolate sobs. No words were spoken, no thoughts shared, as they sat separate, each trying to recover from the passion they had experienced.

The countess found her wits first. A bottle of water was lowered on a rope. "Untie it," the countess called down. "Then tie the rope to the creature's wrists so we can bring her up. You have given me something . . ." Her voice trailed off, the experience had no words to contain it. "I would not have you share your cell with a corpse."

He did as she requested. When the body had been raised and the doors shut once again, she looked down at him and spoke graciously, "Whatever you need, I will give, though I will not free you. You reached her, I sensed it. Everything is beginning as it should. Tomorrow, you will share your blood with me and we will see if you speak the truth."

"Of course, Countess."

He sensed Margueri's silent protest and responded with a private message. —I have no reason to refuse the request. Indeed, I will cherish the bond. It will make her pain so much more perfect when I devour her.—

He stood in the center of his prison listening to his captor's footsteps on the tower stairs. Then there was only the smell of smoke from the smoldering torches and the intoxicating scent of Margueri's fear.

CHAPTER
20

As she washed the blood from her body in the grey morning light, Elizabeth's hands shook. Expressions of love, grief, wonder, horror, and joy danced across her face, the shifts of emotion so sudden that she dismissed everyone, even Annika, lest they think her mad.

But it wasn't madness, she knew, only aftershocks like those following a perfect climax with a lover. The very intensity of the night's act had been the reason she had waited to make that final sharing of blood and life. Had she shared herself last night she would have been at that creature's mercy forever. No one, not even an immortal, would play her for a fool.

It had been so long since she had undressed herself, since she had a moment of solitude to look at her body and appraise the damage of her years. Had she really lived half a century? Her breasts had sagged a little but they were still small and high, her waist still thin, and her tiny hands with their long slender fingers still held much of the smoothness of their youth. Her mother had been like her, a beauty until the end. Though she had been nearly sixty when she died not a single sign of grey had marred the chestnut tones of Anna Bathori's hair. Perhaps it was the blood of their immortal ancestors that made them so immune to the years.

The lines around her lips and eyes were the only real disappointment. Perhaps when her immortality was complete, they would vanish leaving her as perfectly beautiful as Catherine and Charles. Dorca knocked lightly on her door, asking if she wished something to eat or drink. She sent the woman away with the order that no one disturb her contemplation, then sat and stared at her eyes in the mirror, dreaming of blood and power and immortality until she heard the quiet promise brushing her mind. Yes, Charles was right. The time had nearly come.

"Tonight," she whispered and felt his quick assent. With an indrawn hiss of pleasure, she slipped between the sheets and slept.

In her room joined to the countess's chambers by a narrow private hall, Ayn Darvulia lay on her bed, thrashing as she fought a magnificent, terrible dream. It began with the face of a woman, an immortal woman with unkempt hair and a perverse seductive smile.

—Catherine— Charles whispered in her mind, then pushed her onward.

. . . She wanders the streets of Paris, barefoot with her clothes in rags that reveal far too much of her body. Laughing, she begs alms from the wealthy passersby until only the desperate and the dissolute still roam the lightless streets. Then she walks through the narrow alleys, letting the coins jangling in her cup and the memory of her eyes lure her victim to her. She plays the game night after night, refusing to choose, letting her victims choose for her, devouring what fate gives her with innocent savagery . . . Hunting . . . killing . . . screaming her lonely passion to the distant stars . . .

—Catherine.—

Ayn found herself panting with excitement. Asleep yet aware, she knew the vision for what it was and the words were no surprise. —This is the woman we touched last night. She is a jealous lover. She will never allow you to share Elizabeth's love.—

"I have been loyal," Ayn said aloud. "I will not desert the countess now."

—Then you will be destroyed. Catherine, like your mistress, takes her pleasure from pain. Would you like to feel how it is to die by fire, Ayn, to have the limbs torn from your body. That is what you will experience in your mind if she heeds my call. And if she does not and the king's men take you instead, you will experience it in fact.—

"Leave me alone!" Ayn demanded, then added softly, "Otherwise, I will tell the countess that you talk to me. She will take action."

—She will do nothing. I will leave you only if you go to her now.—

Ayn did and found her mistress sitting in her usual place in front of her mirror. She was naked with her long hair covering her breasts as she brushed it herself until its blue highlights glowed in the shaft of sunlight falling through the window.

"This morning, I dreamed about her, Ayn. Isn't it wonderful that she will come for me?" As she stood and stretched in a wanton pose so at odds with her usual elegance, it occurred to Ayn that she had never seen the countess naked before. "This was how we lived in her cottage—innocent as the animals she hunted. Like Eve and Lilith before the fall. Ayn, you will love her, you won't be able to help yourself, she is so perfect."

"You sound like a child, Countess," Ayn responded carefully.

"A child?" Elizabeth laughed. "Of course I am a child. Methuselah would be a child compared to her."

— . . . You will be destroyed . . . — Were the words in her mind spoken or memory. No matter. The outcome was beyond her control.

Ayn arranged the countess's hair as she had last night. When she had finished, Dorca helped her dress in the simple white gown she had chosen. Low-cut, with flaring medieval sleeves, it fell straight from the high waist to just above the ankle. As the countess walked, her thighs and pubic cleft were visible through the thin satin fabric. It was a gown for a lover's tryst, a perfect choice for what would happen tonight.

The act demanded some ritual and so Elizabeth went first, carrying the matched short-bladed daggers crisscrossed in her open palms. Ayn followed with a pair of golden goblets, chosen because of their handles and the tight-fitting covers. Dorca, carrying the torch and washed cotton bandages Ayn had told her to hide in her dress, ended the short procession.

When they reached the cavern, only Ayn and Elizabeth entered. Dorca shut the barred doors and stood behind them. While Ayn circled the room lighting the torches, Elizabeth pulled out her key and unlocked the small metal door. Behind it was the lever that controlled the bars capping the cistern. Before she opened them, she called out to her captive, "If you try to escape or disobey me in any way, Dorca will release the cage. If the weight doesn't destroy you, you can watch your lover die."

Above him, Margueri stifled a cry. As always when the countess was present she tried to be as invisible as possible. —I can control Dorca— Charles told Margueri privately, then turned the full power of his mind on the countess. —Not an auspicious way of beginning our merging— he said, his thoughts caressing her.

"Did you think I would trust you? No, I will only let you go when Catherine comes and assures me that you will not harm me, no sooner." She separated the bars only far enough for the goblets to be exchanged while Charles listened carefully, trying to judge the strength of the levers controlling them.

—Send down a torch, Countess, so that when we drink we can see each other clearly.—

She did as he asked, lowering a pair of them in a tall metal holder. He set them in the floor, then sat and waited as the knife and goblet followed. A quick thought of escape was dismissed. The countess was holding the rope and expecting such a move. Far better to wait until the blood tie was perfect and he controlled her completely.

"Tell your servant to stand away near the door. No one should disturb our concentration now."

Ayn stepped back, her eyes narrowing less from the insult than Elizabeth's casual dismissal of it.

Charles lifted the knife in his right hand, holding his arm above the goblet. "Do as I have done," he said. "Then look at me."

She did as he asked, trying to emulate his intense expression that lent such solemnity to this sharing that no other ritual was necessary.

—Usually there is physical contact, since that it not possible, Countess, you must concentrate entirely on me. Open your mind. Feel what I do.—

Last night, he had been inside her, sharing the passion the death had given. Tonight, she was inside him, looking up at herself through his eyes, her hand moving simultaneously with his, raising the knife, slashing down through the flesh.

It amazed her that a cut so deep should cause no pain. He had stolen it, that must be the trick. Or perhaps he did not feel pain as a mortal would—she was in him, after all.

A sound grew in the room, a low steady beat of blood dripping into the cups, each tiny drip into hers echoed by his.

—Fill it, Countess. The more we exchange the more likely the union.— *And the weaker she becomes the more easily I can control the bitch,* he added to himself, sharing the hopeful thought with Margueri.

When the goblets were full, Elizabeth wove the rope through the handles of hers. The length of rope across the top held the cover in place. As it was lowered, the swaying of the rope and the glitter of the torchlight on the gold made a hypnotic effect that dizzied her. She concentrated on his eyes, on the hunger in them, on the moment soon to come.

When she had his goblet resting in her cupped palms, she breathed deeply, recalling Catherine in this sweeter more cloying scent. He did the same with hers, wondering at the familiarity of its scent. Then a single long cry, so high-pitched she would have covered her ears had her hands been free, made the cup in her hand vibrate. The cry went on, echoing in her mind long after the sound had ended, staying with them as they lifted their cups and drank.

And the cry broke into dancing prisms of light that flickered down her veins into her heart, her mind. Blinded by the rapture, she lay back, her senses folding inward to contemplate the wonder of the change, never noticing how the gates to the cistern rolled back a few inches, just far enough to let his body through.

The light faded slowly like one of the brilliant sunsets on the Alföld plains. When it was over, she felt a curious languor, a passion spent. —We must do this again, Countess— he told her.

—Now?—

—Now.—

—Death touched you. You vanquished it once, you must do so again and again until the exchange is complete. Take your knife.—

She did as he asked, stabbing again, watching the blood flow, never noticing that his own cup remained empty. She felt light-headed, faint.

—Lower it, Countess.—

Even when she did, her eyes remained focused on his or on the cup, never on the widened gap. When the rope was just within his reach, Charles leapt from his place on the floor, grabbing it and pulling hard, the sudden jerk threw Elizabeth off balance and she fell forward and would have tumbled into his arms had Ayn not grabbed her shoulders and pulled her back.

Elizabeth, still trapped by her prisoner's mind, saw only the cup overturn, the blood spill. "Fool!" she shrieked and kicked Ayn backward. Ayn fell with her body halfway across the gap at the moment that Charles made another desperate bid for freedom, flinging the lit torch upward. Had Ayn's body not deflected it, the countess's gown might have caught fire instead of the sleeve on Ayn's arm.

As Ayn rolled away from the gap and beat at the fabric with her free hand, Charles leapt upward, grabbing the rope before Elizabeth could let it go, using it and his momentum to reach the bars. His fingers hooked through them a few feet from the center opening, and as Elizabeth sensed his triumph, she pulled her will away from his control. "Dorca! Shut the grate!" she cried, stabbing at his fingers with the knife, then at his bare feet as he tried to force the lever to freeze.

But the metal gears were too strong for him. Though they groaned from his pressure, the grate rolled shut. Desperate, Charles lowered his feet and attempted the final reach for the center. The sudden release of pressure snapped the grate shut, pinning his hand between the closing points. With a cry of agony, he ripped it free and fell.

Ayn's soft moans were drowned by Elizabeth's voice. Shrieking his name, screaming for Catherine, she used the hearth shovel to send a shower of coals through the grate, beating the largest ones through with the back of the shovel. "When Catherine comes, she will tell me how to destroy you," she screamed down at Charles.

"Elizabeth," Ayn whispered and stifled a sob.

Elizabeth looked down at her lover. One arm and both of Ayn's hands were deeply blistered and the side of her face had a long ragged cut from the pointed metal bars of the cistern grate. "Open the gates, Dorca," she called to her servant. "Then take Ayn to her room and tend to her burns."

She waited until the women had gone, then spit into the cistern. "Liar!" she screamed. "Until Catherine comes, I will not look on your face again."

Willing her mind calmer, more frigid than she had ever imagined it could be, Elizabeth walked slowly from the room, the blood flowing from her wrist leaving long dark streaks on her skirt.

CHAPTER
21

I

In the High Tatra region of the Beskid Mountains, retreating Alpine glaciers had formed great crevasses in the rock, an interconnected chain of caves that twisted for miles into the remote peaks. Sudden drop-offs and inland lakes made these unexplorable and the few travelers that happened on them would stand at the entrances and stare into the impenetrable darkness, then, reminded of the oncoming night, depart.

Some travelers were merely cautious. Others might be heeding the tale of the demon that had claimed this darkness, of the nights when an unsuspecting journeyer would hear the wails flowing through the cracks in the mountain—screams of agony, shrieks of desire.

And others might never leave these mountains again for this was Catherine's home, the darkness a labyrinthine web that held her slaves with more surety than any bars could accomplish.

She chose her victims carefully now. Children were too frail and far too much trouble. Those too easily excited would soon fall into madness in the demanding emptiness of her dwelling. But the strong, the stoic, and the beautiful found themselves admitted to a world beyond their imagining.

She would take them on the route she had first followed through her mind. They were carried down into the mountain on a winding path through the darkness, tossed across a chasm where water pounded rocks far below, then were lifted and carted once again. Their only anchor was the body holding them, their only comfort the strength of her grasp, the brush of her soft hair, the warm musky scent of her skin. Usually, they never saw her face until the light grew in their final abode. Then, through eyes tearing from the sudden light, they would look at her in wonder and later examine their prison with as much awe. And once they knew the comforting brilliance of that single room, they could not leave it for the perilous blackness of the lower caves.

Catherine lived in the hugest of the chambers—a great room beneath a smooth rock chimney that rose to the top of the peak. On the ledges close to the floor, she had wedged sections of her Austra window in no particular order and disjointed pieces of St. Lucy threw soothing rainbows of light on prisoners and jailer alike.

Those who failed to please Catherine were killed or simply abandoned in the deep crevasses to die from thirst and starvation. Those who won her favor lived longer. They slept beside her on the thick straw and feather bed with the satin coverlets, their bodies always ready for her use. If they were wise, they worshiped her. In exchange, they had crystalline water to drink from golden goblets, tiny fish with blind milky eyes served raw on plates of silver and glass. For an infrequent privileged slave, she even scavenged, bringing back fruit and vegetables, occasional sweets and wine. When, as she sometimes did, she found herself obsessed with her victim's comfort, she would kill the favored one for she had no desire to ever love a mortal again.

She had lived this way for thirty-five years. She was prepared to continue on in her loneliness for centuries more when Charles made his first desperate call.

She had been hunting for her latest favorite in the settled region of Vazec when the cry reached her. She had always expected Charles to someday seek her and would not have been surprised to find him waiting for her outside her lair or catching her unawares at its center. But never had she expected that faint cry for help from one of the most powerful of her kin. She paused and stared up at the stars, sifting through the images the brief contact had evoked, trying to determine which were real.

Darkness. Pain. Charles. Elizabeth.

Elizabeth.

She had thrust the images from her mind. The call had held

no more substance than a fantasy, after all. Picking up her sack of apples, hard cheese, and sweet mead stolen from some petty noble's larder, she completed the climb to her lair and the night like so many other perfect nights before it.

It began to storm as she reached her lair, great sheets of water that puddled and fell from one window section to another filling the rock pool in the center of Catherine's chamber. She snapped her fingers and pointed at the rising water and Selim rushed to fill the drinking bottles. As always, he avoided all but the quickest glance at her, keeping his eyes downcast, afraid of the shameful passion a direct look at her would reveal.

She had picked him for those eyes—magnificent amber flecked with green and dark lashes so long they seemed to brush his cheeks when he slept. Like the other Iranian Shiites in his company, he had been shamefully treated by his Turkish captors, enough that the group had risked escape and somehow made their way into the Beskids where they lived as outlaws.

Catherine had watched them for days before she made her choice, paralyzing Selim, stealing his voice, and carrying him away while the others slept. At the river that flowed from her mountain, she had stripped off his filthy clothing and ordered him to bathe before she carried him inside. In the weeks that followed, she had grown too attached to him. Perhaps she would kill him tonight.

She unlaced the black cotton suit, one of many the seamstress had made for her before she devoured the woman. Loose-fitting folds covered her from neck to ankle. The hooded collar could be raised and tied to cover everything but her eyes, making her nearly invisible as she moved through the trees. Stepping out of the garment, she unbound her hair, letting it fall freely over her shoulders.

—Selim, look at me.—

He did as she asked. It was better to always do as she asked than to feel the pain her mind inflicted when he disobeyed.

She brushed past him and stepped into the pool, holding out a jeweled hand for him to kiss. "Join me, Selim," she said. "And tell me what you are thinking."

"You know that already."

"Tell me, in your own words. Do not lie."

He sat across from her, his eyes still locked with hers, unable

to look away until she allowed it. "I am thinking that you are
beautiful and frightening like the golden sword my Turkish
master kept mounted beside his bed."

"Do you wish you were with him now?"

"Yes. He had to drug me to use me. You need only look at
me and I do whatever you desire."

She laughed and touched the side of his face, noting how
his eyes closed though he did not try to pull away. Loathing
and rapture; such was the perfection of his captivity. "Go and
light a candle, Selim. Then dry yourself and we will . . ."

Her voice grew soft before the words stopped altogether.
Her eyes focused on the air, her dark brows furrowed with
concentration.

Selim stood at the edge of the pool, afraid to move and
disturb her. "What was it?" he asked when her eyes focused
on him once again.

"Nothing," she replied, her teeth white and moist as she
smiled.

But though she could lie to him or even to herself the blood
tie to her family was too strong to dismiss completely. The cry
she had heard earlier had roused her instinct. The pain she had
felt was real.

And as she pressed her long body against Selim's compact
muscular one, she thought of what it would be like to touch one
of her own again and found herself responding with surprising
longing.

II

Margueri's cage was lowered and opened twice daily so that
she could leave it, stretch, and eat. Dorca and Ficzko were
always present to prevent any chance of escape. Usually the
countess came as well but no other servants entered the room
holding the special prize trapped in its metal lined cell.

In spite of the energy he had used to reach Catherine,
the lives Charles had devoured could sustain him for days.
However, thirst soon became a nagging problem. Margueri
would have shared the water given her but she never had an
opportunity to drop the cup. In desperation, she finally kicked

the water bucket toward the cistern, then watched sadly as the thin stream flowed away from the grate. She would have swept the water toward him, but Dorca kicked her away and she fell on top of the grate, looking through the tiny holes at the pale oval of his face so far beneath her.

—If I were truly in need, Margueri, the countess would give me water. She would have no choice.—

Nonetheless, he sounded thankful for what she had tried to do and she took some comfort from that as she was pushed back into her metal cage and raised above the cistern once again. Then, as always, the bars leading to the chamber shut, the torches burned their last, and the pair were left in darkness. When Elizabeth came again, she brought only a small cup of water and watched Margueri every moment that she drank.

In the endless hours that followed each visit, Margueri and Charles spoke very little. It seemed odd to Margueri that the gulf between them should grow rather than diminish now that they faced true adversity together. Her fantasies had hardened into a painful reality that made even her memories shameful. Perhaps he sensed this, she thought. Or perhaps his silence was a deliberate means of hiding precisely how much he needed what her body could give.

"Charles," she finally called when the darkness had become so pressing that she needed more companionship than this shared misery. "Charles, are you all right?"

—Please, Margueri. Your voice is like the smell of fresh baked bread to a starving man.—

"Charles . . ."

—Or ripe apricots.— He started to laugh.

Cramped and desolate, Margueri tried to bear her nagging pain as stoically as possible, thankful for those infrequent moments when his mind brushed hers helping her to sleep.

By the end of the second week Charles felt true hunger as well as thirst. By the end of the third, he began to search for life. He would have waited longer but his instincts were beginning to center on survival, already less concerned with escape than sustenance. Given his immortality, the second was infinitely more important than the first.

Life was all around him but because of the small size of the holes in the metal grate over his prison, only the most insignificant creatures could reach him. He concentrated on these and soon a thin trickle of mice began their journey down the passages of the Cachtice cellars.

A woman screamed as they passed by her cell, a second yelled for the guards but he continued to call until the floor above him was carpeted with rodents drawn from the passages of the Cachtice cellars. A handful of the tiniest squeezed through the holes in the grate. The others swarmed above him, nipping one another, digging at the metal with their teeth and paws until, responding to his shriek of rage, they began tearing one another's flesh, sending down a sparse dark rain of blood. Charles stripped off his clothes, licking the salty drops from his arms and legs, running his tongue along the rough metal of the floor. When the strongest pangs of hunger finally subsided, Charles sent his sustenance scurrying for the safety of the deepest cisterns. Later, he would call them again.

But the dead remained, and when the countess came to feed Margueri, she saw them, dropped the food, and screamed for her servants. They came and, following her orders, began bricking up one of the two passages into the room. Others built a frame on the second and pounded in heavy metal loops.

Margueri gripped her bars and tried to see Charles through the darkness and the grate, then whispered his name, her voice full of apology for calling to him.

—Hush, Margueri. The metal is only to secure the door. The countess does not intend to let you die.—

As he said this, he knew the countess's intent would make no difference. Margueri would die anyway unless he made the sacrifice now. "You!" he called to Dorca who was feeding the other prisoners. "Tell your mistress I wish to speak to her."

Dorca put down the kettle and walked to the barred door. "She will not come," Dorca called.

"Then tell her that the castle will burn around her. Shall I show you how I can do that?"

Dorca would have laughed but one of her hands twitched, then the arm began moving upward, her fingers ready to claw at her own eyes.

Dorca had taken a breath to scream when he let her go. "Tell the countess what I did," he said.

Though Dorca was half-insane with fear as she babbled the story of what had happened, Elizabeth refused to go. Instead she sat at her mirror, ignoring the shaking woman, opening her mind to her captive. "If you wish to speak, come to me." She said the thought aloud.

The response was faint, forced. She wondered if he had really grown that weak or if this was some trick to lure her to him.

—You must move Margueri's cage. If she stays where she is, I will force her to open her veins so that I may consume her.—

The countess only smiled, noting how pretty she looked today.

—Another life will give me weeks of sustenance. Do you have that time, Countess?—

"You are keeping my enemies away."

—After I kill her, I will summon an army to your gates. Move her. I may not be able to make this request again.—

Then he left her as abruptly as he had come. Elizabeth sat as she had for hours, twining her hair around her fingers, then letting it fall. Annika could do it so perfectly. Annika could do everything so well. But Ayn was wounded; she might even die. Without her solid presence, Elizabeth felt adrift and helpless, a boat with a broken mast.

And the waters had become so stormy. She searched her memories, trying to think of anything Catherine had told her that could help her. But Catherine had never revealed the slightest sign of weakness or affection for anyone but her and had never spoken of her past so Elizabeth had only legends and her wits to guide her now.

"Dorca," she called to the woman still standing beside the door. "Bring me the red-haired woman from Piestany, the one who said she could do hair. And bathe her first, those cellars have such a dank smell."

She waited until the servant had gone, then returned to studying her reflection. "If her death is on my conscience, Charles Austra, it will hardly be the first."

III

The next time she slept, Margueri dreamed that she had died. It was not the horrible experience she had expected; rather, a kind of slow painless drift down and down into nothingness.

Compared to the world she had known for the last five weeks, death was even comforting and for a moment when she woke, she mourned.

But the soft drifting continued, the motion increasing as she tried to push herself to a sitting position.

Her cage was swinging, the uncontrollable rocking of her body providing the thrust. She tried to force herself to be rigid and still but her efforts did not stop her.

Had she somehow become suicidal, driven insane by the darkness and the dull agony? Driven, she thought. The exact word.

"Charles," she called softly and received no reply.

"Charles!" she screamed his name now, realizing what caused the sway.

No response. With only their past to guide her, she rubbed her wrist across one of the points, letting the blood drip through the grate to his waiting lips. The bond tightened. She felt the full measure of his hunger, then his apology as the swaying slowed.

"It's all right," she said. "Perhaps it's even best that I stay here. They give me enough to eat. I can share my life with you."

—It won't be enough. I will kill you and it still won't be enough. The distance diminishes the potency of what you give.—

"Distance means nothing if the emotion is strong enough. Force what you must out of me. Go beyond the pain of our nights in Rouen. I owe you that much."

—Margueri, I came here of my own free will, fighting all the warnings of my instincts because I care for you. If I did not, I would still be in Rouen and you would most likely be dead. No, I will not knowingly destroy your sanity to appease my hunger, not as long as I have any control.—

The cage shook above him. Drops fell on his arm. He licked her tears as he had her blood. Using all the power he still possessed, he called to his captor. —For whatever decency you possess to my family, Countess, take Margueri away!—

He heard the echo of her vocal laughter in her reply. —I thought you wouldn't ask again.—

—Your servants will impale themselves if I demand it. And you will die before I call to Catherine again.—

The threat worked. Elizabeth came with her servants and, ignoring Margueri's protests, pulled her from her cage and shackled one of her arms to a short length of chain attached to a loop beside the main door. Though she never looked down at her prisoner, she did speak to him once, just before she left. "Margueri will be fed through the hole in the door. She will live and you will starve and you will call for Catherine. You have no choice anymore."

Then there was only darkness and a silence broken by the distant thunder of Margueri's pulse. "I love you," she whispered to him after a long while.

"Pity, isn't it?" Charles replied, not caring if she heard.

IV

In the weeks since she had been wounded, Ayn tossed in her bed, her arm slowly healing, her mind wandering through blood-drenched dreams until the delirium passed and she managed to wake. Her legs barely held her as she staggered across her room to the long mirror on her wall, lighting the candles with her good hand, arranging them on the bench beneath it before daring to look at the reflection.

The damage was even worse that she had expected. Bits of hair had been burned from one side of her scalp and the scarring there would make new growth impossible. The cut on her cheek was longer and broader than she'd expected and an angry red keloid had formed over part of it making her smile ugly and uneven. Worst of all, the tissue on her hand had thickened as it healed. She would never be able to bend her fingers again.

Elizabeth loathed deformity. Elizabeth would never love her again.

If she ever truly had.

A terrible thought, perhaps not even her own. In a voice so soft it could scarcely be called a whisper, she said his name, "Charles?"

The reply was faint, strained in a way that made her think of the flesh on her burned fingers when she tried to bend them.
—Was Martin the name of your beloved, Ayn?— he asked.

"Yes," she replied, more softly than before.

—Would you like to know how he died?—

She pressed her arms over her ears as if she could shut out his words. "No," she whispered.

—Klara Bathori drugged you that first night, remember? Then yes, she and her cousin offered Martin a gold piece in exchange for his promised wife. Do you want to know what they did to him when he refused to take it?—

"I will ask Elizabeth. She will tell me the truth."

—Silently, Ayn. Go to her now.—

Perhaps it was her weakness that made her listen. Perhaps it was her own terrible doubt. Unlike the other sleeping rooms, hers was not locked and she walked as softly as she was able across the hall to the countess's room and pushed open the door.

A fire burned in the room's tiny hearth. Elizabeth lay sprawled on a divan in front of it, one hand moving lightly over the bare shoulders of a thin dark-haired girl Ayn had never seen before, kissing her, murmuring endearments. Ayn might have felt some pangs of jealousy but she saw the handle of the knife sticking out from beneath a pillow, waiting for its familiar use.

She kills the women who love her. What would she do to the sex she despises?

Martin. Ayn mouthed the name and retreated as softly as she came.

In her room, staring as her ruined reflection, she dared to ask, "If I free you will you promise to go and leave us in peace?"

—Peace . . . — She heard soft laughter trickling through the response staying with her for the hours she lay, feigning sleep, listening to the silence. After the bell had been rung and the servants had dragged away the body of Elizabeth's latest victim, she still waited until she was certain Elizabeth would be asleep. Then, stealing into the countess's room, she lifted the mirror and found the keys attached to the back.

Carrying a cased candle, she worked her way to the top of the stairs leading to the cellars. There her legs failed her and she slid her body from one to the other until, at the bottom, she dared to try to walk again.

There was only one way into the chamber where Charles was kept and she was not surprised to find the guard absent. She saw the marks where he had tried to pry through the metal and understood that the best means to keep the captive trapped was to be certain he was always alone.

The door had been forced shut and Ayn had to lean all her weight against it to open it far enough to wedge herself between the bars and the wall. Her ruined hand cracked from the effort, leaving a bloodstain on the stones as she forced her body through, then leaned against the stone wall, looking for the strength to go on. She found it in the gleam of hope in Margueri's eyes.

The candle had burned nearly to its base by the time she pushed the smaller key into the tiny door on the wall. But though the key fit, it would not turn. She tried to force it until the soft metal casting began to bend.

"I expected someone to betray me. I never thought it would be you, Ayn."

Ayn whirled and saw the countess standing behind her, her face twisted with rage. She wore her brown wool gown, her killing dress, and she carried the same knife Ayn had seen in her chambers some hours before.

"Would you want me as I am?" Ayn asked, turning her head to show the scar, holding out her ruined hand.

"Annika," the countess sobbed her name. "When you nearly died, I tended you. I wrapped your fingers. I put the wet bandages against your face. Annika, no matter what the deformity, I love you. I would be lost without you."

Ayn held out her arms and moved closer to Elizabeth. "I am so sorry that . . ."

The knife slashed upward, glancing off her ribs. Ayn reeled back, betrayal etched on her face. This was the end. No matter what happened now, this was the end. She turned as Elizabeth slashed at her again, the blade falling on air as Ayn rushed toward the cistern. If she was to die now, she would have one small victory.

"Ayn!" Elizabeth screamed, following her. She would have pulled her back but Ayn had laced her fingers through the metal grate of Charles's prison and used what strength remained to hold on while Elizabeth stabbed her in the places where the blood would not flow onto Charles's waiting lips.

Finally, when Ayn was too weak to hold on any longer, Elizabeth saw her final revenge. She placed Ayn lengthwise against the grate and, taking the good key from her pocket, opened the cistern gates just far enough for Ayn to fall through. "Call to Catherine," she said as she watched her lover fall.

When Charles caught Ayn, she was nearly dead and for that he mourned, not out of any concern for her but for himself. He would prefer to keep her alive for as long as possible. Given the countess's resolve when she left the chamber, Ayn would be the last meal he saw until he was freed.

And as the countess knew, his last chance for any real call for help.

He ran his fingers over Ayn's chest, listening to her heart, feeling her pulse weaken. He lifted her head with one arm to make her breathing easier.

Her soul seemed more wounded than the body dying around it. This surprised him. He had expected some anger for the countess's callous betrayal, some outward sign of hate.

"I need your help now," he whispered, waiting for her understanding before continuing. "We must summon Catherine. I must have your help."

"Help?"

"I need the love you still hold for her. I will use it to call."

"No pain?" she asked. There had been so much pain already.

—No pain. And I will stay with you until the end— he said as gently as his hunger would allow, then moved his arm lower so her head hung back, her neck stretched and waiting. His lips ran the side of it, sensing the strongest pulse for the single deep lethal bite. With Ayn nearly dead already, he would have to devour her life quickly or the blood would be useless to him.

He drank their affection, their years together, their passion, their love. His, Catherine's, Ayn's, Elizabeth's—the memories blended so perfectly together. Ayn responded first with confusion, then with all the force of her devotion.

—Please— she called to Catherine. —Please. She will be so lonely without anyone to love her! Come back!—

This wasn't enough. His instincts sensed the deceit at the root of her call, the doubt that diminished its strength. With effort, he thrust all the agony from his past into his victim.

Ayn was bathed in fire, a fire so terrible that she managed a weak, strangled cry before he grasped her mind completely.

Then, with all the power his mind still possessed, he channeled that betrayal into one final, desperate cry.

—Catherine!— he screamed alone at the moment of Ayn's death. —Catherine! Come back to her!—

CHAPTER
22

I

Two weeks before the Long Night celebration would begin in Cailly, a terrible vision pulled Matthew from his deep dawn slumber. His hands were clenched, his palms bloody from his nails, and his teeth had left deep wounds on the inside of one arm. His mind instinctively moved through the house, touching each of the servants. They still slept. He had not screamed.

At first he thought he'd had a dream, perhaps of his attack so long ago, though after so many years with the memory so deeply buried he hardly expected it to surface now. But as he lay with his eyes closed and his mind focused on the nightmare, he saw that he was not the victim. No, his father lay at his feet and Matthew supplied the bodies, holding their wounds against his father's mouth so that he could drink. Even so, he felt his father's life slipping further, ever further from his mental grasp.

His mind had never assaulted him quite this horribly before. He could never return to sleep now nor, given the hour, seek out his uncle and explain what had happened. Instead, with his mind still racing, he opened a book of poetry by Lope de Vega and attempted to occupy his time.

The distraction did not work. Like a demanding wound that needed life to heal, the vision kept returning, the reason for its persistence just beyond his grasp. Eventually Matthew put down the book and concentrated fully on making sense out of his abrupt derangement.

By the time he reached AustraGlass, he thought he had some insight into the cause. When he sought out his uncle, Steffen quickly noted his agitation and the early hour. —My office?— he asked privately.

Matthew nodded and followed him. There, with bewilderment clear in his expression, Matthew told Steffen what had happened and asked his advice.

"Questions of instinct can never be answered easily, Matthew," Steffen responded, pride evident in his tone.

"If this is instinct, I wish it would go away and never trouble me again," he confessed.

"It will as soon as you understand what the vision means and act accordingly."

Matthew considered all the possible meanings of his nightmare. Only one felt right, though it troubled him to admit it. "My father is in danger. Though I received no cry for help, I know this is true. I believe I have been sensing this for a long time," he said.

"Then you must go to him, yes?"

Half order. Half question. "What?" Matthew asked, astonished. He had been prepared for a lengthy argument.

"If you would rather not go, I will."

Steffen's tone had become urgent. "What is it?" Matthew said.

"The strength of what you experienced. And the fact that you never felt anything like it before."

Matthew nodded. "I will go," he said and immediately felt the gloomy vision lift from him.

"If you travel on foot through the nights, you can be in Vienna in just a few days."

"Steffen, what would happen if I did not act on what I saw?"

"That vision would be a part of your every slumber. Eventually it would invade your waking moments. If the reason was compelling enough, you would have no choice but to end the torment and obey. Now, answer this question if you can. Could you wait until after the solstice to leave?"

Matthew considered this and felt the first faint stirrings inside him. "No," he said.

"A day or two?"

"I'm not certain . . . perhaps," Matthew answered. "Is there any reason I should?"

"None at all. Don't wait for this vision to come again. Leave for Vienna tonight."

Steffen pulled a box from his desk, undid the hidden latch, and counted out two dozen Viennese gold coins. "This will save you any need for exchange. May your journey be easier than the vision that ordered you to it," he said, dropping them into Matthew's hand. "I shared the womb with Charles yet I did not sense this danger. Do not shirk from doing all that must be done." For a moment, his eyes fixed on the amber pendant hanging from Matthew's neck and they both thought of Matthew's mother, the sadness replaced with a new and hopeful pride.

I am being entrusted with my father's life. My mind is stronger than anyone suspected, Matthew thought, *least of all me.*

II

Matthew arrived in Vienna in the middle of the night. Barefoot, his loose dark clothes filthy and dotted with burrs, he stole into James's room with the same silence he had displayed when he scaled the city wall less than an hour before. He roused his cousin with the brush of his mind, then conveyed, as succinctly as possible, what force had drawn him here with such haste.

James padded across the room to his cupboard, pulling out a bottle of water, and poured his cousin a glass before responding gruffly, "Well, you're not the only one looking for Charles. Margueri was in Vienna as well."

"Was?" Matthew could not hide his amazement.

"She has left. I was leaving for Cailly tomorrow night. When I arrived, I intended to ask about her."

—Ask!— Matthew did not dare utter the word lest he wake the house. He could well imagine Monique Vernet's reaction to James's inquiry.

"I haven't seen her for some weeks. The servants tell me that some of her clothes are missing."

"You lost her?" Matthew ran his fingers through his hair, suppressing the thought that he faced an idiot fifteen centuries older than himself.

"If something unlikely had happened to her, I would have heard of it."

"Has she written?"

"Not to me. I sent letters on to Charles but none of them were in her hand."

"And my father? Where is he now?"

"When last he wrote, he was in Sopron finishing Count Nemeth's summer house on the edge of Neusiedler Lake. He intended to go directly from there to the keep and spend the winter with the Old One."

"How far to Sopron?"

"Two hours' run but he's most likely gone by now."

Matthew finished his water, handing his glass to James. "I'm going anyway. Don't give up the solstice to wait for me." He stood, resting his hand on the table a moment too long.

This strong a weariness, as James well knew, could quickly lead to exhaustion and the dawn, with the lethargy it always brought, was only hours away. "Two hours' run unless you are already spent. How long did it take you to travel from Vienna?" he asked.

"Six days."

"A difficult trip. Rest today. Leave for Sopron at dusk."

If he had only been seeking his father, Matthew would have happily done so. But now Margueri was involved and her danger might be far too immediate. He shook his head.

"My servants could provide for your needs."

"I want to reach my father by morning. If I grow too hungry, I'll hunt."

"Matthew, I am sorry," James said, the words reluctantly but sincerely spoken. He held out his arms. "Let me help you."

A surprising invitation but a welcome one. As they held each other, Matthew began to drink, the sweet family blood renewing him as nothing else could. "I'll think of you often," James said with as much concern as one Austra adult would display to another.

Then Matthew was off, his hands and feet pounding the spongy lowland ground as he headed for the lakeshore and Sopron. He reached it just before dawn, then, from the shelter of a stand of trees on the far side of the planned garden, let his mind move through the finished wings of the stone summer house. He searched long after he knew that his father had gone.

The sun was rising, the familiar dawn lethargy nearly impossible to resist. His body screamed for shelter and sleep and food. He would have retreated into the woods and found a shaded place for his morning rest but the gardeners coming to work had already spied him. He waved and, with difficulty, plodded to the house. Once in the entrance hall where he waited to speak to Count Nemeth, he fell onto the nearest chair.

By the time Count Nemeth joined him, Matthew was half-asleep. The count noted his muddy boots, his torn clothing. "We'll speak later," he said to Matthew, then motioned to a servant. "Help him to his kinsman's room, then get him some food and water and stay with him until he dismisses you."

As the man obeyed, the count returned to his own room, dressed, and crossed the hall to where Matthew had been taken.

As he expected, he found Matthew in an exhausted sleep. The servant sat with his head resting on the table in an equally deep slumber. The count noted the marks on the back of the man's neck, then the drops of blood on the pillow. Moving as silently as he was able, the count went to the table and rested his fingertips between the two small wounds, then without a word turned and left.

At dusk, Matthew was summoned to the spacious room the count used as an office while the work was being done. Count Nemeth did not ask him to sit so Matthew stood in the center of the room and stared evenly at the count hoping his eyes could show him what his mind was still too exhausted to try and claim. Fortunately, Count Nemeth came directly to the point.

He unlocked the box on his desk and pulled out the letters Charles had left with him, giving them to Matthew. "Charles Austra asked my advice, I assumed that he had taken it. Now I suspect that he may have gone to Cachtice." He waited until Matthew had read the letters, then asked, "Perhaps you will tell me why a man would be willing to face so powerful a killer without telling anyone where he had gone? A foolish thing to do, and whatever else Charles Austra may be, he is no fool." He stressed the words *whatever else* slightly and now stood staring at Matthew as if expecting some reply.

"Please explain what interest you have in this matter," Matthew responded.

"He entrusted me with these letters. I don't think I need reveal any more."

The count spoke the truth, nonetheless Matthew stood with his head slightly tilted, waiting.

"Very well," the count said with an exasperated sigh. "There is something I wish to show you."

He led Matthew to his dressing rooms and opened what seemed like a closet door. But instead of a closet, the count led him into a room about two meters square. Every wall contained three floor-to-ceiling mirrors giving the clearest reflection Matthew had ever seen. As Matthew stood, marveling at the cost of such vanity, the count continued.

"Charles shared an abhorrence for filth and vermin equal to my own. He never smelled of old sweat. When he wasn't working his clothes were always spotless. He could be more meticulous about fashion though I suppose my own inclinations are too strong in that area. Still, as Charles so often noted, he does not have the degrading social demands of the Hungarian nobility. Here I am, omnipotent in my domain and I still can trust no one with my grooming." He unhooked the corner mirrors and pulled them inward on their hinges until Matthew had a view of himself from every angle. "People are amazed at my perfection. Now I've given away my little secret. Under the circumstances, I trust you will keep it."

"Circumstances?"

"I can see the back of my head, Matthew Austra. I first noted the two odd marks at the hairline on the nape of my neck a few days after your kinsman came here. I made mention of them in my diary as I do all strange physical changes in my person. I noted that they also shrank, then grew larger some days later. At that time, I measured how far apart they were." The count held up a hand, the palm toward Matthew. "I have unfortunate hands, far too large at the knuckles, far too flat at the tips. They belong on a laborer, not an aristocrat, but they do serve one function. Those marks that so concerned me were exactly two and a half fingers wide. The night you came here, my servant acquired two wounds in the same place and nearly the same distance apart. Would you tell me what this means, Matthew Austra?"

Matthew looked down at his hands, smiled, and said nothing. His father had a true talent for choosing the most cunning companions.

"And I note that you share his mannerisms. In the weeks

that he worked here, I don't think I ever saw beyond Charles Austra's front teeth."

"Could we speak of this elsewhere?" Matthew asked. The myriad of reflections were beginning to make him dizzy.

"As you wish." They returned to Matthew's room where the count poured himself a glass of wine from the carafe on the table. "It was the best I could offer, someone ought to drink it," he said with a smirk, then motioned for Matthew to join him at the table. "I don't enjoy being manipulated or deceived, Matthew Austra, but for your kinsman's sake, I am willing to forgive. No one spies on this room. I saw to that when it was built. All you need do is answer yes or no to one question and I will ask nothing else. Do the Mountain Lords exist?"

"Yes," Matthew answered evenly.

After a long silence the count said, "If Charles did go to Cachtice, we must go to Bytca for him."

"You need not trouble yourself."

"Trouble?" Nemeth laughed. "I enjoy being in the center of the storm. Life is so tedious elsewhere. Now rest one more night before we travel to Bytca together."

It would be wrong to go Bytca, Matthew knew, though he could think of no rational reason not to accompany Count Nemeth at least as far as Cachtice. For a moment, he recalled the past, the keep, Catherine.

It didn't surprise him. He thought of her so often now.

This time the thought was not a fleeting one. Her face, perfectly recalled in his memory, had a new background—a place he had never seen before but which he knew was no more than a few nights' run from Bytca. He would let Count Nemeth deliver the letters to Thurzo and he would go on alone to find her. He did not know the part she played in this matter, only that her presence was crucial to his father's safety.

He told the count of his decision to leave as they rode out of Sopron with the count's guards. "It will take you five days of hard riding to reach Bytca," he said. "I don't think I have five days to spare."

"If your kinsman faced that Bathori woman alone and has been trapped, what makes you think you will have better luck?" Count Nemeth asked him.

"I'm not going into Cachtice alone," Matthew responded. Noting the unspoken question in the count's expression, he added, "I don't know where I am going but there is someone I must find."

The count made a long breathy "ahh" of understanding. "The legends speak of instinct. Of course, you must go."

"I would like to leave after dark. I did not want to wait to tell you since there are only three guards. If you were counting on my protection . . ."

"Your protection!" The count laughed honestly. "I have a sword and dagger and I am deadly with both of them. No one will touch us. No one will dare."

The count had sounded too relieved to be rid of him, Matthew thought that evening as he began the first of his night runs. He had sensed some danger from Nemeth but the man had been unwittingly bound to silence and Matthew's instincts were quiet so perhaps it was only the count's overestimation of his own cunning that troubled him—along with the fact that favors from the powerful usually demanded a high price.

No matter. Matthew was certain that Count Nemeth would go to Bytca and present the letters. Before Thurzo acted on them, his father and Margueri had to be freed. Matthew quickened his pace, leaving widely spaced prints in the early October dusting of snow.

The snowfall grew steadily heavier, the wind blew harder, and what had begun as an easy three-night run stretched to a difficult five before Matthew reached the high peaks north and west of Cachtice. With no real destination in mind save this area itself, he lay in the shelter of a close stand of pines, slowed his breathing, and called to her.

At first the only response was the hissing of the wind through the long needles above him, but then he heard her voice, muffled it seemed by the storm, more irritated than curious at his intrusion. Not certain how long she would tolerate the contact, he quickly told her why he had come.

—You sense your father's need?— she responded scornfully. —What does a child, not even first born, know of instinct?—

Certain his anger would make her refusal more likely, he broke the bond and lay as he had been, half-asleep and waiting for her to make the next move. In the hours that followed, the air grew colder and the storm howled its innocent rage to the peaks around him.

Catherine surprised him by coming to him in person. Perhaps she wished to guard her lair, he thought. If he were her, he might do the same. She wore thin black lace as the only covering from the storm. Her body was pale beneath it and when she stood still, she took on the shape of snow on windswept rocks. She did not look at him as she spoke and he thought he understood that too. She wanted no reminders of home until her decision was made. "I have also sensed your father calling and another as well," she said, her eyes focused on the distant peaks.

"I need your help," Matthew responded.

"*He* needs my help, you mean. Why should I give it when he abandoned me?"

Their perspectives were too skewed for Matthew to understand her words let alone answer.

"I thought he cared for me but when I was banished all he talked of was seeing me settled as if I were a child with no power of my own to support me. Never once did he say he would go with me. I've lived well enough without him . . . without any of you."

Her fingers were curled. He wondered if she intended to attack him as she had his father and forced himself to stand his ground, watchful and waiting. "He is being held in Cachtice Castle by the Countess Elizabeth Bathori," he said, not certain why he spoke the words.

Catherine's expression froze. For the first time, she looked at him directly and he saw the loss in her eyes, not for her family but for someone else. Insight came quickly, as strong as the night he had first seen his father in his dreams, but before he could speak Catherine turned and ran. Resigned, he began his lonely journey to Cachtice. The storm gave no sign of abating and he still had three long hours to dawn and sleep.

III

Madame Eva Karoli stood in a bedroom of her brother's estate near Vazec preparing for bed. Though the rest of the family was still awake, she had finished a difficult journey from Bratislava the day before. In the last hours they had abandoned the coach and ridden the remaining miles on horseback, outrunning the worst of the storm. Once Eva had been an expert horsewoman but now, at her age, the vertebrae in her back felt fused by the hard ride, her arches ached from the stirrups, and she needed hours of extra rest.

Eva was brushing out her thin grey hair when she saw the shadow slip through the window and into her room. With a sincere smile of welcome, she turned and held out her arms, kissing a willowy girl on the cheek. "Oh, it's you. I should have been expecting your visit, I suppose."

Though snowflakes still dotted her long dark curls, the girl's feet were bare. A band of exquisite black lace showed beneath the dark traveling cloak she wore. At their first meeting, Eva had assumed that the pale Gypsy girl was a servant. Now the mistake no longer mattered.

Eva Karoli knew nothing about the girl except her name, Catherine, and that Catherine looked forward to their meetings and the time when they would sit and briefly discuss the newest changes in the cities—religion and politics first, then the more interesting world of manners and fashion. Eva never spoke of these visits to anyone, sensing without being told that the charming child-woman would never visit her again should their secret be shared.

Now, as always, Eva was content to lie back on her bed and watch Catherine circle the room, fingering the heavy velvet of Eva's new gown before lifting the sleeves to note their cut. Afterward, with Catherine at her feet, rubbing away the aches, Eva recalled every detail of court. Unlike her own family who merely tolerated her presence, the girl never tired of listening to her. *You could visit me publicly sometime,* she thought petulantly, surprised to see a spark of mischief dance in Catherine's eyes.

"What do you know of the Countess Elizabeth Bathori?" Catherine asked in a deceptively casual tone.

Eva frowned. Catherine had never asked so direct a question before and the countess was the last person she wished to discuss. With a tinge of fear, she wondered if Catherine knew her. "She is in great difficulty. At court there are terrible rumors about her. They say that she murdered the little Countess Zichy." Catherine's expression goaded her on. "Why? She kills her servants, that's why they suspect her. They say she has not been sane for years."

"What do you think, madame?"

"I have known her a long time though hardly very well. She never recovered from her husband's death, that's what I think. Six years, yes, that's how long he's been gone."

Catherine continued kneading Eva's foot.

"They had four children but the youngest died when she was just a child. The other girls married, the son lives in Sarvar with his teacher instead of with his mother. Isn't that odd? They say it's odd at court, anyway.

"Ursula Nadasdy? She died. Anna Bathori? Dead also. Why do you look so surprised? The Countess Elizabeth must be fifty though she hardly looks it. Do I talk to her? I suppose I could though with her standing we hardly move in the same social circles. I *could*, of course, especially now that no one else does but I admit that I'm frightened of her."

"Where does the Countess Elizabeth live?"

"At Cachtice north of Trencin, though I can't imagine why. A piece of rock surrounded by wilderness, that's all it is."

Catherine lowered the woman's feet to the bed and covered them with a blanket. "Are you going so soon?" Eva asked. "You just got here."

When Catherine reached the door, Eva thought of one final item. "Wait! I have something for you." She went to the cupboard and drew out a dress of wine-colored velvet so dark it almost seemed black in the dim candlelight. The flared sleeves had wide cuffs of black Spanish lace.

Catherine lifted it from her arms, pressed it against her lithe body, lovingly fingering the soft fabric. "You had this made for me?" she asked incredulously as if no one had given her a gift before.

"For my niece. I didn't tell her that when I showed it to her because she'll take whatever is given. She hated the color, the neckline was too low, the waist too high. She was right, of course. It would look terrible on her. I must have been thinking of you when I ordered it. I think of you so often now."

"I must give you something unexpected in return." Catherine removed one of her rings and slipped it on Eva's little finger. The warmth of Catherine's body made the gold tingle against her flesh and Eva Karoli stood at her window, fingering its pale blue stone as she watched Catherine's shadow glide swiftly toward the woods.

"Come back," she whispered though, as always, she received no reply.

IV

"What would you do if you were free, Selim?" Catherine asked her companion later that evening.

Selim lay beneath the down coverlets, trying to keep warm. Pulling them tighter around his chest, he rolled onto his side and stared at the single candle, flickering in its glass holder, then at Catherine, magnificent in her new wine-colored gown. She toyed with his mind, he decided. She found as much pleasure in that as from his body. "I don't know," he said truthfully. "They kill Turks in this country in . . ." He tried to leave the thought unfinished.

"In ways that make my caresses seem gentle?" She laughed brightly, her smile broad. He stared at her teeth, wondering how she would use them tonight. She touched their tips with her tongue and he shuddered.

"And I cannot pass for European as you do, that is my curse, I suppose," he added anxiously.

"You could go west. Dark servants have become a sign of wealth in Paris and London. You would be clothed like some eastern pasha and made to sit outside their doors browning in the sun. Would you like that, Selim?"

"I would like to see the sun," he admitted. He had not felt its rays since she had brought him here four months earlier.

"You could go to the Old One's keep. I could send you as a gift. For that alone he might cherish you."

Selim shivered. He had seen the Old One in her visions. "Why do you ask when I am going nowhere?"

"Or I could destroy you now. You would die beautifully, Selim."

Selim shut his eyes. He could feel his pulse pounding against the sides of his neck. She could see it, he knew. She could quicken it or slow it. She could devour him and he would have no choice but to submit.

His captor turned her back on him. "Come, Selim. Unhook my gown," she purred.

The moment he stood, shivering in the cold, he felt her mind whirling around him, felt the warmth of it as if he had slipped inside her like a child back to the womb. This was his real torment, he knew. He would die adoring her.

Hours later, dizzied by her need, he woke and found himself alone in the night. The candle had long since burned away but in the darkness of the cavern lights flickered. He crawled through the narrow crack she used as her doorway and saw the torches strung through the void, lighting his way back to the world.

Disobeying her strictest order, he dressed in one of her dark suits. Then, wrapped in a down coverlet, carrying a sack of gold coins and jewels, he made his way through the twisting cave.

The torches were already sputtering their last when he reached the mouth. There, desolate and free, he sat and looked out at the snow-covered countryside and up at the stars, softly calling her name.

For she was out there in the darkness watching him, sharing his grief, trying to comprehend his loss.

"I would have followed you anywhere, lady, if you had only given me enough freedom to love you," he whispered.

CHAPTER
23

I

Erszi Majorova had raised the brown bear since it had been a tiny cub hardly weaned when its mother had been destroyed. Erszi had fed it broth, then showed it the way of the forest as its mother might have done. Though she had tried not to love it, she had done so anyway for it was a beautiful creature, large and gentle. Perhaps that was even right in its own way. Her love would make the sacrifice so much greater now.

Though the act diluted the power of the ritual, she had drugged the beast with the same tea she had brewed for herself, hoping to allay its fear and pain. Now it lay on its back in front of her crossed legs while she caressed the soft fur of the bear's stretched neck and began the chant.

> *"Great beast with honeyed paws,*
> *gentle all-knowing beast,*
> *farseeing beast,*
> *give me the power that I may touch the heavens,*
> *soar through the star-dappled sky*
> *seeking . . ."*

With tears in her eyes, she made the downward slash through the neck so deftly the animal only shuddered once, its claws leaving two long scratches on her bare arm. Muttering the prayers of sacrifice, she skinned the bear, covered her body with its pelt, and feasted on the heart.

In front of the tiny ritual fire, with the bear's arms and legs bound to hers, its head covering her hair, she drained a cup of the farseeing drug and danced the bear's dance while the name swelled in her.

"Catherine . . . Catherine . . . Catherine . . . Catherine . . ."

As the one-word chant continued, she whirled faster, ever faster, her mind moving out and away, following the rising smoke to the outerworld.

"Catherine . . . come to me . . ."

Another of Catherine's kind answered, his voice audible, near! Erszi snapped into her body and with eyes round from surprise peered into the darkness around her. "Come," she called to him and he stepped from the trees in front of her ritual fire.

She would have known him for what he was even if she had not been summoning his kind. His hair was dark and curled, his skin pale as the legends, his body long and tall. She scurried toward him on hands and knees, kissing his bare feet, then holding up her wrists. "Lord, thank you for coming to me. I offer what I have. I ask that you stay and let me worship you."

"Rise," he said with a soft, oddly embarrassed laugh, then took her hands and pulled her to her feet. "You have been calling Catherine. Tell me why."

"I was asked to call. I did not believe, for that I am sorry, lord. Then the woman responded but only once. Sometimes, I think I reach her but she will not speak." Erszi began to tremble, she could not believe her good fortune.

"Who asked you to call?"

His voice was so beautiful it seemed profane to utter the other's name in his presence. "The Countess Bathori," she blurted and lowered her eyes to where his hands still held hers. The blood of the bear had seeped onto them and dripped off his fingertips reminding her of red apples on new-fallen snow. She looked into his black eyes, glowing from her ritual fire, and for a long time she spoke to him, though later she had no recollection of what she had said.

At dawn, washed and with her hair unbound, she woke on the floor of her cottage with her strange visitor asleep beside her. Her tongue felt thick in her mouth, her vision clouded by something more than the drug she had consumed. She looked down at her wrists and saw the marks of his hunger, then felt the strange pricks on the side of her neck. He had taken what she offered.

The grey morning light fell through the half-open door, diffused by the smoke from the cottage's hearth. Without rising completely from her place on the floor, she pulled the door open, surprised that the Mountain Lord did not react to the light. Indeed, he hardly seemed to breathe at all. She ran her hand over the soft, coal-black curls, over the smooth unmarred skin of his face, over the long fingers with their hard nails. He had used her . . . her!

But when he woke, he would leave her and there were so many questions she wanted to ask. Giving thanks to the gods for her good fortune, she pushed the door shut, crawled to the hearth and drank the rest of the tea she had brewed. Then she sat and waited until she felt the first calming wave of the drug coursing through her before pressing the wound on her wrist against his mouth. Focused inward, she felt part of her life being drawn into him. She closed her eyes and tried to follow but the drug was too strong for her and she slept. Though she expected to find him still beside her when she woke, he had gone leaving only her wounds and the trace of his musky scent to prove that he had ever been here.

II

The winter air around Cachtice crackled from Charles Austra's hunger. At night, when what remained of his powers were at their strongest, he could not help but call and any warm-blooded prey in reach of his mind responded. Servants slept alone in rooms locked from the outside to keep them from trying to go to him. Wolves prowled the forest surrounding Cachtice. Owls and bats were seen circling the inner ward, flinging their bodies against the doors and windows.

"His kinsmen have come for him," Elizabeth would tell the servants, hoping to use their fear to keep them pliant. The ruse only half-worked. The servants who ran off, more terrified by

Elizabeth's captive than the countess herself, had whispered to others of the strange events at Cachtice, adding to the growing legends of the Mountain Lords. Those too frightened to leave had been destroyed, dragged from their locked chambers and down the narrow cellar passages of Cachtice where their screams merged with the frenzied shrieks of Elizabeth's captive. So many died that Dorca and Ficzko could not keep pace with their mistress. The bodies once again remained unburied and a frantic Dorca was spared having to tell her mistress that there were no women left in the cellars only by the timely arrival of ten serving girls sent by the procuress in Bystrica.

Ayn's betrayal and death had given Elizabeth the final push into insanity. Plots were hatching all around her. Though it was foolhardy to leave Cachtice unmanned, what remained of her guards were sent to the town of Cachtice and to nearby Trencin with orders to be constantly on guard for either Thurzo or King Matthias's men. As for Cachtice, Elizabeth guarded it herself, sitting in the high tower, looking out at the snowy countryside beyond the closed barred gates. Once, her daytime grooming had been impeccable. Now, she wore the same clothes day and night. Blood had caked on the hem and sleeves of her brown wool gown and glued together the long unwashed strands of her hair. A sword rested across her knees. She would use it on her enemy, if possible. If not, she would turn it on herself. As for the castle, no one would take that either. Though the outside walls were stone, the inner ones were all of wood, ancient and dry and ready to ignite once the faggots and logs piled in the cellars were set ablaze.

She had placed all her hope on the creature trapped below but whatever protection it could once give had long since ended, whatever calls it had once made to Catherine had not been answered. The mocking words in her mind had ended as well, and when she opened her thoughts to her exotic prisoner, all she detected was a silent agonizing scream of need.

She wished he would die. She had no idea how to kill him.

Always cautious, she ordered a second door installed on the far edge of the tunnel leading to the cistern. As with the main door, she held the only key.

Below her, the gates to the lower-level cells opened and Dorca came out, carrying the buckets of water and stew. After one long final look at the snowy countryside and the setting sun, Elizabeth went down the stairs. Though fear of her prisoner made her weak, morning and evening, true to her promise, she went to tend to Margueri.

She walked alone past the cells holding her doomed prisoners. As soon as she opened the outside door to the tunnel she found herself pulled into the vortex of hunger that surrounded her exotic captive.

As usual, Margueri was not at the grate waiting for Elizabeth. Instead the girl was stretched to the length of her chain, pulling against the bond, trying to reach him. Elizabeth watched, marveling for a moment over the possibilities of so much power, then called to Margueri.

Margueri looked blankly at the grate for a moment, then forced her mind away from her lover's and ran to the door. "Please," she whispered, her voice cracking from grief. "He cannot beg so I will beg for him. Give him something, any animal no matter how small, that will nourish him. Then I know he will call for her. He has no choice now, don't you understand?"

Margueri felt an agonizing stab in her mind. Was he furious that she had moved away from the grate? Was he angry because she begged for him? No matter. As long as they shared the darkness, she would do what she could to save him.

As always, the countess said nothing, passing Margueri food through the bars, then a moist rag so she could wash and wet her lips. Today the rag seemed wetter than usual, and instead of using it, Margueri flung it at the cistern hoping that a few drops at least would fall. She faced the countess once more and pleaded again. "Before Catherine could ignore his plea. But he is starving now, she will have no choice but to come."

"Everyone lies to me," Elizabeth responded.

"She will come but he must have the strength to call her," Margueri responded, the pain in her eyes making it impossible for Elizabeth to know if she told the truth. Without a word, Elizabeth turned her back on the girl and walked toward the outer door while the stone hallway echoed with Margueri's sobs.

Instead of leaving the lower chambers as she usually did, the countess screamed for Ficzko. "We will not wait for full darkness," she said as he hobbled down the hall toward her. "I choose . . ." Her eyes scanned the dozen cells, focusing finally on an older woman who had been there longer than most of the others and a young girl whose constant sobbing had become an irritation to her. She did not even bother to point at them as she brushed past Ficzko and went to the main chamber where the fire always waited for her.

After the screams subsided, Margueri looked over her shoulder and saw the flicker of light through the grate, heard the countess's voice calling her. The magnet that drew her attention to the cistern slowly diminished until Margueri managed to break the pull entirely and run to the grate. The countess passed in two wine bottles corked and filled with a dark red liquid. "The women aren't dead yet," the countess called loudly to Charles. "They will be soon. This is your last chance. Use their lives and summon her."

Elizabeth's eyes glittered in the torchlight as she gave her instructions. "Throw the bottles hard and they will break on the grate." Margueri again stretched to the length of her chain, tossing the bottles as hard as she was able, gratified to hear the shatters followed by the soft tinkle of shards falling into the cistern. The sound continued and Margueri imagined Charles on hands and knees picking through the broken glass, licking every drop of life from the metal floor. She had a sudden vision of how he had looked at her last social in Rouen, magnificent in a peach and grey brocade jacket, his hands brushing back a stray lock of her hair as they walked in her garden, his wide mouth tight as he smiled, promising more of the games they played. "He doesn't deserve this," she whispered, and with no warning even to herself, she flung her body against the bars, stretching her hands through, trying to claw at the countess's face.

Elizabeth stepped back, then whirled as, in the firelit chamber beyond the hallway, her victims screamed. Their long sounds of unremitting terror growing louder and louder until a single nebulous thought, less word than vision, pierced Margueri's mind.

— . . . Catherine . . . —

Margueri watched the countess run back to the main room and the pleasure of her victims, heard her cry of anger, Dorca's hurried excuse that both had died without being touched, a sharp slap followed by Dorca's loud sobs.

The women had been killed by the force of Charles's hunger

and need. Margueri did not question the power of that beast inside him; what she had glimpsed in the past had been growing for weeks. Though it would mean her death, she would go to him and gladly if someone would only make it possible.

"Charles?" Margueri dared to whisper his name for the first time in days.

She felt the quick welcome brush of his mind before the predator within him overpowered his reason once again. Margueri sat with her back against the door, her fingers curled around the metal mounting holding her chain to the wall wondering how much strength she would need to rip it free.

III

Matthew stood in the forest at the edge of the meadow that led to the underground passage into Cachtice. He had been there since midafternoon trying to shake off the strange lethargy that had descended on him. Had he really allowed himself to become this exhausted? More likely the witch had drugged him so that now, though he sensed his father inside the castle, he could not even send a quick comforting message to him. His mind was trapped inside his body and when he considered going inside in this diminished state, his instincts responded with a sharp warning.

Then he heard his father's cry, the hunger and agony so clear that the warnings made no difference any longer. He bounded on hands and feet across the field toward the darkened lower entrance to Cachtice.

The reek of death was all around him as he followed the passage Shiller had described, up the narrow winding tunnel, past the storage rooms, and up a flight of stone steps to the closed bars. A pair of wolves sat with their muzzles pressed between them. Matthew sent them scurrying with an angry snarl, then used his hands and feet to pull a pair of the bars apart far enough for him to slip through. He heard voices in the distance—one harsh and imperious, another servile and soothing, the creak of a hinge. He went on, slower now, until he reached the final turn to the main chamber. He risked a quick glance at the open passage. As he expected, it was also barred.

It had taken him only moments to get through the last barrier.

What could they do to stop him? With so much at risk, did he dare risk it?

A low keening began flowing from a passage deeper within the castle. His father's voice! Though Matthew's mind was unable to reach his father, he still possessed the other Austra senses. With his tone well above the human range of hearing, he called to his father and the keening immediately became a high-pitched cry of victory.

With her hands over her ears, Dorca looked at the passage leading to the cistern, her expression so fearful that it seemed she expected that the countess's prisoner had escaped. Ficzko did the same. Only Elizabeth remained impassive. Her delusions might control her but her memory did not fail her now. The goblet in her hand was vibrating and she knew precisely what it meant.

Pulling a pair of the torches from their holders, she moved closer to the pile of tinder and dry wood. "Come into the light where I can see you," she called down the passage where Matthew was hidden. "Do it now or I will start the fires. I will destroy us all before I let him go."

She only guessed he was here. How could she know? Matthew remained in the shadows.

"Come!" Elizabeth screamed. "Come out or I won't wait to see your face!"

Matthew did as she ordered, stepping into the light, seeing his adversary for the first time. Even now, in her blood-soaked dress, with the red smears across her lips and the wet strands of hair glistening in the torchlight, he sensed the power of the woman, the resolve in her dark eyes.

"You will not have him," she said coldly. "And you will not have me either." She stretched out her hand toward the woodpile. Dorca, sensing her mistress's intent, let out a strangled cry of fear. Elizabeth looked at her servant with disgust. "Not yet, Dorca. Not unless he forces me. We will wait instead though not long." She laughed as if enjoying her servant's fear, then moved closer to the passage where Matthew stood.

"We are at a stalemate, you and I. I suppose that, like your kinsman, you think to control me."

Matthew shook his head. "I would not make that attempt."

"Not even if you could?" She laughed again with an infectious hysteria that made Dorca cry out in terror, then cut it off as quickly, her eyes focused on the black passage behind him. "Do you hear her? Do you feel her?" She walked closer to the gate, breathing hard, then screamed the name, "Catherine!"

Matthew took advantage of the moment. Springing forward, he pried the bars apart with hands and feet, and quickly pushed himself through while the countess retreated toward the ready pyre. His hands were inches from the countess's throat when he heard the cry behind him.

"Stop!"

He spun, staring, as Elizabeth did, at Catherine. Though her feet and arms and neck were bare and her dark hair sparkled from the melted snowflakes, her clothing befitted a fairy queen. She wore the wine-colored velvet Madame Karoli had given her and the necklace of deep amethysts. Each finger had a different ring, a different stone. Elizabeth looked at her with eyes glazed with shock as if she had become one of her own victims while Dorca obeyed Catherine's silent command and lifted the gate. Only Ficzko, understanding that his time was over, retreated in terror through the tunnel leading to the castle.

As the gate rolled upward, Elizabeth dropped the torches to sizzle on the bloody floor, then fell to her knees before Catherine. Catherine gripped her hands and pulled her upright. "For a moment I thought you were one more dream," Elizabeth whispered, looking at their joined hands as if still not certain that Catherine was real.

Catherine shook her head. "You called me."

"For so many years I tried to kill the memory," Elizabeth whispered. "Like you, it will never die. Then I tried to live it but I can't, can I?"

Catherine said nothing, only stood touching her lost lover, her body trembling like a reed in the wind beneath its wine velvet sheath. "You will come with me, away from this place," she said after a while. "You will come and I will share my world with you for as long as you live."

Elizabeth pushed herself out of Catherine's embrace. "This is my home. I will not leave it."

Matthew expected a battle. He moved close to one of the torches and kicked it out of Elizabeth's reach. She whirled and lurched toward him, but Catherine pulled her back, holding her tightly and stroking her hair. "Shhh, Countess," she said in a low voice. "If you let my kinsman go, I will promise that you will never have to leave this place. And I will never desert you."

"Never?"

As she spoke the keening began once more, low sounds of pain and hunger. For the first time, Catherine glanced at Matthew and he detected her concern. "Where are the keys to my kinsman's prison, Elizabeth?" Catherine asked.

"No!" The countess struggled in Catherine's grasp. "If I let him go, he will destroy me."

"No. No." She forced Elizabeth to look directly at her and Matthew sensed that whatever power Catherine possessed was directed at controlling the countess's fear. "I will not let him, I promise."

Could she mean it? Matthew wondered. Could she really deny Charles his vengeance? Matthew would not have dared to try.

"Where are the keys, Elizabeth?" Catherine asked again.

Resigned, Elizabeth gave directions and Matthew rushed up the stairs to retrieve them. When he returned, Catherine was still holding her lost love in her arms, stroking her face, crooning soft words of comfort.

—Count Thurzo's men are riding into the courtyard— he told Catherine privately, then hastily lowered the gate to the upper castle and unlocked the first two doors to his father's prison. Catherine, leading the countess and carrying a torch, followed him into the room where Margueri and Charles were kept.

Margueri sat as she had been earlier, stretched to the length of her chain, her body flat on the stone floor with her feet toward the cistern. She raised her head and stared woodenly at Matthew, no sign of recognition on her face even when he released her. Instead as soon as she was free, she rushed to the edge of the cistern where she knelt, trying to glimpse her lover's face through the metal grate. Matthew, knowing the danger of his father's hunger, rushed to her side and held her tightly. But when he tried to pull her back from the edge, she shook her head and gripped the grate, preparing to fight with what strength she still possessed. "Matthew, please! I'm all right," she said without looking at him. "He and I have shared so many days of darkness. I must see him now. I must!"

As the cistern grate rolled slowly back the torch shed a dim
light on the space below and Margueri saw her lover for the
first time.

The carefully controlled facade had vanished completely. No
trace of humanity remained. Instead, Charles resembled a lean
and hairless cat of almost human form. He had begun biting his
arms in an effort to trick his body into thinking his hunger had
been appeased. The first small wounds had become larger and
deeper as if he could devour a part of himself to survive and they
had only half healed from the blood he had consumed earlier.

As he looked up at his lover and his son, his eyes glowed, not
only with the reflection but with some inner light as well . . .
the light in the eyes of all hungry predators when they detect
the life that would become their next meal.

And at the moment when he was more perfectly himself
than Margueri had ever seen him before, she realized that she
looked on a magnificence she had only glimpsed in the past.
She wanted to turn and run but she could not pull her eyes
away from his face. "Charles?" she called softly.

An instant of recognition, a brief mental caress, then his
instincts overrode his will and responded to her voice with all
the power they still possessed. Matthew's grip on Margueri
weakened. She wrenched her body out of his grasp and fell
without a sound into her lover's waiting arms.

She heard Matthew calling his father's name, and her own.
His voice seemed to come from a great distance and she, like
Charles, ignored him. Her hands pressed against the hollows
of her lover's cheeks as she whispered his name again.

Now that his torment was over he trembled, admitting his
hunger, she thought. With her eyes open and fixed on his, she
raised her head and kissed him. Their lips brushed, then with
a shriek of rage for his weakness, he yielded what remained
of his reason to the power of the beast inside him.

His fingers gripped her tangled hair, pulling back her head.
And while the part of him that cherished her mourned, it was
as impotent as his son looking down with horror from above,
both of them frozen by his body's inexorable need for blood.

Charles felt her growing fear, felt the beast inside him thrilling
to its potency, and with a sudden surge of will, he devoured
her far more quickly and mercifully than the hunger in him

demanded. Her shocked expression softened and she slumped lifeless in his arms.

Control returned as quickly and silently as Margueri's death. With her life and his own rage to fuel him, Charles dug his feet into the three indentations he had made in the metal and in one final leap caught his hands on the edge of the cistern and pulled himself free. He crouched at the edge, one hand flat on the stone floor. With his lover's blood rouging his lips, he raised his head and gave a shriek of rage and defiance, then fixed his eyes on his next victim, the Countess Bathori.

Elizabeth whimpered. Her skin, always pale, became as white as Catherine's and she moved back a step as, without warning, he sprang.

Catherine reacted even faster, thrusting herself between Charles and Elizabeth. "You shall not have her," she declared.

"Not?" Charles repeated, his lips flat, pressed against his teeth, his body aching for its revenge.

But no matter what Catherine had done to him, not matter what sentence the Old One had pronounced, Catherine was his own kind and he would not harm her. But he would not be denied his vengeance either. With the swift wave of one arm and the strength of need, he brushed her aside, the growing power of his mind holding her back far more easily than his instincts had held Matthew only moments before.

Again his eyes trapped his victim, the one he had dreamed of killing through so many long weeks of darkness and pain. He wished he had days to destroy her properly, to milk every drop of agony she could give for Margueri and himself and all the nameless victims she had used to torment him.

Elizabeth made no move to resist as he gripped her shoulders. Instead, with a courage that astonished him, she purred, "Come, first born. The legends say you cannot destroy one of your own kind. Now we will learn the truth of my lineage." A smile touched her lips and she tilted her head back, opening her mind to him, waiting for his attack.

He chose a spot where his fangs would hit a nerve, and as she moaned with the first pain, he magnified it until she was struggling helplessly in his locked arms. But then, as he tried to make the deeper lethal bite, he faltered. With their flesh touching, with their minds merged and focused on death, he could not ignore the truth he had only glimpsed before. He tasted more than human blood!

His blood. His brother's blood. And he knew he held the monster he had once joked would come of those strange bewitching unions a century before. *Life is hardly an abomination,* he had said to Steffen then. How wrong he had been.

With a snarl, he flung the countess away from him. She landed hard against the wall, then slid to the floor. "Monster!" he whispered with disgust.

Though Elizabeth was dazed by the blow, she managed a twisted smile of triumph. "Now we know, Charles Austra," she said, her voice rising as she spoke his name.

"Monster!" he repeated with icy rage. His arms were crossed over his stomach, his body bent forward, his hunger and instinctive recoil battling each other for control. No matter what she was, he wanted nothing more than to do the impossible and devour her.

"I have food in plenty, Charles Austra," Elizabeth called. "The cells of Cachtice are filled with life." She unhooked a ring of keys from her belt and held them out to him. "Go. Feast."

Though Charles's eyes were fixed on the keys, he did not move to take them.

"Charles, the girl was weak. Before you flee, you must feed again," Catherine told him.

"Do the servants upstairs know our name or have you only cried it out to these victims?" Matthew interrupted, speaking for the first time since Margueri had been killed.

Elizabeth shook her head. "Her servants don't know," Catherine answered for her.

"There are men in the castle. We have little time," Matthew repeated the warning he had given Catherine earlier, resignation clear in his voice. Elizabeth responded to the news with an involuntary cry, then fought the fear. Her expression became determined, and icy calm. She would face whatever came.

Catherine looked from Matthew to his father, her brows arched with interest. "He is still so young, isn't he, kinsman," she commented to Charles.

Charles nodded. With sudden resolve, Matthew lifted the keys from the countess's hand and ran down the hall, opening the cells where Elizabeth's victims were kept, pushing a pair of the women into the room where Charles waited to devour them.

• • •

As for the others, Matthew hardly glanced at them. He had neither time nor power to wipe their memories so he did what had to be done, realizing that Catherine had joined the slaughter only when he reached the most distant cell and saw her holding the final victim by her wrists, waiting for him. "You have a long journey yourself," she reminded him. "Take some extra moments with this one."

The tunnel twisted at the end and the stones of her cell were thick. She might not have heard. "Do you know my name?" he asked the girl Catherine thrust against him.

Mute, frightened, she could only shake her head. A simple probe told him that she spoke the truth.

"Then live to tell what the countess did," he said, pushing her away, locking her cell door behind him. As he followed Catherine down the stone corridor toward the main room, he heard the steady boom of wood on metal. Thurzo's men were breaking down the door.

"Hold them back," the countess said to Catherine, her white-knuckled grip on Catherine's hand the only sign of her fear.

"There are too many, Countess. We don't have the power," Catherine responded.

"Then kill them."

"More will only come. Elizabeth, are you certain you will not leave with me?"

"Yes, but you must go." Elizabeth pushed Catherine away from her. "You have no choice. I release you from your promise. Now go!"

With one final loving look at Elizabeth, Catherine turned and followed the men through the main room.

But at the edge of the tunnel leading to the fields below Cachtice, she stopped and faced the castle entrance. Thurzo's men had just broken through, then moved aside so Thurzo could enter first followed closely by Count Nemeth. As Thurzo stepped through the door, he stopped and looked across the torchlit room at the vision standing on the far side of it. As he gaped at Catherine, marveling at her pale beauty, she held up a hand, spread the fingers, and tensed them. The tips hardened, the nails curved downward into claws. She lifted her chin and smiled, revealing her fangs, the blackness of her eyes. A silent shriek of defiance cut through Thurzo's senses. He cried out from the pain of it, then stared in wonder at the woman as her words formed, clear and lilting in his mind, their beauty so at odds with the threat the order implied. —You shall not harm her!—

Count Nemeth had moved behind Thurzo, standing there long enough to glimpse the terrible glory of the woman before she whirled and ran. "Did she speak to you?" Nemeth asked.

"How could you know?" Thurzo replied.

Count Nemeth sidestepped the question. "I think it would be wise to listen to a woman such as that one," he commented instead. Nemeth's eyes focused on the carnage in the center of the room, drawing Thurzo's attention to the pair of victims on the floor, then to Elizabeth who looked so tiny and so pale in the stone archway.

IV

Just before dawn, after hours of viewing her carnage and listening to the garbled tale of the single surviving victim, Count Thurzo walked slowly up the stairs to Elizabeth's chambers. The guards outside her door noted his somber expression and, without waiting for his order, parted to admit him.

He found his cousin sitting quietly at her writing desk, composing letters to her children. In the hours he had been below, Elizabeth had changed into a black Spanish-style gown. The hair that had been so wild and tangled earlier had been pinned into a high severe bun, a style that accentuated her dark and, even now it seemed, sensitive eyes. The effect made her look like a nun, reminding him uncomfortably of the sentence his conscience would no longer let him impose. No, a convent would not be punishment enough for what she had done here.

And though he was no coward and the demon-woman's threat meant little to him, he could not condemn her to death either. To do so would mean her family would forfeit their lands and their honor to the crown. Thurzo, a Lutheran and Elizabeth's cousin through marriage, could not allow such a victory to a Catholic king.

"There will be a trial in four days, Elizabeth," he said to her.

Before he could continue, she stood, her expression haughty. "I welcome it," she said as if she could somehow prove her innocence.

He went on as if he had not heard her. "Though your servants were more than willing to detail all your crimes, a little painful prodding was all it took to convince them to confess their own as well. The trial will be for them. You will not attend."

"Not? I will not be able to defend my name?"

"Defend! Madame, you would destroy it with your ravings and that is something I cannot allow."

"Ravings!" She displayed anger for the first time. "You call them ravings after you saw her face?"

Once again, Thurzo ignored her. "I issue my own sentence on behalf of your children," he said. "You will be banished from their sight and the world's sight forever."

The countess bristled. "I will not leave this place alive," she declared.

Thurzo shook his head. "No, Countess, you never will." He waited for the meaning of his words to become clear before he continued. "You have three private rooms in this tower. You will be confined to them for the rest of your life. Though you will be given food and water and wood for your hearth, you will never look at another's face again. I give you a month, to say your good-byes."

Thurzo had expected some reaction, horror or at least defiance, but Elizabeth acted as if he had said nothing. "It has been a long night, George. Perhaps it's time we both rest. I would order rooms prepared for you and Jules Nemeth but I suspect my servants are all in chains."

If she was inquiring about the fate of Dorca and the others, he would not give her the satisfaction of a direct answer. Instead, he turned and walked to the door with her close behind him. He wondered if she would be desperate enough to try to escape and prepared to hold her back.

He needn't have worried. At the door, she touched her fingers to his cheek in a gesture of familial affection and he thought he detected the faint scent of blood on her skin. Though he did not recoil, his expression grew even harder than it had been and he left without a word.

CHAPTER
24

I

After he had fled with Matthew and Catherine, Charles lay throughout the night and following day in a dark hollow in the woods beyond Cachtice. Though he recovered from his weeks of captivity after only a few hours of near catatonic slumber, he chose to remain in that state, his mind moving inward on its own troubling paths.

He woke when he reached a decision about what he must do and found Catherine pressed against him. —I came to you because I had no choice— she said and kissed him, not with the passion that marked their usual contact, but softly and with gratitude. —Of all the family you are the only one who has the courage to love me. I owed you something for that— she added.

Her words strengthened his resolve. He rolled over and stretched, then looked for Matthew. As he did, he felt Catherine pull away from him. He reached for her but she had already vanished into the trees. His mental cry to her to stop and wait meant nothing. She left as abruptly as she had reentered his life the night before. No matter, he would still do what must be done.

Matthew sat nearby so absorbed in his own thoughts that he did not hear his father approaching until Charles rested a hand on his shoulder. Matthew flinched at the touch, looking for a moment like a small boy expecting to be punished.

"You were thinking of Margueri?" Charles asked.

"And of you. You were raised as Catherine was. You've hunted men for sport. You've used them for food. And then you cared so much for Margueri that you left her rather than destroy her."

"And in the end, my nature rallied. After centuries of life, I am reconciled to that." Charles did not explain that at the moment he felt as if his soul were split in two conflicting halves or that his world was not at all what he had believed it to be. He saw no benefit in raising doubt in his son's mind. Matthew had enough to reflect on already.

"But how did you learn to care at all?" Matthew asked.

Matthew was thinking of Catherine, Charles knew, of the perfect logic of her barbarity. Margueri's face formed in Charles's mind, not as she looked in the last moment of her life but rather on the night in Rouen when he had dared to drop his human facade and see the world as it should but could never be. "How could I have not cared?" he said as he shared the vision with his son. "But this isn't our world, Matthew. No matter how much we would wish it to be otherwise, men die. *And we survive*, Charles added to himself though he did not say the words.

Charles took a deep breath and plunged on with what needed to be said. "I am going home, Matthew. I would like you to return to France and tell the others everything that happened."

Matthew was surprisingly acquiescent. With his instincts newly awakened, with Margueri's death strong in his mind, he understood finally that there were things that each of them needed to face alone.

Four days later, as the first trial convened in Bytca to decide the fate of Elizabeth's accomplices, Charles walked through the open doorway of the family keep.

The servants had died in the years after Catherine had gone. With no one to carry wood nor any human need for warmth, the fires had long since been extinguished and the winter wind howled through the great hall. Though the hall appeared empty, Charles sensed his father here, using his power to hide from his own. "Father, you cannot hide from me," he shouted in the family language, the pitch high and painful, the inflections resolute. He would not go until they had faced one another.

The space above the raised dais shimmered as his father let down his mental cloak. There he sat, staring at some space between his eyes and the empty hearth, refusing to meet his son's eyes as Charles approached him. "You came back," he said with no surprise.

"I had to. There are questions I must ask." Charles sat at his father's feet, took his hand, and swiftly conveyed everything that happened since the day he walked into the Countess Elizabeth's trap. When he had finished, he looked down and noticed for the first time that his father had gripped his hand too hard. His nails had dug into Charles's flesh. Blood flowed.

"You lied, didn't you, Father?" Charles looked directly into the Old One's eyes, his mind probing for some response.

Francis pulled his hand away and raised the mental barrier between them, unwilling or perhaps unable to control his son's wrath.

"Where do we come from, Father?"

"I have no memory of my early life."

"But what of the rest of us? Why is it that during the Long Night, our memories stop with the birth of Denys? Who was his mother? Who was her mother and her mother's mother?"

"That makes no difference to any of you."

"It does!" Charles beat the stone hearth with the flat of one hand. He sent the pillows scattering from the divan. On the walls far above him, a pane of glass cracked from his scream of rage. —Who was that monster I touched in Cachtice?— The words were unspoken now. Fury made him unable to utter them.

"You are my family. You and your kin."

—Where did that woman come from?—

"You are my only family."

"You lie!" Charles turned the full force of his power on his father, compelling him to speak the truth.

Francis could have resisted but he did not try. "If you wish it so," he replied, his voice low and defeated.

"I did not come to challenge you, Father. When you've finished, take the memory from me or seal it so I can never reveal it to the others but give me the satisfaction of knowing the truth if only for one moment."

The Old One's thin body trembled with an emotion that all of Charles's power could not comprehend. Then with a swift decision, he drew Charles onto the dais where they lay side by side. His mind overpowered the present and Charles found himself in a huge cave lined with furs. No fire warmed the space, no torches lit it for the family had no need of light or warmth.

—There were five of us then— Francis began, mind to mind. —There was myself and my four children. We lived in the lesser hills, empty but for us and the beasts and a few isolated tribes. One night the ground began to shake, a tremor that went on for weeks. At first, these were light but later they became stronger. Stones fell from the top of our cave, wounding my infant son as he slept. Luzia, my younger daughter, trembled in my arms . . . no, do not ask to see her face. With effort I have almost forgotten it . . . and though I knew we should not stay where we were, she was too frightened to leave. That night, I hunted alone and as I returned to the the cave we all shared, I saw a fissure rend the hill, a great crack moving toward the shelter. I ran but I was not swift enough. I pulled Luzia from beneath the boulders. The rest were gone, crushed by the opening and closing of the earth.—

His father shook with the force of the memory but still his voice went on, flat and cold in Charles's mind. —Can you guess how frightened I became? Only one life kept me from utter loneliness. Luzia and I spoke of what must be done and, desperate, I went to the Magyar tribes in our domain. I stole their women. I forced them to drink my blood. It changed them. I could sense the change but their children could never be one with us. Yet, I grew to care for my human family. In the end, I even sent them back to their own.—

—And Luzia?— Charles asked.

—She . . . — Francis fought to hold on to a memory so terrible that the vision began to shimmer and fade until he forced it to form once more. —Her time came and when we knew she would bear twin sons, I . . . I did what had to be done. When she delivered them, I did not let her die. Instead, I fed her my blood. I nearly died from her greed before I pulled away. When I mustered my strength, I forced her to drink the blood of every creature I could summon with the call of my mind. When she became stronger, she fought me but I did not let death claim her.—

Charles pulled himself out of his father's mind. Nonetheless, he felt his own rage pounding into his father. "You denied her death? You kept her alive against her will?"

"I did what had to be done! And later she bore again, a son and two daughters. One of them was the grandmother of James and Rachel, the other began the line that has ended with you and Steffen and Claudia."

"And what of the Bathori blood? Catherine speaks of a bond between her and the countess. I sensed it in the woman."

"Catherine's grandmother was half-human. The warrior who sired her was Magyar and conception was only possible because my blood was already in him."

"And his family carried the legend down through the centuries."

"Sometimes I still taste a bit of myself in a Magyar slave. Odd how enduring blood can be."

There had been gaps in the memory, black spaces on the edge of the vision that Charles would not be allowed to comprehend but he had heard enough. "You speak of abominations far worse than what Catherine did in her moments of rage."

"And you intend to bargain with me?"

"Not bargain, request. Like you, Catherine faces an eternity with no one. Have pity on her, Father. Release her from your curse and I promise that if you allow me to keep this memory, I will never reveal what you have told me."

"Do you understand what your promise means?"

"I will never be completely one with my family again? I understand, Father. I would still make this bargain."

"Very well. When Catherine comes to me, I will release her. As to the family, they are free to help her as they wish." He looked at the room and all its treasures, meticulously arranged in harmony with his life. Catherine would destroy that balance for destruction was her only true talent. "The family will curse you for this, you know."

"I know." Charles sat on the edge of the dais, his expression in the pale golden light more troubled than any thought of family censure could evoke. He turned his back on his father, his breathing quickened as the sudden flash of instinct revealed itself fully. He felt like one of the women who saw death waiting—a long way off, yes, but waiting nonetheless. He buried the knowledge, so deep that not even his father could touch it. "May I stay with you, Father?"

"You need not ask."

"I need more than shelter, Father. I need you. Will you hunt with me? Will you be my companion as you were when I was young? Out there surrounded by all those dying souls I . . . forget what I am."

Aloof, cold in his years, the Old One reluctantly held out his arms, drawing his son forward, holding him tightly while Charles trembled against him.

II

As soon as Count Thurzo's arranged trials had ended, the sentences were carried out. Dorca and Helena Jo had their fingers ripped from their hands before they were burned alive. Ficzko was beheaded and his body destroyed in the same fire that killed the other two. Elizabeth's guards were also put to death. As she heard the news from her jailers, she had to suppress the urge to laugh. Thurzo had destroyed the only witnesses who could speak against her. The king could never bring her to trial now.

The days passed with little change in her life. The food was as well prepared by Thurzo's servants as it had been by her own. Her clothing was well kept. An occasional visitor even came to call. Many were simply curious to see the woman who had committed such terrible crimes, others came to whisper their support. Sometimes she was charming, but for the most part, she would stare at her visitors, her dark eyes cold and remote, until she sensed that first moment of fear. She wished she could devour them all.

Finally, when January had nearly ended, Count Thurzo rode from Bytca to see his sentence carried out.

She waited for him in her chambers, dressed in the same severe style as the night she had been arrested, watching the masons cart the bricks to the hall outside her rooms. Though she displayed little emotion, Thurzo said he would allow her one final meal downstairs so that she would not have to stand, watching her prison rise layer by layer.

"A last supper for the condemned, how very pleasant," she said as she walked into the great hall and stood in front of the fire. A portrait of her hung above the mantel and she saw eyes moving from her to the painting. Her lips tightened as she suppressed a smile. She wore this dress deliberately. Every time he came to Cachtice, his eyes would be drawn to the painting, then to the memory of how she looked on her last day in the world.

Though she played her most charming role, he did not take her walking in the garden one last time. Instead, when the supper ended, he followed her up the stairs to where the masons had paused in their work, leaving just enough space to thrust her inside.

She stood, watching as the last bricks were set in place, then walked to the window and looked up at the stars through the narrow slits that remained.

Her future would be little changed from her past. Outside of those few months with Catherine, she had always been alone. She lowered her eyes and with a small sigh of resignation, turned back to the darkness of her rooms.

Intending to prepare for bed, she lit a candle and pulled back the bed drapes and found Catherine there waiting for her, her face just visible beneath the coverlets piled over her.

—It is a big room, is it not?— Catherine conveyed with a quick, sad smile.

"You should not have done this!" Elizabeth said, knowing how much Catherine gave up for her.

—I do as I wish— Catherine responded and held out her arms.

EPILOG

Official records of the time state that Elizabeth Bathori endured her captivity with unusual silence. The guards stationed outside her walled-up door report that she never complained, indeed never spoke at all except to make simple requests.

But in that silence, much was said. The constant exchange between Elizabeth and her perfect lover required no words. Their discussions were that of history, pictures conveyed through Catherine's mind. Their touching was likewise done in silence, their kissing cloaked in the darkness of Elizabeth's chamber. And their privacy was always insured.

They abided three years together. It was likewise reported that Elizabeth's appetite was unusually good until the end. Then, weary of the darkness, weary of the monotony, weary even of Catherine, Elizabeth lay down beside her immortal lover and requested that Catherine end her life.

Afterward, Thurzo's edict was defied. Instead of sealing the single hole into her chamber as the Bathori family had demanded, the wall was ripped down so that Elizabeth could be interred in the crypt with her ancestors. As her body was carried from her chamber, one of the king's guards thought he saw a shadow move toward the door and pass through it. A specter. A soul. He would never be certain and he reported it only in a letter to his daughter for he would not share his foolish beliefs with anyone else.

.And from a vantage point elsewhere in the castle, a servant saw a tall woman draw a long black cloak tightly around her slender body. Then, with head bowed in apparent mourning, she disappeared into the forest surrounding Cachtice Castle. He thought he saw a pair of shadows moving with her through the trees but he could not be sure.

AFTERWORD

I was finishing the last few chapters of *Daughter of the Night* when the Jeffrey Dahmer case broke in my hometown of Milwaukee. It was impossible not to notice the similarities between Bathori and Dahmer—two murderers born four hundred years apart.

Both preyed on members of their own sex. Both practiced some form of cannibalism. Both killed people who were lightly regarded by the law—Elizabeth Bathori, servants who were no more than chattel in sixteenth century Hungary; Jeffrey Dahmer, primarily gay, black men, rovers who would not be missed.

In both cases, the public complained. Clerics denounced Elizabeth Bathori from their pulpits and protested to the crown and were ignored. In Milwaukee, residents of Dahmer's building complained about the stench from his apartment and neighbors tried to keep Dahmer from dragging away a naked bleeding Laotian boy only to have the police ignore their call and hand the young man over to his killer.

But Elizabeth Bathori had the privacy of a castle to conceal her atrocities and the privilege of noble rank to excuse them. Dahmer had a one-bedroom apartment in a crowded city building and his victims were people who should have received equal protection from the authorities.

People must have thought the same in Countess Bathori's era—we live in barbaric, terrifying times.

HISTORICAL NOTE

Though *Daughter Of the Night* is a work of fiction, I have attempted to incorporate as many facts from Elizabeth Bathori's biographies as possible within my novel. In doing this, I encountered a number of difficulties which I feel compelled to explain to my readers.

The first is a minor one. In Eastern Europe in the sixteenth century there was a clear dearth of names for noble children. There are more Elizabeths, Annas, Katarines and, especially, Stephans to fill five novels. Where possible, I used ethnic variations on similar names. In other places, I let the actual names stand. Though this may prove confusing for some readers it will allow others to pursue Elizabeth Bathori's history without having to try and determine whether my fictionalized character *A* was the historian's character *B*.

The second problem is a moral one. Elizabeth Bathori lived in an area of the world where peasants were bound to their land, their lives dependent on their lords' whims. Torturing and killing recalcitrant servants was not only acceptable, in some areas harsh treatment was encouraged, particularly after the peasant revolt in 1514. At the same time, Elizabeth grew up in an enlightened Lutheran family, and in an age when kings could often barely read or write, she was educated in Latin, Greek, and German as well as the other disciplines. As I describe in the novel, she was betrothed at age eleven to a cousin six years her senior who could barely read Hungarian and whom she may have met only briefly. She was pregnant at twelve or thirteen. The father is unknown but, in a case where truth is stranger than fiction, it is believed that her mother-in-law rather than her mother covered up the birth so that the marriage could proceed as planned when Elizabeth was fourteen. After the marriage, Elizabeth kept the Bathori name and her husband was permitted to add her name to his.

Soon after the marriage, Elizabeth imposed a rigid discipline on her household servants, torturing those who did not meet her rigorous demands. Following the death of her husband when she was forty-four, pain became murder and in the next six years, it is estimated that she tortured and killed as many as six hundred women, eating their flesh and drinking their blood, apparently in an attempt to maintain her youth.

Though Elizabeth was never brought to trial, her servants testified to her atrocities. None of them placed the number of her victims higher than eighty-five. However, after the trial a diary believed to be in Elizabeth's handwriting was found listing the names of over six hundred victims. Whether she kept a list of her victims, as so many serial killers do, or whether King Matthias was making one final effort to force her trial is not known.

After their trials, Elizabeth's servants were executed in the manner described in the book. Some days later the women who recruited Elizabeth's victims were also executed as was Erszi Majorova, the witch whose advice had led to Elizabeth's eventual downfall.

These are the facts. I did not alter them. I did, however, choose to skirt many of the gruesome details of Elizabeth Bathori's life and also altered her heritage. If in doing so I made my readers feel somewhat sympathetic to her, I would like to remind them that, during the era in which Elizabeth Bathori lived, nearly two hundred thousand people were executed because they were believed to be witches. Well over ninety percent of the victims were women.

When strengths must be hidden, the result is often perversion.

Surrender to the Vampire's Kiss
SPELLBINDING NOVELS OF THE NIGHT

___RED DEATH by P.N. Elrod___   0-441-71094-8/$4.99
While studying in London, young Jonathan Barrett grows
fascinated with unearthly beauty Nora Jones–even as she
drinks his blood during their nightly trysts. Forced by
impending war to return to America, Jonathan stands ready
to spill his blood for his country. But Nora's kiss has left him
craving the blood of others–for all time...

___GUILTY PLEASURES by Laurell K. Hamilton___
0-441-30483-4/$4.99
"You'll want to read it in one sitting–I did."–P.N. Elrod
Anita Blake holds a license to kill the Undead, driving
vampires to call her The Executioner. But when a serial killer
begins murdering vampires, the most powerful bloodsucker
in town hires Anita to find the killer.

___SHATTERED GLASS by Elaine Bergstrom___
0-441-00074-6/$4.99
*"Bergstrom's vampire is of the breed Anne Rice fans
will love."*–Milwaukee Journal
Stephen Austra is a prominent artist, renowned for his
wondrous restoration of stained glass. He is also a vampire,
but he respects ordinary people and would never hurt a soul.
Or so beautiful Helen Wells would like to believe...